The Horror
of
Northanger Abbey

REVIEWS FOR DAVID WELLING

FOR CINEMA HOUSTON

By allowing us to remember what we lost, Welling refines our perspective on what is worth preserving.

— Aaron Carpenter, *Cite Magazine*

If (the theatre is) clean and comfortable and the interiors don't clash, great, but, hey, who cares. David Welling cares.

— Louis B. Parks, *Houston Chronicle*

Welling has done a great service in preserving memories.

— Russell Herron, reader

FOR MIDWINTER TALES

Midwinter Tales is a literary holiday cookie tray. It's a happy-making jumble of updated seasonal favorites and nuggets that are anything but sweet, all lovingly infused with modern mythology.
— Kathy Biehl, author of *Confessions of a Third-Rate Goddess* and *Eat, Drink & Be Wary*

Get cozy with these *Midwinter Tales*... Welling's stories are rich with relatable characters, vivid settings, and surprising twists along the way.

— Melissa Algood, author of the *Enhanced Being* series

The HORROR of NORTHANGER ABBEY

Jane Austen
&
David Welling

Dedicated to Denise.
A romantic at heart. She hates horror.
They say opposites attract.

ACKNOWLEDGEMENTS:

IT IS A TRUTH UNIVERSALLY ACKNOWLEDGED, that a single writer in possession of a good idea, must be in want of supportive friends. So be it here.

Of course, this book would not be possible without the majesty of Jane Austen whose world this book inhabits. She is the basis of this alternate version, and for that, I am eternally grateful. The other major influence is the dark imaginings of H.P. Lovecraft who is about as far apart in style and substance from Miss Austen as one could be.

It has been a joy to marry the two in this deviation from her well-known plot. In Austen's final edition, the heroine, Catherine Morland, was proven wrong, her suspicions resulting from an active imagination. But what if she was right?

The first draft of this novel was written between January 2010 and August 2011 and has gone through multiple revisions and polishings since then. Much time and hundreds of sources went into fleshing out the background, countryside, mythology, and regional lore of Austen's world and time, blending it with the not-so-natural elements that complete this book. I have attempted to adhere to accuracy when required and to mythos when it came into play.

Thanks to Project Gutenberg for its ongoing work in keeping classic literature alive for new generations. Thanks to Tina Winograd for her editing skills. Thanks to family, friends, associates, fellow writers, and the usual pranksters for their support and love. Of course, thanks to Denise with many hearts.

And thank you, the reader, for taking the path where Jane feared to go.

David Welling
April 2025

Introduction

JANE AUSTEN'S *NORTHANGER ABBEY* is a novel both lost and found. It is one of the six completed novels written during the authoress's lifetime, and while overshadowed by her more popular works such as *Pride and Prejudice* and *Emma*, it still bears all the signature marks of the time and her interpretation of society norms.

It is notable as being her first chronologically completed novel, although often listed as her third, the first two being *Sense and Sensibility* (original title *Elinor and Marianne*) and *Pride and Prejudice* (original title *First Impressions*).

Northanger Abbey was not published until the year after her death and in an entirely different version from the original manuscript. That initial novel had been lost to time—until now.

This literary rediscovery changes the scope of her written output. Originally viewed as a gothic romance that embraced her appreciation of the popular novels and writers of the time—Ann Radcliffe, Horace Walpole, and Frances Burney among them—this precursor to *Northanger Abbey* reveals her original concept as nothing short of a horror story predating the works of Mary Wollstonecraft Shelley and Bram Stoker.

More notably, the specifics contain the same elements used by H.P. Lovecraft over a century later suggesting that he was not the originator of the fabled Cthulhu Mythos.

An abbreviated dateline of her novel is as follows:

Northanger Abbey was originally written between 1798 and 1803 under the title of *Susan*. In 1803, the manuscript was sold to Crosby Publishing in London through her brother, Henry, for £10. Crosby promised an early publication and went as far as to advertise the novel to be released in two volumes.

Years passed with no further word from Crosby, and her book never made it into print (one factor being the high cost of book production. Even paper was expensive, all handmade until the creation of machine-made paper in 1798). In 1809, she wrote to Crosby under the assumed name of Mrs. Ashton Dennis, expressing her concern and offering to supply another manuscript in case the original had been lost.

Richard Crosby replied that no publication timetable had been promised nor set and the publishing house was not obliged to publish the book. Furthermore, he threatened to protect his investment and would take steps to prevent anyone else from publishing the book. He then offered to sell back the rights for the same £10 that was first paid.

For Austen, finding the £10 to re-acquire her novel proved to be difficult. Her father had passed away in 1805 and the family funds were stretched. She finally regained the manuscript in 1813. It then went through a series of rewrites, the most notable alteration being the heroine's name changing from Susan to Catherine.

The passage of time caused Austen to consider the relevance of the novel, and as late as 1817—the year of her death—she wrote to a friend that "Miss Catherine is put on the shelve for the present, and I do not know that she will ever come out."

The year following Jane's death, the prestigious John Murray publishing house acquired both *Northanger Abbey* (an improved title decided upon by her siblings Henry and Cassandra) and *Persuasion* to be published as part of a multiple-volume set.

Much has been debated on the differences between the original version of *Susan* and the final published edition of *Northanger Abbey* as there were no copies of the *Susan* manuscript in existence.

This is no surprise as it has also been difficult to piece together a full account of Austen's life due to the lack of correspondence. Cassandra destroyed a large number of Austen's letters either to ensure the writer's reputation or to protect the family name from Jane's forthright opinions and criticisms.

Of the thousands of letters Austen had penned, fewer than two hundred have been accounted for. It is quite possible that the *Susan* manuscript became one of the casualties of Cassandra's actions.

The story might have ended here except for the discovery in 2001 of a large collection of unpublished manuscripts in the archives of the defunct publishing house of Saxon & Norley. The holdings had been stored untouched in a basement crate blocked from view by a bricked partition, and only during a renovation was it discovered. Among those papers was a copy of *Susan* as credited to Austen (and not to her pseudonym of Ashton Dennis).

How the manuscript found its way there raises many questions. It does not appear to be the first version of *Susan* as written by Austen, partially due to the details given about Bath. Jane visited the city on several occasions. The Austen family moved to Bath in 1801, years after she first wrote *Susan*.

The extended time spent there allowed her to give greater detail to the social life and experiences in the popular city. This suggests but does not prove that the specifics about the resort city may not have appeared in her initial novel.

It is possible that S&N Publishers was approached with the manuscript for publication after she regained control of her property, although there is no documentation to suggest such an action. What is obvious are the major differences between this existing version of *Susan* and the final draft of *Northanger Abbey*.

While the basic storylines are similar, especially in the first two-thirds of the novel, it is full of occult references that have not appeared in any of her other writings. The serial murder subplot was excised and the entire last portion rewritten, completely changing her discoveries at the Tilney abbey.

Furthermore, the supernatural elements are identical in many details to that of Howard Phillips Lovecraft and his works from a century later. This establishes two points: One is that Lovecraft did not invent the Cthulhu Mythos he is credited for. Austen's specifics by name—Al Azif-Azif; the listings of the Great Old Ones such as Nyarlathotep, Yog-Sothoth, Cthulhu, and Hastur, as well as other references to dark magic—are proof that the mythology existed well before the publication of Lovecraft's short stories and novels beginning in 1916 and continuing until his death in 1936.

More importantly, the lore mentioned by both may not be fiction but based on factual occult magical practice. This is an astonishing observation, especially for a writer such as Austen, and it raises the question of how she might have encountered such information. Based on the entirety of her other works, it appears unlikely she created the lore on her own. This essential and detailed part of the *Susan* plot confirms her exposure, although how she gained the knowledge to such a high degree remains a mystery.

Austen eventually completed a rewrite of the novel removing all aspects of the occult and changing the tone from a precursor of a horror novel to the gothic romance style that was popular at the time. Other large sections of the novel remained unchanged, holding to the original framework of the story.

It is this edition that eventually found itself in print and has been a part of Austen's literary legacy in the years since. It is also likely that any early drafts of *Susan* that survived after her death were destroyed by her sister due to the ungodly elements of that work.

Now, we have a complete version of *Susan* as Jane Austen first envisioned it. Only a few editorial changes have been made for modern readers. In keeping with Austen's later preference, the heroine's name has likewise been updated from Susan to Catherine, and with that, the title likewise altered to mirror its well-known counterpart.

Like *Sanditon*, her partially completed final novel, *Susan* represents one of the great what-ifs of her literary output. We may never know what she had in mind for *Sanditon* and its cast of characters, but we can now see the evolution from *Susan* to its final published form.

Here, then, begins the journey into *The Horror of Northanger Abbey*. Turn the page and embark on a very different adventure for Catherine Morland—born in both accounts to be an heroine.

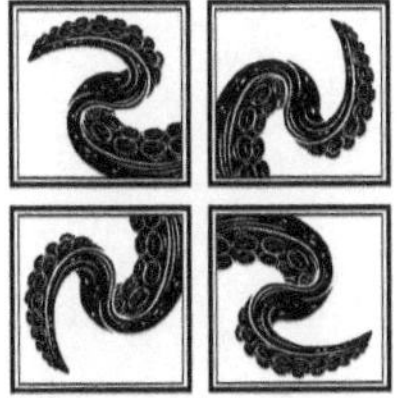

Prologue

WHAT IF Almighty God in Heaven had an epiphany that of man, whom he had formed out of nothingness and had cared for so greatly, lacked the worth of redemption, thus the Lord turned his back? Without divine guidance and mercy, would we be any better off than the lowest creatures to crawl from the sea?

It was a horrible, disconcerting thought that might disquiet the most ardent of faith, pondering its ramifications. So it did, and Brother Christopher spent many a restless night wrestling with the question, but never more than in recent weeks. That he, a man who had taken his vows early in life and lived the ensuing years in fervent devotion, should face such thoughts that might shatter the core of his resolve, was unthinkable. Then, again, the recent turn of events at the abbey had brought him to contemplate these issues more than ever before.

A shadow had befallen the monastery and all who dwelt within. Would that some answer to prayer give resolution, or at the very least, an element of hope, was all that he might hope for?

"Darkness is the tempter of man's soul, and only through the Light of God can be found salvation," he reminded himself and followed this with another repetition of faith. "Pater noster, qui es in caelis, sanctificetur nomen tuum. Adveniat regnum tuum. Fiat voluntas tua, sicut in caelo et in terra." The heavens answered in no uncertain terms with a fresh round of thunder that resounded even within the solid stone walls of the abbey.

He should have been asleep by now. Dawn would arrive soon enough, with the ritual chores of tending the garden, full of its bounty of medicinal herbs, fruits, and vegetables, which gave sustenance to the order, followed by the first mass of the day. In opposition to his desire, nature would have none of it.

Even if he were to quiet his mind to the point of slumber, the torrential rainfall, accompanied by the cacophony of thunder, made it impossible. He could not see the flashes of light that streaked across the night sky, his small chamber having no windows, but he did not need the visual to know of its existence. Acceptance was a part of devotion, so he acknowledged that he would be excessively tired in the morning. Thus was the Will of God.

Gardening was no effort to his mind. It offered him a means of communion with nature, it also being an aspect of the Almighty. He did his work without complaint and accepted every bead of sweat as part of his contrition. It was his calling, just as other brothers had found ties to their individual labors.

Brother Andre had an exceptional talent for duties in the kitchen along with other household chores. Others in the congregation, such as Brothers Nigel and Michael, found their calling in the learning. This was Brother Bernard's specialty as well, but his true gift was in the translating and reproduction of ancient manuscripts.

Bernard was a superb artist, indeed a gift from above. That he was fluent in three different languages added to his value within the monastery. Much of his time, outside of the daily masses and meals, was spent laboriously copying texts from other languages while adding decorative flourishes to each page with an eye for detail that went beyond mere talent.

Christopher thought the world of the boy, who being something of twenty and an unknown scattering of years, was still much younger than he. Indeed, he thought of Bernard, not as a fellow brother of the faith, but as a son.

Again, another round of thunder sounded from outside, accompanying the fierce rainfall, which rumbled for many seconds, reaching a crescendo at one point, then leveled into the background of the rain against stone. Sound played games within the confines of the abbey, echoing against walls so as to carry great distances. A brother's call, sounding like he was only feet away, might be several rooms apart, whereas other nearby sounds could fade completely, all due to the configuration of the walls.

As to the storm, it might be heard from every part of the enclosure, and seemed all the louder from deep within, as if the walls were able to amplify the sound.

Brother Christopher rose from his bed and paced his chamber, small and sparsely furnished as it was, in hopes that he might put his thoughts to rest, and perhaps get a few hours sleep before daybreak.

The source of his worries centered on Brother Bernard, who in recent weeks no longer seemed to be himself, and in retrospect it was easy to pinpoint both the date and the cause of this transformation. There was no denying that his concerns were based on an ancient manuscript that had been assigned to Bernard for translation and reproduction.

It had been brought to the abbey through Prior Terrance, having gained the approval of Abbot Peter for the task, and was an ancient text of unknown origin, masked in darkness and mystery. Unlike other manuscripts that crossed the threshold of the abbey, this was a foul document, wholly supernatural in its source from all that were able to discern, and there was much debate over its being kept within the monastery.

Such a manuscript did not honour the name of Almighty God and thus should be wholly destroyed. It was, however, argued that as bearers of history and knowledge, no matter what the source, it was a responsibility to know what evils there were in the world to better confront them. This latter argument won, and Prior Terrance selected Brother Bernard specifically for the task in translation from its ancient tongue, and to copy it into words that might be fully understood.

That decision had been more than a fortnight hence, and young Brother Bernard had become a changed man. It did not come all at once, but by degrees. He began spending less time at his other duties and at mealtime, showing up for mass as briefly as possible, and becoming less communicative—all the while spending more time at work on the manuscript.

It was further noted that he was often seen talking to himself as if in fervent prayer; however, from all indications, this was not of any prayer of which they knew. Brother Christopher had noticed the variance almost immediately, but by the time he had chosen to confront the younger brother directly, there already were some outward signs of malnutrition.

Bernard appeared gaunt, with hollow circles around his eyes, yet when asked in concern for his health and how the labors appeared to be wearing heavy on him, he answered that he was perfectly fine and that no concern was necessary. Further questioning only agitated the young man.

Christopher was not convinced and soon brought it to the attention of the Abbot, explaining how so much time spent around a specimen of such ill repute could not be a practice worthy of a child of the Lord. "I agree with you," noted Abbot Peter, "but mysterious are the ways of God and his works. The efforts upon which our brother is tasked should continue, so I would ask you to look after him and see that he spends more time out of doors, and time of social interaction with his fellow brothers, and in prayer. His work will be done soon enough, and then we may be rid of the thing of which you speak. I, for one, will be quite satisfied to see it go."

Such advice, while well meant, was problematic to put into action as Brother Bernard had become increasingly resolute to his given intentions, nor was Christopher able to gain help from his brethren, particularly Prior Terrance, who had been pushing Bernard along for a speedy completion of his work. Thus, in the last few days, Bernard had been seen hardly at all, spending his waking hours at work on the text.

Upon occasion when Christopher entered the scriptorium, he would hastily cover his work with blank parchment as if keeping a great secret away from prying eyes.

These events led to the present and contributed to Brother Christopher's inability to sleep, full in the knowledge that such was not meant to be the will of the Divine. He had been tasked with looking after the youth, and it was upon his shoulders to find a solution. If only a resolution was clear.

Then came another loud crack of thunder, far more pronounced than before, but with a strange undertone. Only when the thunder faded and the secondary sound continued, did Christopher comprehend that it was not an intonation related to the forces of nature. This was a scream, as terrifying as imaginable, that extended far beyond what might be produced from a normal intake of breath.

And as it continued, it seemed to become even more distorted, the sound garbled, even wet, the noise produced as if choking.

At once, Christopher raced from the door of his chamber, hurrying down the corridor toward the source of the sound. Even as he ran, he knew where the noise originated, that being the scriptorium.

He burst through the door, initially finding the room quite empty, but the sound more pronounced than ever. Multiple candles near the table cast long shadows throughout, offering ample illumination to the area, and occasional flashes of light burst through the small window.

On the far table, he saw the horrid manuscript, but immediately noticed the pages marked with a splattering of red, and in drawing closer, knew it to be blood mixed with bits of tissue. Then he saw, on the floor behind the table, a pair of legs, still convulsing, and the screams now reduced to a slushy inarticulate call.

Slowly, Brother Christopher approached the body, seeing more of the lower torso, until a full reveal caused him to freeze in his tracks. Brother Bernard, for it must have been him, recognizable from the garments he wore, was splayed upon the stone floor, surrounded in a spilt and expanding pool of blood, the body still twitching.

The true horror was not in the body itself, as from the neck down, all looked as proper; but where his head should have been, the true unspeakable nightmare was visible. Bernard's head appeared to have exploded, showering everything in close proximity with specs of flesh and bone, and in its place was a seeming mass of writhing skin.

Taking a hesitant step closer, Christopher was able to see in greater detail that which had erupted out of the brother's collar; it might be best described as a series of undulating tentacles, covered in blood, but in substance not of normal flesh, and of a material almost gelatinous. The tentacles were textured with smaller formations, each moving on its own, and only after looking closely did Christopher realize that these were smaller mouths, opening and closing independently of the others, and producing a sickly sucking sound.

A commotion erupted behind Christopher as his fellow brothers arrived, each alarmed at the sound, and then in abject terror from the sight before them. The last to arrive, Brother Nigel, held a torch aloft, having brought it along for greater light in the dim passages. Only Prior Terrance, standing near the back, showed no emotion but took in the scene in stone-faced silence.

Knowing what was required, Brother Christopher took the torch from Nigel, stepped up to the convulsing form of their brother, and began a recitation of the last rites. He then set the torch to Bernard's garments, allowing the flames to consume the form, and deliverance into the merciful hands of God.

With his free hand, he scooped all that was on the table—the manuscript, the translation so carefully rendered by Bernard, and even the ink-covered quills, brushing them onto the body where they, too, were taken by the flames.

Dark smoke rose, darkening the ceiling and moving outward, even as the brethren worked to salvage the remaining furniture and other parchments from the room. And having rescued all that was deemed worthy to save, they exited, pulling the door shut behind them, leaving the flames to do their holy work and cleanse the room through fire of all its evil.

CHAPTER

NO ONE WHO had ever seen Catherine Morland in her infancy would have supposed her born to be an heroine. Her situation in life, the character of her father and mother, her own person and disposition, were all equally against her. To think of her reaching adulthood, set to encounter any sort of adventure, suspense, storybook villain, or dashing, gentlemanly rescuer, would be a point of pure imaginative fantasy.

Fewer would be able to correctly predict how she could have responded when faced with such escapades; to do so would have taken something as equally fanciful as a crystal ball. Therefore, neither family, friends, nor other acquaintances could possibly know of the unspeakable horrors she would encounter at the time of her seventeenth year.

Her father was a clergyman, without being neglected, or poor, and a very respectable man, though his name was Richard—and he had never been handsome. He had a considerable independence besides two good livings—and he was not in the least addicted to locking up his daughters. Her mother was a woman of useful plain sense, with a good temper, and, what is more remarkable, with a good constitution. She had three sons before Catherine was born; and instead of dying in bringing the latter into the world, as anybody might expect, she still lived on—lived to have six children more—to see them growing up around her, and to enjoy excellent health herself.

A family of ten children will be always called a fine family, where there are heads and arms and legs enough for the number; but the Morlands had little other right to the word, for they were in general very plain, and Catherine, for many years of her life, as plain as any. She had a thin awkward figure, a sallow skin without colour, dark lank hair, and strong features—so much for her person; and not less unpropitious for heroism seemed her mind. She was fond of all boy's plays, and greatly preferred cricket not merely to dolls, but to the more heroic enjoyments of infancy, nursing a dormouse, feeding a canary-bird, or watering a rose-bush. Indeed she had no taste for a garden; and if she gathered flowers at all, it was chiefly for the pleasure of mischief—at least so it was conjectured from her always preferring those which she was forbidden to take. Such were her propensities—her abilities were quite as extraordinary. She never could learn or understand anything before she was taught; and sometimes not even then, for she was often inattentive, and occasionally stupid. Her mother was three months in teaching her only to repeat the "Beggar's Petition"; and after all, her next sister, Sally, could say it better than she did. Not that Catherine was always stupid—by no means; she learnt the fable of "The Hare and Many Friends" as quickly as any girl in England. Her mother wished her to learn music; and Catherine was sure she should like it, for she was very fond of tinkling the keys of the old forlorn spinnet; so, at eight years old she began. She learnt a year, and could not bear it; and Mrs. Morland, who did not insist on her daughters being accomplished in spite of incapacity or distaste, allowed her to leave off. The day which dismissed the music-master was one of the happiest of Catherine's life. Her taste for drawing was not superior; though whenever she could obtain the outside of a letter from her mother or seize upon any other odd piece of paper, she did what she could in that way, by drawing houses and trees, hens and chickens, all very much like one another. Writing and accounts she was taught by her father; French by her mother: her proficiency in either was not remarkable, and she shirked her lessons in both whenever she could. What a strange, unaccountable character!—for with all these symptoms of profligacy at ten years old, she had neither a bad heart nor a bad temper, was seldom stubborn, scarcely ever quarrelsome, and very kind to the little ones, with few interruptions of tyranny; she was moreover noisy and wild, hated confinement and cleanliness, and loved nothing so well in the world as rolling down the green slope at the back of the house.

Such was Catherine Morland at ten. At fifteen, appearances were mending; she began to curl her hair and long for balls; her complexion improved, her features were softened by plumpness and colour, her eyes gained more animation, and her figure more consequence. Her love of dirt gave way to an inclination for finery, and she grew clean as she grew smart; she had now the pleasure of sometimes hearing her father and mother remark on her personal improvement.

"Catherine grows quite a good-looking girl—she is almost pretty today," were words which caught her ears now and then; and how welcome were the sounds! To look almost pretty is an acquisition of higher delight to a girl who has been looking plain the first fifteen years of her life than a beauty from her cradle can ever receive.

Mrs. Morland was a very good woman, and wished to see her children everything they ought to be; but her time was so much occupied in lying-in and teaching the little ones, that her elder daughters were inevitably left to shift for themselves; and it was not very wonderful that Catherine, who had by nature nothing heroic about her, should prefer cricket, baseball, riding on horseback, and running about the country at the age of fourteen, to books—or at least books of information—for, provided that nothing like useful knowledge could be gained from them, provided they were all story and no reflection, she had never any objection to books at all. But from fifteen to seventeen she was in training for an heroine; she read all such works as heroines must read to supply their memories with those quotations which are so serviceable and so soothing in the vicissitudes of their eventful lives.

From Pope, she learnt to censure those who

"bear about the mockery of woe."

From Gray, that

"Many a flower is born to blush unseen,
And waste its fragrance on the desert air."

From Thompson, that—

"It is a delightful task
To teach the young idea how to shoot."

And from Shakespeare she gained a great store of information—amongst the rest, that—

"Trifles light as air,
Are, to the jealous, confirmation strong,
As proofs of Holy Writ."

That

> *"The poor beetle, which we tread upon,*
> *In corporal sufferance feels a pang as great*
> *As when a giant dies."*

And that a young woman in love always looks—

> *"like Patience on a monument*
> *Smiling at Grief."*

While her education began under the tutelage of these authors, thus refining her mind and broadening her awareness, it was through the reading of novels that she found her true passion.

Yes, novels; for I will not adopt that ungenerous and impolitic custom so common with novel-writers, of degrading by their contemptuous censure the very performances, to the number of which they are themselves adding—joining with their greatest enemies in bestowing the harshest epithets on such works, and scarcely ever permitting them to be read by their own heroine, who, if she accidentally take up a novel, is sure to turn over its insipid pages with disgust. Alas! If the heroine of one novel be not patronized by the heroine of another, from whom can she expect protection and regard? I cannot approve of it. Let us leave it to the reviewers to abuse such effusions of fancy at their leisure, and over every new novel to talk in threadbare strains of the trash with which the press now groans.

Let us not desert one another; we are an injured body. Although our productions have afforded more extensive and unaffected pleasure than those of any other literary corporation in the world, no species of composition has been so much decried. From pride, ignorance, or fashion, our foes are almost as many as our readers. And while the abilities of the nine-hundredth abridger of the History of England, or of the man who collects and publishes in a volume some dozen lines of Milton, Pope, and Prior, with a paper from the Spectator, and a chapter from Sterne, are eulogized by a thousand pens—there seems almost a general wish of decrying the capacity and undervaluing the labour of the novelist, and of slighting the performances which have only genius, wit, and taste to recommend them. "I am no novel-reader—I seldom look into novels—Do not imagine that I often read novels—It is really very well for a novel." Such is the common cant. "And what are you reading, Miss—?" "Oh! It is only a novel!"

replies the young lady, while she lays down her book with affected indifference, or momentary shame. "It is only Cecilia, or Camilla, or Belinda"; or, in short, only some work in which the greatest powers of the mind are displayed, in which the most thorough knowledge of human nature, the happiest delineation of its varieties, the liveliest effusions of wit and humour, are conveyed to the world in the best-chosen language.

Now, had the same young lady been engaged with a volume of the Spectator, instead of such a work, how proudly would she have produced the book, and told its name; though the chances must be against her being occupied by any part of that voluminous publication, of which either the matter or manner would not disgust a young person of taste: the substance of its papers so often consisting in the statement of improbable circumstances, unnatural characters, and topics of conversation which no longer concern anyone living; and their language, too, frequently so coarse as to give no very favourable idea of the age that could endure it.

As Catherine had stored up a wealth of quotations from the more respectable volumes, she now added a great deal more from the authors she loved the best.

Francis Lathom told her to

> *"Swear then, for I have a tale of most mysterious nature to unfold, swear thou wilt be secret."*

From Ann Radcliffe, that

> *"The passions are the seeds of vices as well as of virtues, from which either may spring, accordingly as they are nurtured. Unhappy they who have never been taught the art to govern them!"*

From Eleanor Sleath, that

> *"This heavy calamity, inflicted upon him by the violence of unregulated passions, had an effect upon his mind as powerful as it was instantaneous."*

Even the great bard, Shakespeare, continued to entice her growth as a woman, with words such as

> *"Graze on my lips; and if those hills be dry, stray lower, where the pleasant fountains lie."*

And

> *"Hereafter, in a better world than this, I shall desire more love and knowledge of you."*

And

> *"Were kisses all the joys in bed, one woman would another wed."*

In short, Catherine found novels to be the b's and e's.

So far her improvement was sufficient—and in many other points she came on exceedingly well; for though she could not write sonnets, she brought herself to read them; and though there seemed no chance of her throwing a whole party into raptures by a prelude on the pianoforte, of her own composition, she could listen to other people's performance with very little fatigue. Her greatest deficiency was in the pencil—she had no notion of drawing—not enough even to attempt a sketch of her lover's profile, that she might be detected in the design. There she fell miserably short of the true heroic height. At present she did not know her own poverty, for she had no lover to portray. She had reached the age of seventeen, without having seen one amiable youth who could call forth her sensibility, without having inspired one real passion, and without having excited even any admiration but what was very moderate and very transient. This was strange indeed! But strange things may be generally accounted for if their cause be fairly searched out. There was not one lord in the neighbourhood; no—not even a baronet. There was not one family among their acquaintance who had reared and supported a boy accidentally found at their door—not one young man whose origin was unknown. Her father had no ward, and the squire of the parish no children.

But when a young lady is to be an heroine, the perverseness of forty surrounding families cannot prevent her. Something must and will happen to throw a hero in her way.

Mr. Allen, who owned the chief of the property about Fullerton, the village in Wiltshire where the Morlands lived, was ordered to Bath for the benefit of a gouty constitution—and his lady, a good-humoured woman, fond of Miss Morland, and probably aware that if adventures will not befall a young lady in her own village, she must seek them abroad, invited her to go with them. Mr. and Mrs. Morland were all compliance, and Catherine all happiness.

Bath was adventure. Bath was elegant sociality and balls held in lush assembly rooms with ladies dressed in the finest, all esteemed as diamonds of the first water, and every gentleman a nonesuch. Bath was everything she might have dreamed of, and brought her all the closer to the excitement of that found in her precious books. Indeed, Bath had it all and soon she would be a part of it.

CHAPTER

Two

NO BOOK WAS EVER created equal. The common understanding among both the learned and those with more hair than wit held that books might come in all shapes and sizes. Some arrived large while others small, some filled with short verse and perhaps a decorative flourish or two, while others expanded in subject to being thick tomes of voluminous, even laborious text. Their contents might be the lightest of fare, or the novels of such horrid and scandalous events, these being the same ones that Catherine was so fond of. Indeed, a world of variety could be found within the pages of a single volume.

Then, again, some books were born to be bad, bad to the core—and one more than most.

Few knew of its existence but of those who did, this singular book was a dark treasure much sought after. Its origins were of question, but generally credited to be the work of a maddened poet of Arabian descent during the period of the Ommiade caliphs, circa 700 A.D.

Prior to the writing of the book, the Yemen-born Abdul Alhazred spent considerable time in travels and learning, having visited the ruins of Babylon and Memphis, and spent a decade of solitude in the Arabian great southern desert, known also as the Roba el Khaliyeh—the empty space of the ancients—as well as the Dahna region, both believed to be inhabited Aby the most foul of spirits. His journeys also took him to Irem, the City of Pillars, and more importantly, to the ruins of an unnamed desert town. Here, he claimed to have discovered the secrets of the ancients. Alhazred returned to Damascus and spent his final years there.

It was here that he wrote the book, originally titled *Al Azif-azif*. His death was enigmatic, having disappeared without a trace around 738 A.D.

Equally mysterious was the book itself, which became a sought-after intelligence to the philosophers of the age, and thus gained considerable circulation. In 950 A.D., a Greek translation was completed under a different name by Theodorus Philetas of Constantinople but was suppressed and burned a century later by the patriarch Michael Cerularius. It reappeared as a Latin translation by Olaus Wormius in 1228, which was banned, along with its Greek counterpart, by Pope Gregory IX in 1232 A.D. This Latin text was reprinted in black letter in the fifteenth century, most likely in Germany, and then again in Spain in the seventeenth century. Likewise, a reprinting of the Greek text took place in Italy sometime between 1500 and 1550.

Few copies of the book were known to have survived, outside of private collectors and book owners, and editions at the British Museum and the Bibliothèque Nationale in France. Attempts at suppression and destruction throughout the centuries since its original writing served to reduce its numbers to the unhappy few, but despite these attempts, *Al Azif-azif* did survive, as did those who followed its messages, understood its meaning, and lived their lives in nature to its text.

Not surprisingly, Catherine Morland was not familiar with the book under any of its names, it being hardly the type of volume she would have sought out on her own. Nor would she have found it at any of the libraries or shelves that sported such writers as Ann Radcliffe, Eliza Parsons, Regina Maria Roche, or Ludwig Flammenberg. She would not find the book on her terms, either by chance or by necessity—but in due time, *Al Azif-azif* would find her.

CHAPTER

Three

IN ADDITION to what has been already said of Catherine Morland's personal and mental endowments, when about to be launched into all the difficulties and dangers of a six weeks' residence in Bath, it may be stated, for the reader's more certain information, lest the following pages should otherwise fail of giving any idea of what her character is meant to be, that her heart was affectionate; her disposition cheerful and open, without conceit or affectation of any kind—her manners just removed from the awkwardness and shyness of a girl; her person pleasing, and, when in good looks, pretty—and her mind about as ignorant and uninformed as the female mind at seventeen usually is.

When the hour of departure drew near, the maternal anxiety of Mrs. Morland will be naturally supposed to be most severe. A thousand alarming presentiments of evil to her beloved Catherine from this terrific separation must oppress her heart with sadness, and drown her in tears for the last day or two of their being together; and advice of the most important and applicable nature must of course flow from her wise lips in their parting conference in her closet. Cautions against the violence of such noblemen and baronets as delight in forcing young ladies away to some remote farm-house, must, at such a moment, relieve the fulness of her heart. Who would not think so? But Mrs. Morland knew so little of lords and baronets, that she entertained no notion of their general mischievousness, and was wholly unsuspicious of danger to her daughter from their machinations. Her cautions were confined to the following points. "I beg, Catherine, you will always wrap yourself up very warm about the throat, when you come from the rooms at night; and I wish you would try to keep some account of the money you spend; I will give you this little book on purpose."

Sally, or rather Sarah (for what young lady of common gentility will reach the age of sixteen without altering her name as far as she can?), must from situation be at this time the intimate friend and confidante of her sister. It is remarkable, however, that she neither insisted on Catherine's writing by every post, nor exacted her promise of transmitting the character of every new acquaintance. This oversight might have been youthful forgetfulness, and mindful of their confidentiality, Catherine assured her that she would write of every detail and interesting conversation that Bath might produce – providing, of course, there be time to do so, as she expected every moment of every day to be filled. Everything indeed relative to this important journey was done, on the part of the Morlands, with a degree of moderation and composure, which seemed rather consistent with the common feelings of common life, than with the refined susceptibilities, the tender emotions which the first separation of an heroine from her family ought always to excite. Her father, instead of giving her an unlimited order on his banker, or even putting an hundred pounds bank-bill into her hands, gave her only ten guineas, and promised her more when she wanted it.

Under these unpromising auspices, the parting took place, and the journey began. It was performed with suitable quietness and uneventful safety. Neither robbers nor tempests befriended them, nor one lucky overturn to introduce them to the hero. Nothing more alarming occurred than a fear, on Mrs. Allen's side, of having once left her clogs behind her at an inn, and that fortunately proved to be groundless.

Despite the lack of adventure on their journey, Catherine passed the time by staring out the carriage at the passing countryside and imagining all sorts of scenarios, usually involving the aforementioned robbers, tempests, and heroes.

At any moment, a group of masked ruffians might appear on horseback, forcing the carriage to a stop before plundering its passengers for their valuables. The lead robber, wearing a partial mask that left his lower face revealed would target Catherine for his own, and she would find herself being carried off, gazing up at that half-hooded face.

Ah, but such a face, and based on the scant portion revealed, how handsome he might be once purged of his disguise. The feeling she experienced was one of fear and uncertainty, but also one of delicious excitement. On and on, the daydreams continued, each a variation of the previous, but all with the same end.

They arrived at Bath. Catherine was all eager delight—her eyes were here, there, everywhere, as they approached its fine and striking environs, and afterwards drove through those streets which conducted them to the hotel. She was come to be happy, and she felt happy already.

They were soon settled in comfortable lodgings in Pulteney Street.

It is now expedient to give some description of Mrs. Allen, that the reader may be able to judge in what manner her actions will hereafter tend to promote the general distress of the work, and how she will, probably, contribute to reduce poor Catherine to all the desperate wretchedness of which a last volume is capable—whether by her imprudence, vulgarity, or jealousy—whether by intercepting her letters, ruining her character, or turning her out of doors.

Mrs. Allen was one of that numerous class of females, whose society can raise no other emotion than surprise at there being any men in the world who could like them well enough to marry them. She had neither beauty, genius, accomplishment, nor manner. The air of a gentlewoman, a great deal of quiet, inactive good temper, and a trifling turn of mind were all that could account for her being the choice of a sensible, intelligent man like Mr. Allen. In one respect she was admirably fitted to introduce a young lady into public, being as fond of going everywhere and seeing everything herself as any young lady could be. Dress was her passion. She had a most harmless delight in being fine; and our heroine's entree into life could not take place till after three or four days had been spent in learning what was mostly worn, and her chaperone was provided with a dress of the newest fashion. Catherine too made some purchases herself, and when all these matters were arranged, the important evening came which was to usher her into the Upper Rooms. Her hair was cut and dressed by the best hand, her clothes put on with care, and both Mrs. Allen and her maid declared she looked quite as she should do. With such encouragement, Catherine hoped at least to pass uncensured through the crowd. As for admiration, it was always very welcome when it came, but she did not depend on it.

Mrs. Allen was so long in dressing that they did not enter the ballroom till late. The season was full, the room crowded, and the two ladies squeezed in as well as they could. As for Mr. Allen, he repaired directly to the card-room, and left them to enjoy a mob by themselves. With more care for the safety of her new gown than for the comfort of her protegee, Mrs. Allen made her way through the throng of men by the door, as swiftly as the necessary caution would allow; Catherine, however, kept close at her side, and linked her arm too firmly within her friend's to be torn asunder by any common effort of a struggling assembly. But to her utter amazement she found that to proceed along the room was by no means the way to disengage themselves from the crowd; it seemed rather to increase as they went on, whereas she had imagined that when once fairly within the door, they should easily find seats and be able to watch the dances with perfect convenience. But this was far from being the case, and though by unwearied diligence they gained even the top of the room, their situation was just the same; they saw nothing of the dancers but the high feathers of some of the ladies. Still they moved on—something better was yet in view; and by a continued exertion of strength and ingenuity they found themselves at last in the passage behind the highest bench. Here there was something less of crowd than below; and hence Miss Morland had a comprehensive view of all the company beneath her, and of all the dangers of her late passage through them. It was a splendid sight, and she began, for the first time that evening, to feel herself at a ball: she longed to dance, but she had not an acquaintance in the room. Mrs. Allen did all that she could do in such a case by saying very placidly, every now and then, "I wish you could dance, my dear—I wish you could get a partner." For some time her young friend felt obliged to her for these wishes; but they were repeated so often, and proved so totally ineffectual, that Catherine grew tired at last, and would thank her no more.

They were not long able, however, to enjoy the repose of the eminence they had so laboriously gained. Everybody was shortly in motion for tea, and they must squeeze out like the rest. Catherine began to feel something of disappointment—she was tired of being continually pressed against by people, the generality of whose faces possessed nothing to interest, and with all of whom she was so wholly unacquainted that she could not relieve the irksomeness of imprisonment by the exchange of a syllable with any of her fellow captives; and when at last arrived in the tea-room, she felt yet more the awkwardness of having no party to join, no acquaintance to claim, no gentleman to assist them. They saw nothing of Mr. Allen; and after looking about them in vain for a more eligible situation, were obliged to sit down at the end of a table, at which a large party were already placed, without having anything to do there, or anybody to speak to, except each other.

Mrs. Allen congratulated herself, as soon as they were seated, on having preserved her gown from injury. "It would have been very shocking to have it torn," said she, "would not it? It is such a delicate muslin. For my part I have not seen anything I like so well in the whole room, I assure you."

"How uncomfortable it is," whispered Catherine, "not to have a single acquaintance here!"

"Yes, my dear," replied Mrs. Allen, with perfect serenity, "it is very uncomfortable indeed."

"What shall we do? The gentlemen and ladies at this table look as if they wondered why we came here—we seem forcing ourselves into their party."

"Aye, so we do. That is very disagreeable. I wish we had a large acquaintance here."

"I wish we had any—it would be somebody to go to."

"Very true, my dear; and if we knew anybody we would join them directly. The Skinners were here last year—I wish they were here now."

"Had not we better go away as it is? Here are no tea-things for us, you see."

"No more there are, indeed. How very provoking! But I think we had better sit still, for one gets so tumbled in such a crowd! How is my head, my dear? Somebody gave me a push that has hurt it, I am afraid."

"No, indeed, it looks very nice. But, dear Mrs. Allen, are you sure there is nobody you know in all this multitude of people? I think you must know somebody."

"I don't, upon my word—I wish I did. I wish I had a large acquaintance here with all my heart, and then I should get you a partner. I should be so glad to have you dance. There goes a strange-looking woman! What an odd gown she has got on! How old-fashioned it is! Look at the back."

After some time they received an offer of tea from one of their neighbours; it was thankfully accepted, and this introduced a light conversation with the gentleman who offered it, which was the only time that anybody spoke to them during the evening, till they were discovered and joined by Mr. Allen when the dance was over.

"Well, Miss Morland," said he, directly, "I hope you have had an agreeable ball."

"Very agreeable indeed," she replied, vainly endeavouring to hide a great yawn.

"I wish she had been able to dance," said his wife; "I wish we could have got a partner for her. I have been saying how glad I should be if the Skinners were here this winter instead of last; or if the Parrys had come, as they talked of once, she might have danced with George Parry. I am so sorry she has not had a partner!"

"We shall do better another evening I hope," was Mr. Allen's consolation.

The company began to disperse when the dancing was over—enough to leave space for the remainder to walk about in some comfort; and now was the time for an heroine, who had not yet played a very distinguished part in the events of the evening, to be noticed and admired. Every five minutes, by removing some of the crowd, gave greater openings for her charms. She was now seen by many young men who had not been near her before. Not one, however, started with rapturous wonder on beholding her, no whisper of eager inquiry ran round the room, nor was she once called a divinity by anybody. Yet Catherine was in very good looks, and had the company only seen her three years before, they would now have thought her exceedingly handsome.

She was looked at, however, and with some admiration; for, in her own hearing, two gentlemen pronounced her to be a pretty girl. Such words had their due effect; she immediately thought the evening pleasanter than she had found it before—her humble vanity was contented—she felt more obliged to the two young men for this simple praise than a true-quality heroine would have been for fifteen sonnets in celebration of her charms, and went to her chair in good humour with everybody, and perfectly satisfied with her share of public attention.

CHAPTER

Four

THE PARTICULARS OF Imogen Carlson could not have been any more different from that of Miss Morland. As one had come to Bath by invitation to enjoy
all the pleasures and finery the city had to offer, the other called it home and only
experienced its entertainments secondhand through observation of the social
class in which she played no part.

One viewed life through the naivety of youth and inexperience with all the
hopes and expectations of a happy life, a loving husband, and prosperous surroundings, while the other had become prematurely wise to the streets and bore
no prospects to hope for. As one honed her skills as a sometime heroine, the
other resigned her lot in life as that of a victim of circumstance–and on this same
night that Catherine Morland experienced her first taste of Bath, Imogen Carlson
breathed her last.

The Carlson family was of the common working class with little to offer to
the future of either Imogen or her younger brother or sister. The father spent his
days doing whatever jobs he could find and his nights under the weight of the
bottle, while the mother cared for their small home and labored with linen work
for those who might use her services. He was rough in his exterior, brash and
distant in nature, but with enough consideration for those immediately around
him to make home life tolerable, if not bearable.

Both Mr. and Mrs. Carlson knew that their means of life depended on the
prosperity of Bath and its inhabitants. They lived to serve and passed this understanding of the world to their offspring.

Imogen, at seven and twenty years of age, was still a jewel. The toil of the days had not diminished the vibrancy of her appearance, and she attracted the eyes of many a gentleman just as much as she did when she was sixteen. Her eyes were wide and blue, tinged with specks of tan, accented by thick lashes, and with a complexion still considered quite fair. The whole was framed by waves of lush brown hair.

Her figure likewise found favor, even if not accented by the latest in fashion as were many in Bath. The only dampener to the whole was her demeanor, both quiet and solemn, having taken in early on what her future held. For as she might still hope to find love and marriage, a home of her own and a knight to take her from all she had known, she somehow knew deep down that it was not to be. Her few acquaintances that might have borne fruit never bloomed, and she came to accept that she would bear out her future in the same manner as her past and that the best days of her youth had long since passed.

For all this, everyone who knew Imogen considered her a sweet girl, a charming girl, and one that would make any prospective husband happy. True, she rarely smiled anymore, but when she did, it illuminated the room.

To wish her a storybook ending with the shining knight would be utmost on anyone's lips, but for all those who might have carried her off to some happy ending, she instead met up with the worst sort that she could have encountered. Words were spoken, promises made, hopes and expectations raised, and Imogen even began to think that her life was about to change. In this, she was right, but with an end beyond her imagination.

So swayed was she in her affection that she gave of her heart completely, as well as that most precious thing that is only a woman's to give, not knowing that her devotion was being taken advantage of in the most callous way.

In her last moments, she screamed as loud as she might, hoping that someone might hear—and then the blade slit her throat, the cry became thick and garbled as it mixed with blood, and all her hopes and fears came to an abrupt end. Nearby, there were the unexpected screeches of nightjars, a curious fact within the confines of the city as the nocturnal birds tended to populate the more rural areas.

Imogen's body was dumped into the River Avon, far from anyone who might have heard her final call.

CHAPTER
Five

EVERY MORNING NOW brought its regular duties—shops were to be visited; some new part of the town to be looked at; and the pump-room to be attended, where they paraded up and down for an hour, looking at everybody and speaking to no one. The wish of a numerous acquaintance in Bath was still uppermost with Mrs. Allen, and she repeated it after every fresh proof, which every morning brought, of her knowing nobody at all.

They made their appearance in the Lower Rooms; and here fortune was more favourable to our heroine. The master of the ceremonies introduced to her a very gentlemanlike young man as a partner; his name was Tilney. He seemed to be about four or five and twenty, was rather tall, had a pleasing countenance, a very intelligent and lively eye, and, if not quite handsome, was very near it. His address was good, and Catherine felt herself in high luck. There was little leisure for speaking while they danced; but when they were seated at tea, she found him as agreeable as she had already given him credit for being. He talked with fluency and spirit—and there was an archness and pleasantry in his manner which interested, though it was hardly understood by her. After chatting some time on such matters as naturally arose from the objects around them, he suddenly addressed her with—"I have hitherto been very remiss, madam, in the proper attentions of a partner here; I have not yet asked you how long you have been in Bath; whether you were ever here before; whether you have been at the Upper Rooms, the theatre, and the concert; and how you like the place altogether. I have been very negligent—but are you now at leisure to satisfy me in these particulars? If you are I will begin directly."

"You need not give yourself that trouble, sir."

"No trouble, I assure you, madam." Then forming his features into a set smile, and affectedly softening his voice, he added, with a simpering air, "Have you been long in Bath, madam?"

"About a week, sir," replied Catherine, trying not to laugh.

"Really!" with affected astonishment.

"Why should you be surprised, sir?"

"Why, indeed!" said he, in his natural tone. "But some emotion must appear to be raised by your reply, and surprise is more easily assumed, and not less reasonable than any other. Now let us go on. Were you never here before, madam?"

"Never, sir."

"Indeed! Have you yet honoured the Upper Rooms?"

"Yes, sir, I was there last Monday."

"Have you been to the theatre?"

"Yes, sir, I was at the play on Tuesday."

"To the concert?"

"Yes, sir, on Wednesday."

"And are you altogether pleased with Bath?"

"Yes—I like it very well."

"Now I must give one smirk, and then we may be rational again." Catherine turned away her head, not knowing whether she might venture to laugh. "I see what you think of me," said he gravely—"I shall make but a poor figure in your journal tomorrow."

"My journal!"

"Yes, I know exactly what you will say: Friday, went to the Lower Rooms; wore my sprigged muslin robe with blue trimmings—plain black shoes—appeared to much advantage; but was strangely harassed by a queer, half-witted man, who would make me dance with him, and distressed me by his nonsense."

"Indeed I shall say no such thing."

"Shall I tell you what you ought to say?"

"If you please."

"I danced with a very agreeable young man, introduced by Mr. King; had a great deal of conversation with him—seems a most extraordinary genius—hope I may know more of him. That, madam, is what I wish you to say."

"But, perhaps, I keep no journal."

"Perhaps you are not sitting in this room, and I am not sitting by you. These are points in which a doubt is equally possible. Not keep a journal! How are your absent cousins to understand the tenour of your life in Bath without one? How are the civilities and compliments of every day to be related as they ought to be, unless noted down every evening in a journal? How are your various dresses to be remembered, and the particular state of your complexion, and curl of your hair to be described in all their diversities, without having constant recourse to a journal? My dear madam, I am not so ignorant of young ladies' ways as you wish to believe me; it is this delightful habit of journaling which largely contributes to form the easy style of writing for which ladies are so generally celebrated. Everybody allows that the talent of writing agreeable letters is peculiarly female. Nature may have done something, but I am sure it must be essentially assisted by the practice of keeping a journal."

Catherine was not to be found out so easily, and therefore, avoided the direct question. "The writing of letters is essential when away from one's family," she answered. "Indeed, I have taken to writing my younger sister, Sally, and conveying all of my activities while I have been here, for she would be as eager to be here as I. In this way, she can share in the experience as best as possible." Catherine paused, and then said in doubt, "I have sometimes thought whether ladies do write so much better letters than gentlemen! That is—I should not think the superiority was always on our side."

"As far as I have had opportunity of judging, it appears to me that the usual style of letter-writing among women is faultless, except in three particulars."

"And what are they?"

"A general deficiency of subject, a total inattention to stops, and a very frequent ignorance of grammar."

"Upon my word! I need not have been afraid of disclaiming the compliment. You do not think too highly of us in that way."

"I should no more lay it down as a general rule that women write better letters than men, than that they sing better duets, or draw better landscapes. In every power, of which taste is the foundation, excellence is pretty fairly divided between the sexes."

They were interrupted by Mrs. Allen: "My dear Catherine," said she, "do take this pin out of my sleeve; I am afraid it has torn a hole already; I shall be quite sorry if it has, for this is a favourite gown, though it cost but nine shillings a yard."

"That is exactly what I should have guessed it, madam," said Mr. Tilney, looking at the muslin.

"Do you understand muslins, sir?"

"Particularly well; I always buy my own cravats, and am allowed to be an excellent judge; and my sister has often trusted me in the choice of a gown. I bought one for her the other day, and it was pronounced to be a prodigious bargain by every lady who saw it. I gave but five shillings a yard for it, and a true Indian muslin."

Mrs. Allen was quite struck by his genius. "Men commonly take so little notice of those things," said she; "I can never get Mr. Allen to know one of my gowns from another. You must be a great comfort to your sister, sir."

"I hope I am, madam."

"And pray, sir, what do you think of Miss Morland's gown?"

"It is very pretty, madam," said he, gravely examining it; "but I do not think it will wash well; I am afraid it will fray."

"How can you," said Catherine, laughing, "be so—" She had almost said "strange."

"I am quite of your opinion, sir," replied Mrs. Allen; "and so I told Miss Morland when she bought it."

"But then you know, madam, muslin always turns to some account or other; Miss Morland will get enough out of it for a handkerchief, or a cap, or a cloak. Muslin can never be said to be wasted. I have heard my sister say so forty times, when she has been extravagant in buying more than she wanted, or careless in cutting it to pieces."

"Bath is a charming place, sir; there are so many good shops here. We are sadly off in the country; not but what we have very good shops in Salisbury, but it is so far to go—eight miles is a long way; Mr. Allen says it is nine, measured nine; but I am sure it cannot be more than eight; and it is such a fag—I come back tired to death. Now, here one can step out of doors and get a thing in five minutes."

Mr. Tilney was polite enough to seem interested in what she said; and she kept him on the subject of muslins till the dancing recommenced. Catherine feared, as she listened to their discourse, that he indulged himself a little too much with the foibles of others. "What are you thinking of so earnestly?" said he, as they walked back to the ballroom; "not of your partner, I hope, for, by that shake of the head, your meditations are not satisfactory."

Catherine coloured, and said, "I was not thinking of anything."

"That is artful and deep, to be sure; but I had rather be told at once that you will not tell me."

"Well then, I will not."

"Thank you; for now we shall soon be acquainted, as I am authorized to tease you on this subject whenever we meet, and nothing in the world advances intimacy so much."

They danced again; and, when the assembly closed, parted, on the lady's side at least, with a strong inclination for continuing the acquaintance. Whether she thought of him so much, while she drank her warm wine and water, and prepared herself for bed, as to dream of him when there, cannot be ascertained; but I hope it was no more than in a slight slumber, or a morning doze at most; for if it be true, as a celebrated writer has maintained, that no young lady can be justified in falling in love before the gentleman's love is declared,* it must be very improper that a young lady should dream of a gentleman before the gentleman is first known to have dreamt of her. How proper Mr. Tilney might be as a dreamer or a lover had not yet perhaps entered Mr. Allen's head, but that he was not objectionable as a common acquaintance for his young charge he was on inquiry satisfied; for he had early in the evening taken pains to know who her partner was, and had been assured of Mr. Tilney's being a clergyman, and of a very respectable family in Gloucestershire.

As to Catherine's dreams, it can be told that they were most pleasant in nature, leaving her well-rested in the morning and eager for the activities of the new day. Nowhere in her slumbers was there a hint of the dark shadows that would soon cloud those dreams.

CHAPTER

Six

My dearest Sally,

As you shall ever and always shall be known to me as such, for no other name could replace that which I have held you in such affection. Please offer no argument in this account but simply let it be, as I will ever and always be your Cathy.

I am well overdue in my writings, and as I am sure you are all in eagerness to know of my stay so far, I will keep it to those little particulars that I know you will find most interesting.

I have little to say of the travel to Bath, which was long and uneventful, excepting the view of the splendid countryside. Upon our arrival, Mr. Allen set us into our lodgings, which are quite pleasant, and with its location on Pulteney Street, offers a lovely view of the thoroughfare.

From here, we are able to travel west across Pulteney Bridge to the Assembly Rooms, they being all that you might imagine, and all the other places worth visiting.

I would like to say that we set there immediately, but this was not to be, as I was required to accompany Mrs. Allen to the various shops so that we might appear properly dressed for the events. I feel like a princess for wearing the latest fashion, and my hair has been cut and put up so you would hardly recognize me. All of this required several days' worth of preparation.

Our first evening out was amazing, even though the room was so full of people, we could scarcely move, and as we knew no one else at the ballroom, we spent most of the time keeping each other company. There was no dancing to be had that evening.

Our subsequent day's outings proved to be more satisfactory, and at our visit to the Lower Rooms, I was introduced to a singularly agreeable young man by the name of Tilney, who speaks the most fascinating nonsense and asked me to dance.

He suggested that I might write of him in my journal and describe him as half-witted and queer, but feel just as witless for being unable to keep up with his thoughts. In truth, he may be as queer as he claims, but I think that he only makes light of himself, and I find him all the more charming for it.

I wish you were here, as I know you would be equally enthralled with Bath. Upon my return, I will give you all the minute details, far more than I can presently put on paper. Be well and give my love to all.

Your sister,
Cathy

CHAPTER
Seven

WITH MORE THAN usual eagerness did Catherine hasten to the pump-room the next day, secure within herself of seeing Mr. Tilney there before the morning were over, and ready to meet him with a smile; but no smile was demanded—Mr. Tilney did not appear. Every creature in Bath, except himself, was to be seen in the room at different periods of the fashionable hours; crowds of people were every moment passing in and out, up the steps and down; people whom nobody cared about, and nobody wanted to see; and he only was absent. "What a delightful place Bath is," said Mrs. Allen as they sat down near the great clock, after parading the room till they were tired; "and how pleasant it would be if we had any acquaintance here."

This sentiment had been uttered so often in vain that Mrs. Allen had no particular reason to hope it would be followed with more advantage now; but we are told to "despair of nothing we would attain," as "unwearied diligence our point would gain"; and the unwearied diligence with which she had every day wished for the same thing was at length to have its just reward, for hardly had she been seated ten minutes before a lady of about her own age, who was sitting by her, and had been looking at her attentively for several minutes, addressed her with great complaisance in these words: "I think, madam, I cannot be mistaken; it is a long time since I had the pleasure of seeing you, but is not your name Allen?" This question answered, as it readily was, the stranger pronounced hers to be Thorpe; and Mrs. Allen immediately recognized the features of a former schoolfellow and intimate, whom she had seen only once since their respective marriages, and that many years ago. Their joy on this meeting was very great, as well it might, since they had been contented to know nothing of each other for the last fifteen years. Compliments on good looks now passed; and, after observing how time had slipped away since they were last together, how little they had thought of meeting in Bath, and what a pleasure it was to see an old friend, they proceeded to make inquiries and give intelligence as to their families, sisters, and cousins, talking both together, far more ready to give than to receive information, and each hearing very little of what the other said. Mrs. Thorpe, however, had one great advantage as a talker, over Mrs. Allen, in a family of children; and when she expatiated on the talents of her sons, and the beauty of her daughters, when she related their different situations and views—that John was at Oxford, Edward at Merchant Taylors', and William at sea—and all of them more beloved and respected in their different station than any other three beings ever were, Mrs. Allen had no similar information to give, no similar triumphs to press on the unwilling and unbelieving ear of her friend, and was forced to sit and appear to listen to all these maternal effusions, consoling herself, however, with the discovery, which her keen eye soon made, that the lace on Mrs. Thorpe's pelisse was not half so handsome as that on her own.

"Here come my dear girls," cried Mrs. Thorpe, pointing at three smart-looking females who, arm in arm, were then moving towards her. "My dear Mrs. Allen, I long to introduce them; they will be so delighted to see you: the tallest is Isabella, my eldest; is not she a fine young woman? The others are very much admired too, but I believe Isabella is the handsomest."

The Miss Thorpes were introduced; and Miss Morland, who had been for a short time forgotten, was introduced likewise. The name seemed to strike them all; and, after speaking to her with great civility, the eldest young lady observed aloud to the rest, "How excessively like her brother Miss Morland is!"

"The very picture of him indeed!" cried the mother—and "I should have known her anywhere for his sister!" was repeated by them all, two or three times over. For a moment Catherine was surprised; but Mrs. Thorpe and her daughters had scarcely begun the history of their acquaintance with Mr. James Morland, before she remembered that her eldest brother had lately formed an intimacy with a young man of his own college, of the name of Thorpe; and that he had spent the last week of the Christmas vacation with his family, near London.

The whole being explained, many obliging things were said by the Miss Thorpes of their wish of being better acquainted with her; of being considered as already friends, through the friendship of their brothers, etc., which Catherine heard with pleasure, and answered with all the pretty expressions she could command; and, as the first proof of amity, she was soon invited to accept an arm of the eldest Miss Thorpe, and take a turn with her about the room. Catherine was delighted with this extension of her Bath acquaintance, and almost forgot Mr. Tilney while she talked to Miss Thorpe. Friendship is certainly the finest balm for the pangs of disappointed love.

Their conversation turned upon those subjects, of which the free discussion has generally much to do in perfecting a sudden intimacy between two young ladies: such as dress, balls, flirtations, and quizzes. Miss Thorpe, however, being four years older than Miss Morland, and at least four years better informed, had a very decided advantage in discussing such points; she could compare the balls of Bath with those of Tunbridge, its fashions with the fashions of London; could rectify the opinions of her new friend in many articles of tasteful attire; could discover a flirtation between any gentleman and lady who only smiled on each other; and point out a quiz through the thickness of a crowd. These powers received due admiration from Catherine, to whom they were entirely new; and the respect which they naturally inspired might have been too great for familiarity, had not the easy gaiety of Miss Thorpe's manners, and her frequent expressions of delight on this acquaintance with her, softened down every feeling of awe, and left nothing but tender affection. Their increasing attachment was not to be satisfied with half a dozen turns in the pump-room, but required, when they all quitted it together, that Miss Thorpe should accompany Miss Morland to the very door of Mr. Allen's house; and that they should there part with a most affectionate and lengthened shake of hands, after learning, to their mutual relief, that they should see each other across the theatre at night, and say their prayers in the same chapel the next morning. Catherine then ran directly upstairs, and watched Miss Thorpe's progress down the street from the drawing-room window; admired the graceful spirit of her walk, the fashionable air of her figure and dress; and felt grateful, as well she might, for the chance which had procured her such a friend.

Mrs. Thorpe was a widow, and not a very rich one; she was a good-humoured, well-meaning woman, and a very indulgent mother. Her eldest daughter had great personal beauty, and the younger ones, by pretending to be as handsome as their sister, imitating her air, and dressing in the same style, did very well.

This brief account of the family is intended to supersede the necessity of a long and minute detail from Mrs. Thorpe herself, of her past adventures and sufferings, which might otherwise be expected to occupy the three or four following chapters; in which the worthlessness of lords and attorneys might be set forth, and conversations, which had passed twenty years before, be minutely repeated.

CHAPTER

Eight

THE EVENING WAS already well underway when Catherine and the Allens set out for the theatre, and aside from the usual bustle in the streets, there seemed to be a strange calm to the evening. Even Mrs. Allen, who normally would fail to notice such subtleties as this, commented that the air seemed "much too still for the city." Catherine gave it no notice, as Bath was still the latest realm of adventure, and each moment brought about something new.

As they drew close to the Pulteney Bridge, their carriage slowed due to a gathering of onlookers at one side. Catherine immediately grew attentive to the activities, and after the carriage had come to a full stop, she stepped down to get a closer look followed by Mr. Allen.

It was evident from the observations of the crowd that the source of their attention resided in the waters directly below the bridge. Catherine worked her way to its edge, then peered down to the dark waters below. Two small boats were positioned in the area just outside of the bridge foundation, each bearing two officers who were attempting to pull a shape from the water. It took a full minute for her to comprehend that the object of their attention was a human body, immediately bringing forth an audible gasp from her lips. Moments later, the body was pulled upward into the boat, allowing Catherine an unobstructed view of the corpse.

Some sights are meant to be forgotten. This was one such image. The remains were that of a woman, whose body had been mutilated in a manner most heinous. Clots of mud clung to her hair and clothes, partially covering the strange symbols that appeared to be inscribed upon the body.

Catherine recognized that the girl had been quite handsome; even a death such as this could not obscure that fact. Equally obvious was that she did not come to her end in any natural fashion. In all, Catherine saw the body for only a few seconds, yet the frightful vision would last a lifetime.

At this point, Mr. Allen pulled her away and led her back to the carriage, stating that the spectacle was hardly the sort of thing that she should be witness to. By the time she took to her seat, she was in tears, feeling the full impact of that life that had been lost, and all of the infinite possibilities of a future that would never happen.

They made their way to the theatre, and both Allens hoped that the performance might help to restore Catherine to her former self. By increments, she managed to find her pleasant manners, although the scene at the bridge never fully left her during the remainder of the evening.

As to be expected, Catherine was not so much engaged at the theatre that evening, in returning the nods and smiles of Miss Thorpe, though they certainly claimed much of her leisure, as her mind invariably wandered back to the scene at the bridge. It was an event that would give full account to, not now, but later when she and Isabella might talk in confidence. There was so much that she felt, and so much she could not quite define, that it would require a closed audience, so for the present, she allowed the conversation to flit from one idle subject to another.

In addition, there was another object to her attention that even the events at the bridge could not wash away, and thus she would repeatedly look with an inquiring eye for Mr. Tilney in every box which her eye could reach; but she looked in vain. Mr. Tilney was no fonder of the play than the pump-room. She hoped to be more fortunate the next day; and when her wishes for fine weather were answered by seeing a beautiful morning, she hardly felt a doubt of it; for a fine Sunday in Bath empties every house of its inhabitants, and all the world appears on such an occasion to walk about and tell their acquaintance what a charming day it is.

As soon as divine service was over, the Thorpes and Allens eagerly joined each other; and after staying long enough in the pump-room to discover that the crowd was insupportable, and that there was not a genteel face to be seen, which everybody discovers every Sunday throughout the season, they hastened away to the Crescent, to breathe the fresh air of better company. Here Catherine and Isabella, arm in arm, again tasted the sweets of friendship in an unreserved conversation; they talked much, and with much enjoyment; but again was Catherine disappointed in her hope of reseeing her partner. He was nowhere to be met with; every search for him was equally unsuccessful, in morning lounges or evening assemblies; neither at the Upper nor Lower Rooms, at dressed or undressed balls, was he perceivable; nor among the walkers, the horsemen, or the curricle-drivers of the morning. His name was not in the pump-room book, and curiosity could do no more. He must be gone from Bath. Yet he had not mentioned that his stay would be so short! This sort of mysteriousness, which is always so becoming in a hero, threw a fresh grace in Catherine's imagination around his person and manners, and increased her anxiety to know more of him. From the Thorpes she could learn nothing, for they had been only two days in Bath before they met with Mrs. Allen. It was a subject, however, in which she often indulged with her fair friend, from whom she received every possible encouragement to continue to think of him; and his impression on her fancy was not suffered therefore to weaken. Isabella was very sure that he must be a charming young man, and was equally sure that he must have been delighted with her dear Catherine, and would therefore shortly return. She liked him the better for being a clergyman, "for she must confess herself very partial to the profession"; and something like a sigh escaped her as she said it. Perhaps Catherine was wrong in not demanding the cause of that gentle emotion—but she was not experienced enough in the finesse of love, or the duties of friendship, to know when delicate raillery was properly called for, or when a confidence should be forced.

Mrs. Allen was now quite happy—quite satisfied with Bath. She had found some acquaintance, had been so lucky too as to find in them the family of a most worthy old friend; and, as the completion of good fortune, had found these friends by no means so expensively dressed as herself. Her daily expressions were no longer, "I wish we had some acquaintance in Bath!" They were changed into, "How glad I am we have met with Mrs. Thorpe!" and she was as eager in promoting the intercourse of the two families, as her young charge and Isabella themselves could be; never satisfied with the day unless she spent the chief of it by the side of Mrs. Thorpe, in what they called conversation, but in which there was scarcely ever any exchange of opinion, and not often any resemblance of subject, for Mrs. Thorpe talked chiefly of her children, and Mrs. Allen of her gowns.

The progress of the friendship betwen Catherine and Isabella was quick as its beginning had been warm, and they passed so rapidly through every gradation of increasing tenderness that there was shortly no fresh proof of it to be given to their friends or themselves. They called each other by their Christian name, were always arm in arm when they walked, pinned up each other's train for the dance, and were not to be divided in the set; and if a rainy morning deprived them of other enjoyments, they were still resolute in meeting in defiance of wet and dirt, and shut themselves up, to read novels together.

Isabella had a particular appetite for them, describing particular scenes with delicious relish, and the more horrendous they were, the better. In this, Catherine had an ideal confidant, even if the source of their discussions was fictitious and bore no direct relation to their true circumstance.

"Oh, don't stop now," Catherine exclaimed on one damp morning when Isabella paused in her reading of *The Lost Chamber of Meinster Castle.* "I must know what happens next."

The two had found solitude in Catherine's room, with the soft drizzle of rain outside to set the mood. Catherine sat on her bed, holding a comforting pillow to her chest, while her friend relaxed in a nearby chair with the book in hand. Isabella giggled, cleared her throat, and continued in the recitation.

> "I have secured the key," Gerta whispered after closing the door. "Are you sure you want to do this?"
>
> A feeling of nervousness overtook Dora, to the degree that she could not immediately answer, so she responded with a nod of her head. The danger behind such an adventure could be great if they were discovered, and yet so intense was her curiosity that she declared it worth the risk.
>
> She averted her gaze, fear mounting upon itself, but felt an entrusting hand placed on hers and she knew she would not venture forth alone. The time had come, and without a word, they retrieved the candles from the mantle and moved quietly into the corridor.

Isabella cast a glance at Catherine, whose eyes were wide with captivated interest, and with a smile, read on, describing the passage of Gerta and Dora through the hallways of the ancient castle. As if to give its consent to the story, the outside rain picked up its pace.

> With the most delicate of footsteps, they made their way down multiple floors of the structure, far more than they thought existed, until they were sure to be on a level beneath the earth itself. The walls gave confirmation of this with its cool dampness, as well as the absence of any windows to offer light. Equally evident was the disuse of these passages with a solid coating of dust, while the webbings of many generations of

spiders stretched above their heads. Minimal light offered by their twin candles created deep shadows, swallowing whole portions of the corridor. It occurred to Dora that should their lights go out, they would be plunged into absolute darkness, and must feel their way along the walls to find their way back to the lit spaces above. One uncomfortable thought led to the next, including the possibility of becoming lost in these winding passages, and she could no longer suppress a whimper.

"Be strong, Dora," whispered Gerta. "We are nearly there."

Initially hidden in the darkness, the door came into view with worn metal framing and a formidable lock set to one side. Gerta wasted no time in trying the key, and at first, the lock seemed frozen and would not move, but soon gave way with a discernible click. She pushed on the door and it gave with an extended creak of iron against iron that resonated throughout the subterranean passageway. With that, they were in.

Again, Isabella stopped and looked over to see if her recitations were doing justice to the novel. With more excitement than she might have otherwise shown, Catherine nearly shouted, "Yes, continue! What will happen next?"

Isabella teased her by leafing through the next few pages, inspecting each one silently, and casting knowing glances while letting out an occasional gasp. Catherine responded by slapping her pillow in agitation, and as she could not stand the suspense any longer, Isabella began anew.

The unnerving darkness of the corridor paled in comparison to the dense black that awaited them inside the chamber, which while small, had numerous alcoves and indentions that made the room all the more mysterious. Most notable were the three additional doors, one set to each wall, and an open window inset with iron bars, behind which was yet another wall, this one of stone. This was most peculiar due to its position under ground level and therefore without the need of a window.

With no openings for a draft, the smoke from the candles drifted serenely upward in a straight vertical line. Equally absent was any noise except for the echoes of their footsteps against the stone flooring. In all, the antiquity of the room with its lack of furnishings made the environment all the more frightening.

Without warning, a gust arose and extinguished both of the candles, leaving them both in darkness. Gerta and Dora reached for one another in need of reassurance but they never connected, fingers passing fingers as ships might in the night. Gerta attempted to scream, but her cry was stifled by an unseen hand that had risen from behind and clutched her face. This was followed by the reverberations of footsteps moving away, along with the sound of something heavy dragged across the floor.

After that, Dora remained alone with the silence and the darkness.

As the day progressed, the rain lessened and was eventually exhausted, giving way to warm sunlight and the bluest of skies. In all, the afternoon was a perfect one for activities out of doors, and indeed, much of Bath did just that. Even with this enticement, Catherine and her friend found it hard to leave the confines of her room, so engrossed were they in the adventures inside Meinster Castle, and the unknown fate of its heroine.

CHAPTER

Nine

AMAZING THINGS, newspapers.

No sooner might an individual–with intentions to be fully knowledgeable of all the latest events worth knowing, and being astute to political, economic, and social trends–digest all there was to know of the day, it would then be that the latest edition of the periodical would appear, thus rendering all the previously accumulated information out of date.

Still tacky from freshly set ink, the paper would offer up a fresh set of details to be consumed, digested, and used as a topic of conversation while demonstrating how clever the possessor of such information indeed was, within the period before the next edition.

Such was the nature of newspapers, with any town of worth being represented by at least one; Bath was no different, offering up news of importance through the pages of its *Bath Journal*. This periodical served as a reputable institution, having been in business since 1743 with a combination of topical stories, social listings, advertisements, and letters. Most astounding to this publication was that it managed to endure.

After all, Bath served as a center of popular activity, having lured a steady flow of visitors from far and wide under the guise of its wholesome remedies but it was most notable for its social environment. Therefore, reason suggested that in a center such as this, ripe with tête-à-têtes and idle gossip, and nary a secret left unspoken of, how could a newspaper ever hope to compete– but compete it did with much success, and for the gentlemen of any sensibility, it served as a source more reputable that the second-hand words of Mrs. Smith or Mrs. Jones.

Few doubted that the recent discovery of the body floating in the waters of the Avon would be given some coverage, and so it came to be. The story found its way into print as one of the smaller stories, it being less important than the social events taking place that week, and suffering from the literary embellishments so often used by its journalists. The story ran as follows:

Excerpt from the Bath Journal, August 7

BODY RECOVERED IN AVON RIVER

The most sorrowful of instances occurred two nights ago, that being the body of a woman found floating in the River Avon. The discovery was made by Mr. Andrew Jeffries, a recently arrived visitor to this city for reasons of health, who took on the habit of being observant to every detail around him, and thus noticed the figure in the water near the Pulteney Bridge. Mr. Jeffries acted with haste in securing additional help, and several boats were soon employed to reach the source of their attention.

The body has been identified as Imogen Carlson. The identity was confirmed by her father, Philippe Roger Carlson of Bath, who had previously notified the authorities that his daughter had gone missing. The source of her death is not known although it is strongly suspected that it was not of natural causes. Mr. Carlson stated that he had no reason to suspect anyone, as his daughter was held in high esteem and so it is believed that the implications to her death may be accidental.

Those who found the body have been reticent to divulge more details. It is known that Miss Carlson was twenty-seven years of age and was neither married nor in any form of engagement at the time of her death. It is estimated that the body had been in the water for several days, putting her death on or around the first or second of August.

The discovery at the Pulteney Bridge attracted a large number of observers, but an interrogation of those indicated that none were familiar with her. As mentioned previously in this newspaper, Bath is a safe and secure city, and its residents can rest assured of their well-being. This unfortunate incident should not in any way suggest to them otherwise.

Listed in the same edition of the journal was this lesser story, also given only a small amount of space, and most likely inserted into the paper as a means of filling space prior to publication.

A burglary took place in the early morning hours at a small business on James Street. There were no witnesses to the crime, and no one occupied the shop at the time, leaving the intruder ample time to enter and rummage for valuables. Access was gained by breaking the window adjoining the door and releasing the lock.

The proprietor of the store, Mr. Thorley Gainsborough, confirmed that while the burglar left the interior in a disheveled state, having thrown items from the shelves and drawers onto the floor, there appears to have been nothing stolen.

Mr. Gainsborough was understandably upset at the invasion and remained in a nervous state during the entire time of the investigation. It was also noted that a locked safe in the rear of the building remained locked, although the intruder tried unsuccessfully to force the lock. Gainsborough, who has the only key to the safe box, confirmed this. Because of an absence of witnesses, no further evidence of the perpetrator's identity, and nothing of value missing from the shop, there will be no further inquiry. Mr. Gainsborough is a dealer of vintage books, antiques, and other sought-after items.

CHAPTER

THE FOLLOWING CONVERSATION, which took place between the two friends in the pump-room one morning, after an acquaintance of eight or nine days, is given as a specimen of their very warm attachment, and of the delicacy, discretion, originality of thought, and literary taste which marked the reasonableness of that attachment.

They met by appointment; and as Isabella had arrived nearly five minutes before her friend, her first address naturally was, "My dearest creature, what can have made you so late? I have been waiting for you at least this age!"

"Have you, indeed! I am very sorry for it; but really I thought I was in very good time. It is but just one. I hope you have not been here long?"

"Oh! These ten ages at least. I am sure I have been here this half hour. But now, let us go and sit down at the other end of the room, and enjoy ourselves. I have an hundred things to say to you. In the first place, I was so afraid it would rain this morning, just as I wanted to set off; it looked very showery, and that would have thrown me into agonies! Do you know, I saw the prettiest hat you can imagine, in a shop window in Milsom Street just now—very like yours, only with coquelicot ribbons instead of green; I quite longed for it. But, my dearest Catherine, what have you been doing with yourself all this morning? Have you gone on with *Udolpho*?"

"Yes, I have been reading it ever since I woke; and I am got to the black veil."

"Are you, indeed? How delightful! Oh! I would not tell you what is behind the black veil for the world! Are not you wild to know?"

"Oh! Yes, quite; what can it be? But do not tell me—I would not be told upon any account. I know it must be a skeleton, I am sure it is Laurentina's skeleton. Oh! I am delighted with the book! I should like to spend my whole life in reading it. I assure you, if it had not been to meet you, I would not have come away from it for all the world."

"Dear creature! How much I am obliged to you; and when you have finished *Udolpho*, we will read the Italian together; and I have made out a list of ten or twelve more of the same kind for you."

"Have you, indeed! How glad I am! What are they all?"

"I will read you their names directly; here they are, in my pocketbook. *Castle of Wolfenbach, Clermont, Mysterious Warnings, Necromancer of the Black Forest, Midnight Bell, Orphan of the Rhine*, and *Horrid Mysteries*. Those will last us some time."

"Yes, pretty well; but are they all horrid, are you sure they are all horrid?"

"Yes, quite sure; for a particular friend of mine, a Miss Andrews, a sweet girl, one of the sweetest creatures in the world, has read every one of them. I wish you knew Miss Andrews, you would be delighted with her. She is netting herself the sweetest cloak you can conceive. I think her as beautiful as an angel, and I am so vexed with the men for not admiring her! I scold them all amazingly about it."

"Scold them! Do you scold them for not admiring her?"

"Yes, that I do. There is nothing I would not do for those who are really my friends. I have no notion of loving people by halves; it is not my nature. My attachments are always excessively strong. I told Captain Hunt at one of our assemblies this winter that if he was to tease me all night, I would not dance with him, unless he would allow Miss Andrews to be as beautiful as an angel. The men think us incapable of real friendship, you know, and I am determined to show them the difference. Now, if I were to hear anybody speak slightingly of you, I should fire up in a moment: but that is not at all likely, for you are just the kind of girl to be a great favourite with the men."

"Oh, dear!" cried Catherine, colouring. "How can you say so?"

"I know you very well; you have so much animation, which is exactly what Miss Andrews wants, for I must confess there is something amazingly insipid about her. Oh! I must tell you, that just after we parted yesterday, I saw a young man looking at you so earnestly—I am sure he is in love with you." Catherine coloured, and disclaimed again. Isabella laughed. "It is very true, upon my honour, but I see how it is; you are indifferent to everybody's admiration, except that of one gentleman, who shall be nameless. Nay, I cannot blame you"—speaking more seriously—"your feelings are easily understood. Where the heart is really attached, I know very well how little one can be pleased with the attention of anybody else. Everything is so insipid, so uninteresting, that does not relate to the beloved object! I can perfectly comprehend your feelings."

"But you should not persuade me that I think so very much about Mr. Tilney, for perhaps I may never see him again."

"Not see him again! My dearest creature, do not talk of it. I am sure you would be miserable if you thought so!"

"No, indeed, I should not. I do not pretend to say that I was not very much pleased with him; but while I have *Udolpho* to read, I feel as if nobody could make me miserable. Oh! The dreadful black veil! My dear Isabella, I am sure there must be Laurentina's skeleton behind it."

At once, the secrets behind the veil with the possible skeletal corpse triggered familiar images of the Pulteney Bridge and the waterlogged body covered in blood and wet earth, causing Catherine to stop in mid-thought. Her thoughts must have been all too apparent to Isabella, as it immediately drew a reaction.

"My dearest Catherine, are you all right?" she said, reaching out with both hands to give comfort. "You have suddenly gone quite pale."

"Yes, I think so, but there is something that I have been meaning to tell you. Indeed, I have spoken little of it since its occurrence a week back. Do accept my apologies for not confiding in you sooner, but it is still such a shock for me, even to think of it. Oh, the monstrosity of it all. Nor did I feel comfortable recounting the details to you at any time with other company present. But now let me tell you all, for I have been bearing these memories alone for too long."

Catherine gave a full account of the events at the bridge, and as might be expected, Isabella took to the news with profound fascination, much like she would to the plot from one of her horrid novels. "Too shocking," she exclaimed. "Too shocking. And you were there to see all of this. What do you make of it? How do you think she came to such a dreadful end?"

"I should hardly know, but it could not have been from any ordinary cause. I do wish I could purge the whole affair from my memory. Time and again, I find my thoughts going to this poor unfortunate woman, and what her final moments were. It has kept me up these last few nights when the room is dark and quiet, and I am waiting for sleep to take me. That is when she is most on my mind, even though I try my best not to dwell on her."

"And have you heard anything further since then?"

"Not a word, but to be truthful, it makes me fear for my safety. Can it be that Bath is such a dangerous place?"

Isabella threw off such ideas with a wave of her hand. "I should think it is safe enough, and there are always plenty of people around to ward off any wickedness. I assure you that you are quite secure. As to that poor creature, how might she have come to such an end? Surely not a lover's quarrel of disastrous results? Perhaps some gentleman had fallen hopelessly in love with her, but she was not equal in her disposition to him, and in a fit of maddened passion, he acted beyond his control. Might it have been ruffians who came upon her when she least expected it, or they might have thought her a princess and were determined to hold her ransom? Dearest me, could it have been someone she knew, someone so close that she never would have expected it?"

As she talked, Isabella's excitement grew as did the possible scenarios she concocted as to the woman's demise, while paying less attention to the severity of the event, or its effect on Miss Morland.

"And to think that you did not tell me any of this for the whole week we have been together," Isabella exclaimed. "I would have thought you would have confided in me the very moment it happened, as we are the dearest of friends and there cannot be any secrets between us. I should think I would tell you everything in my life, from the smallest detail, even the scraping of butter onto bread in the morning."

"I have wanted to, but it is so horrid to dwell upon. I wish I could get the image out of my mind. Yet I know of no one else to speak of this to as it bothers the Allens just as much, and they prefer me not to discuss it."

"Perhaps you might bring it up with your Mr. Tilney, as he might have a stronger constitution, and I know how well you would prefer his comfort." The comment succeeded in causing Catherine's cheeks to redden.

Soon enough, the story had run its course, and Isabella dismissed the subject with no more concern, treating the whole affair as if it had been a part of a fictitious volume. Indeed, she shifted the subject back to the books at hand, considering them part and parcel of the same thing.

"It is so odd to me, that you should never have read *Udolpho* before; but I suppose Mrs. Morland objects to novels."

"No, she does not," responded Catherine. "She very often reads Sir Charles Grandison herself; but new books do not fall in our way."

"Sir Charles Grandison! That is an amazing horrid book bore, is it not? I remember Miss Andrews could not get through the first volume, and I cannot say I blame her."

"It is not like *Udolpho* at all; but yet I think it is very entertaining."

"Do you indeed! You surprise me; I thought it had not been readable. But, my dearest Catherine, have you settled what to wear on your head tonight? I am determined at all events to be dressed exactly like you. The men take notice of that sometimes, you know."

"But it does not signify if they do," said Catherine, very innocently.

"Signify! Oh, heavens! I make it a rule never to mind what they say. They are very often amazingly impertinent if you do not treat them with spirit, and make them keep their distance."

"Are they? Well, I never observed that. They always behave very well to me."

"Oh! They give themselves such airs. They are the most conceited creatures in the world, and think themselves of so much importance! By the by, though I have thought of it a hundred times, I have always forgot to ask you what is your favourite complexion in a man. Do you like them best dark or fair?"

"I hardly know. I never much thought about it. Something between both, I think. Brown—not fair, and—and not very dark."

"Very well, Catherine. That is exactly he. I have not forgot your description of Mr. Tilney—'a brown skin, with dark eyes, and rather dark hair.' Well, my taste is different. I prefer light eyes, and as to complexion—do you know—I like a sallow better than any other. You must not betray me, if you should ever meet with one of your acquaintance answering that description."

"Betray you! What do you mean?"

"Nay, do not distress me. I believe I have said too much. Let us drop the subject."

Catherine, in some amazement, complied, and after remaining a few moments silent, was on the point of reverting to what interested her at that time rather more than anything else in the world, Laurentina's skeleton, when her friend prevented her, by saying, "For heaven's sake! Let us move away from this end of the room. Do you know, there are two odious young men who have been staring at me this half hour. They really put me quite out of countenance. Let us go and look at the arrivals. They will hardly follow us there."

Away they walked to the book; and while Isabella examined the names, it was Catherine's employment to watch the proceedings of these alarming young men.

"They are not coming this way, are they? I hope they are not so impertinent as to follow us. Pray let me know if they are coming. I am determined I will not look up."

In a few moments Catherine, with unaffected pleasure, assured her that she need not be longer uneasy, as the gentlemen had just left the pump-room.

"And which way are they gone?" said Isabella, turning hastily round. "One was a very good-looking young man."

"They went towards the church-yard."

"Well, I am amazingly glad I have got rid of them! And now, what say you to going to Edgar's Buildings with me, and looking at my new hat? You said you should like to see it."

Catherine readily agreed. "Only," she added, "perhaps we may overtake the two young men."

"Oh! Never mind that. If we make haste, we shall pass by them presently, and I am dying to show you my hat."

"But if we only wait a few minutes, there will be no danger of our seeing them at all."

"I shall not pay them any such compliment, I assure you. I have no notion of treating men with such respect. That is the way to spoil them."

Catherine had nothing to oppose against such reasoning; and therefore, to show the independence of Miss Thorpe, and her resolution of humbling the sex, they set off immediately as fast as they could walk, in pursuit of the two young men.

CHAPTER
Eleven

HALF A MINUTE conducted them through the pump-yard to the archway, opposite Union Passage; but here they were stopped. Everybody acquainted with Bath may remember the difficulties of crossing Cheap Street at this point; it is indeed a street of so impertinent a nature, so unfortunately connected with the great London and Oxford roads, and the principal inn of the city, that a day never passes in which parties of ladies, however important their business, whether in quest of pastry, millinery, or even (as in the present case) of young men, are not detained on one side or other by carriages, horsemen, or carts. This evil had been felt and lamented, at least three times a day, by Isabella since her residence in Bath; and she was now fated to feel and lament it once more, for at the very moment of coming opposite to Union Passage, and within view of the two gentlemen who were proceeding through the crowds, and threading the gutters of that interesting alley, they were prevented crossing by the approach of a gig, driven along on bad pavement by a most knowing-looking coachman with all the vehemence that could most fitly endanger the lives of himself, his companion, and his horse.

"Oh, these odious gigs!" said Isabella, looking up. "How I detest them." But this detestation, though so just, was of short duration, for she looked again and exclaimed, "Delightful! Mr. Morland and my brother!"

"Good heaven! 'Tis James!" was uttered at the same moment by Catherine; and, on catching the young men's eyes, the horse was immediately checked with a violence which almost threw him on his haunches, and the servant having now scampered up, the gentlemen jumped out, and the equipage was delivered to his care.

Catherine, by whom this meeting was wholly unexpected, received her brother with the liveliest pleasure; and he, being of a very amiable disposition, and sincerely attached to her, gave every proof on his side of equal satisfaction, which he could have leisure to do, while the bright eyes of Miss Thorpe were incessantly challenging his notice; and to her his devoirs were speedily paid, with a mixture of joy and embarrassment which might have informed Catherine, had she been more expert in the development of other people's feelings, and less simply engrossed by her own, that her brother thought her friend quite as pretty as she could do herself.

John Thorpe, who in the meantime had been giving orders about the horses, soon joined them, and from him she directly received the amends which were her due; for while he slightly and carelessly touched the hand of Isabella, on her he bestowed a whole scrape and half a short bow. He was a stout young man of middling height, who, with a plain face and ungraceful form, seemed fearful of being too handsome unless he wore the dress of a groom, and too much like a gentleman unless he were easy where he ought to be civil, and impudent where he might be allowed to be easy. He took out his watch: "How long do you think we have been running it from Tetbury, Miss Morland?"

"I do not know the distance." Her brother told her that it was twenty-three miles.

"Three and twenty!" cried Thorpe. "Five and twenty if it is an inch." Morland remonstrated, pleaded the authority of road-books, innkeepers, and milestones; but his friend disregarded them all; he had a surer test of distance. "I know it must be five and twenty," said he, "by the time we have been doing it. It is now half after one; we drove out of the inn-yard at Tetbury as the town clock struck eleven; and I defy any man in England to make my horse go less than ten miles an hour in harness; that makes it exactly twenty-five."

"You have lost an hour," said Morland; "it was only ten o'clock when we came from Tetbury."

"Ten o'clock! It was eleven, upon my soul! I counted every stroke. This brother of yours would persuade me out of my senses, Miss Morland; do but look at my horse; did you ever see an animal so made for speed in your life?" (The servant had just mounted the carriage and was driving off.) "Such true blood! Three hours and a half indeed coming only three and twenty miles! Look at that creature, and suppose it possible if you can."

"He does look very hot, to be sure."

"Hot! He had not turned a hair till we came to Walcot Church; but look at his forehand; look at his loins; only see how he moves; that horse cannot go less than ten miles an hour: tie his legs and he will get on. What do you think of my gig, Miss Morland? A neat one, is not it? Well hung; town-built; I have not had it a month. It was built for a Christchurch man, a friend of mine, a very good sort of fellow; he ran it a few weeks, till, I believe, it was convenient to have done with it. I happened just then to be looking out for some light thing of the kind, though I had pretty well determined on a curricle too; but I chanced to meet him on Magdalen Bridge, as he was driving into Oxford, last term: 'Ah! Thorpe,' said he, 'do you happen to want such a little thing as this? It is a capital one of the kind, but I am cursed tired of it.' 'Oh! Damn,' said I; 'I am your man; what do you ask?' And how much do you think he did, Miss Morland?"

"I am sure I cannot guess at all."

"Curricle-hung, you see; seat, trunk, sword-case, splashing-board, lamps, silver moulding, all you see complete; the iron-work as good as new, or better. He asked fifty guineas; I closed with him directly, threw down the money, and the carriage was mine."

"And I am sure," said Catherine, "I know so little of such things that I cannot judge whether it was cheap or dear."

"Neither one nor t'other; I might have got it for less, I dare say; but I hate haggling, and poor Freeman wanted cash."

"That was very good-natured of you," said Catherine, quite pleased.

"Oh! Damn it, when one has the means of doing a kind thing by a friend, I hate to be pitiful."

An inquiry now took place into the intended movements of the young ladies; and, on finding whither they were going, it was decided that the gentlemen should accompany them to Edgar's Buildings, and pay their respects to Mrs. Thorpe. James and Isabella led the way; and so well satisfied was the latter with her lot, so contentedly was she endeavouring to ensure a pleasant walk to him who brought the double recommendation of being her brother's friend, and her friend's brother, so pure and uncoquettish were her feelings, that, though they overtook and passed the two offending young men in Milsom Street, she was so far from seeking to attract their notice, that she looked back at them only three times.

John Thorpe kept of course with Catherine, and, after a few minutes' silence, renewed the conversation about his gig. "You will find, however, Miss Morland, it would be reckoned a cheap thing by some people, for I might have sold it for ten guineas more the next day; Jackson, of Oriel, bid me sixty at once; Morland was with me at the time."

"Yes," said Morland, who overheard this; "but you forget that your horse was included."

"My horse! Oh. Damn it! I would not sell my horse for a hundred. Are you fond of an open carriage, Miss Morland?"

"Yes, very; I have hardly ever an opportunity of being in one; but I am particularly fond of it."

"I am glad of it; I will drive you out in mine every day."

"Thank you," said Catherine, in some distress, from a doubt of the propriety of accepting such an offer.

"I will drive you up Lansdown Hill tomorrow."

"Thank you; but will not your horse want rest?"

"Rest! He has only come three and twenty miles today; all nonsense; nothing ruins horses so much as rest; nothing knocks them up so soon. No, no; I shall exercise mine at the average of four hours every day while I am here."

"Shall you indeed!" said Catherine very seriously. "That will be forty miles a day."

"Forty! Aye, fifty, for what I care. Well, I will drive you up Lansdown tomorrow; mind, I am engaged."

"How delightful that will be!" cried Isabella, turning round. "My dearest Catherine, I quite envy you; but I am afraid, brother, you will not have room for a third."

"A third indeed! No, no; I did not come to Bath to drive my sisters about; that would be a good joke, faith! Morland must take care of you."

This brought on a dialogue of civilities between the other two; but Catherine heard neither the particulars nor the result. Her companion's discourse now sunk from its hitherto animated pitch to nothing more than a short decisive sentence of praise or condemnation on the face of every woman they met; and Catherine, after listening and agreeing as long as she could, with all the civility and deference of the youthful female mind, fearful of hazarding an opinion of its own in opposition to that of a self-assured man, especially where the beauty of her own sex is concerned, ventured at length to vary the subject by a question which had been long uppermost in her thoughts; it was, "Have you ever read *Udolpho*, Mr. Thorpe?"

"*Udolpho*! Oh, Lord! Not I; I never read novels; I have something else to do."

Catherine, humbled and ashamed, was going to apologize for her question, but he prevented her by saying, "Novels are all so full of nonsense and stuff; there has not been a tolerably decent one come out since *Tom Jones*, except *The Monk*; I read that t'other day; but as for all the others, they are the stupidest things in creation."

"I think you must like *Udolpho*, if you were to read it; it is so very interesting."

"Not I, faith! No, if I read any, it shall be Mrs. Radcliffe's; her novels are amusing enough; they are worth reading; some fun and nature in them."

"*Udolpho* was written by Mrs. Radcliffe," said Catherine, with some hesitation, from the fear of mortifying him.

"No sure; was it? Aye, I remember, so it was; I was thinking of that other stupid book, written by that woman they make such a fuss about, she who married the French emigrant."

"I suppose you mean Camilla?"

"Yes, that's the book; such unnatural stuff! An old man playing at see-saw, I took up the first volume once and looked it over, but I soon found it would not do; indeed I guessed what sort of stuff it must be before I saw it: as soon as I heard she had married an emigrant, I was sure I should never be able to get through it."

"I have never read it."

"You had no loss, I assure you; it is the horridest nonsense you can imagine; there is nothing in the world in it but an old man's playing at see-saw and learning Latin; upon my soul there is not."

This critique, the justness of which was unfortunately lost on poor Catherine, brought them to the door of Mrs. Thorpe's lodgings, and the feelings of the discerning and unprejudiced reader of Camilla gave way to the feelings of the dutiful and affectionate son, as they met Mrs. Thorpe, who had descried them from above, in the passage. "Ah, Mother! How do you do?" said he, giving her a hearty shake of the hand. "Where did you get that quiz of a hat? It makes you look like an old witch. Here is Morland and I come to stay a few days with you, so you must look out for a couple of good beds somewhere near." And this address seemed to satisfy all the fondest wishes of the mother's heart, for she received him with the most delighted and exulting affection. On his two younger sisters he then bestowed an equal portion of his fraternal tenderness, for he asked each of them how they did, and observed that they both looked very ugly.

These manners did not please Catherine; but he was James's friend and Isabella's brother; and her judgment was further bought off by Isabella's assuring her, when they withdrew to see the new hat, that John thought her the most charming girl in the world, and by John's engaging her before they parted to dance with him that evening. Had she been older or vainer, such attacks might have done little; but, where youth and diffidence are united, it requires uncommon steadiness of reason to resist the attraction of being called the most charming girl in the world, and of being so very early engaged as a partner; and the consequence was that, when the two Morlands, after sitting an hour with the Thorpes, set off to walk together to Mr. Allen's, and James, as the door was closed on them, said, "Well, Catherine, how do you like my friend Thorpe?" instead of answering, as she probably would have done, had there been no friendship and no flattery in the case, "I do not like him at all," she directly replied, "I like him very much; he seems very agreeable."

"He is as good-natured a fellow as ever lived; a little of a rattle; but that will recommend him to your sex, I believe: and how do you like the rest of the family?"

"Very, very much indeed: Isabella particularly."

"I am very glad to hear you say so; she is just the kind of young woman I could wish to see you attached to; she has so much good sense, and is so thoroughly unaffected and amiable; I always wanted you to know her; and she seems very fond of you. She said the highest things in your praise that could possibly be; and the praise of such a girl as Miss Thorpe even you, Catherine," taking her hand with affection, "may be proud of."

"Indeed I am," she replied; "I love her exceedingly, and am delighted to find that you like her too. You hardly mentioned anything of her when you wrote to me after your visit there."

"Because I thought I should soon see you myself. I hope you will be a great deal together while you are in Bath. She is a most amiable girl; such a superior understanding! How fond all the family are of her; she is evidently the general favourite; and how much she must be admired in such a place as this—is not she?"

"Yes, very much indeed, I fancy; Mr. Allen thinks her the prettiest girl in Bath."

"I dare say he does; and I do not know any man who is a better judge of beauty than Mr. Allen. I need not ask you whether you are happy here, my dear Catherine; with such a companion and friend as Isabella Thorpe, it would be impossible for you to be otherwise; and the Allens, I am sure, are very kind to you?"

"Yes, very kind; I never was so happy before; and now you are come it will be more delightful than ever; how good it is of you to come so far on purpose to see me."

James accepted this tribute of gratitude, and qualified his conscience for accepting it too, by saying with perfect sincerity, "Indeed, Catherine, I love you dearly."

Inquiries and communications concerning brothers and sisters, the situation of some, the growth of the rest, and other family matters now passed between them, and continued, with only one small digression on James's part, in praise of Miss Thorpe, till they reached Pulteney Street, where he was welcomed with great kindness by Mr. and Mrs. Allen, invited by the former to dine with them, and summoned by the latter to guess the price and weigh the merits of a new muff and tippet. A pre-engagement in Edgar's Buildings prevented his accepting the invitation of one friend, and obliged him to hurry away as soon as he had satisfied the demands of the other. The time of the two parties uniting in the Octagon Room being correctly adjusted, Catherine was then left to the luxury of a raised, restless, and frightened imagination over the pages of *Udolpho*, lost from all worldly concerns of dressing and dinner, incapable of soothing Mrs. Allen's fears on the delay of an expected dressmaker, and having only one minute in sixty to bestow even on the reflection of her own felicity, in being already engaged for the evening.

CHAPTER

JOHN THORPE'S ACCOUNT of acquiring his gig at a price neither "cheap nor dear" was in perfect keeping to his general view of commerce; all worldly items might be had at a price, depending on the needs of buyer and seller, and it was only in finding that point of agreement that the sale might be completed, the item under consideration being anything from a mansion to a sewing needle.

The curricle was nothing more than the latest purchase made by Thorpe, just as he had likewise sold off other items in his possession. As to the true value of such an item, a bargain was infinitely preferable, and he would never owe up to being taken advantage of, even if he had been; his self-importance would have prevented it, such being the nature of a rattle.

This method of buying and selling off possessions from one individual to another was vastly different from that of normal commerce, in which such acts were conducted on a daily basis as a means of theoretically making the seller richer and the buyer poorer for it, and thereby providing a means of continued income. In the former, it was simply a way of relieving oneself of that singular item that was of no further use to the party. Such acts were quite common, as part of an open market between gentlemen.

These two variations on a business theme were hardly the only forms of marketing, some of which fell into the more unsavory forms of illicit trade, contraband, and the sale of fellow humans in one method or another.

This black market catered to a very different clientele, and as to be expected, functioned with its own set of rules, discretion being chief among them. Catherine would have known nothing about this, nor even John Thorpe, except in its most superficial forms, however as it existed far and wide around the world, so it had its place in Bath.

Among the many products dealt with in this underground commerce, were the "black books," a market of volumes that were extremely rare, often quite old, and generally quite offensive to a general reader. One might assume that such tomes would be detailed records of pornea and sexual deviancy, and in some cases, such lewd accounts could be found, but the whole of such books dealt with subjects far older and more disturbing than such base instincts. These were the books that only a few academicians and scholars knew of and would rarely speak but an equally small number of private collectors also were aware of the documents and sought them out for their private motivations.

Al Azif-azif was one such book, possibly the darkest and most recognizable, at least under its translated Greek name of *Necronomicon* circa 950 A.D. but it hardly was the only one of notoriety. *The Pnakotic Manuscripts* were to be of such ancient a history as to have predated man—or so it was said. *De Vermis Mysteriis* by the alchemist Ludwig Prinn was of a more recent origin, but its contents stemmed from equally arcane sources, and its author put to death for his practices in the late 15th or early 16th century.

Liber Ivonis was assumed to have been written in a now forgotten language, to which the Latin translation was best known, but only in fragments. *The Cthäat Aquadingen* was first documented in Germany around 400 A.D., a translation into Latin between the 11th and 12th century, and an English version some two hundred years after that, the title translated roughly into *Beings of the Water*.

What unified these diverse artifacts was that of a common mythology as detailed and lavish as the myriad of stories of other cultures, but preceding them by countless thousands of years. A closer comparison might even suggest that the origins of the classical mythologies were derived from these ancient legends.

The gods and goddesses of Greek myths had been well documented, particularly through literary sources such as Homer's *Iliad* and *Odyssey*, and the stories so often repeated that even children tutored in history and the classics could recite their names, abilities, and domains. What young boy would not want to be the mighty Zeus, the supreme ruler of the gods and lord of the sky, or Poseidon, god of the water realm and second in power to Zeus—although fewer lads would choose to identify themselves with Hades, lord of the underworld.

Likewise, those girls of better education might have found favor with Hera, wife and sister to Zeus, and a protector to the institute of marriage. With a few more years behind them, the more passionate of these young ladies, having discovered the sleeping goddess within them, might have shifted their allegiances to the allure of Aphrodite, the luminous goddess of love, desire, and beauty.

As the gods in these legends were great and powerful, so were the creatures, all mysterious, sometimes enchanting, but often terrible to behold. Lord Poseidon held dominion over the creatures of the sea, from the nymphs of the ocean to the beastly Cetus, a sea monster of enormous size that also appeared in other traditions.

In Norse myth, a similar gargantuan—known as the Kraken—was described as the size of a floating island, and able to pull boats into the watery depths from the violent whirlpool it created as it descended. Common to its many variations was the description of it as a horrendous thing with many tentacles, suggesting that the stories might have originated from sightings of a giant squid.

In every culture far and wide, the resident mythology bore accounts of fearsome beasts that might chill the bones of the most stout of men. So clear were these tales that for the most observant of historians, a monstrous lineage could be traced from one race to another.

In Mesopotamian mythology, there were the Scorpion men, born of a giant serpent, who were representatives of chaos and the saltwater ocean, and there was Dagon, the god of vegetation, described as half fish and half man. To the Nordic lands was Aegir, god of the sea, and his wife, Ran, who dragged men to their deaths with her net. Egypt had its specific roster of deities, from Ra, the god of the sun bearing the head of a falcon, and Osiris, the god of the dead, to Sekhmet, the god of destruction, while Anuket, was honoured as a goddess to the Nile River.

It was suggested that these were the secondary mythologies of the Earth, pale ghosts to the murky legends that came before, with origins that predated man, and that the tentacled horrors of later fables were in fact the beings of this older time. To the foundation of the stories, there was required an element of truth, and the entities that later appeared in one set of fables after another had actually existed—or so some claimed. In truth, these were just stories and nothing more, this being the consensus of a larger number of academics, and as they were the majority, they assuredly were correct.

As to the mythos, it went as follows, the accounts taken as accurate and factual as it might—or might not be. Before the gods and goddesses of Rome and Greece, before the deities of Egypt and Mesopotamia, were the Great Old Ones, beings that held sway over the various continents of the Earth, only to lose their grip and be exiled to realms just outside the material plane by the Elder Gods.

The origin of these Ancient Ones was uncertain, although generally theorized that they were not of this world, but far beyond the stars visible to human eye, nor could any records be deemed accurate as their existence upon the Earth predated man. As to the documentation of these beings, derived from the architectural ruins of great cities and relics that were allegedly built either for or by the Old Ones, its accuracy was of as dubious a nature as the legends themselves. Indeed, the remains of these cyclopean stones buried deep within the earth, or far under the sea—or even the remnants scattered across islands in the Pacific, were as highly doubted as the originators themselves.

Of the Old Ones, it was said that they were not dead but sleeping, entombed in a netherworld within those very cities that had been constructed for them, or outside of time itself, and each—as with Zeus, Poseidon, and the like—bore their realms and servants. There the similarities ended; comparing the omnipotence of Zeus would have been a stretch to Yog-Sothoth, the Beyond One, a derivative of the Arabic phrase "Yaji Ash-Shuthath," and alternately described as limitless in scope, or as the gate, and both key and guardian to the gate.

The complete roster of gods, demi-gods, minions, and beasts read like the checklist from the mind of one dislodged from reality; Nyarlathotep, the crawling chaos and messenger to the Old Ones; Shub Niggurath, the black goat of a thousand young; the blind idiot god, Azathoth; Hastur, the unspeakable one; Zhar, the twin obscenities; Ithaqua, the wind-walker; and Cthulhu, high priest to the Ancient Ones.

Cthulhu, it should be added, had long been a point of fixation for the small number of academics in search of evidence proving the existence of Atlantis, Lemuria, Mu, and other fabled lost civilizations. According to the black books, Cthulhu, like the other Old Ones, was imprisoned by a race of beings far older than they, and rested in a state of perpetual dreaming in the sunken city of R'lyeh, waiting through the centuries to be woken. Thus this couplet from *Al Azif-azif* became a topic of debate in certain secret circles:

> *"That is not dead which can eternal lie.*
> *And with strange aeons even death may die."*

Even its appearance might have been surmised from bits mentioned in various texts, illustrating a colossal being not of flesh and blood but of something altogether different, mountainous in size, with rudimentary bat-like wings and a scaly torso, suggesting simultaneously that of a dragon, octopus, and human.

Most attention was paid to the repulsive squid-like head writhing with engorged tentacles. Other accounts simply identified the shape as something impossible to describe in crude words.

Even in translated editions, some passages were left in their original foreign script. An oft-repeated phrase directly attributed to this particular legend read as follows:

"Ph'nglui mglw'nafh Cthulhu R'lyeh wgah'nagl fhtagn"

The English translation to the above, which appeared not dissimilar to the couplet from *Al Azif-azif,* read as "In his house at R'lyeh, dead Cthulhu waits dreaming," with this entire phrase sometimes shortened to "Cthulhu fhtagn" or "Cthulhu waits dreaming."

Common also to these many books of ill repute, and to the archaic fables in which they spoke, was the suggestion that it might be the role of mortal man to revere these beings as the true original gods of the Earth and to endeavor to bridge the barrier between worlds, thereby restoring the Great Old Ones to their rightful place. Depending on the translation of certain texts, it was even believed that the rituals and methodologies for such deeds were there in print, and all was in readiness for when the stars were properly aligned—and for the men bold enough to take on the task.

In response to all this, from scholars and theoreticians far and wide, came the simple word, "Twaddle!" There was no doubt to it being utter rubbish, felt these most studied of minds, and they knew that they were absolutely right. After all, as previously mentioned, they were of the majority.

CHAPTER

Thirteen

THE REMAINING TIME prior to Catherine's departure passed quickly, in spite of her seduction into the pages of *Udolpho* and Mrs. Allen's distress over the dressmaker, who arrived and set things right with only minutes to spare, however, the party from Pulteney Street reached the Upper Rooms in very good time. The Thorpes and James Morland were there only two minutes before them; and Isabella having gone through the usual ceremonial of meeting her friend with the most smiling and affectionate haste, of admiring the set of her gown, and envying the curl of her hair, they followed their chaperones, arm in arm, into the ballroom, whispering to each other whenever a thought occurred, and supplying the place of many ideas by a squeeze of the hand or a smile of affection.

The dancing began within a few minutes after they were seated; and James, who had been engaged quite as long as his sister, was very importunate with Isabella to stand up; but John was gone into the card-room to speak to a friend, and nothing, she declared, should induce her to join the set before her dear Catherine could join it too. "I assure you," said she, "I would not stand up without your dear sister for all the world; for if I did we should certainly be separated the whole evening." Catherine accepted this kindness with gratitude, and they continued as they were for three minutes longer, when Isabella, who had been talking to James on the other side of her, turned again to his sister and whispered, "My dear creature, I am afraid I must leave you, your brother is so amazingly impatient to begin; I know you will not mind my going away, and I dare say John will be back in a moment, and then you may easily find me out." Catherine, though a little disappointed, had too much good nature to make any opposition, and the others rising up, Isabella had only time to press her friend's hand and say, "Good-bye, my dear love," before they hurried off. The younger Miss Thorpes being also dancing, Catherine was left to the mercy of Mrs. Thorpe and Mrs. Allen, between whom she now remained. She could not help being vexed at the non-appearance of Mr. Thorpe, for she not only longed to be dancing, but was likewise aware that, as the real dignity of her situation could not be known, she was sharing with the scores of other young ladies still sitting down all the discredit of wanting a partner. To be disgraced in the eye of the world, to wear the appearance of infamy while her heart is all purity, her actions all innocence, and the misconduct of another the true source of her debasement, is one of those circumstances which peculiarly belong to the heroine's life, and her fortitude under it what particularly dignifies her character. Catherine had fortitude too; she suffered, but no murmur passed her lips.

From this state of humiliation, she was roused, at the end of ten minutes, to a pleasanter feeling, by seeing, not Mr. Thorpe, but Mr. Tilney, within three yards of the place where they sat; he seemed to be moving that way, but he did not see her, and therefore the smile and the blush, which his sudden reappearance raised in Catherine, passed away without sullying her heroic importance. He looked as handsome and as lively as ever, and was talking with interest to a fashionable and pleasing-looking young woman, who leant on his arm, and whom Catherine immediately guessed to be his sister; thus unthinkingly throwing away a fair opportunity of considering him lost to her forever, by being married already. But guided only by what was simple and probable, it had never entered her head that Mr. Tilney could be married; he had not behaved, he had not talked, like the married men to whom she had been used; he had never mentioned a wife, and he had acknowledged a sister. From these circumstances sprang the instant conclusion of his sister's now being by his side; and therefore, instead of turning of a deathlike paleness and falling in a fit on Mrs. Allen's bosom, Catherine sat erect, in the perfect use of her senses, and with cheeks only a little redder than usual.

Mr. Tilney and his companion, who continued, though slowly, to approach, were immediately preceded by a lady, an acquaintance of Mrs. Thorpe; and this lady stopping to speak to her, they, as belonging to her, stopped likewise, and Catherine, catching Mr. Tilney's eye, instantly received from him the smiling tribute of recognition. She returned it with pleasure, and then advancing still nearer, he spoke both to her and Mrs. Allen, by whom he was very civilly acknowledged.

"I am very happy to see you again, sir, indeed; I was afraid you had left Bath." He thanked her for her fears, and said that he had quitted it for a week, on the very morning after his having had the pleasure of seeing her.

"Well, sir, and I dare say you are not sorry to be back again, for it is just the place for young people—and indeed for everybody else too. I tell Mr. Allen, when he talks of being sick of it, that I am sure he should not complain, for it is so very agreeable a place, that it is much better to be here than at home at this dull time of year. I tell him he is quite in luck to be sent here for his health."

"And I hope, madam, that Mr. Allen will be obliged to like the place, from finding it of service to him."

"Thank you, sir. I have no doubt that he will. A neighbour of ours, Dr. Skinner, was here for his health last winter, and came away quite stout."

"That circumstance must give great encouragement."

"Yes, sir—and Dr. Skinner and his family were here three months; so I tell Mr. Allen he must not be in a hurry to get away."

Here they were interrupted by a request from Mrs. Thorpe to Mrs. Allen, that she would move a little to accommodate Mrs. Hughes and Miss Tilney with seats, as they had agreed to join their party. This was accordingly done, Mr. Tilney still continuing standing before them; and after a few minutes' consideration, he asked Catherine to dance with him. This compliment, delightful as it was, produced severe mortification to the lady; and in giving her denial, she expressed her sorrow on the occasion so very much as if she really felt it that had Thorpe, who joined her just afterwards, been half a minute earlier, he might have thought her sufferings rather too acute. The very easy manner in which he then told her that he had kept her waiting did not by any means reconcile her more to her lot; nor did the particulars which he entered into while they were standing up, of the horses and dogs of the friend whom he had just left, and of a proposed exchange of terriers between them, interest her so much as to prevent her looking very often towards that part of the room where she had left Mr. Tilney. Of her dear Isabella, to whom she particularly longed to point out that gentleman, she could see nothing. They were in different sets. She was separated from all her party, and away from all her acquaintance; one mortification succeeded another, and from the whole she deduced this useful lesson, that to go previously engaged to a ball does not necessarily increase either the dignity or enjoyment of a young lady. From such a moralizing strain as this, she was suddenly roused by a touch on the shoulder, and turning round, perceived Mrs. Hughes directly behind her, attended by Miss Tilney and a gentleman. "I beg your pardon, Miss Morland," said she, "for this liberty—but I cannot anyhow get to Miss Thorpe, and Mrs. Thorpe said she was sure you would not have the least objection to letting in this young lady by you." Mrs. Hughes could not have applied to any creature in the room more happy to oblige her than Catherine. The young ladies were introduced to each other, Miss Tilney expressing a proper sense of such goodness, Miss Morland with the real delicacy of a generous mind making light of the obligation; and Mrs. Hughes, satisfied with having so respectably settled her young charge, returned to her party.

Miss Tilney had a good figure, a pretty face, and a very agreeable countenance; and her air, though it had not all the decided pretension, the resolute stylishness of Miss Thorpe's, had more real elegance. Her manners showed good sense and good breeding; they were neither shy nor affectedly open; and she seemed capable of being young, attractive, and at a ball without wanting to fix the attention of every man near her, and without exaggerated feelings of ecstatic delight or inconceivable vexation on every little trifling occurrence. Catherine, interested at once by her appearance and her relationship to Mr. Tilney, was desirous of being acquainted with her, and readily talked therefore whenever she could think of anything to say, and had courage and leisure for saying it. But the hindrance thrown in the way of a very speedy intimacy, by the frequent want of one or more of these requisites, prevented their doing more than going through the first rudiments of an acquaintance, by informing themselves how well the other liked Bath, how much she admired its buildings and surrounding country, whether she drew, or played, or sang, and whether she was fond of riding on horseback.

The two dances were scarcely concluded before Catherine found her arm gently seized by her faithful Isabella, who in great spirits exclaimed, "At last I have got you. My dearest creature, I have been looking for you this hour. What could induce you to come into this set, when you knew I was in the other? I have been quite wretched without you."

"My dear Isabella, how was it possible for me to get at you? I could not even see where you were."

"So I told your brother all the time—but he would not believe me. Do go and see for her, Mr. Morland, said I—but all in vain—he would not stir an inch. Was not it so, Mr. Morland? But you men are all so immoderately lazy! I have been scolding him to such a degree, my dear Catherine, you would be quite amazed. You know I never stand upon ceremony with such people."

"Look at that young lady with the white beads round her head," whispered Catherine, detaching her friend from James. "It is Mr. Tilney's sister."

"Oh! Heavens! You don't say so! Let me look at her this moment. What a delightful girl! I never saw anything half so beautiful! But where is her all-conquering brother? Is he in the room? Point him out to me this instant, if he is. I die to see him. Mr. Morland, you are not to listen. We are not talking about you."

"But what is all this whispering about? What is going on?"

"There now, I knew how it would be. You men have such restless curiosity! Talk of the curiosity of women, indeed! 'Tis nothing. But be satisfied, for you are not to know anything at all of the matter."

"And is that likely to satisfy me, do you think?"

"Well, I declare I never knew anything like you. What can it signify to you, what we are talking of. Perhaps we are talking about you; therefore I would advise you not to listen, or you may happen to hear something not very agreeable."

In this commonplace chatter, which lasted some time, the original subject seemed entirely forgotten; and though Catherine was very well pleased to have it dropped for a while, she could not avoid a little suspicion at the total suspension of all Isabella's impatient desire to see Mr. Tilney. When the orchestra struck up a fresh dance, James would have led his fair partner away, but she resisted. "I tell you, Mr. Morland," she cried, "I would not do such a thing for all the world. How can you be so teasing; only conceive, my dear Catherine, what your brother wants me to do. He wants me to dance with him again, though I tell him that it is a most improper thing, and entirely against the rules. It would make us the talk of the place, if we were not to change partners."

"Upon my honour," said James, "in these public assemblies, it is as often done as not."

"Nonsense, how can you say so? But when you men have a point to carry, you never stick at anything. My sweet Catherine, do support me; persuade your brother how impossible it is. Tell him that it would quite shock you to see me do such a thing; now would not it?"

"No, not at all; but if you think it wrong, you had much better change."

"There," cried Isabella, "you hear what your sister says, and yet you will not mind her. Well, remember that it is not my fault, if we set all the old ladies in Bath in a bustle. Come along, my dearest Catherine, for heaven's sake, and stand by me." And off they went, to regain their former place. John Thorpe, in the meanwhile, had walked away; and Catherine, ever willing to give Mr. Tilney an opportunity of repeating the agreeable request which had already flattered her once, made her way to Mrs. Allen and Mrs. Thorpe as fast as she could, in the hope of finding him still with them—a hope which, when it proved to be fruitless, she felt to have been highly unreasonable. "Well, my dear," said Mrs. Thorpe, impatient for praise of her son, "I hope you have had an agreeable partner."

"Very agreeable, madam."

"I am glad of it. John has charming spirits, has not he?"

"Did you meet Mr. Tilney, my dear?" said Mrs. Allen.

"No, where is he?"

"He was with us just now, and said he was so tired of lounging about, that he was resolved to go and dance; so I thought perhaps he would ask you, if he met with you."

"Where can he be?" said Catherine, looking round; but she had not looked round long before she saw him leading a young lady to the dance.

"Ah! He has got a partner; I wish he had asked you," said Mrs. Allen; and after a short silence, she added, "he is a very agreeable young man."

"Indeed he is, Mrs. Allen," said Mrs. Thorpe, smiling complacently; "I must say it, though I am his mother, that there is not a more agreeable young man in the world."

This inapplicable answer might have been too much for the comprehension of many; but it did not puzzle Mrs. Allen, for after only a moment's consideration, she said, in a whisper to Catherine, "I dare say she thought I was speaking of her son."

Catherine was disappointed and vexed. She seemed to have missed by so little the very object she had had in view; and this persuasion did not incline her to a very gracious reply, when John Thorpe came up to her soon afterwards and said, "Well, Miss Morland, I suppose you and I are to stand up and jig it together again."

"Oh, no; I am much obliged to you, our two dances are over; and, besides, I am tired, and do not mean to dance any more."

"Do not you? Then let us walk about and quiz people. Come along with me, and I will show you the four greatest quizzers in the room; my two younger sisters and their partners. I have been laughing at them this half hour."

Again Catherine excused herself; and at last he walked off to quiz his sisters by himself. The rest of the evening she found very dull; Mr. Tilney was drawn away from their party at tea, to attend that of his partner; Miss Tilney, though belonging to it, did not sit near her, and James and Isabella were so much engaged in conversing together that the latter had no leisure to bestow more on her friend than one smile, one squeeze, and one "dearest Catherine."

CHAPTER

IN ECCLESIASTES CHAPTER 3, it is written that there is a time for everything, and a season for every activity under the heavens, "a time to weep and a time to laugh, a time to mourn and a time to dance." Without giving the passage any thought, Miss Morland had found the evening not right under the heavens for dancing, at least with the object of her wishes, and therefore found mourning more favourable due to his lack thereof.

All about Catherine, however, the dance was timely and welcome, even with those closest to her; Isabella and brother James managed to combine laughter into their own intimate time together on the dance floor, while Mr. Tilney had found a partner that Catherine could not help but feel a flush of jealousy for, even though she was well aware that the lady had done nothing improper in the acceptance, nor could she fault her.

Such is the way of a dance, as life might be considered to be one. The choices people make, how they act to others as well as how they carry themselves, their show of compassion as well as moments of rashness, likes, dislikes, and entreaties of the heart—all this is but part of the dance. So it has been since the beginning and will continue until the last step has been taken. It might be said of life, then, that the dance is all there is.

Over its history, dancing had served many functions, but all revolved around the means of expression and non-verbal communication between animals and humans alike. It played a major part in the Roman Bacchanalia, records of which were left in the many frescos of the time. For the people of ancient Egypt, it served as a means of recreation, often displayed by street performers, but also in work, as laborers moved in rhythm to drums and melodies. In Eastern countries, the adorned ones of the harem danced to the pleasure of their men. Moving back to earlier times, sacred rituals were performed, from fertility dances to the rites meant to appease the gods. Sometimes, a sacrifice was required.

In its earliest forms, the movements were a means of demonstrating attraction to the opposite sex, an aspect that continued through to the present. The cotillions, country dances, and quadrilles so popular in Bath were merely more respectable forms of the same, with a high emphasis put on proper decorum. There were rules of etiquette to be observed both on the floor and off, how and when a lady might be asked to dance, how many dances might be permitted, etcetera, but underneath these manners, there was still the underpinnings of attraction and passion.

Catherine certainly gave no consideration to the many guises that the ubiquitous dance had taken, from the earliest days of human existence to her evening of frustration over a missed partner. There was no thought of ancient traditions, harvest celebrations, pagan rituals, or the ecstatic trance dances embraced by certain religious groups in some far-off countries to her East.

No, for her, a dance was something magical and exciting, especially when the person to be danced with was the one of particular favor, and if she knew of the less-than-savory dancing rituals of the past, it only would have come from her beloved novels.

Of the true sacrificial rites, in which the blood of humans and animals alike were spilled to gain favor with the deities, and the razor edge of the knife cut deep against the skin, there could be found the dance. Set to the ritual chanting and invocation, the swaying of bodies as one, the quickening heartbeats of all involved, and the final scream of agony from the chosen one, the participants danced, all as one in joy and fervent devotion— for here, the dance of life was intertwined with the dance of death.

Then there were the other sacrifices, in which dying under the blade would be preferable to the obscenity summoned and how it claimed the offering as its own.

CHAPTER
Fifteen

THE PROGRESS OF Catherine's unhappiness from the events of the evening was as follows. It appeared first in a general dissatisfaction with everybody about her, while she remained in the rooms, which speedily brought on considerable weariness and a violent desire to go home. This, on arriving in Pulteney Street, took the direction of extraordinary hunger, and when that was appeased, changed into an earnest longing to be in bed; such was the extreme point of her distress; for when there she immediately fell into a sound sleep which lasted nine hours, and from which she awoke perfectly revived, in excellent spirits, with fresh hopes and fresh schemes. The first wish of her heart was to improve her acquaintance with Miss Tilney, and almost her first resolution, to seek her for that purpose, in the pump-room at noon. In the pump-room, one so newly arrived in Bath must be met with, and that building she had already found so favourable for the discovery of female excellence, and the completion of female intimacy, so admirably adapted for secret discourses and unlimited confidence, that she was most reasonably encouraged to expect another friend from within its walls. Her plan for the morning thus settled, she sat quietly down to her book after breakfast, resolving to remain in the same place and the same employment till the clock struck one; and from habitude very little incommoded by the remarks and ejaculations of Mrs. Allen, whose vacancy of mind and incapacity for thinking were such, that as she never talked a great deal, so she could never be entirely silent; and, therefore, while she sat at her work, if she lost her needle or broke her thread, if she heard a carriage in the street, or saw a speck upon her gown, she must observe it aloud, whether there were anyone at leisure to answer her or not. At about half past twelve, a remarkably loud rap drew her in haste to the window, and scarcely had she time to inform Catherine of there being two open carriages at the door, in the first only a servant, her brother driving Miss Thorpe in the second, before John Thorpe came running upstairs, calling out, "Well, Miss Morland, here I am. Have you been waiting long? We could not come before; the old devil of a coachmaker was such an eternity finding out a thing fit to be got into, and now it is ten thousand to one but they break down before we are out of the street. How do you do, Mrs. Allen? A famous ball last night, was not it? Come, Miss Morland, be quick, for the others are in a confounded hurry to be off. They want to get their tumble over."

"What do you mean?" said Catherine. "Where are you all going to?"

"Going to? Why, you have not forgot our engagement! Did not we agree together to take a drive this morning? What a head you have! We are going up Claverton Down."

"Something was said about it, I remember," said Catherine, looking at Mrs. Allen for her opinion; "but really I did not expect you."

"Not expect me! That's a good one! And what a dust you would have made, if I had not come."

Catherine's silent appeal to her friend, meanwhile, was entirely thrown away, for Mrs. Allen, not being at all in the habit of conveying any expression herself by a look, was not aware of its being ever intended by anybody else; and Catherine, whose desire of seeing Miss Tilney again could at that moment bear a short delay in favour of a drive, and who thought there could be no impropriety in her going with Mr. Thorpe, as Isabella was going at the same time with James, was therefore obliged to speak plainer. "Well, ma'am, what do you say to it? Can you spare me for an hour or two? Shall I go?"

"Do just as you please, my dear," replied Mrs. Allen, with the most placid indifference. Catherine took the advice, and ran off to get ready. In a very few minutes she reappeared, having scarcely allowed the two others time enough to get through a few short sentences in her praise, after Thorpe had procured Mrs. Allen's admiration of his gig; and then receiving her friend's parting good wishes, they both hurried downstairs. "My dearest creature," cried Isabella, to whom the duty of friendship immediately called her before she could get into the carriage, "you have been at least three hours getting ready. I was afraid you were ill. What a delightful ball we had last night. I have a thousand things to say to you; but make haste and get in, for I long to be off."

Catherine followed her orders and turned away, but not too soon to hear her friend exclaim aloud to James, "What a sweet girl she is! I quite dote on her."

"You will not be frightened, Miss Morland," said Thorpe, as he handed her in, "if my horse should dance about a little at first setting off. He will, most likely, give a plunge or two, and perhaps take the rest for a minute; but he will soon know his master. He is full of spirits, playful as can be, but there is no vice in him."

Catherine did not think the portrait a very inviting one, but it was too late to retreat, and she was too young to own herself frightened; so, resigning herself to her fate, and trusting to the animal's boasted knowledge of its owner, she sat peaceably down, and saw Thorpe sit down by her. Everything being then arranged, the servant who stood at the horse's head was bid in an important voice "to let him go," and off they went in the quietest manner imaginable, without a plunge or a caper, or anything like one. Catherine, delighted at so happy an escape, spoke her pleasure aloud with grateful surprise; and her companion immediately made the matter perfectly simple by assuring her that it was entirely owing to the peculiarly judicious manner in which he had then held the reins, and the singular discernment and dexterity with which he had directed his whip. Catherine, though she could not help wondering that with such perfect command of his horse, he should think it necessary to alarm her with a relation of its tricks, congratulated herself sincerely on being under the care of so excellent a coachman; and perceiving that the animal continued to go on in the same quiet manner, without showing the smallest propensity towards any unpleasant vivacity, and (considering its inevitable pace was ten miles an hour) by no means alarmingly fast, gave herself up to all the enjoyment of air and exercise of the most invigorating kind, in a fine mild day of February, with the consciousness of safety. A silence of several minutes succeeded their first short dialogue; it was broken by Thorpe's saying very abruptly, "Old Allen is as rich as a Jew—is not he?" Catherine did not understand him—and he repeated his question, adding in explanation, "Old Allen, the man you are with."

"Oh! Mr. Allen, you mean. Yes, I believe, he is very rich."

"And no children at all?"

"No—not any."

"A famous thing for his next heirs. He is your godfather, is not he?"

"My godfather! No."

"But you are always very much with them."

"Yes, very much."

"Aye, that is what I meant. He seems a good kind of old fellow enough, and has lived very well in his time, I dare say; he is not gouty for nothing. Does he drink his bottle a day now?"

"His bottle a day! No. Why should you think of such a thing? He is a very temperate man, and you could not fancy him in liquor last night?"

"Lord help you! You women are always thinking of men's being in liquor. Why, you do not suppose a man is overset by a bottle? I am sure of this—that if everybody was to drink their bottle a day, there would not be half the disorders in the world there are now. It would be a famous good thing for us all."

"I cannot believe it."

"Oh! Lord, it would be the saving of thousands. There is not the hundredth part of the wine consumed in this kingdom that there ought to be. Our foggy climate wants help."

"And yet I have heard that there is a great deal of wine drunk in Oxford."

"Oxford! There is no drinking at Oxford now, I assure you. Nobody drinks there. You would hardly meet with a man who goes beyond his four pints at the utmost. Now, for instance, it was reckoned a remarkable thing, at the last party in my rooms, that upon an average we cleared about five pints a head. It was looked upon as something out of the common way. Mine is famous good stuff, to be sure. You would not often meet with anything like it in Oxford—and that may account for it. But this will just give you a notion of the general rate of drinking there."

"Yes, it does give a notion," said Catherine warmly, "and that is, that you all drink a great deal more wine than I thought you did. However, I am sure James does not drink so much."

This declaration brought on a loud and overpowering reply, of which no part was very distinct, except the frequent exclamations, amounting almost to oaths, which adorned it, and Catherine was left, when it ended, with rather a strengthened belief of there being a great deal of wine drunk in Oxford, and the same happy conviction of her brother's comparative sobriety.

Thorpe's ideas then all reverted to the merits of his own equipage, and she was called on to admire the spirit and freedom with which his horse moved along, and the ease which his paces, as well as the excellence of the springs, gave the motion of the carriage. She followed him in all his admiration as well as she could. To go before or beyond him was impossible. His knowledge and her ignorance of the subject, his rapidity of expression, and her diffidence of herself put that out of her power; she could strike out nothing new in commendation, but she readily echoed whatever he chose to assert, and it was finally settled between them without any difficulty that his equipage was altogether the most complete of its kind in England, his carriage the neatest, his horse the best goer, and himself the best coachman. "You do not really think, Mr. Thorpe," said Catherine, venturing after some time to consider the matter as entirely decided, and to offer some little variation on the subject, "that James's gig will break down?"

"Break down! Oh! Lord! Did you ever see such a little tittuppy thing in your life? There is not a sound piece of iron about it. The wheels have been fairly worn out these ten years at least—and as for the body! Upon my soul, you might shake it to pieces yourself with a touch. It is the most devilish little rickety business I ever beheld! Thank God! we have got a better. I would not be bound to go two miles in it for fifty thousand pounds."

"Good heavens!" cried Catherine, quite frightened. "Then pray let us turn back; they will certainly meet with an accident if we go on. Do let us turn back, Mr. Thorpe; stop and speak to my brother, and tell him how very unsafe it is."

"Unsafe! Oh, lord! What is there in that? They will only get a roll if it does break down; and there is plenty of dirt; it will be excellent falling. Oh, curse it! The carriage is safe enough, if a man knows how to drive it; a thing of that sort in good hands will last above twenty years after it is fairly worn out. Lord bless you! I would undertake for five pounds to drive it to York and back again, without losing a nail."

Catherine listened with astonishment; she knew not how to reconcile two such very different accounts of the same thing; for she had not been brought up to understand the propensities of a rattle, nor to know to how many idle assertions and impudent falsehoods the excess of vanity will lead. Her own family were plain, matter-of-fact people who seldom aimed at wit of any kind; her father, at the utmost, being contented with a pun, and her mother with a proverb; they were not in the habit therefore of telling lies to increase their importance, or of asserting at one moment what they would contradict the next. She reflected on the affair for some time in much perplexity, and was more than once on the point of requesting from Mr. Thorpe a clearer insight into his real opinion on the subject; but she checked herself, because it appeared to her that he did not excel in giving those clearer insights, in making those things plain which he had before made ambiguous; and, joining to this, the consideration that he would not really suffer his sister and his friend to be exposed to a danger from which he might easily preserve them, she concluded at last that he must know the carriage to be in fact perfectly safe, and therefore would alarm herself no longer. By him the whole matter seemed entirely forgotten; and all the rest of his conversation, or rather talk, began and ended with himself and his own concerns. He told her of horses which he had bought for a trifle and sold for incredible sums; of racing matches, in which his judgment had infallibly foretold the winner; of shooting parties, in which he had killed more birds (though without having one good shot) than all his companions together; and described to her some famous day's sport, with the fox-hounds, in which his foresight and skill in directing the dogs had repaired the mistakes of the most experienced huntsman, and in which the boldness of his riding, though it had never endangered his own life for a moment, had been constantly leading others into difficulties, which he calmly concluded had broken the necks of many.

Little as Catherine was in the habit of judging for herself, and unfixed as were her general notions of what men ought to be, she could not entirely repress a doubt, while she bore with the effusions of his endless conceit, of his being altogether completely agreeable. It was a bold surmise, for he was Isabella's brother; and she had been assured by James that his manners would recommend him to all her sex; but in spite of this, the extreme weariness of his company, which crept over her before they had been out an hour, and which continued unceasingly to increase till they stopped in Pulteney Street again, induced her, in some small degree, to resist such high authority, and to distrust his powers of giving universal pleasure.

When they arrived at Mrs. Allen's door, the astonishment of Isabella was hardly to be expressed, on finding that it was too late in the day for them to attend her friend into the house: "Past three o'clock!" It was inconceivable, incredible, impossible! And she would neither believe her own watch, nor her brother's, nor the servant's; she would believe no assurance of it founded on reason or reality, till Morland produced his watch, and ascertained the fact; to have doubted a moment longer then would have been equally inconceivable, incredible, and impossible; and she could only protest, over and over again, that no two hours and a half had ever gone off so swiftly before, as Catherine was called on to confirm; Catherine could not tell a falsehood even to please Isabella; but the latter was spared the misery of her friend's dissenting voice, by not waiting for her answer. Her own feelings entirely engrossed her; her wretchedness was most acute on finding herself obliged to go directly home. It was ages since she had had a moment's conversation with her dearest Catherine; and, though she had such thousands of things to say to her, it appeared as if they were never to be together again; so, with smiles of most exquisite misery, and the laughing eye of utter despondency, she bade her friend adieu and went on.

Catherine found Mrs. Allen just returned from all the busy idleness of the morning, and was immediately greeted with, "Well, my dear, here you are," a truth which she had no greater inclination than power to dispute; "and I hope you have had a pleasant airing?"

"Yes, ma'am, I thank you; we could not have had a nicer day."

"So Mrs. Thorpe said; she was vastly pleased at your all going."

"You have seen Mrs. Thorpe, then?"

"Yes, I went to the pump-room as soon as you were gone, and there I met her, and we had a great deal of talk together. She says there was hardly any veal to be got at market this morning, it is so uncommonly scarce."

"Did you see anybody else of our acquaintance?"

"Yes; we agreed to take a turn in the Crescent, and there we met Mrs. Hughes, and Mr. and Miss Tilney walking with her."

"Did you indeed? And did they speak to you?"

"Yes, we walked along the Crescent together for half an hour. They seem very agreeable people. Miss Tilney was in a very pretty spotted muslin, and I fancy, by what I can learn, that she always dresses very handsomely. Mrs. Hughes talked to me a great deal about the family."

"And what did she tell you of them?"

"Oh! A vast deal indeed; she hardly talked of anything else."

"Did she tell you what part of Gloucestershire they come from?"

"Yes, she did; but I cannot recollect now. But they are very good kind of people, and very rich. Mrs. Tilney was a Miss Drummond, and she and Mrs. Hughes were schoolfellows; and Miss Drummond had a very large fortune; and, when she married, her father gave her twenty thousand pounds, and five hundred to buy wedding-clothes. Mrs. Hughes saw all the clothes after they came from the warehouse."

"And are Mr. and Mrs. Tilney in Bath?"

"Yes, I fancy they are, but I am not quite certain. Upon recollection, however, I have a notion they are both dead; at least the mother is; yes, I am sure Mrs. Tilney is dead, because Mrs. Hughes told me there was a very beautiful set of pearls that Mr. Drummond gave his daughter on her wedding-day and that Miss Tilney has got now, for they were put by for her when her mother died."

"And is Mr. Tilney, my partner, the only son?"

"I cannot be quite positive about that, my dear; I have some idea he is; but, however, he is a very fine young man, Mrs. Hughes says, and likely to do very well."

Catherine inquired no further; she had heard enough to feel that Mrs. Allen had no real intelligence to give, and that she was most particularly unfortunate herself in having missed such a meeting with both brother and sister. Could she have foreseen such a circumstance, nothing should have persuaded her to go out with the others; and, as it was, she could only lament her ill luck, and think over what she had lost, till it was clear to her that the drive had by no means been very pleasant and that John Thorpe himself was quite disagreeable.

CHAPTER
Sixteen

My dearest Sally,

Once again, sweet sister, I have been remiss in my correspondence, and feel terribly inconsiderate for not writing to you on a regular basis. You, whom I tell everything when we are together. Yet I must confess that the days have been so filled with activities, and Bath is a place of such enchantment, that I can offer no sound explanation for my silence other than my selfish diversions. Please accept my apologies along with this overdue summation of my time here.

I have so much to tell that I am at a loss for where to start, so I shall begin with what you would be most familiar with, that being our dear brother, James, who is in Bath as well. He arrived with a friend of his from Oxford, of whom I shall return to shortly, except to state that his name is John Thorpe. I could not have been more surprised at their appearance, but I am pleased in every way at having another relation in town. Should this be a trend, the whole of our family might be in Bath by week's end.

I have made some additional acquaintances, to which much of my time has been taken up. By chance, Mrs. Allen met up with a school friend from her youth, along with her daughters, to whom I have become acquainted, and in particular the oldest whose name is Isabella Thorpe. Together we have shared in many of the entertainments of Bath, and have found interests common to us both, including a mutual love for reading, and as you know my preference on the subject, I need not detail further. By now, I am sure you have noticed the similarity of names, and indeed, it is no coincidence, as Isabella is sister to the same John Thorpe who arrived with my brother.

I should also mention that James appears to find Isabella quite favourable, but for now, let that be our secret.

We attended the Upper Rooms the other evening and I saw Mr. Tilney once more, but unfortunately was not able to converse with him at length, to which I was very disappointed. As before, he was most charming, and less strange than he seemed upon our initial meeting. However, I was able to meet his sister, Eleanor Tilney, who was quite pretty and most kind to me in our conversation. I like her immensely.

I had hoped to find her on the following day but instead found myself on a coach ride with Mr. Thorpe, Isabella, and James. I have not made up my mind as of yet concerning Mr. Thorpe; he appears to have many opinions on every subject, oftentimes in conflict with what he has already said. I find it all very disconcerting.

Now I must come to an event that was most upsetting and still haunts me if I allow the memory to surface. I was en route to the theatre with the Allens when we came across the body of a woman being dredged from the river. I saw it quite clearly, and though nothing further was said of her, I am sure that she came to her end through the most foul of deeds. I will not detail it here on paper, but the sight was the most horrible thing I have ever witnessed, to such an extent that I wish I could purge from my memory.

I apologize for ending this letter on such a dismal note, so let me say how much I miss you and Mum and Papa, and I look forward to seeing you upon my return. Please write to me and tell me of any activities I have missed.

With all my love,
Cathy

CHAPTER

Seventeen

THE ALLENS, THORPES, AND MORLANDS all met in the evening at the theatre; and, as Catherine and Isabella sat together, there was then an opportunity for the latter to utter some few of the many thousand things which had been collecting within her for communication in the immeasurable length of time which had divided them. "Oh, heavens! My beloved Catherine, have I got you at last?" was her address on Catherine's entering the box and sitting by her. "Now, Mr. Morland," for he was close to her on the other side, "I shall not speak another word to you all the rest of the evening; so I charge you not to expect it. My sweetest Catherine, how have you been this long age? But I need not ask you, for you look delightfully. You really have done your hair in a more heavenly style than ever; you mischievous creature, do you want to attract everybody? I assure you, my brother is quite in love with you already; and as for Mr. Tilney—but that is a settled thing—even your modesty cannot doubt his attachment now; his coming back to Bath makes it too plain. Oh! What would not I give to see him! I really am quite wild with impatience. My mother says he is the most delightful young man in the world; she saw him this morning, you know; you must introduce him to me. Is he in the house now? Look about, for heaven's sake! I assure you, I can hardly exist till I see him."

"No," said Catherine, "he is not here; I cannot see him anywhere."

"Oh, horrid! Am I never to be acquainted with him? How do you like my gown? I think it does not look amiss; the sleeves were entirely my own thought. Do you know, I get so immoderately sick of Bath; your brother and I were agreeing this morning that, though it is vastly well to be here for a few weeks, we would not live here for millions. We soon found out that our tastes were exactly alike in preferring the country to every other place; really, our opinions were so exactly the same, it was quite ridiculous! There was not a single point in which we differed; I would not have had you by for the world; you are such a sly thing, I am sure you would have made some droll remark or other about it."

"No, indeed I should not."

"Oh, yes you would indeed; I know you better than you know yourself. You would have told us that we seemed born for each other, or some nonsense of that kind, which would have distressed me beyond conception; my cheeks would have been as red as your roses; I would not have had you by for the world."

"Indeed you do me injustice; I would not have made so improper a remark upon any account; and besides, I am sure it would never have entered my head."

Isabella smiled incredulously and talked the rest of the evening to James.

Catherine's resolution of endeavouring to meet Miss Tilney again continued in full force the next morning; and till the usual moment of going to the pump-room, she felt some alarm from the dread of a second prevention. But nothing of that kind occurred, no visitors appeared to delay them, and they all three set off in good time for the pump-room, where the ordinary course of events and conversation took place; Mr. Allen, after drinking his glass of water, joined some gentlemen to talk over the politics of the day and compare the accounts of their newspapers; and the ladies walked about together, noticing every new face, and almost every new bonnet in the room. The female part of the Thorpe family, attended by James Morland, appeared among the crowd in less than a quarter of an hour, and Catherine immediately took her usual place by the side of her friend. James, who was now in constant attendance, maintained a similar position, and separating themselves from the rest of their party, they walked in that manner for some time, till Catherine began to doubt the happiness of a situation which, confining her entirely to her friend and brother, gave her very little share in the notice of either. They were always engaged in some sentimental discussion or lively dispute, but their sentiment was conveyed in such whispering voices, and their vivacity attended with so much laughter, that though Catherine's supporting opinion was not unfrequently called for by one or the other, she was never able to give any, from not having heard a word of the subject. At length however she was empowered to disengage herself from her friend, by the avowed necessity of speaking to Miss Tilney, whom she most joyfully saw just entering the room with Mrs. Hughes, and whom she instantly joined, with a firmer determination to be acquainted, than she might have had courage to command, had she not been urged by the disappointment of the day before. Miss Tilney met her with great civility, returned her advances with equal goodwill, and they continued talking together as long as both parties remained in the room; and though in all probability not an observation was made, nor an expression used by either which had not been made and used some thousands of times before, under that roof, in every Bath season, yet the merit of their being spoken with simplicity and truth, and without personal conceit, might be something uncommon.

"How well your brother dances!" was an artless exclamation of Catherine's towards the close of their conversation, which at once surprised and amused her companion.

"Henry!" she replied with a smile. "Yes, he does dance very well."

"He must have thought it very odd to hear me say I was engaged the other evening, when he saw me sitting down. But I really had been engaged the whole day to Mr. Thorpe." Miss Tilney could only bow. "You cannot think," added Catherine after a moment's silence, "how surprised I was to see him again. I felt so sure of his being quite gone away."

"When Henry had the pleasure of seeing you before, he was in Bath but for a couple of days. He came only to engage lodgings for us."

"That never occurred to me; and of course, not seeing him anywhere, I thought he must be gone. Was not the young lady he danced with on Monday a Miss Smith?"

"Yes, an acquaintance of Mrs. Hughes."

"I dare say she was very glad to dance. Do you think her pretty?"

"Not very."

"He never comes to the pump-room, I suppose?"

"Yes, sometimes; but he has rid out this morning with my father."

Mrs. Hughes now joined them, and asked Miss Tilney if she was ready to go. "I hope I shall have the pleasure of seeing you again soon," said Catherine. "Shall you be at the cotillion ball tomorrow?"

"Perhaps we—Yes, I think we certainly shall."

"I am glad of it, for we shall all be there." This civility was duly returned; and they parted—on Miss Tilney's side with some knowledge of her new acquaintance's feelings, and on Catherine's, without the smallest consciousness of having explained them.

She went home very happy. The morning had answered all her hopes, and the evening of the following day was now the object of expectation, the future good. What gown and what head-dress she should wear on the occasion became her chief concern. She cannot be justified in it. Dress is at all times a frivolous distinction, and excessive solicitude about it often destroys its own aim. Catherine knew all this very well; her great aunt had read her a lecture on the subject only the Christmas before; and yet she lay awake ten minutes on Wednesday night debating between her spotted and her tamboured muslin, and nothing but the shortness of the time prevented her buying a new one for the evening. This would have been an error in judgment, great though not uncommon, from which one of the other sex rather than her own, a brother rather than a great aunt, might have warned her, for man only can be aware of the insensibility of man towards a new gown. It would be mortifying to the feelings of many ladies, could they be made to understand how little the heart of man is affected by what is costly or new in their attire; how little it is biased by the texture of their muslin, and how unsusceptible of peculiar tenderness towards the spotted, the sprigged, the mull, or the jackonet. Woman is fine for her own satisfaction alone. No man will admire her the more, no woman will like her the better for it. Neatness and fashion are enough for the former, and a something of shabbiness or impropriety will be most endearing to the latter. But not one of these grave reflections troubled the tranquillity of Catherine.

She entered the rooms on Thursday evening with feelings very different from what had attended her thither the Monday before. She had then been exulting in her engagement to Thorpe, and was now chiefly anxious to avoid his sight, lest he should engage her again; for though she could not, dared not expect that Mr. Tilney should ask her a third time to dance, her wishes, hopes, and plans all centred in nothing less. Every young lady may feel for my heroine in this critical moment, for every young lady has at some time or other known the same agitation. All have been, or at least all have believed themselves to be, in danger from the pursuit of someone whom they wished to avoid; and all have been anxious for the attentions of someone whom they wished to please. As soon as they were joined by the Thorpes, Catherine's agony began; she fidgeted about if John Thorpe came towards her, hid herself as much as possible from his view, and when he spoke to her pretended not to hear him. The cotillions were over, the country-dancing beginning, and she saw nothing of the Tilneys.

"Do not be frightened, my dear Catherine," whispered Isabella, "but I am really going to dance with your brother again. I declare positively it is quite shocking. I tell him he ought to be ashamed of himself, but you and John must keep us in countenance. Make haste, my dear creature, and come to us. John is just walked off, but he will be back in a moment."

Catherine had neither time nor inclination to answer. The others walked away, John Thorpe was still in view, and she gave herself up for lost. That she might not appear, however, to observe or expect him, she kept her eyes intently fixed on her fan; and a self-condemnation for her folly, in supposing that among such a crowd they should even meet with the Tilneys in any reasonable time, had just passed through her mind, when she suddenly found herself addressed and again solicited to dance, by Mr. Tilney himself. With what sparkling eyes and ready motion she granted his request, and with how pleasing a flutter of heart she went with him to the set, may be easily imagined. To escape, and, as she believed, so narrowly escape John Thorpe, and to be asked, so immediately on his joining her, asked by Mr. Tilney, as if he had sought her on purpose!—it did not appear to her that life could supply any greater felicity.

Scarcely had they worked themselves into the quiet possession of a place, however, when her attention was claimed by John Thorpe, who stood behind her. "Heyday, Miss Morland!" said he. "What is the meaning of this? I thought you and I were to dance together."

"I wonder you should think so, for you never asked me."

"That is a good one, by Jove! I asked you as soon as I came into the room, and I was just going to ask you again, but when I turned round, you were gone! This is a cursed shabby trick! I only came for the sake of dancing with you, and I firmly believe you were engaged to me ever since Monday. Yes; I remember, I asked you while you were waiting in the lobby for your cloak. And here have I been telling all my acquaintance that I was going to dance with the prettiest girl in the room; and when they see you standing up with somebody else, they will quiz me famously."

"Oh, no; they will never think of me, after such a description as that."

"By heavens, if they do not, I will kick them out of the room for block-heads. What chap have you there?" Catherine satisfied his curiosity. "Tilney," he repeated. "Hum—I do not know him. A good figure of a man; well put together. Does he want a horse? Here is a friend of mine, Sam Fletcher, has got one to sell that would suit anybody. A famous clever animal for the road—only forty guineas. I had fifty minds to buy it myself, for it is one of my maxims always to buy a good horse when I meet with one; but it would not answer my purpose, it would not do for the field. I would give any money for a real good hunter. I have three now, the best that ever were backed. I would not take eight hundred guineas for them. Fletcher and I mean to get a house in Leicestershire, against the next season. It is so damn uncomfortable, living at an inn."

This was the last sentence by which he could weary Catherine's attention, for he was just then borne off by the resistless pressure of a long string of passing ladies. Her partner now drew near, and said, "That gentleman would have put me out of patience, had he stayed with you half a minute longer. He has no business to withdraw the attention of my partner from me. We have entered into a contract of mutual agreeableness for the space of an evening, and all our agreeableness belongs solely to each other for that time. Nobody can fasten themselves on the notice of one, without injuring the rights of the other. I consider a country-dance as an emblem of marriage. Fidelity and complaisance are the principal duties of both; and those men who do not choose to dance or marry themselves, have no business with the partners or wives of their neighbours."

"But they are such very different things!"

"—That you think they cannot be compared together."

"To be sure not. People that marry can never part, but must go and keep house together. People that dance only stand opposite each other in a long room for half an hour."

"And such is your definition of matrimony and dancing. Taken in that light certainly, their resemblance is not striking; but I think I could place them in such a view. You will allow, that in both, man has the advantage of choice, woman only the power of refusal; that in both, it is an engagement between man and woman, formed for the advantage of each; and that when once entered into, they belong exclusively to each other till the moment of its dissolution; that it is their duty, each to endeavour to give the other no cause for wishing that he or she had bestowed themselves elsewhere, and their best interest to keep their own imaginations from wandering towards the perfections of their neighbours, or fancying that they should have been better off with anyone else. You will allow all this?"

"Yes, to be sure, as you state it, all this sounds very well; but still they are so very different. I cannot look upon them at all in the same light, nor think the same duties belong to them."

"In one respect, there certainly is a difference. In marriage, the man is supposed to provide for the support of the woman, the woman to make the home agreeable to the man; he is to purvey, and she is to smile. But in dancing, their duties are exactly changed; the agreeableness, the compliance are expected from him, while she furnishes the fan and the lavender water. That, I suppose, was the difference of duties which struck you, as rendering the conditions incapable of comparison."

"No, indeed, I never thought of that."

"Then I am quite at a loss. One thing, however, I must observe. This disposition on your side is rather alarming. You totally disallow any similarity in the obligations; and may I not thence infer that your notions of the duties of the dancing state are not so strict as your partner might wish? Have I not reason to fear that if the gentleman who spoke to you just now were to return, or if any other gentleman were to address you, there would be nothing to restrain you from conversing with him as long as you chose?"

"Mr. Thorpe is such a very particular friend of my brother's, that if he talks to me, I must talk to him again; but there are hardly three young men in the room besides him that I have any acquaintance with."

"And is that to be my only security? Alas, alas!"

"Nay, I am sure you cannot have a better; for if I do not know anybody, it is impossible for me to talk to them; and, besides, I do not want to talk to anybody."

"Now you have given me a security worth having; and I shall proceed with courage. Do you find Bath as agreeable as when I had the honour of making the inquiry before?"

"Yes, quite—more so, indeed."

"More so! Take care, or you will forget to be tired of it at the proper time. You ought to be tired at the end of six weeks."

"I do not think I should be tired, if I were to stay here six months."

"Bath, compared with London, has little variety, and so everybody finds out every year. 'For six weeks, I allow Bath is pleasant enough; but beyond that, it is the most tiresome place in the world.' You would be told so by people of all descriptions, who come regularly every winter, lengthen their six weeks into ten or twelve, and go away at last because they can afford to stay no longer."

"Well, other people must judge for themselves, and those who go to London may think nothing of Bath. But I, who live in a small retired village in the country, can never find greater sameness in such a place as this than in my own home; for here are a variety of amusements, a variety of things to be seen and done all day long, which I can know nothing of there."

"You are not fond of the country."

"Yes, I am. I have always lived there, and always been very happy. But certainly there is much more sameness in a country life than in a Bath life. One day in the country is exactly like another."

"But then you spend your time so much more rationally in the country."

"Do I?"

"Do you not?"

"I do not believe there is much difference."

"Here you are in pursuit only of amusement all day long."

"And so I am at home—only I do not find so much of it. I walk about here, and so I do there; but here I see a variety of people in every street, and there I can only go and call on Mrs. Allen."

Mr. Tilney was very much amused.

"Only go and call on Mrs. Allen!" he repeated. "What a picture of intellectual poverty! However, when you sink into this abyss again, you will have more to say. You will be able to talk of Bath, and of all that you did here."

"Oh! Yes. I shall never be in want of something to talk of again to Mrs. Allen, or anybody else. I really believe I shall always be talking of Bath, when I am at home again—I do like it so very much. If I could but have Papa and Mamma, and the rest of them here, I suppose I should be too happy! James's coming (my eldest brother) is quite delightful—and especially as it turns out that the very family we are just got so intimate with are his intimate friends already. Oh! Who can ever be tired of Bath?"

"Not those who bring such fresh feelings of every sort to it as you do. But papas and mammas, and brothers, and intimate friends are a good deal gone by, to most of the frequenters of Bath—and the honest relish of balls and plays, and everyday sights, is past with them." Here their conversation closed, the demands of the dance becoming now too importunate for a divided attention.

Soon after their reaching the bottom of the set, Catherine perceived herself to be earnestly regarded by a gentleman who stood among the lookers-on, immediately behind her partner. He was a very handsome man, of a commanding aspect, past the bloom, but not past the vigour of life; and with his eye still directed towards her, she saw him presently address Mr. Tilney in a familiar whisper. Confused by his notice, and blushing from the fear of its being excited by something wrong in her appearance, she turned away her head. But while she did so, the gentleman retreated, and her partner, coming nearer, said, "I see that you guess what I have just been asked. That gentleman knows your name, and you have a right to know his. It is General Tilney, my father."

Catherine's answer was only "Oh!"—but it was an "Oh!" expressing everything needful: attention to his words, and perfect reliance on their truth. With real interest and strong admiration did her eye now follow the general, as he moved through the crowd, and "How handsome a family they are!" was her secret remark.

In chatting with Miss Tilney before the evening concluded, a new source of felicity arose to her. She had never taken a country walk since her arrival in Bath. Miss Tilney, to whom all the commonly frequented environs were familiar, spoke of them in terms which made her all eagerness to know them too; and on her openly fearing that she might find nobody to go with her, it was proposed by the brother and sister that they should join in a walk, some morning or other. "I shall like it," she cried, "beyond anything in the world; and do not let us put it off—let us go tomorrow." This was readily agreed to, with only a proviso of Miss Tilney's, that it did not rain, which Catherine was sure it would not. At twelve o'clock, they were to call for her in Pulteney Street; and "Remember—twelve o'clock," was her parting speech to her new friend. Of her other, her older, her more established friend, Isabella, of whose fidelity and worth she had enjoyed a fortnight's experience, she scarcely saw anything during the evening. Yet, though longing to make her acquainted with her happiness, she cheerfully submitted to the wish of Mr. Allen, which took them rather early away, and her spirits danced within her, as she danced in her chair all the way home.

CHAPTER

Eighteen

THE BONDS OF FRIENDSHIP, whether they be the fruit of long and enduring companionship, or the sprouts set from new acquaintances, share the same unchanging element, which is that the interest in perpetuating the relationship must be held by both parties. True, they may not be fully equal, and seldom are, as no two people are exactly alike, nor are their emotional propensities; one is always bound to feel more than the other. Yet the fact remains that it is still a unification that requires a minimum of two.

It is at the beginning of such an acquaintance that a great deal of guessing is required, usually in how one is perceived by the other, be it favourable or not, and how to be seen in the most agreeable terms. To do so necessitates an understanding of the alternate party and their place in the world, how they feel, their likes and dislikes, their history, triumphs and despairs, idiosyncrasies and quirks, and all of the other things that when added together into a single whole, makes that person unique unto themselves.

In addition, the forging of new ties often means putting forth the effort of not making a fool of oneself, which can oftentimes happen through sheer nervousness over not doing that very thing. A single word spoken at the wrong time, or a gesture improperly given can assuredly raise the colour of the cheeks faster than any other method in proper company. In the nature of relations, a person wants to know exactly how they are perceived in the eyes of others.

In her short time in Bath, Catherine had managed to make the acquaintance of two sets of potential friends, both in the form of sister and brother, and with each one came its unique level of guesswork, although the first to make her acquaintance, Isabella, required the least amount of analysis. With her constant expressions of attention, Catherine surmised (without actually giving it any deep thought) how that affection was worn on the sleeve as clearly as her patterned muslin. She accepted Miss Thorpe's constant declarations of attention to her, their interlinking of arms, and the terms of such a cherishing nature as "my dearest creature," repeated so often as to be her real name. If Isabella strayed in her attention, as when James was near, Catherine could forgive without any forethought due to the source of the diversion, as she had always been compliant as far as her brother was concerned.

There was no subtlety in Isabella; so strong were her pronouncements that without quite knowing how to describe the impressions, Catherine felt after each encounter that she had been run over by a racing carriage of endearments, and left to pick herself up from the dust. Even with this in consideration, Isabella was a friend and sister to her brother's friend. Nothing more needed to be said.

As to Isabella's brother, Catherine had more difficulty in determining what she should make of him. As he was both a good friend to her own brother, as well as sibling to her own friend, any clear opinion was altered by their own good associations.

Then there were the Tilneys, to which the prospect of a continued acquaintance brought about such excitement to Catherine, but also a great degree of the aforementioned guesswork. The opportunity to become better acquainted with the sister, Eleanor, would be wonderful indeed, and from the brief time they had spent together, she felt encouraged by the possibility of a friendship. What struck her was the extreme difference in temperament between Eleanor and Isabella, and it was this observation that made her want all the more to make a good impression while avoiding any accidental faux pas in her presence.

As to Henry Tilney, well, yes—the thoughts could make her blush.

As stated previously, the development of any friendship must come likewise from both parties, and while it might not be a contract as binding as that of a dance as noted by Mr. Tilney with its principles of fidelity and complaisance, nor of the ramifications of that of a marriage, the potentials of a friendship might outweigh both in terms of length of duration, commitment, and overall attraction. For Miss Morland, a cultivation of such an intimacy with both of the Tilneys was of utmost importance.

The question of it being felt equally by the opposing party, either in varying degrees in one or the other, or in unified and shared opinion, might best be answered by the conversation held by brother and sister later the same evening. The discussion took place after they had left the cotillion ball, having been informed by their father that he had grown tired—although restlessness or boredom might have been more accurate descriptions—and he was ready to depart immediately, as should they. Following a short ride back to their lodgings in relative silence, and their father retiring to his quarters, the two were able to speak openly without concern of being overheard.

"I see you met with a new acquaintance this evening," Henry began.

Eleanor knew immediately to whom he was referring. "Yes," she answered in the simplest of responses but with much more said underneath, and immediately understood by the other. Theirs was a unique relationship, even among siblings, deep in caring for one another and a familiarity so well developed that they often did not need to speak with words in order to communicate with the other. A simple gesture, a change in tone, or a glance could reveal volumes.

"And did you find her agreeable?

"Yes. Quite agreeable."

"And did you speak of anything of importance?"

"In what manner do you mean?" She smiled, knowing how he was baiting her, as was his nature, and likewise played along.

"Might have you spoken of, oh, the pleasantness of the weather?"

"We might have, only that it might not rain tomorrow."

"A well-justified desire. Did you speak of her stay in Bath?"

"Perhaps we might have."

"And?"

"Her stay has been pleasant," she answered.

"Her lodgings have been comfortable?"

"I do not recall discussing the subject, however, my impression is yes."

"I see. And were there any other subjects of interest brought up? Likes? Dislikes?"

"I know where you are going with this, dear brother. You, who have made mention of her well before this evening, and even after your initial excursion to Bath, thereby leaving little doubt in my mind as to who she is. But do not think that you can so easily work on me for any additional information. Our conversation was ours alone."

"Oh, dear," Henry exclaimed in mock amazement. "It must have been scandalous."

"You know me better than that, as I you." Eleanor paused, and with the mildest of smiles, offered, "She does think you a fine dancer."

"Then I shall be quite content to be in her good opinion as to my ability to put one foot in front of the other, and shall sleep peacefully this evening." He returned the smile, and after laying his hand on her arm, repeated the question. "And did you find her agreeable?"

Her response was likewise the same, but as with his question, the meaning was different. "Yes. I found her most agreeable. I thank you for asking."

"I do worry about you."

She patted his hand. "I know."

They retired soon thereafter, with each knowing considerably more from their discourse, and true to his word, Henry's thoughts being on the welfare of his sister.

Fate has a way of dispersing conditions without any true rhyme or reason, and it is left to each individual to deal with the circumstances as they might. For Eleanor, those conditions had produced an existence lacking in the companionship she might have desired, and with Henry as her best confidant for all the hopes and fears that a lady might otherwise impart to another of the same sex; because of this, she kept much of her feelings to herself. For his part, Henry tried to be all he might be for her, but his specific obligations, being a man as well as a brother, were distinct barriers not to be cleared.

So it was with the appearance of Miss Morland, to whom he had already become acquainted, that a fervent hope had materialized of some sort of friendship to develop with Eleanor. True, their stay in Bath was temporary, but for their visit, it might prove to be a welcome respite to her solitude, and he could think of no one else more favourable to be in her good graces.

Naturally, there was always the chance of her meeting a gentleman to which she would find favor, Bath being a constant succession of balls, theatrical performances, and other social gatherings, but he knew that this was not a probability. There was an elusive nature to Eleanor whenever an eligible man was near, for reasons comprehended in their intricacies only by the two. Anyway, the main individual of whom approval must be given would be that of the general. Previous experience had proven that quite well.

There was a young man who had captured her interest. They met during his stay at their estate in Gloucestershire. Michael Everett had arrived with his father, a merchant of wine and spirits who was based in one of the smaller coastal towns in the eastern part of the country, and who had entered into a business arrangement with the general while establishing a secondary trade to the south in Cornwall.

The elder Everett had been successful in his commerce, partially due to his proximity to the dock and arrangements with the port's master regarding incoming cargo. True, the port was located in one of the more secluded towns along the coast; however, this seemed to work in the merchant's favor. So, too, were the secondary ports he had established a business with, including the southmost one in the vicinity of Seaham near the town of Newquay.

Due to the details to be worked out with General Tilney, along with other related business to be handled while in Gloucestershire, he was offered the hospitality of the estate. The younger Everett was early in the learning of the trade from the father and was brought along as part of his education.

Michael Everett was indeed handsome, with large blue eyes that seemed to be forever alert, a trait handed down from father to son, but as the younger was quite dashing, the father was far less in appearance, suggesting that the whole of his good looks must have originated from the mother's side than the father's. However, set side by side, father and son could easily be matched by the iridescent quality of their eyes—although the fathers had grown quite large, and with a roughened, almost scale-like complexion, his overall appearance might be politely described as peculiar.

It came as no surprise that Miss Tilney might be smitten with young Everett. He was charming to a fault, and in every way possible a perfect match for Eleanor, save one, that being a situation inferior to hers, thus making any possible engagement impossible. That they were aware of this did not soften the affection that they both had for one another nor had the elapsed time since then changed their opinion of the other, even with the knowledge that either might eventually be betrothed to a person other than themselves. Knowing that her father would frown upon any continued communication, they nevertheless continued to do so discreetly, and even Henry had played a part in their letters, offering to act as a courier on more than one occasion.

For his part, Henry had hoped that his sister might eventually come to terms with the hopelessness of the situation, but would not do anything to dissuade her heart, as that was for her alone to consider. With this prior history, it was more than understandable how she would receive other gentlemen if they were to visit her home, or if she were at any form of public event, which certainly included the most recent stay at Bath. She was, as expected, agreeable and kind to all, but to offers of any sort, she most politely declined.

If Eleanor Tilney managed to carry an air of solitude, even when in the middle of a crowded room, it was not without its reasons. And as much as she loved her brother, it would be so nice to have another confidant, preferably of the same gender.

"Yes," Eleanor repeated after a minute. "I do find Miss Morland very agreeable, as I strongly believe that you do as well." Her eyes met his as she asked in confirmation of the answer, "Do you not?"

Henry did not reply. There was no need. He simply smiled.

CHAPTER

Nineteen

THE MORROW BROUGHT a very sober-looking morning, the sun making only a few efforts to appear, and Catherine augured from it everything most favourable to her wishes. A bright morning so early in the year, she allowed, would generally turn to rain, but a cloudy one foretold improvement as the day advanced. She applied to Mr. Allen for confirmation of her hopes, but Mr. Allen, not having his own skies and barometer about him, declined giving any absolute promise of sunshine. She applied to Mrs. Allen, and Mrs. Allen's opinion was more positive. "She had no doubt in the world of its being a very fine day, if the clouds would only go off, and the sun keep out."

At about eleven o'clock, however, a few specks of small rain upon the windows caught Catherine's watchful eye, and "Oh! dear, I do believe it will be wet," broke from her in a most desponding tone.

"I thought how it would be," said Mrs. Allen.

"No walk for me today," sighed Catherine; "but perhaps it may come to nothing, or it may hold up before twelve."

"Perhaps it may, but then, my dear, it will be so dirty."

"Oh! That will not signify; I never mind dirt."

"No," replied her friend very placidly, "I know you never mind dirt."

After a short pause, "It comes on faster and faster!" said Catherine, as she stood watching at a window.

"So it does indeed. If it keeps raining, the streets will be very wet."

"There are four umbrellas up already. How I hate the sight of an umbrella!"

"They are disagreeable things to carry. I would much rather take a chair at any time."

"It was such a nice-looking morning! I felt so convinced it would be dry!"

"Anybody would have thought so indeed. There will be very few people in the pump-room, if it rains all the morning. I hope Mr. Allen will put on his greatcoat when he goes, but I dare say he will not, for he had rather do anything in the world than walk out in a greatcoat; I wonder he should dislike it, it must be so comfortable."

The rain continued—fast, though not heavy. Catherine went every five minutes to the clock, threatening on each return that, if it still kept on raining another five minutes, she would give up the matter as hopeless. The clock struck twelve, and it still rained. "You will not be able to go, my dear."

"I do not quite despair yet. I shall not give it up till a quarter after twelve. This is just the time of day for it to clear up, and I do think it looks a little lighter. There, it is twenty minutes after twelve, and now I shall give it up entirely. Oh! That we had such weather here as they had at Udolpho, or at least in Tuscany and the south of France!—the night that poor St. Aubin died!—such beautiful weather!"

At half past twelve, when Catherine's anxious attention to the weather was over and she could no longer claim any merit from its amendment, the sky began voluntarily to clear. A gleam of sunshine took her quite by surprise; she looked round; the clouds were parting, and she instantly returned to the window to watch over and encourage the happy appearance. Ten minutes more made it certain that a bright afternoon would succeed, and justified the opinion of Mrs. Allen, who had "always thought it would clear up." But whether Catherine might still expect her friends, whether there had not been too much rain for Miss Tilney to venture, must yet be a question.

It was too dirty for Mrs. Allen to accompany her husband to the pump-room; he accordingly set off by himself, and Catherine had barely watched him down the street when her notice was claimed by the approach of the same two open carriages, containing the same three people that had surprised her so much a few mornings back.

"Isabella, my brother, and Mr. Thorpe, I declare! They are coming for me perhaps—but I shall not go—I cannot go indeed, for you know Miss Tilney may still call." Mrs. Allen agreed to it. John Thorpe was soon with them, and his voice was with them yet sooner, for on the stairs he was calling out to Miss Morland to be quick. "Make haste! Make haste!" as he threw open the door. "Put on your hat this moment—there is no time to be lost—we are going to Bristol. How d'ye do, Mrs. Allen?"

"To Bristol! Is not that a great way off? But, however, I cannot go with you today, because I am engaged; I expect some friends every moment." This was of course vehemently talked down as no reason at all; Mrs. Allen was called on to second him, and the two others walked in, to give their assistance. "My sweetest Catherine, is not this delightful? We shall have a most heavenly drive. You are to thank your brother and me for the scheme; it darted into our heads at breakfast-time, I verily believe at the same instant; and we should have been off two hours ago if it had not been for this detestable rain. But it does not signify, the nights are moonlight, and we shall do delightfully. Oh! I am in such ecstasies at the thoughts of a little country air and quiet! So much better than going to the Lower Rooms. We shall drive directly to Clifton and dine there; and, as soon as dinner is over, if there is time for it, go on to Kingsweston."

"I doubt our being able to do so much," said Morland.

"You croaking fellow!" cried Thorpe. "We shall be able to do ten times more. Kingsweston! Aye, and Blaize Castle too, and anything else we can hear of; but here is your sister says she will not go."

"Blaize Castle!" cried Catherine. "What is that'?"

"The finest place in England—worth going fifty miles at any time to see."

"What, is it really a castle, an old castle?"

"The oldest in the kingdom."

"But is it like what one reads of?"

"Exactly—the very same."

"But now really—are there towers and long galleries?"

"By dozens."

"Then I should like to see it; but I cannot—I cannot go."

"Not go! My beloved creature, what do you mean'?"

"I cannot go, because"—looking down as she spoke, fearful of Isabella's smile—"I expect Miss Tilney and her brother to call on me to take a country walk. They promised to come at twelve, only it rained; but now, as it is so fine, I dare say they will be here soon."

"Not they indeed," cried Thorpe; "for, as we turned into Broad Street, I saw them—does he not drive a phaeton with bright chestnuts?"

"I do not know indeed."

"Yes, I know he does; I saw him. You are talking of the man you danced with last night, are not you?"

"Yes.

"Well, I saw him at that moment turn up the Lansdown Road, driving a smart-looking girl."

"Did you indeed?"

"Did upon my soul; knew him again directly, and he seemed to have got some very pretty cattle too."

"It is very odd! But I suppose they thought it would be too dirty for a walk."

"And well they might, for I never saw so much dirt in my life. Walk! You could no more walk than you could fly! It has not been so dirty the whole winter; it is ankle-deep everywhere."

Isabella corroborated it: "My dearest Catherine, you cannot form an idea of the dirt; come, you must go; you cannot refuse going now."

"I should like to see the castle; but may we go all over it? May we go up every staircase, and into every suite of rooms?"

"Yes, yes, every hole and corner."

"But then, if they should only be gone out for an hour till it is dryer, and call by and by?"

"Make yourself easy, there is no danger of that, for I heard Tilney hallooing to a man who was just passing by on horseback, that they were going as far as Wick Rocks."

"Then I will. Shall I go, Mrs. Allen?"

"Just as you please, my dear. Mind you, stay clear of Severnford. It is not a safe place, so I have been told."

The comment snared young Thorpe's attention. "Why, pray tell? What form of danger might we find?"

Mrs. Allen stiffened. "That I cannot say. All I have heard has been in whispers as if the vicinity is unholy, township and castle alike, but I have heard no specifics."

"Another castle," exclaimed Thorpe, but Mrs. Allen held steadfast in her resolve.

"Catherine, promise me that you will not venture anywhere near Severnford. Remember, you are in my charge. I must look after your care."

With a look at her companions, she nodded. "I give you my word. But if the Tilneys should come? Oh, shall I go?"

"Mrs. Allen, you must persuade her to go," was the general cry. Mrs. Allen was not inattentive to it: "Well, my dear," said she, "suppose you go." And in two minutes they were off.

Catherine's feelings, as she got into the carriage, were in a very unsettled state; divided between regret for the loss of one great pleasure, and the hope of soon enjoying another, almost its equal in degree, however unlike in kind. She could not think the Tilneys had acted quite well by her, in so readily giving up their engagement, without sending her any message of excuse. It was now but an hour later than the time fixed on for the beginning of their walk; and, in spite of what she had heard of the prodigious accumulation of dirt in the course of that hour, she could not from her own observation help thinking that they might have gone with very little inconvenience. To feel herself slighted by them was very painful. On the other hand, the delight of exploring an edifice like Udolpho, as her fancy represented Blaize Castle to be, was such a counterpoise of good as might console her for almost anything.

They passed briskly down Pulteney Street, and through Laura Place, without the exchange of many words. Thorpe talked to his horse, and she meditated, by turns, on broken promises and broken arches, phaetons and false hangings, Tilneys and trap-doors. As they entered Argyle Buildings, however, she was roused by this address from her companion, "Who is that girl who looked at you so hard as she went by?"

"Who? Where?"

"On the right-hand pavement—she must be almost out of sight now." Catherine looked round and saw Miss Tilney leaning on her brother's arm, walking slowly down the street. She saw them both looking back at her. "Stop, stop, Mr. Thorpe," she impatiently cried; "it is Miss Tilney; it is indeed. How could you tell me they were gone? Stop, stop, I will get out this moment and go to them." But to what purpose did she speak? Thorpe only lashed his horse into a brisker trot; the Tilneys, who had soon ceased to look after her, were in a moment out of sight round the corner of Laura Place, and in another moment she was herself whisked into the marketplace.

Still, however, and during the length of another street, she entreated him to stop. "Pray, pray stop, Mr. Thorpe. I cannot go on. I will not go on. I must go back to Miss Tilney." But Mr. Thorpe only laughed, smacked his whip, encouraged his horse, made odd noises, and drove on; and Catherine, angry and vexed as she was, having no power of getting away, was obliged to give up the point and submit. Her reproaches, however, were not spared. "How could you deceive me so, Mr. Thorpe? How could you say that you saw them driving up the Lansdown Road? I would not have had it happen so for the world. They must think it so strange, so rude of me! To go by them, too, without saying a word! You do not know how vexed I am; I shall have no pleasure at Clifton, nor in anything else. I had rather, ten thousand times rather, get out now, and walk back to them. How could you say you saw them driving out in a phaeton?" Thorpe defended himself very stoutly, declared he had never seen two men so much alike in his life, and would hardly give up the point of its having been Tilney himself.

Their drive, even when this subject was over, was not likely to be very agreeable. Catherine's complaisance was no longer what it had been in their former airing. She listened reluctantly, and her replies were short. Blaize Castle remained her only comfort; towards that, she still looked at intervals with pleasure; though rather than be disappointed of the promised walk, and especially rather than be thought ill of by the Tilneys, she would willingly have given up all the happiness which its walls could supply—the happiness of a progress through a long suite of lofty rooms, exhibiting the remains of magnificent furniture, though now for many years deserted—the happiness of being stopped in their way along narrow, winding vaults, by a low, grated door; or even of having their lamp, their only lamp, extinguished by a sudden gust of wind, and of being left in total darkness. In the meanwhile, they proceeded on their journey without any mischance, and had been only a short ways past Saltford when they heard the screeching of birds from a distant field.

"I dare say someone nearby has just kicked the bucket," said Thorpe with a casual nod to the collective noise. The statement confounded Catherine, who had still not come to terms with his nature of saying things that were not wholly accurate and was therefore at a loss to his meaning.

"I'm sure I don't understand," she replied.

"The birds. It means that death is in the air." When she further pronounced her ignorance, he let out a sigh of amazement. "Surely you have heard stories about the nightjars, and how they gather when someone is on the verge of death in order to steal the poor unfortunate's soul. If you lose your soul to the nightjars, you will never find peace. I've heard of them since I was a child."

"I can't say that I have.

"There you have it then. When you are on your deathbed, pray not to be taken by the feathered beasts from hell."

"But did you truly call them nightjars?"

"Indeed, I did. No mistake about that."

"But it is late in the afternoon, and are not nightjars nocturnal creatures? I thought that they only come out at dusk or just before the sun rises—and if so, what we just heard could not possibly be a nightjar."

Thorpe shifted uncomfortably, seeing as how his attempt to get a rise from Catherine had failed. "Yes, well, it might be another breed. What is one bird to another? Anyway, it is just a silly fairy story and nothing more."

With that, they resumed their silence to one another for a distance that seemed much longer than it actually was and were within view of the town of Keynsham, when a halloo from Morland, who was behind them, made his friend pull up, to know what was the matter. The others then came close enough for conversation, and Morland said, "We had better go back, Thorpe; it is too late to go on today; your sister thinks so as well as I. We have been exactly an hour coming from Pulteney Street, very little more than seven miles; and, I suppose, we have at least eight more to go. It will never do. We set out a great deal too late. We had much better put it off till another day, and turn round."

"It is all one to me," replied Thorpe rather angrily; and instantly turning his horse, they were on their way back to Bath.

"If your brother had not got such a damned beast to drive," said he soon afterwards, "we might have done it very well. My horse would have trotted to Clifton within the hour, if left to himself, and I have almost broke my arm with pulling him in to that cursed broken-winded jade's pace. Morland is a fool for not keeping a horse and gig of his own."

"No, he is not," said Catherine warmly, "for I am sure he could not afford it."

"And why cannot he afford it?"

"Because he has not money enough."

"And whose fault is that?"

"Nobody's, that I know of." Thorpe then said something in the loud, incoherent way to which he had often recourse, about its being a damned thing to be miserly; and that if people who rolled in money could not afford things, he did not know who could, which Catherine did not even endeavour to understand. Disappointed of what was to have been the consolation for her first disappointment, she was less and less disposed either to be agreeable herself or to find her companion so; and they returned to Pulteney Street without her speaking twenty words.

As she entered the house, the footman told her that a gentleman and lady had called and inquired for her a few minutes after her setting off; that, when he told them she was gone out with Mr. Thorpe, the lady had asked whether any message had been left for her; and on his saying no, had felt for a card, but said she had none about her, and went away. Pondering over these heart-rending tidings, Catherine walked slowly upstairs. At the head of them she was met by Mr. Allen, who, on hearing the reason of their speedy return, said, "I am glad your brother had so much sense; I am glad you are come back. It was a strange, wild scheme."

They all spent the evening together at Thorpe's. Catherine was disturbed and out of spirits; but Isabella seemed to find a pool of commerce, in the fate of which she shared, by private partnership with Morland, a very good equivalent for the quiet and country air of an inn at Clifton. Her satisfaction, too, in not being at the Lower Rooms was spoken more than once. "How I pity the poor creatures that are going there! How glad I am that I am not amongst them! I wonder whether it will be a full ball or not! They have not begun dancing yet. I would not be there for all the world. It is so delightful to have an evening now and then to oneself. I dare say it will not be a very good ball. I know the Mitchells will not be there. I am sure I pity everybody that is. But I dare say, Mr. Morland, you long to be at it, do not you? I am sure you do. Well, pray do not let anybody here be a restraint on you. I dare say we could do very well without you; but you men think yourselves of such consequence."

Catherine could almost have accused Isabella of being wanting in tenderness towards herself and her sorrows, so very little did they appear to dwell on her mind, and so very inadequate was the comfort she offered. "Do not be so dull, my dearest creature," she whispered. "You will quite break my heart. It was amazingly shocking, to be sure; but the Tilneys were entirely to blame. Why were not they more punctual? It was dirty, indeed, but what did that signify? I am sure John and I should not have minded it. I never mind going through anything, where a friend is concerned; that is my disposition, and John is just the same; he has amazing strong feelings. Good heavens! What a delightful hand you have got! Kings, I vow! I never was so happy in my life! I would fifty times rather you should have them than myself."

And now I may dismiss my heroine to the sleepless couch, which is the true heroine's portion; to a pillow strewed with thorns and wet with tears. And lucky may she think herself, if she get another good night's rest in the course of the next three months.

CHAPTER

Twenty

THE GREATEST IRONY of their failed excursion was entirely lost upon Catherine, who had built up such grand expectations of the castle they were to visit. Hers were born of romantic concepts but were hardly based on any real fact. Part of this was due to a youthful and imaginative mind, however equal fault and responsibility for the preconceived ideas may be leveled on Mr. Thorpe, who prompted such flights through his descriptions. Indeed, the reality was so far different from his encouragements, had she reached the grounds, she would have surely been disappointed.

As locations go, Blaize Castle bore hardly any mystery. It was far from the oldest castle in England, as Thorpe had claimed, nor did it contain the dozens of towers and long galleries as promised. In actuality, it was just over half a century in age, making it a mere infant compared to the regal giants of old. True, the land surrounding the structure could boast of historical activity, if not any major importance, at one time populated by farmers during the Neolithic Period, and activity continuing through the ages to the hill-forts inhabited by Romans.

As to mysteries, hauntings, or other events attached to the castle, there was little to recommend. If Miss Morland had expected an edifice such as *Udolpho*, or a mere hint of melodrama, she would have left with the visions groundless.

In this respect, her disdain for historical accounts proved to be a failure to her fancied interests. Had she been more knowledgeable of the many legends of the isles, she would have known to look elsewhere, for the true mysteries, many of them unspoken, could be found in the areas far and wide, far surpassing what she might have read in her dear novels, including *Udolpho* and *Meinster Castle*.

Among the oldest of these in popular knowledge were the ancient stone circles and barrows scattered in multitudes across the country, from pillars of massive height to the diminutive groupings that sat low into the earth. Lost in meaning due to their antiquity, they likewise were a part of everyday life for many across the isles, as ordinary as the neighbouring trees. How they came to be, what purpose they might have had at the time of their construct, who the people were who erected the stones, and when they ceased to serve their original functions were all questions that were both considered with serious intent by academics and passed off as nonessential details by the general populace. Regardless of what was thought of them, the sites remained just as they had for thousands of years.

By far the most notable of these was the set of monolithic standing stones located on Salisbury Plain in Wiltshire, the five trilothons made all the more unusual by the size of the horizontal formations resting on top of the upright ends. Catherine had seen the ancient site with her family when she was younger, but she spent most of the time running between the columns, shouting "olly olly oxen free" while hiding from Sally, rather than contemplating the mysteries of the ages.

Her later memories of it were scattered, as to be expected from one of that age, but still more intact than her younger brothers and sisters. With an additional half dozen years behind her when she made the trip, she most likely would have been bestowed with more awe of her surroundings.

Outside of this one excursion, she had little opportunity to see any of the few formations in the region: Avebury, a few miles out of Malborough, a ritual space used for ancient fertility rites; the Rollright Stones in Oxfordshire with its stories of the circle being a king and his army who were turned to stone by a powerful magician in the course of their march, or its tree that once was a witch, now transformed and whose branches contained potent healing powers; and the rings of Stanton Drew, a close nine miles west of Bath, whose stones were purportedly the remnant of a wedding rite whose revelers carried their celebrations into the Sabbath.

The greater number of these ancient sites were collected in the upper regions of the isle, of Scotland, Ireland, Wales, and to the far southwest. So few of these were to be found in the south-central region that they disappeared completely once a traveler passed the stones in Wiltshire, creating another layer to the mystery. Still, the sites remained, just as they had, in vast numbers across the land, and each with its legend attached to it.

As with all folklore, there was usually some basis to its origin, upon which the sometimes fanciful stories would flourish. In other cases, the stories were mere allegory for something more essential to the people of the time. Lastly, the legends might be wholly authentic to the source. It was largely believed that they were the sites of ancient temples, used by the natives for dancing, prayer, astronomical observations, fertility rituals—be it a plentiful crop or a plentiful womb—and the horrific acts of animal and human sacrifice.

Near the Welsh coast in Gwydnedd, stood the ancient pillar known as the Druid's Circle, with tales of the sacrifice of children there accepted as truth, no doubt due to the finding of small bones at the site. Scorhill also served as a locale for blood sacrifice, to the degree that horses were still bothered by the scent of the blood that saturated the stone, thus making it impossible to ride through the site. Over and again, the legends repeated across the land, in Aberdeenshire and West Lothian, the counties of Ireland, Derbyshire, Cumberland, and across the Hebrides.

How these structures came to be was another unanswered question, although most gave it no mind. The gigantic stones were, to put it simply, there, always had been there, and were of no further concern. This was for the academics to ponder, and theorize how their forebears might have constructed such monuments, and have moved them from the ancient quarries into their final designated spots. To date, there had been no reasonable answer given, resulting in the popular acceptance of the architecture as an unquestioned part of the landscape. Still, the origin of these blocks led way to myths, including the many variations similar to Stanton Drew and of maidens being turned to stone for dancing on the Sabbath. The elegant circle in Swinside, sometimes called Sunkenkirk, carried its fable of being constructed by the Devil, and how the stones were sunk deep into the ground so as not to be used as a foundation for a church.

Just as the rings of stone manifested their specific lore, so did other relics of the olden times, carried on to the present in the form of burrows, abandoned castles, and cemeteries. The ruins of Pomerai Castle were avoided after dark, with whispers of the two sisters, one unattractive but older and mistress of the castle, and the other beautiful beyond measure. Both fell in love with the same man and in a fit of jealousy, the older imprisoned her sister in the dungeon and allowed her to starve to death. It was this doomed sister who was said to still walk the grounds, and if seen, could cause madness to the unlucky witness. To show its disdain for the structure, Heaven left the structure in ruins the previous century with a bolt of lightning.

The remnants of the Augustinian Bolton Priory in Yorkshire were likewise avoided, and those who lingered would tell of dark forces at work and a ghostly figure in black. Also in Yorkshire, there stood Whitby Abbey and its spectral coach pulled by four headless horses. Even Catherine had read Walter Scott's doomed account of Constance de Beverley, and how her figure still roamed the site. In Cornwall, the phantom of a Druid priest was said to haunt a prehistoric burial mound on the Bodmin Moor and would assail the occasional traveler with an enchanted drink. Most legendary was that of Pendragon Castle in Cumbria, said to be the father of King Arthur, and an undiscovered treasure hidden deep within the foundation of the ruins.

Some of these sites were born evil, while others inherited their foul reputation from the deeds of men, and were forevermore unable to shake off the lingering aura of those acts. The blood spilt contaminated the very ground, and left a permanent stain that might be witnessed only out of the corner of one's eye or when the sun had faded from view. Be it the acts of anger, betrayal, jealousy, or woe—or the ritual of pagan sacrifice—these realms could never be wholly claimed again in purity by the living.

Or so the legends spoke.

CHAPTER

Twenty-One

"MRS. ALLEN," said Catherine the next morning, "will there be any harm in my calling on Miss Tilney today? I shall not be easy till I have explained everything."

"Go, by all means, my dear; only put on a white gown; Miss Tilney always wears white."

Catherine cheerfully complied, and being properly equipped, was more impatient than ever to be at the pump-room, that she might inform herself of General Tilney's lodgings, for though she believed they were in Milsom Street, she was not certain of the house, and Mrs. Allen's wavering convictions only made it more doubtful. To Milsom Street she was directed, and having made herself perfect in the number, hastened away with eager steps and a beating heart to pay her visit, explain her conduct, and be forgiven; tripping lightly through the church-yard, and resolutely turning away her eyes, that she might not be obliged to see her beloved Isabella and her dear family, who, she had reason to believe, were in a shop hard by.

She reached the house without any impediment, looked at the number, knocked at the door, and inquired for Miss Tilney. The man believed Miss Tilney to be at home, but was not quite certain. Would she be pleased to send up her name? She gave her card. In a few minutes the servant returned, and with a look which did not quite confirm his words, said he had been mistaken, for that Miss Tilney was walked out. Catherine, with a blush of mortification, left the house. She felt almost persuaded that Miss Tilney was at home, and too much offended to admit her; and as she retired down the street, could not withhold one glance at the drawing-room windows, in expectation of seeing her there, but no one appeared at them.

At the bottom of the street, however, she looked back again, and then, not at a window, but issuing from the door, she saw Miss Tilney herself. She was followed by a gentleman, whom Catherine believed to be her father, and they turned up towards Edgar's Buildings. Catherine, in deep mortification, proceeded on her way. She could almost be angry herself at such angry incivility; but she checked the resentful sensation; she remembered her own ignorance. She knew not how such an offence as hers might be classed by the laws of worldly politeness, to what a degree of unforgivingness it might with propriety lead, nor to what rigours of rudeness in return it might justly make her amenable.

Dejected and humbled, she had even some thoughts of not going with the others to the theatre that night; but it must be confessed that they were not of long continuance, for she soon recollected, in the first place, that she was without any excuse for staying at home; and, in the second, that it was a play she wanted very much to see. To the theatre accordingly they all went; no Tilneys appeared to plague or please her; she feared that, amongst the many perfections of the family, a fondness for plays was not to be ranked; but perhaps it was because they were habituated to the finer performances of the London stage, which she knew, on Isabella's authority, rendered everything else of the kind "quite horrid." She was not deceived in her own expectation of pleasure; the comedy so well suspended her care that no one, observing her during the first four acts, would have supposed she had any wretchedness about her. On the beginning of the fifth, however, the sudden view of Mr. Henry Tilney and his father, joining a party in the opposite box, recalled her to anxiety and distress.

The stage could no longer excite genuine merriment—no longer keep her whole attention. Every other look upon an average was directed towards the opposite box; and, for the space of two entire scenes, did she thus watch Henry Tilney, without being once able to catch his eye. No longer could he be suspected of indifference for a play; his notice was never withdrawn from the stage during two whole scenes. At length, however, he did look towards her, and he bowed— but such a bow! No smile, no continued observance attended it; his eyes were immediately returned to their former direction. Catherine was restlessly miserable; she could almost have run round to the box in which he sat and forced him to hear her explanation. Feelings rather natural than heroic possessed her; instead of considering her own dignity injured by this ready condemnation— instead of proudly resolving, in conscious innocence, to show her resentment towards him who could harbour a doubt of it, to leave to him all the trouble of seeking an explanation, and to enlighten him on the past only by avoiding his sight, or flirting with somebody else—she took to herself all the shame of misconduct, or at least of its appearance, and was only eager for an opportunity of explaining its cause.

The play concluded—the curtain fell—Henry Tilney was no longer to be seen where he had hitherto sat, but his father remained, and perhaps he might be now coming round to their box. She was right; in a few minutes he appeared, and, making his way through the then thinning rows, spoke with like calm politeness to Mrs. Allen and her friend. Not with such calmness was he answered by the latter: "Oh! Mr. Tilney, I have been quite wild to speak to you, and make my apologies. You must have thought me so rude; but indeed it was not my own fault, was it, Mrs. Allen? Did not they tell me that Mr. Tilney and his sister were gone out in a phaeton together? And then what could I do? But I had ten thousand times rather have been with you; now had not I, Mrs. Allen?"

"My dear, you tumble my gown," was Mrs. Allen's reply.

Her assurance, however, standing sole as it did, was not thrown away; it brought a more cordial, more natural smile into his countenance, and he replied in a tone which retained only a little affected reserve: "We were much obliged to you at any rate for wishing us a pleasant walk after our passing you in Argyle Street: you were so kind as to look back on purpose."

"But indeed I did not wish you a pleasant walk; I never thought of such a thing; but I begged Mr. Thorpe so earnestly to stop; I called out to him as soon as ever I saw you; now, Mrs. Allen, did not—Oh! You were not there; but indeed I did; and, if Mr. Thorpe would only have stopped, I would have jumped out and run after you."

Is there a Henry in the world who could be insensible to such a declaration? Henry Tilney at least was not. With a yet sweeter smile, he said everything that need be said of his sister's concern, regret, and dependence on Catherine's honour. "Oh! Do not say Miss Tilney was not angry," cried Catherine, "because I know she was; for she would not see me this morning when I called; I saw her walk out of the house the next minute after my leaving it; I was hurt, but I was not affronted. Perhaps you did not know I had been abere."

"I was not within at the time; but I heard of it from Eleanor, and she has been wishing ever since to see you, to explain the reason of such incivility; but perhaps I can do it as well. It was nothing more than that my father—they were just preparing to walk out, and he being hurried for time, and not caring to have it put off—made a point of her being denied. That was all, I do assure you. She was very much vexed, and meant to make her apology as soon as possible."

Catherine's mind was greatly eased by this information, yet a something of solicitude remained, from which sprang the following question, thoroughly artless in itself, though rather distressing to the gentleman: "But, Mr. Tilney, why were you less generous than your sister? If she felt such confidence in my good intentions, and could suppose it to be only a mistake, why should you be so ready to take offence?"

"Me! I take offence!"

"Nay, I am sure by your look, when you came into the box, you were angry."

"I angry! I could have no right."

"Well, nobody would have thought you had no right who saw your face." He replied by asking her to make room for him, and talking of the play.

He remained with them some time, and was only too agreeable for Catherine to be contented when he went away. Before they parted, however, it was agreed that the projected walk should be taken as soon as possible; and, setting aside the misery of his quitting their box, she was, upon the whole, left one of the happiest creatures in the world.

While talking to each other, she had observed with some surprise that John Thorpe, who was never in the same part of the house for ten minutes together, was engaged in conversation with General Tilney; and she felt something more than surprise when she thought she could perceive herself the object of their attention and discourse. What could they have to say of her? She feared General Tilney did not like her appearance: she found it was implied in his preventing her admittance to his daughter, rather than postpone his own walk a few minutes. "How came Mr. Thorpe to know your father?" was her anxious inquiry, as she pointed them out to her companion. He knew nothing about it; but his father, like every military man, had a very large acquaintance.

At a point in their conversation, she looked to Thorpe and the general, only to find them both staring back at her. The exchange lasted hardly a second before the two dropped their gaze, while still engaged in focused consultation. The experience left Catherine perplexed, concluding that they must have been looking at Henry, no doubt he being the subject of their exchange. After all, why would she be singled out as a topic of interest?

When the entertainment was over, Thorpe came to assist them in getting out. Catherine was the immediate object of his gallantry; and, while they waited in the lobby for a chair, he prevented the inquiry which had travelled from her heart almost to the tip of her tongue, by asking, in a consequential manner, whether she had seen him talking with General Tilney: "He is a fine old fellow, upon my soul! Stout, active—looks as young as his son. I have a great regard for him, I assure you: a gentleman-like, good sort of fellow as ever lived."

"But how came you to know him?"

"Know him! There are few people much about town that I do not know. I have met him forever at the Bedford; and I knew his face again today the moment he came into the billiard-room. One of the best players we have, by the by; and we had a little touch together, though I was almost afraid of him at first: the odds were five to four against me; and, if I had not made one of the cleanest strokes that perhaps ever was made in this world—I took his ball exactly—but I could not make you understand it without a table; however, I did beat him. A very fine fellow; as rich as a Jew. I should like to dine with him; I dare say he gives famous dinners. But what do you think we have been talking of? You. Yes, by heavens! And the general thinks you the finest girl in Bath."

"Oh! Nonsense! How can you say so?"

"And what do you think I said?"—lowering his voice—"well done, general, said I; I am quite of your mind."

Here Catherine, who was much less gratified by his admiration than by General Tilney's, was not sorry to be called away by Mr. Allen. Thorpe, however, would see her to her chair, and, till she entered it, continued the same kind of delicate flattery, in spite of her entreating him to have done.

That General Tilney, instead of disliking, should admire her, was very delightful; and she joyfully thought that there was not one of the family whom she need now fear to meet. The evening had done more, much more, for her than could have been expected.

CHAPTER
Twenty-Two

GENERAL TILNEY STOOD at the window in his lodgings on Milsom Street, looking out at the lights of Bath. While quite late into the night—or early in the morning, depending on which side of the day one happened to reside— he remained wide awake, having pressing matters on his mind, and finding the cityscape a good companion to his thoughts.

Despite the hour, the locality still glowed with light, as was usually the case for being a city that never managed to put itself to sleep. For the general, rest would eventually come, but it could wait for now.

He took a sip of wine, his glass nearly drained. The dark liquid acted as an excellent accompaniment to contemplation, although his partiality extended to a good scotch, the latter best suited for when he was either sociable or in an agitated mood. Like the choice between game or fish, billiards or cards, he might find one more suitable to his disposition than the other. He raised the goblet, allowing the illumination from city to play along the bevels of the glass, shifting along the edges as he moved it from side to side.

"The whole of life is always in motion," he thought as he examined the refracted light, "as are the deeds of man. It is the choices we make, and the opportunities that come to us, that define us, and let us set straight our purpose."

His consideration had been on the events of the evening, and a set of circumstances wholly unplanned, but with ramifications that could work well in his favor. His current position might allow for a shifting of elements before him, and the more he considered it, the more auspicious it appeared.

He first noticed his son speaking with a young lady two days earlier, and he had initially given it little thought, but soon noticed the direct attention the young man gave in her behalf. True, this was not uncommon, as Henry was often seen dancing or in conversation with the fairer sex, but the event was notable enough to prompt the general to later ask him to whom he had spoken so attentively. Thus, he was first made known of Miss Catherine Morland, and although he said not a word to Henry of his opinion, he did find that she was quite pretty. His son could choose far worse in terms of appearance. Few other particulars were given at that time, the son only stating that she was new to Bath and he had met her only recently.

Miss Morland made her appearance the following day only indirectly, referenced by his son and daughter in plans to go for a walk together, to which they were delayed by the morning rain. Upon their return, there was no further mention of either the walk or their being joined by the young lady.

The general, being attentive to other matters, did not think to ask, and gave her no mind until this morning, when young Miss Morland appeared unexpectedly at their doorstep in hopes of visiting with Eleanor. Poor timing, indeed, as he was set to leave the house, and as he was dressed and ready, and with Eleanor set as well, he would not be delayed. In quick order, he gave word that his daughter was not at home, and to send Miss Morland on her way. Eleanor was disappointed when told of his directive, but she held her words, as she well should out of respect. He would have no less of his daughter.

With this outlay of events, the same Miss Morland, of whom he had no knowledge a week prior, now became such a fixture of reference that the general could not avoid notice—made all the more evident as she had found her way to the theatre earlier this evening and once more engaged the attentions of his son. Noting also the attentive nature that Henry again bestowed upon the lady, the general's curiosity compelled action to additional details of her background. Fortune, if not outrageous then simply precise, played its part in this matter with the appearance of a young man who appeared to be fully knowledgeable of her.

This chance meeting came by and by when the elder Tilney noticed the young gentleman staring at Miss Morland and Henry from a distance, and with an expression that suggested some amount of displeasure. Being an excellent judge of appearances and how the language of one's body might reveal their inner thoughts, Tilney suspected some relation to the lady and approached the man, asking him if he was of any acquaintance to young Morland. At once, the young man's countenance changed, becoming agreeable, if not with some airs about him.

"Indeed, I am, sir," he exclaimed, giving forth her name, and his familiarity with her, as well as his close friendship with her brother. The general and the young man exchanged proper introductions, after which John Thorpe continued to proudly elaborate on his knowledge of the Morlands, prompted by further questions by the general. For his part, Thorpe was most happy to be on speaking terms with a man of General Tilney's importance.

Being at that time not only in daily expectation of Morland's engaging Isabella, but likewise, pretty well resolved upon marrying Catherine himself, Thorpe's vanity induced him to represent the family as yet more wealthy than his vanity and avarice had made him believe them. With whomsoever he was, or was likely to be connected, his own consequence always required that theirs should be great, and as his intimacy with any acquaintance grew, so regularly grew their fortune.

The expectations of his friend Morland, therefore, from the first overrated, had ever since his introduction to Isabella been gradually increasing; and by merely adding twice as much for the grandeur of the moment, by doubling what he chose to think the amount of Mr. Morland's preferment, trebling his private fortune, bestowing a rich aunt, and sinking half the children, he was able to represent the whole family to the general in a most respectable light.

For Catherine, however, the peculiar object of the general's curiosity, and his own speculations, he had yet something more in reserve, and the ten or fifteen thousand pounds, which her father could give her would be a pretty addition to Mr. Allen's estate. Her intimacy there had made him seriously determine on her being handsomely legacied hereafter; and to speak of her therefore as the almost acknowledged future heiress of Fullerton naturally followed.

Thus did the general walk away from the conversation with a resolution beginning to form in his mind, while unaware of the inaccuracy of the details. Already had he discerned a liking towards Miss Morland in the countenance of his son; and thankful for Mr. Thorpe's communication, he almost instantly determined to spare no pains in weakening young Thorpe's boasted interest and ruining his dearest hopes. By the time Tilney had returned to Milsom Street, an agenda was already well set, and it was this objective falling into alignment with his other plans that had kept him up to this hour.

He had always been adept at the management of multiple strategies, an ability that had suited him well throughout his military career, and one interwoven throughout the other aspects of his life. It required an element of dimensional forethought akin to a chess game, and the moving of various pieces to their best advantage. A rook set at the right position, with the bishop just so, could make all the difference. How he handled his personal life and that of his family was of little difference from the order given to the regiment. Now a new piece had been added to the chessboard, and he saw clearly how a few proper moves could place him to a greater advantage.

There had always been the matter of his offspring being properly settled in their adulthood, and Henry had already established himself to his duties at the parsonage in Woodston. To date, he had not given serious consideration to any one lady for engagement and wedded bliss, which would also bring great comfort to the general. In all ways, the younger Tilney was upstanding and respectable, yet the general found him as one who was perhaps too virtuous for his own good, and therefore not to be taken into full confidence in the ways of the world.

Indeed, the general had seen many things in the course of his travels and knew well the underside of life. For Henry, the best thing would be to get him married and thus set on his particular path.

By comparison, there was Frederick. Of the general's three children, it was Frederick who was most like him, being similar in mind, and thus had become something more than a son. Like the general, he had taken to the military and was reaping its rewards. In fact, the general gave him little concern regarding his well-being; Frederick could take care of himself and was quite vocal about the fact.

As to Eleanor, there might come a day when she would be betrothed and leave the nest for good. For the present, the general was quite content with things as they were and preferred to keep her in her place. He was mostly a man of solitude in his own home, but he liked to have her company, it breaking the monotony, even if he often found her to be too sedate and whimpering for his taste. Still, she was his daughter, and with a resemblance to her mother that had a way of digging deep, even with the passing years.

"Enough," he reprimanded himself, aware of where the thoughts were shifting. There were pressing matters at hand that required his attention, the manipulation of Miss Morland being but a small one of them. That should be an easy matter, as he had forced the motions of entire legions in his time. Since she was from a fine and wealthy stock, a match would be advantageous to him, as well as young Henry—and who could predict what might come; she might even teach the boy a few things. She certainly had the body for it.

General Tilney finished off the remaining wine and turned from the window with its view of a city of perpetual change and infinite possibilities.

CHAPTER
Twenty-Three

MONDAY, Tuesday, Wednesday, Thursday, Friday, and Saturday have now passed in review before the reader; the events of each day, its hopes and fears, mortifications and pleasures, have been separately stated, and the pangs of Sunday only now remain to be described, and close the week. The Clifton scheme had been deferred, not relinquished, and on the afternoon's crescent of this day, it was brought forward again. In a private consultation between Isabella and James, the former of whom had particularly set her heart upon going, and the latter no less anxiously placed his upon pleasing her, it was agreed that, provided the weather were fair, the party should take place on the following morning; and they were to set off very early, in order to be at home in good time. The affair thus determined, and Thorpe's approbation secured, Catherine only remained to be apprised of it. She had left them for a few minutes to speak to Miss Tilney. In that interval the plan was completed, and as soon as she came again, her agreement was demanded; but instead of the gay acquiescence expected by Isabella, Catherine looked grave, was very sorry, but could not go. The engagement which ought to have kept her from joining in the former attempt would make it impossible for her to accompany them now. She had that moment settled with Miss Tilney to take their proposed walk tomorrow; it was quite determined, and she would not, upon any account, retract. But that she must and should retract was instantly the eager cry of both the Thorpes; they must go to Clifton tomorrow, they would not go without her, it would be nothing to put off a mere walk for one day longer, and they would not hear of a refusal. Catherine was distressed, but not subdued. "Do not urge me, Isabella. I am engaged to Miss Tilney. I cannot go." This availed nothing. The same arguments assailed her again; she must go, she should go, and they would not hear of a refusal. "It would be so easy to tell Miss Tilney that you had just been reminded of a prior engagement, and must only beg to put off the walk till Tuesday."

"No, it would not be easy. I could not do it. There has been no prior engagement." But Isabella became only more and more urgent, calling on her in the most affectionate manner, addressing her by the most endearing names. She was sure her dearest, sweetest Catherine would not seriously refuse such a trifling request to a friend who loved her so dearly. She knew her beloved Catherine to have so feeling a heart, so sweet a temper, to be so easily persuaded by those she loved. But all in vain; Catherine felt herself to be in the right, and though pained by such tender, such flattering supplication, could not allow it to influence her. Isabella then tried another method. She reproached her with having more affection for Miss Tilney, though she had known her so little a while, than for her best and oldest friends, with being grown cold and indifferent, in short, towards herself. "I cannot help being jealous, Catherine, when I see myself slighted for strangers, I, who love you so excessively! There is nothing I would not do for those whom I love, and once my affections are placed, it is not in the power of anything to change them. But I believe my feelings are stronger than anybody's; I am sure they are too strong for my own peace; and to see myself supplanted in your friendship by strangers does cut me to the quick, I own. These Tilneys seem to swallow up everything else."

Catherine thought this reproach equally strange and unkind. Was it the part of a friend thus to expose her feelings to the notice of others? Isabella appeared to her ungenerous and selfish, regardless of everything but her own gratification. These painful ideas crossed her mind, though she said nothing. Isabella, in the meanwhile, had applied her handkerchief to her eyes; and Morland, miserable at such a sight, could not help saying, "Nay, Catherine. I think you cannot stand out any longer now. The sacrifice is not much; and to oblige such a friend—I shall think you quite unkind, if you still refuse."

This was the first time of her brother's openly siding against her, and anxious to avoid his displeasure, she proposed a compromise. If they would only put off their scheme till Tuesday, which they might easily do, as it depended only on themselves, she could go with them, and everybody might then be satisfied. But "No, no, no!" was the immediate answer; "that could not be, for Thorpe did not know that he might not go to town on Tuesday." Catherine was sorry, but could do no more; and a short silence ensued, which was broken by Isabella, who in a voice of cold resentment said, "Very well, then there is an end of the party. If Catherine does not go, I cannot. I cannot be the only woman. I would not, upon any account in the world, do so improper a thing."

"Catherine, you must go," said James.

"But why cannot Mr. Thorpe drive one of his other sisters? I dare say either of them would like to go."

"Thank ye," cried Thorpe, "but I did not come to Bath to drive my sisters about, and look like a fool. No, if you do not go, damn me if I do. I only go for the sake of driving you."

"That is a compliment which gives me no pleasure." But her words were lost on Thorpe, who had turned abruptly away.

The three others still continued together, walking in a most uncomfortable manner to poor Catherine; sometimes not a word was said, sometimes she was again attacked with supplications or reproaches, and her arm was still linked within Isabella's, though their hearts were at war. At one moment she was softened, at another irritated; always distressed, but always steady.

"I did not think you had been so obstinate, Catherine," said James; "you were not used to be so hard to persuade; you once were the kindest, best-tempered of my sisters."

"I hope I am not less so now," she replied, very feelingly; "but indeed I cannot go. If I am wrong, I am doing what I believe to be right."

"I suspect," said Isabella, in a low voice, "there is no great struggle."

Catherine's heart swelled; she drew away her arm, and Isabella made no opposition. Thus passed a long ten minutes, till they were again joined by Thorpe, who, coming to them with a gayer look, said, "Well, I have settled the matter, and now we may all go tomorrow with a safe conscience. I have been to Miss Tilney, and made your excuses."

"You have not!" cried Catherine.

"I have, upon my soul. Left her this moment. Told her you had sent me to say that, having just recollected a prior engagement of going to Clifton with us tomorrow, you could not have the pleasure of walking with her till Tuesday. She said very well, Tuesday was just as convenient to her; so there is an end of all our difficulties. A pretty good thought of mine—hey?"

Isabella's countenance was once more all smiles and good humour, and James too looked happy again.

"A most heavenly thought indeed! Now, my sweet Catherine, all our distresses are over; you are honourably acquitted, and we shall have a most delightful party."

"This will not do," said Catherine; "I cannot submit to this. I must run after Miss Tilney directly and set her right."

Isabella, however, caught hold of one hand, Thorpe of the other, and remonstrances poured in from all three. Even James was quite angry. When everything was settled, when Miss Tilney herself said that Tuesday would suit her as well, it was quite ridiculous, quite absurd, to make any further objection.

"I do not care. Mr. Thorpe had no business to invent any such message. If I had thought it right to put it off, I could have spoken to Miss Tilney myself. This is only doing it in a ruder way; and how do I know that Mr. Thorpe has—He may be mistaken again perhaps; he led me into one act of rudeness by his mistake on Friday. Let me go, Mr. Thorpe; Isabella, do not hold me."

Thorpe told her it would be in vain to go after the Tilneys; they were turning the corner into Brock Street, when he had overtaken them, and were at home by this time.

"Then I will go after them," said Catherine; "wherever they are I will go after them. It does not signify talking. If I could not be persuaded into doing what I thought wrong, I never will be tricked into it." And with these words she broke away and hurried off. Thorpe would have darted after her, but Morland withheld him. "Let her go, let her go, if she will go. She is as obstinate as—"

Thorpe never finished the simile, for it could hardly have been a proper one.

Away walked Catherine in great agitation, as fast as the crowd would permit her, fearful of being pursued, yet determined to persevere. As she walked, she reflected on what had passed. It was painful to her to disappoint and displease them, particularly to displease her brother; but she could not repent her resistance. Setting her own inclination apart, to have failed a second time in her engagement to Miss Tilney, to have retracted a promise voluntarily made only five minutes before, and on a false pretence too, must have been wrong. She had not been withstanding them on selfish principles alone, she had not consulted merely her own gratification; that might have been ensured in some degree by the excursion itself, by seeing Blaize Castle; no, she had attended to what was due to others, and to her own character in their opinion. Her conviction of being right, however, was not enough to restore her composure; till she had spoken to Miss Tilney she could not be at ease; and quickening her pace when she got clear of the Crescent, she almost ran over the remaining ground till she gained the top of Milsom Street. So rapid had been her movements that in spite of the Tilneys' advantage in the outset, they were but just turning into their lodgings as she came within view of them; and the servant still remaining at the open door, she used only the ceremony of saying that she must speak with Miss Tilney that moment, and hurrying by him proceeded upstairs. Then, opening the first door before her, which happened to be the right, she immediately found herself in the drawing-room with General Tilney, his son, and daughter. Her explanation, defective only in being—from her irritation of nerves and shortness of breath—no explanation at all, was instantly given. "I am come in a great hurry—It was all a mistake—I never promised to go—I told them from the first I could not go.—I ran away in a great hurry to explain it.—I did not care what you thought of me.—I would not stay for the servant."

The business, however, though not perfectly elucidated by this speech, soon ceased to be a puzzle. Catherine found that John Thorpe had given the message; and Miss Tilney had no scruple in owning herself greatly surprised by it. But whether her brother had still exceeded her in resentment, Catherine, though she instinctively addressed herself as much to one as to the other in her vindication, had no means of knowing. Whatever might have been felt before her arrival, her eager declarations immediately made every look and sentence as friendly as she could desire.

The affair thus happily settled, she was introduced by Miss Tilney to her father, and received by him with such ready, such solicitous politeness as recalled Thorpe's information to her mind, and made her think with pleasure that he might be sometimes depended on. To such anxious attention was the general's civility carried, that not aware of her extraordinary swiftness in entering the house, he was quite angry with the servant whose neglect had reduced her to open the door of the apartment herself. "What did William mean by it? He should make a point of inquiring into the matter." And if Catherine had not most warmly asserted his innocence, it seemed likely that William would lose the favour of his master forever, if not his place, by her rapidity.

After sitting with them a quarter of an hour, she rose to take leave, and was then most agreeably surprised by General Tilney's asking her if she would do his daughter the honour of dining and spending the rest of the day with her. Miss Tilney added her own wishes. Catherine was greatly obliged; but it was quite out of her power. Mr. and Mrs. Allen would expect her back every moment. The general declared he could say no more; the claims of Mr. and Mrs. Allen were not to be superseded; but on some other day he trusted, when longer notice could be given, they would not refuse to spare her to her friend. "Oh, no; Catherine was sure they would not have the least objection, and she should have great pleasure in coming." The general attended her himself to the street-door, saying everything gallant as they went downstairs, admiring the elasticity of her walk, which corresponded exactly with the spirit of her dancing, and paid compliment to her dress, as simple and plain as it was, noting that he was an excellent judge of fabric. Remembering Henry's discussion of muslin when they first met, she came to the conclusion that an appreciation of fashion must run in the family. Bidding her well when they parted, the general bestowed upon her one of the most graceful bows she had ever beheld.

Catherine, delighted by all that had passed, proceeded gaily to Pulteney Street, walking, as she concluded, with great elasticity, though she had never thought of it before. She reached home without seeing anything more of the offended party; and now that she had been triumphant throughout, had carried her point, and was secure of her walk, she began (as the flutter of her spirits subsided) to doubt whether she had been perfectly right. A sacrifice was always noble; and if she had given way to their entreaties, she should have been spared the distressing idea of a friend displeased, a brother angry, and a scheme of great happiness to both destroyed, perhaps through her means. To ease her mind, and ascertain by the opinion of an unprejudiced person what her own conduct had really been, she took occasion to mention before Mr. Allen the half-settled scheme of her brother and the Thorpes for the following day. Mr. Allen caught at it directly. "Well," said he, "and do you think of going too?"

"No; I had just engaged myself to walk with Miss Tilney before they told me of it; and therefore you know I could not go with them, could I?"

"No, certainly not; and I am glad you do not think of it. These schemes are not at all the thing. Young men and women driving about the country in open carriages! Now and then it is very well; but going to inns and public places together! It is not right; and I wonder Mrs. Thorpe should allow it. I am glad you do not think of going; I am sure Mrs. Morland would not be pleased. Mrs. Allen, are not you of my way of thinking? Do not you think these kind of projects objectionable?"

"Yes, very much so indeed. Open carriages are nasty things. A clean gown is not five minutes' wear in them. You are splashed getting in and getting out; and the wind takes your hair and your bonnet in every direction. I hate an open carriage myself."

"I know you do; but that is not the question. Do not you think it has an odd appearance, if young ladies are frequently driven about in them by young men, to whom they are not even related?"

"Yes, my dear, a very odd appearance indeed. I cannot bear to see it."

"Dear madam," cried Catherine, "then why did not you tell me so before? I am sure if I had known it to be improper, I would not have gone with Mr. Thorpe at all; but I always hoped you would tell me, if you thought I was doing wrong."

"And so I should, my dear, you may depend on it; for as I told Mrs. Morland at parting, I would always do the best for you in my power. But one must not be over particular. Young people will be young people, as your good mother says herself. You know I wanted you, when we first came, not to buy that sprigged muslin, but you would. Young people do not like to be always thwarted."

"But this was something of real consequence; and I do not think you would have found me hard to persuade."

"As far as it has gone hitherto, there is no harm done," said Mr. Allen; "and I would only advise you, my dear, not to go out with Mr. Thorpe any more."

"That is just what I was going to say," added his wife.

Catherine, relieved for herself, felt uneasy for Isabella, and after a moment's thought, asked Mr. Allen whether it would not be both proper and kind in her to write to Miss Thorpe, and explain the indecorum of which she must be as insensible as herself; for she considered that Isabella might otherwise perhaps be going to Clifton the next day, in spite of what had passed. Mr. Allen, however, discouraged her from doing any such thing. "You had better leave her alone, my dear; she is old enough to know what she is about, and if not, has a mother to advise her. Mrs. Thorpe is too indulgent beyond a doubt; but, however, you had better not interfere. She and your brother choose to go, and you will be only getting ill will."

Catherine submitted, and though sorry to think that Isabella should be doing wrong, felt greatly relieved by Mr. Allen's approbation of her own conduct, and truly rejoiced to be preserved by his advice from the danger of falling into such an error herself. Her escape from being one of the party to Clifton was now an escape indeed; for what would the Tilneys have thought of her, if she had broken her promise to them in order to do what was wrong in itself, if she had been guilty of one breach of propriety, only to enable her to be guilty of another?

CHAPTER

Twenty-Four

BATH HAD LONG AGO established itself as a destination location, as much for pleasure as for medicinal purposes, and even to the degree of it being said in jest that one would welcome the pain of gout as a valid excuse to take on the journey. While its social calendar might have grown out of the healing waters of which the city was famous, the full roster of activities forged ahead with little attention given to the ailments of its members. Bath, it might be said, was a world unto itself with no regard for what might transpire outside.

With all the abundant activity throughout the day, well into the evening, and on to the next where the schedule would repeat once more, it would come as some surprise that anyone might want to venture beyond its perimeter for other diversions. The excursion to Clifton so campaigned for by John Thorpe and his company was an example of the breaking free of ritual. For those who had spent enough time in Bath, or were keen for fresh excitement, such alternatives might be sought. By comparison, Clifton had neither the scale nor the grandiose nature of Bath, however, it was unique in its quiet way. For the Thorpes, it was more the journey than the end destination that appealed to them, with the miles to and from the sites as passive entertainment to pleasant company. This certainly suited James and Isabella well, as did John, with his own preferred but unwilling companion.

Clifton was charming enough on its own merits, located just a mile west of Bristol, with an impressive view of the vessels that passed along the River Avon and of the lands of Somersetshire. While it had its distinct history, it was not of the grand highs and lows to be found in London, nor was it detracted by the scandal and rumors that haunted other smaller townships throughout the isles; of these latter unfortunate locations, the mysteries and rumors could fill multiple volumes and never be complete. A large number of these villages could be found throughout the Severn Valley, up beyond the River Severn and far to the topmost reaches of distant Scotland.

Mrs. Allen knew only a partial history of secluded Severnford, through idle gossip while in the pump room. When she attempted to discover more, the informant raised a finger to her lips.

"We do not talk about Severnford. The devil holds sway with the villagers. They keep to themselves and we to ours. It has always been this way."

"But you make it sound as if they merely like their privacy. What could be wrong with that?"

"It is more than that. The nearby castle was once used for the foulest of rituals. It was once the home of Sir Gilbert Morley. It is said that he practiced dark magic and imprisoned demons of the most indescribable kind in the basement beneath the castle walls."

"And you believe this?"

"That is only one story among many. I tell you this: God has abandoned Severnford." With that, she made the sign of the cross.

Severnford had solid company for myth and legend. Cursed as well in the eyes of the locals was the decrepit abandoned church in Temphill with its stories about those who had descended into the catacombs under the structure, and who were doomed to never escape the city, but to forever walk the streets, only to find them somehow bend inwards, always leading back to the same spot.

To the east of Brichester, somber Goatswood existed only for itself as most residents of Exham and other neighbouring towns avoided even the subject. Some spoke of its unusual town square, the center of which stood an ancient metal pylon some fifty feet high with a large convex lens at its top, a relic from ancient Roman times, and used for pagan ceremonies.

In the woods nearby was a crater, apparently from a meteor that had fallen from the sky in the 17th century, the location used afterward as a site for occult worship. The coven had been summarily discovered and executed by Witchfinder General Matthew Hopkins. Nearby residents still considered the site to be evil.

To another direction beyond Brichester were the so-named Devil Stones, a series of rock formations that stretched up a plateau for several hundred feet forming a crude staircase, at the top of which were a trio of ancient stone towers. It was said that Satan walked the world by way of those steps.

If anything, the Severn Valley seemed to be a central zone for superstitions, from the mysterious cult around Lakeside Terrace to the equally disturbing local legends about Clotton and Camside, the latter being newsworthy even in recent times for its expulsion of one of its residents for practicing a form of science deemed unacceptable by the community. Yet such activity was hardly limited to the borders of the valley. In distant Ireland were tales told in hushed whispers of the primeval horror that pervaded the bog in Kilderry, while in Wales, the town of Caermaen in Monmouthshire was believed to be the ancient site of worship to the great horned god. Another cult, directly related to the Picts, could likewise be traced across the islands of Argyll and Bute in Scotland.

Upon closer examination, it came as no great surprise as to the large number of mysterious locations scattered throughout the isles, as the land's very history, rich and varied as it was, exaggerated both the positive and negative aspects of the past. Indeed, the relics to be found near and far could be traced back to the early days of man's existence, and well before that, dating to the dawn of the planet. As to the aged monuments, their mysteries remained as enigmatic as ever before.

Such was the stone structure on a vast property near Adaraborne, situated along the coast in Norfolk, and comprised of what was once a great mansion now reduced to remnants of its former self. Surrounding the castle-like structure were a series of circular stone fences, also partially intact due to the weathering of the ages. Most notable was the formation in the center of the building, a pit of ancient construction, and of a distinctly different make than the surrounding building. Measuring a good fifteen feet across from stone to stone, its depth was by contrast, immeasurable. By appearances, it appeared as nothing but a black pit with no apparent bottom, a misnomer since the sound of lapping waves might sometimes be heard echoing against its walls. The origin of the structure was uncertain, with some evidence linking it to Roman times, but just as possible was it to be a relic even at that age. On some of the stones surrounding the pit were weathered engravings and languages now lost, and figures comparable to mythological entities being half man and half fish. Such an image might bring up mermen of recognizable myths such as Neptune, Triton, or Dagon.

While its history was questionable, what was certain was its unsavory reputation. Adaraborne, the village, was largely avoided by all outside of the area, as were the early residents of the town—this for reasons that were not entirely clear, outside of general disgust, even prejudice to them as a whole. While it did not appear to be based on any form of national or racial affiliation, they were treated with the same disrespect as given to those of offending heredity.

True, it was rumored that some of the wives had come originally from Fiji, Polynesia, and other tropical islands, for what degree that might have had on the reputation of the folk. Descriptions were likewise vague, only suggesting that they carried an aroma—as well as the appearance—of fish. These insults were further defined in the villagers having wide mouths but the thinnest of lips, even a roughened skin similar to scales, as well as overly large eyes that either lacked lids and lashes or bore them at the bare minimum. When spoken of in jest, it was said that the fish of the sea were infinitely more handsome —and pleasant to be in the presence of—than the inhabitants of Adaraborne.

Those villages closest to Adaraborne—Somerset to the south, North Walsham to the west, and further north, Cromer and Runton—took an approach of avoidance with anything dealing with their neighbouring town although contact was nevertheless unavoidable from time to time, leading to further rumors based on those interactions, and thereby mixing some elements of truth with a large dose of fancy.

By all appearance, the feelings were mutual, and the townsfolk in question preferred to keep their affairs to themselves. Little was known of their activities outside of farming and fishing done for commerce and sustenance. Eventually, some of the residents moved away or disappeared altogether. Others chose to abandon their homestead in favor of a new life across the ocean in America, among them the Marshes, and certain members of the Wayghte families, whose legacy stretched across multiple countries, and of those who made the voyage, later adopted the name of Waite.

Well into the present, Adaraborne remained a shunned location, as were its citizens, and acted as much a deterrent for visitation as Clifton was in the positive. Had it been within a morning's ride from Bath, there was little doubt that John and James would not have given it any consideration as a destination.

CHAPTER

Twenty-Five

THE NEXT MORNING WAS FAIR, and Catherine almost expected another attack from the assembled party. With Mr. Allen to support her, she felt no dread of the event: but she would gladly be spared a contest, where victory itself was painful, and was heartily rejoiced therefore at neither seeing nor hearing anything of them. The Tilneys called for her at the appointed time; and no new difficulty arising, no sudden recollection, no unexpected summons, no impertinent intrusion to disconcert their measures, my heroine was most unnaturally able to fulfil her engagement, though it was made with the hero himself. They determined on walking round Beechen Cliff, that noble hill whose beautiful verdure and hanging coppice render it so striking an object from almost every opening in Bath.

"I never look at it," said Catherine, as they walked along the side of the river, "without thinking of the south of France."

"You have been abroad then?" said Henry, a little surprised.

"Oh! No, I only mean what I have read about. It always puts me in mind of the country that Emily and her father travelled through, in *The Mysteries of Udolpho*. But you never read novels, I dare say?"

"Why not?"

"Because they are not clever enough for you—gentlemen read better books."

"The person, be it gentleman or lady, who has not pleasure in a good novel, must be intolerably stupid. I have read all Mrs. Radcliffe's works, and most of them with great pleasure. *The Mysteries of Udolpho*, when I had once begun it, I could not lay down again; I remember finishing it in two days—my hair standing on end the whole time."

"Yes," added Miss Tilney, "and I remember that you undertook to read it aloud to me, and that when I was called away for only five minutes to answer a note, instead of waiting for me, you took the volume into the Hermitage Walk, and I was obliged to stay till you had finished it."

"Thank you, Eleanor—a most honourable testimony. You see, Miss Morland, the injustice of your suspicions. Here was I, in my eagerness to get on, refusing to wait only five minutes for my sister, breaking the promise I had made of reading it aloud, and keeping her in suspense at a most interesting part, by running away with the volume, which, you are to observe, was her own, particularly her own. I am proud when I reflect on it, and I think it must establish me in your good opinion."

"I am very glad to hear it indeed, and now I shall never be ashamed of liking *Udolpho* myself. But I really thought before, young men despised novels amazingly."

"It is amazingly; it may well suggest amazement if they do—for they read nearly as many as women. I myself have read hundreds and hundreds. Do not imagine that you can cope with me in a knowledge of Julias and Louisas. If we proceed to particulars, and engage in the never-ceasing inquiry of 'Have you read this?' and 'Have you read that?' I shall soon leave you as far behind me as—what shall I say?—I want an appropriate simile.—as far as your friend Emily herself left poor Valancourt when she went with her aunt into Italy. Consider how many years I have had the start of you. I had entered on my studies at Oxford, while you were a good little girl working your sampler at home!"

"Not very good, I am afraid," Catherine managed to interject.

"So, yes. I am as fond of Mrs. Radcliffe as I am the works of Danielle Monlaur; *The Lost Chamber of Meinster Castle*, of course, *The Secrets of Bray*, and *The Shadows at Elstree Cottage*."

"And I just recently read *Meinster Castle*. It kept me up all the night. But now really, do not you think *Udolpho* the nicest book in the world?"

"The nicest—by which I suppose you mean the neatest. That must depend upon the binding."

"Henry," said Miss Tilney, "you are very impertinent. Miss Morland, he is treating you exactly as he does his sister. He is forever finding fault with me, for some incorrectness of language, and now he is taking the same liberty with you. The word 'nicest,' as you used it, did not suit him; and you had better change it as soon as you can, or we shall be overpowered with Johnson and Blair all the rest of the way."

"I am sure," cried Catherine, "I did not mean to say anything wrong; but it is a nice book, and why should not I call it so?"

"Very true," said Henry, "and this is a very nice day, and we are taking a very nice walk, and you are two very nice young ladies. Oh! It is a very nice word indeed! It does for everything. Originally perhaps it was applied only to express neatness, propriety, delicacy, or refinement—people were nice in their dress, in their sentiments, or their choice. But now every commendation on every subject is comprised in that one word."

"While, in fact," cried his sister, "it ought only to be applied to you, without any commendation at all. You are more nice than wise. Come, Miss Morland, let us leave him to meditate over our faults in the utmost propriety of diction, while we praise *Udolpho* in whatever terms we like best. It is a most interesting work. You are fond of that kind of reading?"

"To say the truth, I do not much like any other."

"Indeed!"

"That is, I can read poetry and plays, and things of that sort, and do not dislike travels. But history, real solemn history, I cannot be interested in. Can you?"

"Yes, I am fond of history."

"I wish I were too. I read it a little as a duty, but it tells me nothing that does not either vex or weary me. The quarrels of popes and kings, with wars or pestilences, in every page; the men all so good for nothing, and hardly any women at all—it is very tiresome: and yet I often think it odd that it should be so dull, for a great deal of it must be invention. The speeches that are put into the heroes' mouths, their thoughts and designs—the chief of all this must be invention, and invention is what delights me in other books."

"Historians, you think," said Miss Tilney, "are not happy in their flights of fancy. They display imagination without raising interest. I am fond of history—and am very well contented to take the false with the true. In the principal facts they have sources of intelligence in former histories and records, which may be as much depended on, I conclude, as anything that does not actually pass under one's own observation; and as for the little embellishments you speak of, they are embellishments, and I like them as such. If a speech be well drawn up, I read it with pleasure, by whomsoever it may be made—and probably with much greater, if the production of Mr. Hume or Mr. Robertson, than if the genuine words of Caractacus, Agricola, or Alfred the Great."

"You are fond of history! And so are Mr. Allen and my father; and I have two brothers who do not dislike it. So many instances within my small circle of friends is remarkable! At this rate, I shall not pity the writers of history any longer. If people like to read their books, it is all very well, but to be at so much trouble in filling great volumes, which, as I used to think, nobody would willingly ever look into, to be labouring only for the torment of little boys and girls, always struck me as a hard fate; and though I know it is all very right and necessary, I have often wondered at the person's courage that could sit down on purpose to do it."

"That little boys and girls should be tormented," said Henry, "is what no one at all acquainted with human nature in a civilized state can deny; but in behalf of our most distinguished historians, I must observe that they might well be offended at being supposed to have no higher aim, and that by their method and style, they are perfectly well qualified to torment readers of the most advanced reason and mature time of life. I use the verb 'to torment,' as I observed to be your own method, instead of 'to instruct,' supposing them to be now admitted as synonymous."

"You think me foolish to call instruction a torment, but if you had been as much used as myself to hear poor little children first learning their letters and then learning to spell, if you had ever seen how stupid they can be for a whole morning together, and how tired my poor mother is at the end of it, as I am in the habit of seeing almost every day of my life at home, you would allow that 'to torment' and 'to instruct' might sometimes be used as synonymous words."

"Very probably. But historians are not accountable for the difficulty of learning to read; and even you yourself, who do not altogether seem particularly friendly to very severe, very intense application, may perhaps be brought to acknowledge that it is very well worth-while to be tormented for two or three years of one's life, for the sake of being able to read all the rest of it. Consider—if reading had not been taught, Mrs. Radcliffe would have written in vain—or perhaps might not have written at all."

Catherine assented—and a very warm panegyric from her on that lady's merits closed the subject. The Tilneys were soon engaged in another on which she had nothing to say. They were viewing the country with the eyes of persons accustomed to drawing, and decided on its capability of being formed into pictures, with all the eagerness of real taste. Here Catherine was quite lost. She knew nothing of drawing—nothing of taste: and she listened to them with an attention which brought her little profit, for they talked in phrases which conveyed scarcely any idea to her. The little which she could understand, however, appeared to contradict the very few notions she had entertained on the matter before. It seemed as if a good view were no longer to be taken from the top of an high hill, and that a clear blue sky was no longer a proof of a fine day. She was heartily ashamed of her ignorance. A misplaced shame. Where people wish to attach, they should always be ignorant. To come with a well-informed mind is to come with an inability of administering to the vanity of others, which a sensible person would always wish to avoid. A woman especially, if she have the misfortune of knowing anything, should conceal it as well as she can.

The advantages of natural folly in a beautiful girl have been already set forth by the capital pen of a sister author; and to her treatment of the subject I will only add, in justice to men, that though to the larger and more trifling part of the sex, imbecility in females is a great enhancement of their personal charms, there is a portion of them too reasonable and too well informed themselves to desire anything more in woman than ignorance. But Catherine did not know her own advantages—did not know that a good-looking girl, with an affectionate heart and a very ignorant mind, cannot fail of attracting a clever young man, unless circumstances are particularly untoward. In the present instance, she confessed and lamented her want of knowledge, declared that she would give anything in the world to be able to draw; and a lecture on the picturesque immediately followed, in which his instructions were so clear that she soon began to see beauty in everything admired by him, and her attention was so earnest that he became perfectly satisfied of her having a great deal of natural taste. He talked of foregrounds, distances, and second distances—side-screens and perspectives—lights and shades; and Catherine was so hopeful a scholar that when they gained the top of Beechen Cliff, she voluntarily rejected the whole city of Bath as unworthy to make part of a landscape. Delighted with her progress, and fearful of wearying her with too much wisdom at once, Henry suffered the subject to decline, and by an easy transition from a piece of rocky fragment and the withered oak which he had placed near its summit, to oaks in general, to forests, the enclosure of them, waste lands, crown lands and government, he shortly found himself arrived at politics; and from politics, it was an easy step to silence. The general pause which succeeded his short disquisition on the state of the nation was put an end to by Catherine, who, in rather a solemn tone of voice, uttered these words, "I have heard that something very shocking indeed will soon come out in London."

Miss Tilney, to whom this was chiefly addressed, was startled, and hastily replied, "Indeed! And of what nature?"

"That I do not know, nor who is the author. I have only heard that it is to be more horrible than anything we have met with yet."

"Good heaven! Where could you hear of such a thing?"

"A particular friend of mine had an account of it in a letter from London yesterday. It is to be uncommonly dreadful. I shall expect murder and everything of the kind."

"You speak with astonishing composure! But I hope your friend's accounts have been exaggerated; and if such a design is known beforehand, proper measures will undoubtedly be taken by government to prevent its coming to effect."

"Government," said Henry, endeavouring not to smile, "neither desires nor dares to interfere in such matters. There must be murder; and government cares not how much."

The ladies stared. He laughed, and added, "Come, shall I make you understand each other, or leave you to puzzle out an explanation as you can? No—I will be noble. I will prove myself a man, no less by the generosity of my soul than the clearness of my head. I have no patience with such of my sex as disdain to let themselves sometimes down to the comprehension of yours. Perhaps the abilities of women are neither sound nor acute—neither vigorous nor keen. Perhaps they may want observation, discernment, judgment, fire, genius, and wit."

"Miss Morland, do not mind what he says; but have the goodness to satisfy me as to this dreadful riot."

"Riot! What riot?"

"My dear Eleanor, the riot is only in your own brain. The confusion there is scandalous. Miss Morland has been talking of nothing more dreadful than a new publication which is shortly to come out, in three duodecimo volumes, two hundred and seventy-six pages in each, with a frontispiece to the first, of two tombstones and a lantern—do you understand? And you, Miss Morland—my stupid sister has mistaken all your clearest expressions. You talked of expected horrors in London—and instead of instantly conceiving, as any rational creature would have done, that such words could relate only to a circulating library, she immediately pictured to herself a mob of three thousand men assembling in St. George's Fields, the Bank attacked, the Tower threatened, the streets of London flowing with blood, a detachment of the Twelfth Light Dragoons (the hopes of the nation) called up from Northampton to quell the insurgents, and the gallant Captain Frederick Tilney, in the moment of charging at the head of his troop, knocked off his horse by a brickbat from an upper window. Forgive her stupidity. The fears of the sister have added to the weakness of the woman; but she is by no means a simpleton in general."

Catherine looked grave. "And now, Henry," said Miss Tilney, "that you have made us understand each other, you may as well make Miss Morland understand yourself—unless you mean to have her think you intolerably rude to your sister, and a great brute in your opinion of women in general. Miss Morland is not used to your odd ways."

"I shall be most happy to make her better acquainted with them."

"No doubt; but that is no explanation of the present."

"What am I to do?"

"You know what you ought to do. Clear your character handsomely before her. Tell her that you think very highly of the understanding of women."

"Miss Morland, I think very highly of the understanding of all the women in the world—especially of those—whoever they may be—with whom I happen to be in company."

"That is not enough. Be more serious."

"Miss Morland, no one can think more highly of the understanding of women than I do. In my opinion, nature has given them so much that they never find it necessary to use more than half."

"We shall get nothing more serious from him now, Miss Morland. He is not in a sober mood. But I do assure you that he must be entirely misunderstood, if he can ever appear to say an unjust thing of any woman at all, or an unkind one of me."

It was no effort to Catherine to believe that Henry Tilney could never be wrong. His manner might sometimes surprise, but his meaning must always be just: and what she did not understand, she was almost as ready to admire, as what she did. The whole walk was delightful, and though it ended too soon, its conclusion was delightful too; her friends attended her into the house, and Miss Tilney, before they parted, addressing herself with respectful form, as much to Mrs. Allen as to Catherine, petitioned for the pleasure of her company to dinner on the day after the next. No difficulty was made on Mrs. Allen's side, and the only difficulty on Catherine's was in concealing the excess of her pleasure.

The morning had passed away so charmingly as to banish all her friendship and natural affection, for no thought of Isabella or James had crossed her during their walk. When the Tilneys were gone, she became amiable again, but she was amiable for some time to little effect; Mrs. Allen had no intelligence to give that could relieve her anxiety; she had heard nothing of any of them. Towards the end of the morning, however, Catherine, having occasion for some indispensable yard of ribbon which must be bought without a moment's delay, walked out into the town, and in Bond Street overtook the second Miss Thorpe as she was loitering towards Edgar's Buildings between two of the sweetest girls in the world, who had been her dear friends all the morning. From her, she soon learned that the party to Clifton had taken place. "They set off at eight this morning," said Miss Anne, "and I am sure I do not envy them their drive. I think you and I are very well off to be out of the scrape. It must be the dullest thing in the world, for there is not a soul at Clifton at this time of year. Belle went with your brother, and John drove Maria."

Catherine spoke the pleasure she really felt on hearing this part of the arrangement.

"Oh! yes," rejoined the other, "Maria is gone. She was quite wild to go. She thought it would be something very fine. I cannot say I admire her taste; and for my part, I was determined from the first not to go, if they pressed me ever so much."

Catherine, a little doubtful of this, could not help answering, "I wish you could have gone too. It is a pity you could not all go."

"Thank you; but it is quite a matter of indifference to me. Indeed, I would not have gone on any account. I was saying so to Emily and Sophia when you overtook us."

Catherine was still unconvinced; but glad that Anne should have the friendship of an Emily and a Sophia to console her, she bade her adieu without much uneasiness, and returned home, pleased that the party had not been prevented by her refusing to join it, and very heartily wishing that it might be too pleasant to allow either James or Isabella to resent her resistance any longer.

CHAPTER

Twenty-Six

My dearest Sarah,

As I must most disappointedly surrender to your most fervent entreaties, so strong they are in determination and resolve, I have no choice but to abandon that name to which I have known you since childhood. Henceforth, you shall now be my Sarah, as you have wished—although in my mind, I will still be crying Sally, Sally, Sally.

I thank you for your sweet note, and I am so pleased you are doing well. I think of you often and wish you were here. Did Papa and Mamma get the letter I sent them? I have not heard anything in return, but regardless, give them my love and affection. I am distressed to hear about little George taking a tumble, and can only hope that his leg will mend itself soon. It is hard enough at his age to sit still for an hour, so the weeks it will take for the bone to heal will surely seem like an eternity. For all the running about I did when I was his age, I can only express dismay at not breaking a few myself.

I have had the opportunity to spend more time with Miss Tilney and her brother, and have become increasingly fond of them both. They are quite well-read, even to the extent that she spoke of her love of history, a subject that I still find so dreadfully dull, that I must admire anyone who can find fascination in it. We took a lovely walk at Beechen Cliff this morning, an enchanting hill that rises over the city, and it remains one of the highlights of my time here in Bath. That the excursion had been rescheduled once and almost postponed a second time was due to an uncompromising weather condition as well as some misunderstandings with my brother and the Thorpes. When I return, perhaps I will tell you all the small particulars, but suffice it to say that I know that I can sometimes be too easily persuaded for my own good. I must work on this.

As to Mr. Tilney, I find him all the more agreeable, and with a sense of humour that I do not always understand, but he is kind and does not hold my ignorance against me, to which I am most indebted. I have also met his father, a general of some importance from what I can tell, and he appears to be most hospitable, even asking if I would join them for dinner—to which I was unable due to a prior engagement with the Allens. He can be quite charming, but he also has a quality about him that I cannot yet explain, a stern intensity in his gaze, so I have not become fully comfortable in his presence. This, I hope, shall pass.

It is late, and I am soon to retire, so I will end here by wishing you, Papa, Mama, Harriet, George, and his leg all my love.

Your dearest Cathy

CHAPTER
Twenty-Seven

EARLY THE NEXT DAY, a note from Isabella, speaking peace and tenderness in every line, and entreating the immediate presence of her friend on a matter of the utmost importance, hastened Catherine, in the happiest state of confidence and curiosity, to Edgar's Buildings. The two youngest Miss Thorpes were by themselves in the parlour; and, on Anne's quitting it to call her sister, Catherine took the opportunity of asking the other for some particulars of their yesterday's party. Maria desired no greater pleasure than to speak of it; and Catherine immediately learnt that it had been altogether the most delightful scheme in the world, that nobody could imagine how charming it had been, and that it had been more delightful than anybody could conceive. Such was the information of the first five minutes; the second unfolded thus much in detail—that they had driven directly to the York Hotel, ate some soup, and bespoke an early dinner, walked down to the pump-room, tasted the water, and laid out some shillings in purses and spars; thence adjoined to eat ice at a pastry-cook's, and hurrying back to the hotel, swallowed their dinner in haste, to prevent being in the dark; and then had a delightful drive back, only the moon was not up, and it rained a little, and Mr. Morland's horse was so tired he could hardly get it along.

Catherine listened with heartfelt satisfaction. It appeared that Blaize Castle had never been thought of; and, as for all the rest, there was nothing to regret for half an instant. Maria's intelligence concluded with a tender effusion of pity for her sister Anne, whom she represented as insupportably cross, from being excluded the party.

"She will never forgive me, I am sure; but, you know, how could I help it? John would have me go, for he vowed he would not drive her, because she had such thick ankles. I dare say she will not be in good humour again this month; but I am determined I will not be cross; it is not a little matter that puts me out of temper."

Isabella now entered the room with so eager a step, and a look of such happy importance, as engaged all her friend's notice. Maria was without ceremony sent away, and Isabella, embracing Catherine, thus began: "Yes, my dear Catherine, it is so indeed; your penetration has not deceived you. Oh! That arch eye of yours! It sees through everything."

Catherine replied only by a look of wondering ignorance.

"Nay, my beloved, sweetest friend," continued the other, "compose yourself. I am amazingly agitated, as you perceive. Let us sit down and talk in comfort. Well, and so you guessed it the moment you had my note? Sly creature! Oh! My dear Catherine, you alone, who know my heart, can judge of my present happiness. Your brother is the most charming of men. I only wish I were more worthy of him. But what will your excellent father and mother say? Oh! Heavens! When I think of them I am so agitated!"

Catherine's understanding began to awake: an idea of the truth suddenly darted into her mind; and, with the natural blush of so new an emotion, she cried out, "Good heaven! My dear Isabella, what do you mean? Can you—can you really be in love with James?"

This bold surmise, however, she soon learnt comprehended but half the fact. The anxious affection, which she was accused of having continually watched in Isabella's every look and action, had, in the course of their yesterday's party, received the delightful confession of an equal love. Her heart and faith were alike engaged to James. Never had Catherine listened to anything so full of interest, wonder, and joy. Her brother and her friend engaged! New to such circumstances, the importance of it appeared unspeakably great, and she contemplated it as one of those grand events, of which the ordinary course of life can hardly afford a return. The strength of her feelings she could not express; the nature of them, however, contented her friend. The happiness of having such a sister was their first effusion, and the fair ladies mingled in embraces and tears of joy.

Delighting, however, as Catherine sincerely did in the prospect of the connection, it must be acknowledged that Isabella far surpassed her in tender anticipations. "You will be so infinitely dearer to me, my Catherine, than either Anne or Maria: I feel that I shall be so much more attached to my dear Morland's family than to my own."

This was a pitch of friendship beyond Catherine.

"You are so like your dear brother," continued Isabella, "that I quite doted on you the first moment I saw you. But so it always is with me; the first moment settles everything. The very first day that Morland came to us last Christmas—the very first moment I beheld him—my heart was irrecoverably gone. I remember I wore my yellow gown, with my hair done up in braids; and when I came into the drawing-room, and John introduced him, I thought I never saw anybody so handsome before."

Here Catherine secretly acknowledged the power of love; for, though exceedingly fond of her brother, and partial to all his endowments, she had never in her life thought him handsome.

"I remember too, Miss Andrews drank tea with us that evening, and wore her puce-coloured sarsenet; and she looked so heavenly that I thought your brother must certainly fall in love with her; I could not sleep a wink all right for thinking of it. Oh! Catherine, the many sleepless nights I have had on your brother's account! I would not have you suffer half what I have done! I am grown wretchedly thin, I know; but I will not pain you by describing my anxiety; you have seen enough of it. I feel that I have betrayed myself perpetually—so unguarded in speaking of my partiality for the church! But my secret I was always sure would be safe with you."

Catherine felt that nothing could have been safer; but ashamed of an ignorance little expected, she dared no longer contest the point, nor refuse to have been as full of arch penetration and affectionate sympathy as Isabella chose to consider her. Her brother, she found, was preparing to set off with all speed to Fullerton, to make known his situation and ask consent; and here was a source of some real agitation to the mind of Isabella. Catherine endeavoured to persuade her, as she was herself persuaded, that her father and mother would never oppose their son's wishes. "It is impossible," said she, "for parents to be more kind, or more desirous of their children's happiness; I have no doubt of their consenting immediately."

"Morland says exactly the same," replied Isabella; "and yet I dare not expect it; my fortune will be so small; they never can consent to it. Your brother, who might marry anybody!"

Here Catherine again discerned the force of love.

"Indeed, Isabella, you are too humble. The difference of fortune can be nothing to signify."

"Oh! My sweet Catherine, in your generous heart I know it would signify nothing; but we must not expect such disinterestedness in many. As for myself, I am sure I only wish our situations were reversed. Had I the command of millions, were I mistress of the whole world, your brother would be my only choice."

This charming sentiment, recommended as much by sense as novelty, gave Catherine a most pleasing remembrance of all the heroines of her acquaintance; and she thought her friend never looked more lovely than in uttering the grand idea. "I am sure they will consent," was her frequent declaration; "I am sure they will be delighted with you."

"For my own part," said Isabella, "my wishes are so moderate that the smallest income in nature would be enough for me. Where people are really attached, poverty itself is wealth; grandeur I detest: I would not settle in London for the universe. A cottage in some retired village would be ecstasy. There are some charming little villas about Richmond."

"Richmond!" cried Catherine. "You must settle near Fullerton. You must be near us."

"I am sure I shall be miserable if we do not. If I can but be near you, I shall be satisfied. But this is idle talking! I will not allow myself to think of such things, till we have your father's answer. Morland says that by sending it tonight to Salisbury, we may have it tomorrow. Tomorrow? I know I shall never have courage to open the letter. I know it will be the death of me."

A reverie succeeded this conviction—and when Isabella spoke again, it was to resolve on the quality of her wedding-gown.

Their conference was put an end to by the anxious young lover himself, who came to breathe his parting sigh before he set off for Wiltshire. Catherine wished to congratulate him, but knew not what to say, and her eloquence was only in her eyes. From them, however, the eight parts of speech shone out most expressively, and James could combine them with ease. Impatient for the realization of all that he hoped at home, his adieus were not long; and they would have been yet shorter, had he not been frequently detained by the urgent entreaties of his fair one that he would go. Twice was he called almost from the door by her eagerness to have him gone. "Indeed, Morland, I must drive you away. Consider how far you have to ride. I cannot bear to see you linger so. For heaven's sake, waste no more time. There, go, go—I insist on it."

The two friends, with hearts now more united than ever, were inseparable for the day; and in schemes of sisterly happiness the hours flew along. Mrs. Thorpe and her son, who were acquainted with everything, and who seemed only to want Mr. Morland's consent, to consider Isabella's engagement as the most fortunate circumstance imaginable for their family, were allowed to join their counsels, and add their quota of significant looks and mysterious expressions to fill up the measure of curiosity to be raised in the unprivileged younger sisters. To Catherine's simple feelings, this odd sort of reserve seemed neither kindly meant, nor consistently supported; and its unkindness she would hardly have forborne pointing out, had its inconsistency been less their friend; but Anne and Maria soon set her heart at ease by the sagacity of their "I know what"; and the evening was spent in a sort of war of wit, a display of family ingenuity, on one side in the mystery of an affected secret, on the other of undefined discovery, all equally acute.

Catherine was with her friend again the next day, endeavouring to support her spirits and while away the many tedious hours before the delivery of the letters; a needful exertion, for as the time of reasonable expectation drew near, Isabella became more and more desponding, and before the letter arrived, had worked herself into a state of real distress. But when it did come, where could distress be found? "I have had no difficulty in gaining the consent of my kind parents, and am promised that everything in their power shall be done to forward my happiness," were the first three lines, and in one moment all was joyful security. The brightest glow was instantly spread over Isabella's features, all care and anxiety seemed removed, her spirits became almost too high for control, and she called herself without scruple the happiest of mortals.

Mrs. Thorpe, with tears of joy, embraced her daughter, her son, her visitor, and could have embraced half the inhabitants of Bath with satisfaction. Her heart was overflowing with tenderness. It was "dear John" and "dear Catherine" at every word; "dear Anne and dear Maria" must immediately be made sharers in their felicity; and two "dears" at once before the name of Isabella were not more than that beloved child had now well earned. John himself was no skulker in joy. He not only bestowed on Mr. Morland the high commendation of being one of the finest fellows in the world, but swore off many sentences in his praise.

The letter, whence sprang all this felicity, was short, containing little more than this assurance of success; and every particular was deferred till James could write again. But for particulars Isabella could well afford to wait. The needful was comprised in Mr. Morland's promise; his honour was pledged to make everything easy; and by what means their income was to be formed, whether landed property were to be resigned, or funded money made over, was a matter in which her disinterested spirit took no concern. She knew enough to feel secure of an honourable and speedy establishment, and her imagination took a rapid flight over its attendant felicities. She saw herself at the end of a few weeks, the gaze and admiration of every new acquaintance at Fullerton, the envy of every valued old friend in Putney, with a carriage at her command, a new name on her tickets, and a brilliant exhibition of hoop rings on her finger.

When the contents of the letter were ascertained, John Thorpe, who had only waited its arrival to begin his journey to London, prepared to set off. "Well, Miss Morland," said he, on finding her alone in the parlour, "I am come to bid you good-bye." Catherine wished him a good journey. Without appearing to hear her, he walked to the window, fidgeted about, hummed a tune, and seemed wholly self-occupied.

"Shall not you be late at Devizes?" said Catherine. He made no answer; but after a minute's silence burst out with, "A famous good thing this marrying scheme, upon my soul! A clever fancy of Morland's and Belle's. What do you think of it, Miss Morland? I say it is no bad notion."

"I am sure I think it a very good one."

"Do you? That's honest, by heavens! I am glad you are no enemy to matrimony, however. Did you ever hear the old song 'Going to One Wedding Brings on Another?' I say, you will come to Belle's wedding, I hope."

"Yes; I have promised your sister to be with her, if possible."

"And then you know"—twisting himself about and forcing a foolish laugh—"I say, then you know, we may try the truth of this same old song."

"May we? But I never sing. Well, I wish you a good journey. I dine with Miss Tilney today, and must now be going home."

"Nay, but there is no such confounded hurry. Who knows when we may be together again? Not but that I shall be down again by the end of a fortnight, and a devilish long fortnight it will appear to me."

"Then why do you stay away so long?" replied Catherine—finding that he waited for an answer.

"That is kind of you, however—kind and good-natured. I shall not forget it in a hurry. But you have more good nature and all that, than anybody living, I believe. A monstrous deal of good nature, and it is not only good nature, but you have so much, so much of everything; and then you have such—upon my soul, I do not know anybody like you."

"Oh! dear, there are a great many people like me, I dare say, only a great deal better. Good morning to you."

"But I say, Miss Morland, I shall come and pay my respects at Fullerton before it is long, if not disagreeable."

"Pray do. My father and mother will be very glad to see you."

"And I hope—I hope, Miss Morland, you will not be sorry to see me."

"Oh! dear, not at all. There are very few people I am sorry to see. Company is always cheerful."

"That is just my way of thinking. Give me but a little cheerful company, let me only have the company of the people I love, let me only be where I like and with whom I like, and the devil take the rest, say I. And I am heartily glad to hear you say the same. But I have a notion, Miss Morland, you and I think pretty much alike upon most matters."

"Perhaps we may; but it is more than I ever thought of. And as to most matters, to say the truth, there are not many that I know my own mind about."

"By Jove, no more do I. It is not my way to bother my brains with what does not concern me. My notion of things is simple enough. Let me only have the girl I like, say I, with a comfortable house over my head, and what care I for all the rest? Fortune is nothing. I am sure of a good income of my own; and if she had not a penny, why, so much the better."

"Very true. I think like you there. If there is a good fortune on one side, there can be no occasion for any on the other. No matter which has it, so that there is enough. I hate the idea of one great fortune looking out for another. And to marry for money I think the wickedest thing in existence. Good day. We shall be very glad to see you at Fullerton, whenever it is convenient." And away she went. It was not in the power of all his gallantry to detain her longer. With such news to communicate, and such a visit to prepare for, her departure was not to be delayed by anything in his nature to urge; and she hurried away, leaving him to the undivided consciousness of his own happy address, and her explicit encouragement.

The agitation which she had herself experienced on first learning her brother's engagement made her expect to raise no inconsiderable emotion in Mr. and Mrs. Allen, by the communication of the wonderful event. How great was her disappointment! The important affair, which many words of preparation ushered in, had been foreseen by them both ever since her brother's arrival; and all that they felt on the occasion was comprehended in a wish for the young people's happiness, with a remark, on the gentleman's side, in favour of Isabella's beauty, and on the lady's, of her great good luck. It was to Catherine the most surprising insensibility. The disclosure, however, of the great secret of James's going to Fullerton the day before, did raise some emotion in Mrs. Allen. She could not listen to that with perfect calmness, but repeatedly regretted the necessity of its concealment, wished she could have known his intention, wished she could have seen him before he went, as she should certainly have troubled him with her best regards to his father and mother, and her kind compliments to all the Skinners.

CHAPTER

Twenty-Eight

Excerpt from the Bath Journal

MAN OF BUSINESS FOUND DEAD IN SHOP

On Monday last, the body of Mr. Thorley Gainsborough was found inside his place of business on James Street. The cause of death has not yet been established. It may be remembered that a burglary recently took place in his shop, to which the account was noted in this journal, and the perpetrator of the crime never apprehended. Mr. Gainsborough was no stranger to Bath, having operated out of his establishment for many years.

The unexpected passing of Thorley Gainsborough presented a source of controversy for the few individuals privy to the full details of the case. Those who made the initial discovery, the ones who followed through in the details, the removal of the remains, and the procedures leading up to the burial, all had formed their own opinions, or at the very least, had questions as to his demise. Not that it was often discussed by them; instead, the subject was avoided, and if it was given deeper consideration, it was of somber thoughts most likely kept to themselves. As for the general population of Bath, the notice in the newspaper was as much information as to be offered, and the death was eventually passed off as due to a bad constitution.

Those more familiar with Gainsborough had their doubts, as he had always been considered unsavory, this being one of the more complimentary terms given in his favor. Generally unkempt, he ran his shop with a similar upkeep as his appearance, and displayed a gruff personality that would hardly warm itself to polite society. Those attracted to his shop were most often patronizing due to a particular quest rather than a casual shopping excursion, thus his clientele could be of an equally questionable background. This was not to state that he only attracted the dregs of society, as many of the volumes, furniture, and objects d'art were of a price targeting only those with a substantial income. What he came by were usually unusual, often rare, and mostly one-of-a-kind, thus the value could be put to equal measure.

It came as no surprise that his shop might be vandalized, as his reputation for antiquities was well known although it would take a well-educated thief in the realm of such artifacts to pawn them in any effective fashion. More to the point, it would take a good amount of nerve, as Gainsborough also had a history of dealings with things that even the most hardened of criminals would not be enticed with. In general, they left him be, more from fear than anything else, which explained volumes in those circles.

When the break-in occurred, attention was given far more than might be surmised. Like attracts like (or at least pays attention to what the other is doing) so the elements of disrepute paid considerable mind to where the trail might lead. In the end, there was no substantive resolution. Any suspicions were most likely left to Gainsborough himself, and as he kept his secrets, no one else was the wiser.

Gainsborough held to his solitude; no past history of common knowledge, no immediate family to speak of, no wife nor children, nor even a woman that he might boast of to keep company. The whole of his life, as far as anyone knew, was that of his dealings and nothing more.

When questioned about the previous attempted robbery, he was just as silent, even so nervous as to hardly speak. It was later surmised that he knew more than he was willing to say, but if he knew the true mechanisms of the incident, despite any apprehension on his part, he was determined to keep it private. This gave all the more impression of his involvement with elements that were criminal at most, assuredly not respectable, and questionable at the very least.

As to his death, the first indication came from the shop, which remained closed and locked for a succession of days, and although this might not have been considered unusual, with him travelling or otherwise disposed of, it was cause for those who arrived to try the door and peer in through the window. It was this action that allowed one curious seeker to see what appeared to be the lower half of a body extending out from behind a set of shelves. Soon thereafter, the door to the establishment was forced, access gained, and the discovery made.

At first, the entry was barred by the horrendous stench that permeated the interior, no doubt originating from the state of the body and the lack of circulation inside the building. On top of this was another altogether more repulsive odor, that of a fish-like nature so common around the docks of the coastal regions. The whole caused one man to refuse to enter the shop and remained only to assist from outside the structure. This left two other men to enter, holding handkerchiefs against their faces to withstand the oppressive smell. Once they had moved beyond the bookshelf positioned in the middle of the room were they able to take in the whole extent of the horror.

The body was indeed that of Thorley Gainsborough, although it was initially hard to make a solid identification. His lower torso—that which had been initially seen through the shop window—remained relatively intact but the rest of the body had been mutilated beyond imagination, with portions scattered across the floor in all directions and dark stains covering everything in close proximity. The portion of an ear found on the writing desk atop a business ledger caused one of the men to rush out from the building, hand firmly across his mouth, and his eyes wide from what he had just witnessed —leaving the other man quite uncomfortably alone.

What was most distressing to the discovery was that the injuries, as massive as they were, did not seem to come from any external source, and no simple explanation could be offered on how the man came to this state. What those attending agreed upon was that from all visual evidence, it appeared as if the blunt force came from within, and in such a violent nature as to splatter Thorley Gainsborough in all directions.

The one other point noticed was a small one, but possibly of major importance, that being the key ring that Gainsborough would have had on his person or had laid somewhere nearby, was missing from the scene. He would have needed the shop key to enter the building, just as he would have taken it to lock up as he always did upon leaving. There was little doubt that whosoever had done the poor soul in had lifted the set of keys and locked the door on the way out. What was also evident was the additional use the keys played a part in, as the strongbox located in the rear of the building had been unlocked and left wide open.

Whatever resided in the safe had been removed, and more than likely was of such importance to have cost Thorley Gainsborough his life.

CHAPTER
Twenty-Nine

CATHERINE'S EXPECTATIONS of pleasure from her visit in Milsom Street were so very high that disappointment was inevitable; and accordingly, though she was most politely received by General Tilney, and kindly welcomed by his daughter, though Henry was at home, and no one else of the party, she found, on her return, without spending many hours in the examination of her feelings, that she had gone to her appointment preparing for happiness which it had not afforded. Instead of finding herself improved in acquaintance with Miss Tilney, from the intercourse of the day, she seemed hardly so intimate with her as before; instead of seeing Henry Tilney to greater advantage than ever, in the ease of a family party, he had never said so little, nor been so little agreeable; and, in spite of their father's great civilities to her—in spite of his thanks, invitations, and compliments—it had been a release to get away from him. It puzzled her to account for all this. It could not be General Tilney's fault. That he was perfectly agreeable and good-natured, and altogether a very charming man, did not admit of a doubt, for he was tall and handsome, and Henry's father. He could not be accountable for his children's want of spirits, or for her want of enjoyment in his company. The former she hoped at last might have been accidental, and the latter she could only attribute to her own stupidity. Isabella, on hearing the particulars of the visit, gave a different explanation: "It was all pride, pride, insufferable haughtiness and pride! She had long suspected the family to be very high, and this made it certain. Such insolence of behaviour as Miss Tilney's she had never heard of in her life! Not to do the honours of her house with common good breeding! To behave to her guest with such superciliousness! Hardly even to speak to her!"

"But it was not so bad as that, Isabella; there was no superciliousness; she was very civil."

"Oh! Don't defend her! And then the brother, he, who had appeared so attached to you! Good heavens! Well, some people's feelings are incomprehensible. And so he hardly looked once at you the whole day?"

"I do not say so; but he did not seem in good spirits."

"How contemptible! Of all things in the world inconstancy is my aversion. Let me entreat you never to think of him again, my dear Catherine; indeed he is unworthy of you."

"Unworthy! I do not suppose he ever thinks of me."

"That is exactly what I say; he never thinks of you. Such fickleness! Oh! How different to your brother and to mine! I really believe John has the most constant heart."

"But as for General Tilney, I assure you it would be impossible for anybody to behave to me with greater civility and attention; it seemed to be his only care to entertain and make me happy."

"Oh! I know no harm of him; I do not suspect him of pride. I believe he is a very gentleman-like man. John thinks very well of him, and John's judgment—"

"Well, I shall see how they behave to me this evening; we shall meet them at the rooms."

"And must I go?"

"Do not you intend it? I thought it was all settled."

"Nay, since you make such a point of it, I can refuse you nothing. But do not insist upon my being very agreeable, for my heart, you know, will be some forty miles off. And as for dancing, do not mention it, I beg; that is quite out of the question. Charles Hodges will plague me to death, I dare say; but I shall cut him very short. Ten to one but he guesses the reason, and that is exactly what I want to avoid, so I shall insist on his keeping his conjecture to himself."

Isabella's opinion of the Tilneys did not influence her friend; she was sure there had been no insolence in the manners either of brother or sister; and she did not credit there being any pride in their hearts. The evening rewarded her confidence; she was met by one with the same kindness, and by the other with the same attention, as heretofore: Miss Tilney took pains to be near her, and Henry asked her to dance.

Having heard the day before in Milsom Street that their elder brother, Captain Tilney, was expected almost every hour, she was at no loss for the name of a very fashionable-looking, handsome young man, whom she had never seen before, and who now evidently belonged to their party. She looked at him with great admiration, and even supposed it possible that some people might think him handsomer than his brother, though, in her eyes, his air was more assuming, and his countenance less prepossessing. His taste and manners were beyond a doubt decidedly inferior; for, within her hearing, he not only protested against every thought of dancing himself, but even laughed openly at Henry for finding it possible. From the latter circumstance it may be presumed that, whatever might be our heroine's opinion of him, his admiration of her was not of a very dangerous kind; not likely to produce animosities between the brothers, nor persecutions to the lady. He cannot be the instigator of the three villains in horsemen's greatcoats, by whom she will hereafter be forced into a travelling-chaise and four, which will drive off with incredible speed. Catherine, meanwhile, undisturbed by presentiments of such an evil, or of any evil at all, except that of having but a short set to dance down, enjoyed her usual happiness with Henry Tilney, listening with sparkling eyes to everything he said; and, in finding him irresistible, becoming so herself.

At the end of the first dance, Captain Tilney came towards them again, and, much to Catherine's dissatisfaction, pulled his brother away. They retired whispering together; and, though her delicate sensibility did not take immediate alarm, and lay it down as fact, that Captain Tilney must have heard some malevolent misrepresentation of her, which he now hastened to communicate to his brother, in the hope of separating them forever, she could not have her partner conveyed from her sight without very uneasy sensations. Her suspense was of full five minutes' duration; and she was beginning to think it a very long quarter of an hour, when they both returned, and an explanation was given, by Henry's requesting to know if she thought her friend, Miss Thorpe, would have any objection to dancing, as his brother would be most happy to be introduced to her. Catherine, without hesitation, replied that she was very sure Miss Thorpe did not mean to dance at all. The cruel reply was passed on to the other, and he immediately walked away.

"Your brother will not mind it, I know," said she, "because I heard him say before that he hated dancing; but it was very good-natured in him to think of it. I suppose he saw Isabella sitting down, and fancied she might wish for a partner; but he is quite mistaken, for she would not dance upon any account in the world."

Henry smiled, and said, "How very little trouble it can give you to understand the motive of other people's actions."

"Why? What do you mean?"

"With you, it is not, How is such a one likely to be influenced, What is the inducement most likely to act upon such a person's feelings, age, situation, and probable habits of life considered—but, How should I be influenced, What would be my inducement in acting so and so?"

"I do not understand you."

"Then we are on very unequal terms, for I understand you perfectly well."

"Me? Yes; I cannot speak well enough to be unintelligible."

"Bravo! An excellent satire on modern language."

"But pray tell me what you mean."

"Shall I indeed? Do you really desire it? But you are not aware of the consequences; it will involve you in a very cruel embarrassment, and certainly bring on a disagreement between us.

"No, no; it shall not do either; I am not afraid."

"Well, then, I only meant that your attributing my brother's wish of dancing with Miss Thorpe to good nature alone convinced me of your being superior in good nature yourself to all the rest of the world."

Catherine blushed and disclaimed, and the gentleman's predictions were verified. There was a something, however, in his words which repaid her for the pain of confusion; and that something occupied her mind so much that she drew back for some time, forgetting to speak or to listen, and almost forgetting where she was.

At length, her thoughts drifted to that in which she had wanted to discuss with Mr. Tilney since its occurrence, that being the discovery of the body in the river; now with the opportunity there before her, she found herself unsure of how to broach the subject.

"Mr. Tilney?" she said in a manner revealing her uncertainty, and one to gain his ear. After he had responded in kind and his attention in place, she continued.

"I have been wanting to speak about something I witnessed after my arrival in Bath. It has been on my mind ever since, so much so that I thought you might offer some other perspective. Indeed, I would have spoken of it during our walk the other day, except that I would not have wanted to upset your sister, and she already became alarmed when I suggested that something horrible was to come from London shortly."

"Yes, I found it all rather amusing, even though it was at sweet Eleanor's expense; she is a dear sister, and with a quickness of mind, so when something so obvious eludes her, I cannot help but be mischievous. It is to her good nature that she puts up with my amusements. But what is this encounter of yours that might have upset her so?"

"Is the world so bad a place with us in it? What I mean to say is that all of the sordid cruelties that I have read about--"

"Do you refer to the newspapers and events of the day or your novels?"

"Yes, my novels, for perhaps that is as good a place to start. Are they an accurate portrayal of what exists in the world?"

He rubbed his fingers across his chin as if indicating great thought, before responding. "A very astute question: is fiction like the real world? Of course, what you have read is based purely on a person's imagination, but the basis of that can surely be derived from true events, if that is what you mean to ask. Do I think that people are entombed in hidden chambers, or that flutists play music merely to confound the listener to the source of the melody? Perhaps, but I doubt that it would be an everyday occurrence. I do not quite see where you are leading me with this question, so might you offer some insight into your meaning?"

"Of course," she answered. "I should be more direct in this instance." With that, she detailed to him the full account of her experience, the trip to the theatre coming to a halt at the bridge, her observation of the boats below, the retrieval of the girl from the waters, and the wretched condition of the body.

As she spoke, he became attentive to the extreme, paying attention to every word, and occasionally asking about a particular point for clarity. When she finished her account, and added how despite her best efforts to the contrary, she had been unable to rid herself of the vision, he offered a gentle smile as comfort.

"No doubt, you would like to free your mind, but I can reassure you that even the stoutest of men used to the horrors of war would have trouble letting go of such a sight. I feel all the more for you, having had such an experience, and as to your question about the cruelty of the world, it does exist as you have seen. Whether it can be measured by your books is another matter altogether, as they are imaginings not necessarily based in reality."

"But the markings on her body? Surely those were not accidental?"

"As I was not there to see it firsthand, I would be unable to form an opinion, however as it has already been a burden to you without being of any direct relation, I would think it best to dwell on it no longer. All of your concerns in the matter will not serve any purpose, neither to her nor to your well-being. Would you not agree?"

"I suppose you are right, but it is hard to do so."

"What gives you the impression that anything in life should be easy? All of the greatest pleasures are the ones that have been earned."

Catherine nodded in understanding, if not in total agreement, considering the depth of his meaning, allowing some minutes to pass in silent contemplation, till, roused by the voice of Isabella, she looked up and saw her with Captain Tilney preparing to give them hands across.

Isabella shrugged her shoulders and smiled, the only explanation of this extraordinary change which could at that time be given; but as it was not quite enough for Catherine's comprehension, she spoke her astonishment in very plain terms to her partner.

"I cannot think how it could happen! Isabella was so determined not to dance."

"And did Isabella never change her mind before?"

"Oh! But, because—And your brother! After what you told him from me, how could he think of going to ask her?"

"I cannot take surprise to myself on that head. You bid me be surprised on your friend's account, and therefore I am; but as for my brother, his conduct in the business, I must own, has been no more than I believed him perfectly equal to. The fairness of your friend was an open attraction; her firmness, you know, could only be understood by yourself."

"You are laughing; but, I assure you, Isabella is very firm in general."

"It is as much as should be said of anyone. To be always firm must be to be often obstinate. When properly to relax is the trial of judgment; and, without reference to my brother, I really think Miss Thorpe has by no means chosen ill in fixing on the present hour."

The friends were not able to get together for any confidential discourse till all the dancing was over; but then, as they walked about the room arm in arm, Isabella thus explained herself: "I do not wonder at your surprise; and I am really fatigued to death. He is such a rattle! Amusing enough, if my mind had been disengaged; but I would have given the world to sit still."

"Then why did not you?"

"Oh! My dear! It would have looked so particular; and you know how I abhor doing that. I refused him as long as I possibly could, but he would take no denial. You have no idea how he pressed me. I begged him to excuse me, and get some other partner—but no, not he; after aspiring to my hand, there was nobody else in the room he could bear to think of; and it was not that he wanted merely to dance, he wanted to be with me. Oh! Such nonsense! I told him he had taken a very unlikely way to prevail upon me; for, of all things in the world, I hated fine speeches and compliments; and so—and so then I found there would be no peace if I did not stand up. Besides, I thought Mrs. Hughes, who introduced him, might take it ill if I did not: and your dear brother, I am sure he would have been miserable if I had sat down the whole evening. I am so glad it is over! My spirits are quite jaded with listening to his nonsense: and then, being such a smart young fellow, I saw every eye was upon us."

"He is very handsome indeed."

"Handsome! Yes, I suppose he may. I dare say people would admire him in general; but he is not at all in my style of beauty. I hate a florid complexion and dark eyes in a man. However, he is very well. Amazingly conceited, I am sure. I took him down several times, you know, in my way."

When the young ladies next met, they had a far more interesting subject to discuss. James Morland's second letter was then received, and the kind intentions of his father fully explained. A living, of which Mr. Morland was himself patron and incumbent, of about four hundred pounds yearly value, was to be resigned to his son as soon as he should be old enough to take it; no trifling deduction from the family income, no niggardly assignment to one of ten children. An estate of at least equal value, moreover, was assured as his future inheritance.

James expressed himself on the occasion with becoming gratitude; and the necessity of waiting between two and three years before they could marry, being, however unwelcome, no more than he had expected, was borne by him without discontent. Catherine, whose expectations had been as unfixed as her ideas of her father's income, and whose judgment was now entirely led by her brother, felt equally well satisfied, and heartily congratulated Isabella on having everything so pleasantly settled.

"It is very charming indeed," said Isabella, with a grave face. "Mr. Morland has behaved vastly handsome indeed," said the gentle Mrs. Thorpe, looking anxiously at her daughter. "I only wish I could do as much. One could not expect more from him, you know. If he finds he can do more by and by, I dare say he will, for I am sure he must be an excellent good-hearted man. Four hundred is but a small income to begin on indeed, but your wishes, my dear Isabella, are so moderate, you do not consider how little you ever want, my dear."

"It is not on my own account I wish for more; but I cannot bear to be the means of injuring my dear Morland, making him sit down upon an income hardly enough to find one in the common necessaries of life. For myself, it is nothing; I never think of myself."

"I know you never do, my dear; and you will always find your reward in the affection it makes everybody feel for you. There never was a young woman so beloved as you are by everybody that knows you; and I dare say when Mr. Morland sees you, my dear child—but do not let us distress our dear Catherine by talking of such things. Mr. Morland has behaved so very handsome, you know. I always heard he was a most excellent man; and you know, my dear, we are not to suppose but what, if you had had a suitable fortune, he would have come down with something more, for I am sure he must be a most liberal-minded man."

"Nobody can think better of Mr. Morland than I do, I am sure. But everybody has their failing, you know, and everybody has a right to do what they like with their own money." Catherine was hurt by these insinuations. "I am very sure," said she, "that my father has promised to do as much as he can afford."

Isabella recollected herself. "As to that, my sweet Catherine, there cannot be a doubt, and you know me well enough to be sure that a much smaller income would satisfy me. It is not the want of more money that makes me just at present a little out of spirits; I hate money; and if our union could take place now upon only fifty pounds a year, I should not have a wish unsatisfied. Ah! my Catherine, you have found me out. There's the sting. The long, long, endless two years and half that are to pass before your brother can hold the living."

"Yes, yes, my darling Isabella," said Mrs. Thorpe, "we perfectly see into your heart. You have no disguise. We perfectly understand the present vexation; and everybody must love you the better for such a noble honest affection."

Catherine's uncomfortable feelings began to lessen. She endeavoured to believe that the delay of the marriage was the only source of Isabella's regret; and when she saw her at their next interview as cheerful and amiable as ever, endeavoured to forget that she had for a minute thought otherwise. James soon followed his letter, and was received with the most gratifying kindness.

While accepting Isabella's disappointment on the extended wait, Catherine found herself, nevertheless, concerned about all the involved parties, how her brother might fare during the extended courtship, and if there were any underlying issues to her friend's distress. Her apprehension over close friends was mirrored in an equal manner by Mr. Tilney, to whom she had taken into such confidence during the social, but here the similarities ended. She was concerned largely with things as they were to come, whereas he had been attentive to events of the past. For her, it was the entwining of two separate lives; for him, it was for a life now snuffed out. She dwelt on the words spoken and what they might mean. He considered what could no longer be said.

Tilney was fervent in his hopes of Miss Morland putting all thoughts of the Pulteney Bridge incident out of her mind, while just as confident that she would be unable to do so. How could she? For that matter, how could anyone with any sense of compassion or humanity? It was the best parcel of advice he felt he might offer, based on the circumstances, but of little applicable value.

For all the consideration given to the other, the final outcome of their conversation was that instead of one person left with the most unpleasant of thoughts, there were now two, the difference being that he was privy to additional information that she was thankfully unaware of. It was for this reason that he had listened so attentively when she had recounted her experience and had even questioned her on several specific points.

Indeed, the world could be a cruel place, in answer to her question—but not the answer he would have offered to her. This cruelty was balanced out in equal measure by all other traits of the human condition: love, hate, joy, pain, the deepest pits of depression, as well as the greatest heights of ecstasy. Yet all the equality of these experiences could never make the unsavory aspects of man's existence any less foul.

Thus, Henry was now accessory to Catherine's ill-timed experience, and so bothered was he in its subject that he found it equally hard to shed the thoughts from his mind, largely because of proximity, the deceased girl most likely meeting her end in Bath. Yes, Henry was acquainted with the arcane symbols that had been found on her body, and had known of its discovery, having read about it in the newspaper, but what the paper had left out were those particulars of her remains. The revelation of the markings through her description raised his concern, for the fact that this was assuredly not an isolated event.

Similar occurrences had taken place over the last year, not in Bath but in London, a sprawling city more likely to be host to such vicious activities and covered with less decorum and more specifics in its periodicals. It had been through those accounts that he had become familiar with the unusual marks.

The unfortunate fact remained that Miss Morland, by being at a specific place and a specific time, should witness such a sight, and Henry felt all the worse for it, because of all people, she should not be burdened by such realities. Then, again, might the girl at the bridge have been another victim of being at the wrong place at the wrong time, and in her situation, that positioning proved to be fatal.

It all gave evidence that life was but a series of random events, falling as they might in no particular order, but with ramifications that could be most profound. Had predestination played any more a part in Miss Morland's experience at the bridge than his arrival to Bath, leading to their chance meeting? No, there was hardly a master plan to these diverse occurrences, the outcomes of which were equally as random, and to ponder it at any greater depth could be cause for an aching brain; he was ill-equipped to produce an answer, nor did he feel she could either, because in the time he had known her, he had come to believe her to be as sharp of mind as she was upstanding in character, but without experience to back up her convictions.

Every question he had leveled at her, often in response to her questions, validated this judgment, and only increased his good opinion of her. For all her naïveté, she displayed a quality of value and consideration so missing from other ladies of far greater learning and experience, therefore, it contradicted the very advice he had earlier given, of having to work hard for attainment as those qualities of hers had been hers all along without any apparent effort for its gain. With Miss Morland, it simply was.

As to the doomed girl at the bridge, hers was a sad tragedy, and the world was so full of them.

CHAPTER

Thirty

THE ALLENS had now entered on the sixth week of their stay in Bath; and whether it should be the last was for some time a question, to which Catherine listened with a beating heart. To have her acquaintance with the Tilneys end so soon was an evil which nothing could counterbalance. Her whole happiness seemed at stake, while the affair was in suspense, and everything secured when it was determined that the lodgings should be taken for another fortnight. What this additional fortnight was to produce to her beyond the pleasure of sometimes seeing Henry Tilney made but a small part of Catherine's speculation. Once or twice indeed, since James's engagement had taught her what could be done, she had got so far as to indulge in a secret "perhaps," but in general the felicity of being with him for the present bounded her views: the present was now comprised in another three weeks, and her happiness being certain for that period, the rest of her life was at such a distance as to excite but little interest. In the course of the morning which saw this business arranged, she visited Miss Tilney, and poured forth her joyful feelings. It was doomed to be a day of trial. No sooner had she expressed her delight in Mr. Allen's lengthened stay than Miss Tilney told her of her father's having just determined upon quitting Bath by the end of another week. Here was a blow! The past suspense of the morning had been ease and quiet to the present disappointment. Catherine's countenance fell, and in a voice of most sincere concern she echoed Miss Tilney's concluding words, "By the end of another week!"

"Yes, my father can seldom be prevailed on to give the waters what I think a fair trial. He has been disappointed of some friends' arrival whom he expected to meet here, and as he is now pretty well, is in a hurry to get home."

"I am very sorry for it," said Catherine dejectedly; "if I had known this before—"

"Perhaps," said Miss Tilney in an embarrassed manner, "you would be so good—it would make me very happy if—"

The entrance of her father put a stop to the civility, which Catherine was beginning to hope might introduce a desire of their corresponding. After addressing her with his usual politeness, he turned to his daughter and said, "Well, Eleanor, may I congratulate you on being successful in your application to your fair friend?"

"I was just beginning to make the request, sir, as you came in."

"Well, proceed by all means. I know how much your heart is in it. My daughter, Miss Morland," he continued, without leaving his daughter time to speak, "has been forming a very bold wish. We leave Bath, as she has perhaps told you, on Saturday se'nnight. A letter from my steward tells me that my presence is wanted at home; and being disappointed in my hope of seeing the Marquis of Longtown and General Courteney here, some of my very old friends, there is nothing to detain me longer in Bath. And could we carry our selfish point with you, we should leave it without a single regret. Can you, in short, be prevailed on to quit this scene of public triumph and oblige your friend Eleanor with your company in Gloucestershire? I am almost ashamed to make the request, though its presumption would certainly appear greater to every creature in Bath than yourself. Modesty such as yours—but not for the world would I pain it by open praise. If you can be induced to honour us with a visit, you will make us happy beyond expression. 'Tis true, we can offer you nothing like the gaieties of this lively place; we can tempt you neither by amusement nor splendour, for our mode of living, as you see, is plain and unpretending; yet no endeavours shall be wanting on our side to make Northanger Abbey not wholly disagreeable."

Northanger Abbey! These were thrilling words, and wound up Catherine's feelings to the highest point of ecstasy. Her grateful and gratified heart could hardly restrain its expressions within the language of tolerable calmness. To receive so flattering an invitation! To have her company so warmly solicited! Everything honourable and soothing, every present enjoyment, and every future hope was contained in it; and her acceptance, with only the saving clause of Papa and Mamma's approbation, was eagerly given. "I will write home directly," said she, "and if they do not object, as I dare say they will not—"

General Tilney was not less sanguine, having already waited on her excellent friends in Pulteney Street, and obtained their sanction of his wishes. "Since they can consent to part with you," said he, "we may expect philosophy from all the world."

Miss Tilney was earnest, though gentle, in her secondary civilities, and the affair became in a few minutes as nearly settled as this necessary reference to Fullerton would allow.

The circumstances of the morning had led Catherine's feelings through the varieties of suspense, security, and disappointment; but they were now safely lodged in perfect bliss; and with spirits elated to rapture, with Henry at her heart, and Northanger Abbey on her lips, she hurried home to write her letter. Mr. and Mrs. Morland, relying on the discretion of the friends to whom they had already entrusted their daughter, felt no doubt of the propriety of an acquaintance which had been formed under their eye, and sent therefore by return of post their ready consent to her visit in Gloucestershire. This indulgence, though not more than Catherine had hoped for, completed her conviction of being favoured beyond every other human creature, in friends and fortune, circumstance and chance. Everything seemed to cooperate for her advantage. By the kindness of her first friends, the Allens, she had been introduced into scenes where pleasures of every kind had met her. Her feelings, her preferences, had each known the happiness of a return. Wherever she felt attachment, she had been able to create it. The affection of Isabella was to be secured to her in a sister. The Tilneys, they, by whom, above all, she desired to be favourably thought of, outstripped even her wishes in the flattering measures by which their intimacy was to be continued. She was to be their chosen visitor, she was to be for weeks under the same roof with the person whose society she mostly prized—and, in addition to all the rest, this roof was to be the roof of an abbey! Her passion for ancient edifices was next in degree to her passion for Henry Tilney—and castles and abbeys made usually the charm of those reveries which his image did not fill. To see and explore either the ramparts and keep of the one, or the cloisters of the other, had been for many weeks a darling wish, though to be more than the visitor of an hour had seemed too nearly impossible for desire. And yet, this was to happen. With all the chances against her of house, hall, place, park, court, and cottage, Northanger turned up an abbey, and she was to be its inhabitant. Its long, damp passages, its narrow cells and ruined chapel, were to be within her daily reach, and she could not entirely subdue the hope of some traditional legends, some awful memorials of an injured and ill-fated nun.

It was wonderful that her friends should seem so little elated by the possession of such a home, that the consciousness of it should be so meekly borne. The power of early habit only could account for it. A distinction to which they had been born gave no pride. Their superiority of abode was no more to them than their superiority of person.

Many were the inquiries she was eager to make of Miss Tilney; but so active were her thoughts, that when these inquiries were answered, she was hardly more assured than before, of Northanger Abbey having been a richly endowed convent at the time of the Reformation, of its having fallen into the hands of an ancestor of the Tilneys on its dissolution, of a large portion of the ancient building still making a part of the present dwelling although the rest was decayed, or of its standing low in a valley, sheltered from the north and east by rising woods of oak.

CHAPTER
Thirty-One

Dearest Sarah,

This will be the briefest of letters, to which I apologize, but so much has happened since our last correspondence, I do not want to keep you in the dark as to my situation to date. It is the most exciting news; in short, I am to leave Bath as a companion to Miss Tilney, thereby to accompany her, along with her brother and father to their estate in Gloucestershire.

I shall soon take leave of Mr. and Mrs. Allen, who have been so extraordinarily kind and generous throughout my stay. When next I write, it will be from the confines of Northanger Abbey, to which the Tilneys call their home. I can only imagine its appearance, and as you might guess, my anticipation is great. As soon as I have familiarized myself with its many rooms and corridors, every closet and cabinet, I will write again, and disclose its mysterious secrets.

General Tilney has been most kind, while reserved in his attitude. He is a widower, his wife having died some years earlier. He showed me a locket with her portrait inside, which he has worn ever since her death. He must have loved her greatly.

As to the news that you are no doubt aware of, our brother, James, has finally found his match, and is now betrothed to Isabella Thorpe; indeed the same Isabella that I have previously written of, *having become one of my first new friends after my arrival in Bath, and a steady confidant, since you are not by my side. Again, I should state how much there is to tell you once we are reunited. I do hope that you will find her likable, as she is destined to be as much a sister to you as to me, and we will be spending much time together.*

Papa has already given his consent and blessings to the union, with the understanding that it will be two to three years hence before an income is in place and the marriage vows taken. Isabella was disappointed at the wait, and understandably so, for all matters of the heart have no patience, and desire immediate gratification.

There is more to tell, meeting Mr. Tilney's older brother among them, but all this can wait until we are face to face and hand in hand. It has grown late, as I seem to find time to write only at these final hours of the day. Ahead is an adventure to which I am full of excitement, with the most pleasant of company to be with, the only aspect missing in this picture is you.

With all my love,
Cathy

CHAPTER
Thirty-Two

WITH A MIND thus full of happiness, Catherine was hardly aware that two or three days had passed away, without her seeing Isabella for more than a few minutes together. She began first to be sensible of this, and to sigh for her conversation, as she walked along the pump-room one morning, by Mrs. Allen's side, without anything to say or to hear; and scarcely had she felt a five minutes' longing of friendship, before the object of it appeared, and inviting her to a secret conference, led the way to a seat. "This is my favourite place," said she as they sat down on a bench between the doors, which commanded a tolerable view of everybody entering at either; "it is so out of the way."

Catherine, observing that Isabella's eyes were continually bent towards one door or the other, as in eager expectation, and remembering how often she had been falsely accused of being arch, thought the present a fine opportunity for being really so; and therefore gaily said, "Do not be uneasy, Isabella, James will soon be here."

"Psha! My dear creature," she replied, "do not think me such a simpleton as to be always wanting to confine him to my elbow. It would be hideous to be always together; we should be the jest of the place. And so you are going to Northanger! I am amazingly glad of it. It is one of the finest old places in England, I understand. I shall depend upon a most particular description of it."

"You shall certainly have the best in my power to give. But who are you looking for? Are your sisters coming?"

"I am not looking for anybody. One's eyes must be somewhere, and you know what a foolish trick I have of fixing mine, when my thoughts are an hundred miles off. I am amazingly absent; I believe I am the most absent creature in the world. Tilney says it is always the case with minds of a certain stamp."

"But I thought, Isabella, you had something in particular to tell me?"

"Oh! Yes, and so I have. But here is a proof of what I was saying. My poor head, I had quite forgot it. Well, the thing is this: I have just had a letter from John; you can guess the contents."

"No, indeed, I cannot."

"My sweet love, do not be so abominably affected. What can he write about, but yourself? You know he is over head and ears in love with you."

"With me, dear Isabella!"

"Nay, my sweetest Catherine, this is being quite absurd! Modesty, and all that, is very well in its way, but really a little common honesty is sometimes quite as becoming. I have no idea of being so overstrained! It is fishing for compliments. His attentions were such as a child must have noticed. And it was but half an hour before he left Bath that you gave him the most positive encouragement. He says so in this letter, says that he as good as made you an offer, and that you received his advances in the kindest way; and now he wants me to urge his suit, and say all manner of pretty things to you. So it is in vain to affect ignorance."

Catherine, with all the earnestness of truth, expressed her astonishment at such a charge, protesting her innocence of every thought of Mr. Thorpe's being in love with her, and the consequent impossibility of her having ever intended to encourage him. "As to any attentions on his side, I do declare, upon my honour, I never was sensible of them for a moment—except just his asking me to dance the first day of his coming. And as to making me an offer, or anything like it, there must be some unaccountable mistake. I could not have misunderstood a thing of that kind, you know! And, as I ever wish to be believed, I solemnly protest that no syllable of such a nature ever passed between us. The last half hour before he went away! It must be all and completely a mistake—for I did not see him once that whole morning."

"But that you certainly did, for you spent the whole morning in Edgar's Buildings—it was the day your father's consent came—and I am pretty sure that you and John were alone in the parlour some time before you left the house."

"Are you? Well, if you say it, it was so, I dare say—but for the life of me, I cannot recollect it. I do remember now being with you, and seeing him as well as the rest—but that we were ever alone for five minutes—However, it is not worth arguing about, for whatever might pass on his side, you must be convinced, by my having no recollection of it, that I never thought, nor expected, nor wished for anything of the kind from him. I am excessively concerned that he should have any regard for me—but indeed it has been quite unintentional on my side; I never had the smallest idea of it. Pray undeceive him as soon as you can, and tell him I beg his pardon—that is—I do not know what I ought to say—but make him understand what I mean, in the properest way. I would not speak disrespectfully of a brother of yours, Isabella, I am sure; but you know very well that if I could think of one man more than another—he is not the person." Isabella was silent. "My dear friend, you must not be angry with me. I cannot suppose your brother cares so very much about me. And, you know, we shall still be sisters."

"Yes, yes" (with a blush), "there are more ways than one of our being sisters. But where am I wandering to? Well, my dear Catherine, the case seems to be that you are determined against poor John—is not it so?"

"I certainly cannot return his affection, and as certainly never meant to encourage it."

"Since that is the case, I am sure I shall not tease you any further. John desired me to speak to you on the subject, and therefore I have. But I confess, as soon as I read his letter, I thought it a very foolish, imprudent business, and not likely to promote the good of either; for what were you to live upon, supposing you came together? You have both of you something, to be sure, but it is not a trifle that will support a family nowadays; and after all that romancers may say, there is no doing without money. I only wonder John could think of it; he could not have received my last."

"You do acquit me, then, of anything wrong?—You are convinced that I never meant to deceive your brother, never suspected him of liking me till this moment?"

"Oh! As to that," answered Isabella laughingly, "I do not pretend to determine what your thoughts and designs in time past may have been. All that is best known to yourself. A little harmless flirtation or so will occur, and one is often drawn on to give more encouragement than one wishes to stand by. But you may be assured that I am the last person in the world to judge you severely. All those things should be allowed for in youth and high spirits. What one means one day, you know, one may not mean the next. Circumstances change, opinions alter."

"But my opinion of your brother never did alter; it was always the same. You are describing what never happened."

"My dearest Catherine," continued the other without at all listening to her, "I would not for all the world be the means of hurrying you into an engagement before you knew what you were about. I do not think anything would justify me in wishing you to sacrifice all your happiness merely to oblige my brother, because he is my brother, and who perhaps after all, you know, might be just as happy without you, for people seldom know what they would be at, young men especially, they are so amazingly changeable and inconstant. What I say is, why should a brother's happiness be dearer to me than a friend's? You know I carry my notions of friendship pretty high. But, above all things, my dear Catherine, do not be in a hurry. Take my word for it, that if you are in too great a hurry, you will certainly live to repent it. Tilney says there is nothing people are so often deceived in as the state of their own affections, and I believe he is very right. Ah! Here he comes; never mind, he will not see us, I am sure."

Catherine, looking up, perceived Captain Tilney; and Isabella, earnestly fixing her eye on him as she spoke, soon caught his notice. He approached immediately, and took the seat to which her movements invited him. His first address made Catherine start. Though spoken low, she could distinguish, "What! Always to be watched, in person or by proxy!"

"Psha, nonsense!" was Isabella's answer in the same half whisper. "Why do you put such things into my head? If I could believe it—my spirit, you know, is pretty independent."

"I wish your heart were independent. That would be enough for me."

"My heart, indeed! What can you have to do with hearts? You men have none of you any hearts."

"If we have not hearts, we have eyes; and they give us torment enough."

"Do they? I am sorry for it; I am sorry they find anything so disagreeable in me. I will look another way. I hope this pleases you" (turning her back on him); "I hope your eyes are not tormented now."

"Never more so; for the edge of a blooming cheek is still in view—at once too much and too little."

Catherine heard all this, and quite out of countenance, could listen no longer. Amazed that Isabella could endure it, and jealous for her brother, she rose up, and saying she should join Mrs. Allen, proposed their walking. But for this Isabella showed no inclination. She was so amazingly tired, and it was so odious to parade about the pump-room; and if she moved from her seat she should miss her sisters; she was expecting her sisters every moment; so that her dearest Catherine must excuse her, and must sit quietly down again. But Catherine could be stubborn too; and Mrs. Allen just then coming up to propose their returning home, she joined her and walked out of the pump-room, leaving Isabella still sitting with Captain Tilney. With much uneasiness did she thus leave them. It seemed to her that Captain Tilney was falling in love with Isabella, and Isabella unconsciously encouraging him; unconsciously it must be, for Isabella's attachment to James was as certain and well acknowledged as her engagement. To doubt her truth or good intentions was impossible; and yet, during the whole of their conversation her manner had been odd. She wished Isabella had talked more like her usual self, and not so much about money, and had not looked so well pleased at the sight of Captain Tilney. How strange that she should not perceive his admiration! Catherine longed to give her a hint of it, to put her on her guard, and prevent all the pain which her too lively behaviour might otherwise create both for him and her brother.

The compliment of John Thorpe's affection did not make amends for this thoughtlessness in his sister. She was almost as far from believing as from wishing it to be sincere; for she had not forgotten that he could mistake, and his assertion of the offer and of her encouragement convinced her that his mistakes could sometimes be very egregious. In vanity, therefore, she gained but little; her chief profit was in wonder. That he should think it worth his while to fancy himself in love with her was a matter of lively astonishment. Isabella talked of his attentions; she had never been sensible of any; but Isabella had said many things which she hoped had been spoken in haste, and would never be said again; and upon this she was glad to rest altogether for present ease and comfort.

CHAPTER

Thirty-Three

A FEW DAYS PASSED AWAY, and Catherine, though not allowing herself to suspect her friend, could not help watching her closely. The result of her observations was not agreeable. Isabella seemed an altered creature. When she saw her, indeed, surrounded only by their immediate friends in Edgar's Buildings or Pulteney Street, her change of manners was so trifling that, had it gone no farther, it might have passed unnoticed. A something of languid indifference, or of that boasted absence of mind which Catherine had never heard of before, would occasionally come across her; but had nothing worse appeared, that might only have spread a new grace and inspired a warmer interest. But when Catherine saw her in public, admitting Captain Tilney's attentions as readily as they were offered, and allowing him almost an equal share with James in her notice and smiles, the alteration became too positive to be passed over. What could be meant by such unsteady conduct, what her friend could be at, was beyond her comprehension. Isabella could not be aware of the pain she was inflicting; but it was a degree of wilful thoughtlessness which Catherine could not but resent. James was the sufferer. She saw him grave and uneasy; and however careless of his present comfort the woman might be who had given him her heart, to her it was always an object. For poor Captain Tilney too she was greatly concerned. Though his looks did not please her, his name was a passport to her goodwill, and she thought with sincere compassion of his approaching disappointment; for, in spite of what she had believed herself to overhear in the pump-room, his behaviour was so incompatible with a knowledge of Isabella's engagement that she could not, upon reflection, imagine him aware of it. He might be jealous of her brother as a rival, but if more had seemed implied, the fault must have been in her misapprehension. She wished, by a gentle remonstrance, to remind Isabella of her situation, and make her aware of this double unkindness; but for remonstrance, either opportunity or comprehension was always against her. If able to suggest a hint, Isabella could never understand it. In this distress, the intended departure of the Tilney family became her chief consolation; their journey into Gloucestershire was to take place within a few days, and Captain Tilney's removal would at least restore peace to every heart but his own. But Captain Tilney had at present no intention of removing; he was not to be of the party to Northanger; he was to continue at Bath. When Catherine knew this, her resolution was directly made. She spoke to Henry Tilney on the subject, regretting his brother's evident partiality for Miss Thorpe, and entreating him to make known her prior engagement.

"My brother does know it," was Henry's answer.

"Does he? Then why does he stay here?"

He made no reply, and was beginning to talk of something else; but she eagerly continued, "Why do not you persuade him to go away? The longer he stays, the worse it will be for him at last. Pray advise him for his own sake, and for everybody's sake, to leave Bath directly. Absence will in time make him comfortable again; but he can have no hope here, and it is only staying to be miserable."

Henry smiled and said, "I am sure my brother would not wish to do that."

"Then you will persuade him to go away?"

"Persuasion is not at command; but pardon me, if I cannot even endeavour to persuade him. I have myself told him that Miss Thorpe is engaged. He knows what he is about, and must be his own master."

"No, he does not know what he is about," cried Catherine; "he does not know the pain he is giving my brother. Not that James has ever told me so, but I am sure he is very uncomfortable."

"And are you sure it is my brother's doing?"

"Yes, very sure."

"Is it my brother's attentions to Miss Thorpe, or Miss Thorpe's admission of them, that gives the pain?"

"Is not it the same thing?"

"I think Mr. Morland would acknowledge a difference. No man is offended by another man's admiration of the woman he loves; it is the woman only who can make it a torment."

Catherine blushed for her friend, and said, "Isabella is wrong. But I am sure she cannot mean to torment, for she is very much attached to my brother. She has been in love with him ever since they first met, and while my father's consent was uncertain, she fretted herself almost into a fever. You know she must be attached to him."

"I understand: she is in love with James, and flirts with Frederick."

"Oh! no, not flirts. A woman in love with one man cannot flirt with another."

"It is probable that she will neither love so well, nor flirt so well, as she might do either singly. The gentlemen must each give up a little."

After a short pause, Catherine resumed with, "Then you do not believe Isabella so very much attached to my brother?"

"I can have no opinion on that subject."

"But what can your brother mean? If he knows her engagement, what can he mean by his behaviour?"

"You are a very close questioner."

"Am I? I only ask what I want to be told."

"But do you only ask what I can be expected to tell?"

"Yes, I think so; for you must know your brother's heart."

"My brother's heart, as you term it, on the present occasion, I assure you I can only guess at."

"Well?"

"Well! Nay, if it is to be guesswork, let us all guess for ourselves. To be guided by second-hand conjecture is pitiful. The premises are before you. My brother is a lively and perhaps sometimes a thoughtless young man; he has had about a week's acquaintance with your friend, and he has known her engagement almost as long as he has known her."

"Well," said Catherine, after some moments' consideration, "you may be able to guess at your brother's intentions from all this; but I am sure I cannot. But is not your father uncomfortable about it? Does not he want Captain Tilney to go away? Sure, if your father were to speak to him, he would go."

"My dear Miss Morland," said Henry, "in this amiable solicitude for your brother's comfort, may you not be a little mistaken? Are you not carried a little too far? Would he thank you, either on his own account or Miss Thorpe's, for supposing that her affection, or at least her good behaviour, is only to be secured by her seeing nothing of Captain Tilney? Is he safe only in solitude? Or is her heart constant to him only when unsolicited by anyone else? He cannot think this—and you may be sure that he would not have you think it. I will not say, 'Do not be uneasy,' because I know that you are so, at this moment; but be as little uneasy as you can. You have no doubt of the mutual attachment of your brother and your friend; depend upon it, therefore, that real jealousy never can exist between them; depend upon it that no disagreement between them can be of any duration. Their hearts are open to each other, as neither heart can be to you; they know exactly what is required and what can be borne; and you may be certain that one will never tease the other beyond what is known to be pleasant."

Perceiving her still to look doubtful and grave, he added, "Though Frederick does not leave Bath with us, he will probably remain but a very short time, perhaps only a few days behind us. His leave of absence will soon expire, and he must return to his regiment. And what will then be their acquaintance? The mess-room will drink Isabella Thorpe for a fortnight, and she will laugh with your brother over poor Tilney's passion for a month."

Catherine would contend no longer against comfort. She had resisted its approaches during the whole length of a speech, but it now carried her captive. Henry Tilney must know best. She blamed herself for the extent of her fears, and resolved never to think so seriously on the subject again.

Her resolution was supported by Isabella's behaviour in their parting interview. The Thorpes spent the last evening of Catherine's stay in Pulteney Street, and nothing passed between the lovers to excite her uneasiness, or make her quit them in apprehension. James was in excellent spirits, and Isabella most engagingly placid. Her tenderness for her friend seemed rather the first feeling of her heart; but that at such a moment was allowable; and once she gave her lover a flat contradiction, and once she drew back her hand; but Catherine remembered Henry's instructions, and placed it all to judicious affection. The embraces, tears, and promises of the parting fair ones may be fancied.

CHAPTER

Thirty-Four

NEVER BEFORE had Isabella Thorpe felt so vulnerable.

Instinctively, she pulled the bed sheets close against her, as much to find some security in their covering as to suggest some semblance of modesty. A full, unyielding comprehension of what had taken place only minutes before now settled upon her, with all its stark consequences. How had she allowed it to come to this, she wondered, thinking back over the evening? Was her resolve that yielding, or had she, deep down, wanted it as much as he? No, that could not be the case, for as much as she enjoyed catching the attention of the other sex, it had always been all quite innocent, a little flirtation without harm. She would never, not in a thousand years, consider giving of herself until after her vows.

Dear God, it was if as a game she had played suddenly changed its rules, and she was the last to know. This had not been a part of her plan in any form.

The most frightening thing was that she had actually enjoyed it.

After brushing some loose strands of hair from her face, she put on her best guise, projecting a level of confidence, this being another sheet to layer herself with. It was the best she could do, having reached a degree of intimacy that was completely unexpected and unplanned, and therefore unsure of its outcome.

"Why up so soon?" she said while attempting to sound composed. "Will you not come back so that we may talk? I have a thousand things I should like to tell you. Do you not feel the same?"

Frederick Tilney stood on the other side of the room, having buttoned his shirt in silence, and checking his appearance in the mirror. He turned to her and offered something that might have been a smile, but in the dim light, could have as easily been something else.

"And do we have all that much to talk about, or are things best left unspoken? Only a few minutes ago, we said very little, even in closer proximity, although I must confess that you expressed yourself quite well, very eloquent."

She felt a blush come upon her, something she was not frequent to. "I thought we might talk of our plans. Of what the future might bear. Surely you have given that some thought?" Even as she said the words, she felt an emptiness in her stomach. There was something about his manner, an aloof nature that had fascinated her from the beginning, even with his distinct charms. Now it was disconcerting.

He crossed the room, sitting beside her to stroke her hair, but there was a coolness, quite different from how he had touched her earlier. Under his steady gaze, she felt the need to avert her eyes, a sense of modesty again apparent, yet she managed to remain firm, locking her eyes to his. How was it that with him that all her insecurities came to the fore?

"You are such a pretty little thing," he said. "So much to learn, and I could show you so much."

"You speak as if I am a child, but I left that behind me years ago, and surely I can be your equal. Would you not agree?"

"Hardly an equal, but you have proven yourself not a child in certain respects." As emphasis to his words, he ran a hand down the sheet she still clung to, trailing the contours of the body underneath, and causing an involuntary shiver through her spine. Then, with a quick kiss atop her forehead, he was again off from the bed, attending to his own needs.

There was a dull throbbing in her head, along with a slight disorientation, making it hard, even now, to think clearly. Could it have been from the bottle they had drunk earlier? She was not used to any form of drink, but he had persisted, and how could she refuse his attentions? Indeed, he had been so elegant this evening, just as he had during their previous encounters, and then somehow along the way, she seemed to have lost her inhibitions—and her resolve.

Unexpectedly, she thought of James, poor James, and the full ramifications of what had just transpired. Was she not still promised to him? She thought the world of her Mr. Morland, but was he still hers to have now? He had expressed his love in earnest to her, and she to him, yet she had come to wonder if she was truly in love, or was she in love with the idea of his being in love with her. If it were true and pure, then the details of his future income, in addition to their lengthy wait, would not have been a concern. Yet she knew that it was, and on some deep level, she also knew that it was her reason for the continued flirtations, even after their pledges to one another. True, her teasings were so much a part of her nature that it would never be dispensed with, akin to letting go of a close friend, but to what degree had she embraced them after word came from Fullerton?

Mr. Tilney offered such a diversion, and she gave it no real concern in relation to James. But that was not entirely true either, was it? If the right man appeared, he being handsome, agreeable, and well set in his finances, would he be just as good a catch? It now appeared that she had been the one caught, and she was not entirely sure that Tilney was a healthy choice for her. As to James, was that even an option anymore?

She shifted her weight, and feeling the dampness still there on her skin, moved her hand down to the moisture, using the sheets to help wipe the memories away. A variety of feelings washed over her; confusion, fear, remorse, doubt, all of which were thoughts normally far out of her mind. Existence for her had always been rather carefree, leaving her in the luxury of nary a serious thought. Tonight, at this moment, that was all that she had.

Isabella watched Frederick Tilney, full in the realization that whatever she thought of him, he most likely gave far less to her in consideration. So unlike James. So unlike what she could have wanted. Now that she had given of herself, what did it all mean, and what was to happen to her?

With a parting glance, he left the room without another word, leaving Isabella Thorpe to all her thoughts, far more than she had considered at a single time in her entire life.

CHAPTER
Thirty-Five

MR. AND MRS. ALLEN were sorry to lose their young friend, whose good humour and cheerfulness had made her a valuable companion, and in the promotion of whose enjoyment their own had been gently increased. Her happiness in going with Miss Tilney, however, prevented their wishing it otherwise; and, as they were to remain only one more week in Bath themselves, her quitting them now would not long be felt. Mr. Allen attended her to Milsom Street, where she was to breakfast, and saw her seated with the kindest welcome among her new friends; but so great was her agitation in finding herself as one of the family, and so fearful was she of not doing exactly what was right, and of not being able to preserve their good opinion, that, in the embarrassment of the first five minutes, she could almost have wished to return with him to Pulteney Street.

Miss Tilney's manners and Henry's smile soon did away some of her unpleasant feelings; but still she was far from being at ease; nor could the incessant attentions of the general himself entirely reassure her. Nay, perverse as it seemed, she doubted whether she might not have felt less, had she been less attended to. His anxiety for her comfort—his continual solicitations that she would eat, and his often-expressed fears of her seeing nothing to her taste—though never in her life before had she beheld half such variety on a breakfast-table—made it impossible for her to forget for a moment that she was a visitor. She felt utterly unworthy of such respect, and knew not how to reply to it. Her tranquillity was not improved by the general's impatience for the appearance of his eldest son, nor by the displeasure he expressed at his laziness when Captain Tilney at last came down. She was quite pained by the severity of his father's reproof, which seemed disproportionate to the offence; and much was her concern increased when she found herself the principal cause of the lecture, and that his tardiness was chiefly resented from being disrespectful to her. This was placing her in a very uncomfortable situation, and she felt great compassion for Captain Tilney, without being able to hope for his goodwill.

He listened to his father in silence, and attempted not any defense, which confirmed her in fearing that the inquietude of his mind, on Isabella's account, might, by keeping him long sleepless, have been the real cause of his rising late. It was the first time of her being decidedly in his company, and she had hoped to be now able to form her opinion of him; but she scarcely heard his voice while his father remained in the room.

He later regained his normal tone and temperament, but was well out of range of any casual listener, be it Catherine, or by all means his father, and only when Henry approached him in conversation.

"I would venture to say, based on your general appearance," said the younger Tilney, "as something that the tabby might have brought in, that you were sowing your wild oats to a fair degree last night."

Frederick offered up a perfunctory smile, along with something resembling a "Pshaw!" Henry took this, along with the following silence as a nonverbal acknowledgment, and added how the repercussions did not sit well with their father.

"Does anything?" Frederick replied. "Anyway, what would you know of sowing?"

"I may have been raised in an abbey, but not a monastery, so you might give me more credit. It was merely an observation, based on your hurried appearance, which I felt obligated to pass on."

"Then in answer, the evening was pleasant enough."

"A social evening, I am to presume?"

The reply came as a grunt to the affirmative.

"And your company; did you find her quite satisfactory?"

The questioning set the older brother on edge, and he placed his right hand down on a nearby chair, tapping the wood frame with the ring he wore, and drawing Henry's notice. It was an old ring of some antiquarian make, its design quite foreign with a series of geometric and marine shapes, and a circular motive surrounded by wavy lines, the whole made of gold but combined with another alloy unique to most jewelry of the day, giving it a distinctive luster. Henry knew it well, as a trinket of similar origin belonged to Eleanor, it being passed down from mother to daughter. These, along with several other pieces, had been acquired by the general as part of his dealings in trade some years earlier.

"You are driving at something, little brother," said Frederick. "You might best state it outright."

"Only that I was wondering if you might have seen Miss Thorpe recently."

"Ah, so that is your interest. First off, what I do with my time is no one's funeral, and most certainly not yours, however, for what it might mean to you, yes. I have seen something of the lady in question."

"I thought as much. And while it is none of my concern how you might spend your time, or to whom you grace with your company, I thought, as a general courtesy from one to another, to remind you that she is engaged, although this is a fact that you already are aware of."

Frederick chuckled in response, and added with a smug condescension, "I believe that the lady can make her own decisions, and I repeat: it is hardly any concern of yours."

"True enough, however as I am familiar enough with her through mutual friends, I felt that..."

"This is so like you, I am not surprised; far too noble for your own good, and much more like our dear mother."

Henry accepted this as a compliment, knowing that it was not meant that way, as his brother noted his similarity to the patriarch, their likeness in temperament as well as interests.

"And what would our father say about your interest in Miss Thorpe?"

"I suggest that you keep to your mundane interests. For one, you have your own little costume doll to offer your undivided attention to, and a pretty little thing she is, although she strikes me as a bit platitudinous. How pleased you must be for her returning to Northanger."

"At the behest of our father, I might remind you, as a companion to our sister, and while I do find his consideration in this regard a striking change to his normal demeanor, even to wonder if there are deeper motives, I assure you that I played no part in the invitation."

"Yes, a likely answer, but I know you, and she is just the little innocent to make your heart go thumpity-thump. As to my interests, they are mine alone, and I would ask you to bear that in mind."

It was a stalemate and Henry knew it. No entreaties would serve to change his brother's determination. It had never been effective before, nor would it change on this day. He simply nodded and said, "Yes, and I know you."

"No, you don't," replied Frederick. "You never have." He turned and resumed his quiet presence to the remainder of the party.

For her part, Catherine felt sure that it was the general's admonitions that had dampened Henry's mood, and even afterward, so much were his spirits affected, she could distinguish nothing but these words, in a whisper to Eleanor, "How glad I shall be when you are all off."

The bustle of going was not pleasant. The clock struck ten while the trunks were carrying down, and the general had fixed to be out of Milsom Street by that hour. His greatcoat, instead of being brought for him to put on directly, was spread out in the curricle in which he was to accompany his son. The middle seat of the chaise was not drawn out, though there were three people to go in it, and his daughter's maid had so crowded it with parcels that Miss Morland would not have room to sit; and, so much was he influenced by this apprehension when he handed her in, that she had some difficulty in saving her own new writing-desk from being thrown out into the street. At last, however, the door was closed upon the three females, and they set off at the sober pace in which the handsome, highly fed four horses of a gentleman usually perform a journey of thirty miles: such was the distance of Northanger from Bath, to be now divided into two equal stages. Catherine's spirits revived as they drove from the door; for with Miss Tilney she felt no restraint; and, with the interest of a road entirely new to her, of an abbey before, and a curricle behind, she caught the last view of Bath without any regret, and met with every milestone before she expected it. The tediousness of a two hours' wait at Petty France, in which there was nothing to be done but to eat without being hungry, and loiter about without anything to see, next followed— and her admiration of the style in which they travelled, of the fashionable chaise and four—postilions handsomely liveried, rising so regularly in their stirrups, and numerous outriders properly mounted, sunk a little under this consequent inconvenience. Had their party been perfectly agreeable, the delay would have been nothing; but General Tilney, though so charming a man, seemed always a check upon his children's spirits, and scarcely anything was said but by himself; the observation of which, with his discontent at whatever the inn afforded, and his angry impatience at the waiters, made Catherine grow every moment more in awe of him, and appeared to lengthen the two hours into four. At last, however, the order of release was given; and much was Catherine then surprised by the general's proposal of her taking his place in his son's curricle for the rest of the journey: "the day was fine, and he was anxious for her seeing as much of the country as possible."

The remembrance of Mr. Allen's opinion, respecting young men's open carriages, made her blush at the mention of such a plan, and her first thought was to decline it; but her second was of greater deference for General Tilney's judgment; he could not propose anything improper for her; and, in the course of a few minutes, she found herself with Henry in the curricle, as happy a being as ever existed. A very short trial convinced her that a curricle was the prettiest equipage in the world; the chaise and four wheeled off with some grandeur, to be sure, but it was a heavy and troublesome business, and she could not easily forget its having stopped two hours at Petty France. Half the time would have been enough for the curricle, and so nimbly were the light horses disposed to move, that, had not the general chosen to have his own carriage lead the way, they could have passed it with ease in half a minute. But the merit of the curricle did not all belong to the horses; Henry drove so well—so quietly—without making any disturbance, without parading to her, or swearing at them: so different from the only gentleman-coachman whom it was in her power to compare him with! And then his hat sat so well, and the innumerable capes of his greatcoat looked so becomingly important! To be driven by him, next to being dancing with him, was certainly the greatest happiness in the world. In addition to every other delight, she had now that of listening to her own praise; of being thanked at least, on his sister's account, for her kindness in thus becoming her visitor; of hearing it ranked as real friendship, and described as creating real gratitude. His sister, he said, was uncomfortably circumstanced—she had no female companion—and, in the frequent absence of her father, was sometimes without any companion at all.

"But how can that be?" said Catherine. "Are not you with her?"

"Northanger is not more than half my home; I have an establishment at my own house in Woodston, which is nearly twenty miles from my father's, and some of my time is necessarily spent there."

"How sorry you must be for that!"

"I am always sorry to leave Eleanor."

"Yes; but besides your affection for her, you must be so fond of the abbey! After being used to such a home as the abbey, an ordinary parsonage-house must be very disagreeable."

He smiled, and said, "You have formed a very favourable idea of the abbey."

"To be sure, I have. Is not it a fine old place, just like what one reads about?"

"And are you prepared to encounter all the horrors that a building such as 'what one reads about' may produce? Have you a stout heart? Nerves fit for sliding panels and tapestry?"

"Oh! yes—I do not think I should be easily frightened, because there would be so many people in the house—and besides, it has never been uninhabited and left deserted for years, and then the family come back to it unawares, without giving any notice, as generally happens."

"No, certainly. We shall not have to explore our way into a hall dimly lighted by the expiring embers of a wood fire—nor be obliged to spread our beds on the floor of a room without windows, doors, or furniture. But you must be aware that when a young lady is (by whatever means) introduced into a dwelling of this kind, she is always lodged apart from the rest of the family. While they snugly repair to their own end of the house, she is formally conducted by Dorothy, the ancient housekeeper, up a different staircase, and along many gloomy passages, into an apartment never used since some cousin or kin died in it about twenty years before. Can you stand such a ceremony as this? Will not your mind misgive you when you find yourself in this gloomy chamber—too lofty and extensive for you, with only the feeble rays of a single lamp to take in its size—its walls hung with tapestry exhibiting figures as large as life, and the bed, of dark green stuff or purple velvet, presenting even a funereal appearance? Will not your heart sink within you?"

"Oh! But this will not happen to me, I am sure."

"How fearfully will you examine the furniture of your apartment! And what will you discern? Not tables, toilettes, wardrobes, or drawers, but on one side perhaps the remains of a broken lute, on the other a ponderous chest which no efforts can open, and over the fireplace the portrait of some handsome warrior, whose features will so incomprehensibly strike you, that you will not be able to withdraw your eyes from it. Dorothy, meanwhile, no less struck by your appearance, gazes on you in great agitation, and drops a few unintelligible hints. To raise your spirits, moreover, she gives you reason to suppose that the part of the abbey you inhabit is undoubtedly haunted, and informs you that you will not have a single domestic within call. With this parting cordial she curtsies off—you listen to the sound of her receding footsteps as long as the last echo can reach you—and when, with fainting spirits, you attempt to fasten your door, you discover, with increased alarm, that it has no lock."

"Oh! Mr. Tilney, how frightful! This is just like a book! But it cannot really happen to me. I am sure your housekeeper is not really Dorothy. Well, what then?"

"Nothing further to alarm perhaps may occur the first night. After surmounting your unconquerable horror of the bed, you will retire to rest, and get a few hours' unquiet slumber. But on the second, or at farthest the third night after your arrival, you will probably have a violent storm. Peals of thunder so loud as to seem to shake the edifice to its foundation will roll round the neighbouring mountains—and during the frightful gusts of wind which accompany it, you will probably think you discern (for your lamp is not extinguished) one part of the hanging more violently agitated than the rest. Unable of course to repress your curiosity in so favourable a moment for indulging it, you will instantly arise, and throwing your dressing-gown around you, proceed to examine this mystery. After a very short search, you will discover a division in the tapestry so artfully constructed as to defy the minutest inspection, and on opening it, a door will immediately appear—which door, being only secured by massy bars and a pad-lock, you will, after a few efforts, succeed in opening—and, with your lamp in your hand, will pass through it into a small vaulted room."

"No, indeed; I should be too much frightened to do any such thing."

"What! Not when Dorothy has given you to understand that there is a secret subterraneous communication between your apartment and the chapel of St. Anthony, scarcely two miles off? Could you shrink from so simple an adventure? No, no, you will proceed into this small vaulted room, and through this into several others, without perceiving anything very remarkable in either. In one perhaps there may be a dagger, in another a few drops of blood, and in a third the remains of some instrument of torture; but there being nothing in all this out of the common way, and your lamp being nearly exhausted, you will return towards your own apartment. In repassing through the small vaulted room, however, your eyes will be attracted towards a large, old-fashioned cabinet of ebony and gold, which, though narrowly examining the furniture before, you had passed unnoticed. Impelled by an irresistible presentiment, you will eagerly advance to it, unlock its folding doors, and search into every drawer—but for some time without discovering anything of importance—perhaps nothing but a considerable hoard of diamonds. At last, however, by touching a secret spring, an inner compartment will open—a roll of paper appears—you seize it—it contains many sheets of manuscript—you hasten with the precious treasure into your own chamber, but scarcely have you been able to decipher 'Oh! Thou—whomsoever thou mayst be, into whose hands these memoirs of the wretched Matilda may fall'—when your lamp suddenly expires in the socket, and leaves you in total darkness."

"Oh! No, no—do not say so. Well, go on."

But Henry was too much amused by the interest he had raised to be able to carry it farther; he could no longer command solemnity either of subject or voice, and was obliged to entreat her to use her own fancy in the perusal of Matilda's woes. Catherine, recollecting herself, grew ashamed of her eagerness, and began earnestly to assure him that her attention had been fixed without the smallest apprehension of really meeting with what he related. "Miss Tilney, she was sure, would never put her into such a chamber as he had described! She was not at all afraid."

As they drew near the end of their journey, her impatience for a sight of the abbey—for some time suspended by his conversation on subjects very different—returned in full force, and every bend in the road was expected with solemn awe to afford a glimpse of its massy walls of grey stone, rising amidst a grove of ancient oaks, with the last beams of the sun playing in beautiful splendour on its high Gothic windows. But so low did the building stand, that she found herself passing through the great gates of the lodge into the very grounds of Northanger, without having discerned even an antique chimney.

She knew not that she had any right to be surprised, but there was a something in this mode of approach which she certainly had not expected. To pass between lodges of a modern appearance, to find herself with such ease in the very precincts of the abbey, and driven so rapidly along a smooth, level road of fine gravel, without obstacle, alarm, or solemnity of any kind, struck her as odd and inconsistent. She was not long at leisure, however, for such considerations. A sudden scud of rain, driving full in her face, made it impossible for her to observe anything further, and fixed all her thoughts on the welfare of her new straw bonnet; and she was actually under the abbey walls, was springing, with Henry's assistance, from the carriage, was beneath the shelter of the old porch, and had even passed on to the hall, where her friend and the general were waiting to welcome her, without feeling one awful foreboding of future misery to herself, or one moment's suspicion of any past scenes of horror being acted within the solemn edifice. The breeze had not seemed to waft the sighs of the murdered to her; it had wafted nothing worse than a thick mizzling rain; and having given a good shake to her habit, she was ready to be shown into the common drawing-room, and capable of considering where she was.

An abbey! Yes, it was delightful to be really in an abbey! But she doubted, as she looked round the room, whether anything within her observation would have given her the consciousness. The furniture was in all the profusion and elegance of modern taste. The fireplace, where she had expected the ample width and ponderous carving of former times, was contracted to a Rumford, with slabs of plain though handsome marble, and ornaments over it of the prettiest English china. The windows, to which she looked with peculiar dependence, from having heard the general talk of his preserving them in their Gothic form with reverential care, were yet less what her fancy had portrayed. To be sure, the pointed arch was preserved—the form of them was Gothic—they might be even casements—but every pane was so large, so clear, so light! To an imagination which had hoped for the smallest divisions, and the heaviest stone-work, for painted glass, dirt, and cobwebs, the difference was very distressing.

The general, perceiving how her eye was employed, began to talk of the smallness of the room and simplicity of the furniture, where everything, being for daily use, pretended only to comfort, etc.; flattering himself, however, that there were some apartments in the Abbey not unworthy her notice—and was proceeding to mention the costly gilding of one in particular, when, taking out his watch, he stopped short to pronounce it with surprise within twenty minutes of five! This seemed the word of separation, and Catherine found herself hurried away by Miss Tilney in such a manner as convinced her that the strictest punctuality to the family hours would be expected at Northanger.

Returning through the large and lofty hall, they ascended a broad staircase of shining oak, which, after many flights and many landing-places, brought them upon a long, wide gallery. On one side it had a range of doors, and it was lighted on the other by windows which Catherine had only time to discover looked into a quadrangle, before Miss Tilney led the way into a chamber, and scarcely staying to hope she would find it comfortable, left her with an anxious entreaty that she would make as little alteration as possible in her dress.

CHAPTER
Thirty-Six

A MOMENT'S GLANCE was enough to satisfy Catherine that her apartment was very unlike the one which Henry had endeavoured to alarm her by the description of. It was by no means unreasonably large, and contained neither tapestry nor velvet. The walls were papered, the floor was carpeted; the windows were neither less perfect nor more dim than those of the drawing-room below; the furniture, though not of the latest fashion, was handsome and comfortable, and the air of the room altogether far from uncheerful. Her heart instantaneously at ease on this point, she resolved to lose no time in particular examination of anything, as she greatly dreaded disobliging the general by any delay. Her habit therefore was thrown off with all possible haste, and she was preparing to unpin the linen package, which the chaise-seat had conveyed for her immediate accommodation, when her eye suddenly fell on a large high chest, standing back in a deep recess on one side of the fireplace. The sight of it made her start; and, forgetting everything else, she stood gazing on it in motionless wonder, while these thoughts crossed her:

"This is strange indeed! I did not expect such a sight as this! An immense heavy chest! What can it hold? Why should it be placed here? Pushed back too, as if meant to be out of sight! I will look into it—cost me what it may, I will look into it—and directly too—by daylight. If I stay till evening my candle may go out." She advanced and examined it closely: it was of cedar, curiously inlaid with some darker wood, and raised, about a foot from the ground, on a carved stand of the same. The lock was silver, though tarnished from age; at each end were the imperfect remains of handles also of silver, broken perhaps prematurely by some strange violence; and, on the centre of the lid, was a mysterious cipher, in the same metal. Catherine bent over it intently, but without being able to distinguish anything with certainty. She could not, in whatever direction she took it, believe the last letter to be a T; and yet that it should be anything else in that house was a circumstance to raise no common degree of astonishment. If not originally theirs, by what strange events could it have fallen into the Tilney family?

Her fearful curiosity was every moment growing greater; and seizing, with trembling hands, the hasp of the lock, she resolved at all hazards to satisfy herself at least as to its contents. With difficulty, for something seemed to resist her efforts, she raised the lid a few inches; but at that moment a sudden knocking at the door of the room made her, starting, quit her hold, and the lid closed with alarming violence. This ill-timed intruder was Miss Tilney's maid, sent by her mistress to be of use to Miss Morland; and though Catherine immediately dismissed her, it recalled her to the sense of what she ought to be doing, and forced her, in spite of her anxious desire to penetrate this mystery, to proceed in her dressing without further delay. Her progress was not quick, for her thoughts and her eyes were still bent on the object so well calculated to interest and alarm; and though she dared not waste a moment upon a second attempt, she could not remain many paces from the chest. At length, however, having slipped one arm into her gown, her toilette seemed so nearly finished that the impatience of her curiosity might safely be indulged. One moment surely might be spared; and, so desperate should be the exertion of her strength, that, unless secured by supernatural means, the lid in one moment should be thrown back. With this spirit she sprang forward, and her confidence did not deceive her. Her resolute effort threw back the lid, and gave to her astonished eyes the view of a white cotton counterpane, properly folded, reposing at one end of the chest in undisputed possession!

She was gazing on it with the first blush of surprise when Miss Tilney, anxious for her friend's being ready, entered the room, and to the rising shame of having harboured for some minutes an absurd expectation, was then added the shame of being caught in so idle a search. "That is a curious old chest, is not it?" said Miss Tilney, as Catherine hastily closed it and turned away to the glass. "It is impossible to say how many generations it has been here. How it came to be first put in this room I know not, but I have not had it moved, because I thought it might sometimes be of use in holding hats and bonnets. The worst of it is that its weight makes it difficult to open. In that corner, however, it is at least out of the way."

Catherine had no leisure for speech, being at once blushing, tying her gown, and forming wise resolutions with the most violent dispatch. Miss Tilney gently hinted her fear of being late; and in half a minute they ran downstairs together, in an alarm not wholly unfounded, for General Tilney was pacing the drawing-room, his watch in his hand, and having, on the very instant of their entering, pulled the bell with violence, ordered "Dinner to be on table directly!"

Catherine trembled at the emphasis with which he spoke, and sat pale and breathless, in a most humble mood, concerned for his children, and detesting old chests; and the general, recovering his politeness as he looked at her, spent the rest of his time in scolding his daughter for so foolishly hurrying her fair friend, who was absolutely out of breath from haste, when there was not the least occasion for hurry in the world: but Catherine could not at all get over the double distress of having involved her friend in a lecture and been a great simpleton herself, till they were happily seated at the dinner-table, when the general's complacent smiles, and a good appetite of her own, restored her to peace. The dining-parlour was a noble room, suitable in its dimensions to a much larger drawing-room than the one in common use, and fitted up in a style of luxury and expense which was almost lost on the unpractised eye of Catherine, who saw little more than its spaciousness and the number of their attendants. Of the former, she spoke aloud her admiration; and the general, with a very gracious countenance, acknowledged that it was by no means an ill-sized room, and further confessed that, though as careless on such subjects as most people, he did look upon a tolerably large eating-room as one of the necessaries of life; he supposed, however, "that she must have been used to much better-sized apartments at Mr. Allen's?"

"No, indeed," was Catherine's honest assurance; "Mr. Allen's dining-parlour was not more than half as large," and she had never seen so large a room as this in her life. The general's good humour increased. Why, as he had such rooms, he thought it would be simple not to make use of them; but, upon his honour, he believed there might be more comfort in rooms of only half their size. Mr. Allen's house, he was sure, must be exactly of the true size for rational happiness.

The evening passed without any further disturbance, and, in the occasional absence of General Tilney, with much positive cheerfulness. It was only in his presence that Catherine felt the smallest fatigue from her journey; and even then, even in moments of languor or restraint, a sense of general happiness preponderated, and she could think of her friends in Bath without one wish of being with them.

The night was stormy; the wind had been rising at intervals the whole afternoon; and by the time the party broke up, it blew and rained violently. Catherine, as she crossed the hall, listened to the tempest with sensations of awe; and, when she heard it rage round a corner of the ancient building and close with sudden fury a distant door, felt for the first time that she was really in an abbey. Yes, these were characteristic sounds; they brought to her recollection a countless variety of dreadful situations and horrid scenes, which such buildings had witnessed, and such storms ushered in; and most heartily did she rejoice in the happier circumstances attending her entrance within walls so solemn! She had nothing to dread from midnight assassins or drunken gallants. Henry had certainly been only in jest in what he had told her that morning. In a house so furnished, and so guarded, she could have nothing to explore or to suffer, and might go to her bedroom as securely as if it had been her own chamber at Fullerton. Thus wisely fortifying her mind, as she proceeded upstairs, she was enabled, especially on perceiving that Miss Tilney slept only two doors from her, to enter her room with a tolerably stout heart; and her spirits were immediately assisted by the cheerful blaze of a wood fire. "How much better is this," said she, as she walked to the fender—"how much better to find a fire ready lit, than to have to wait shivering in the cold till all the family are in bed, as so many poor girls have been obliged to do, and then to have a faithful old servant frightening one by coming in with a faggot! How glad I am that Northanger is what it is! If it had been like some other places, I do not know that, in such a night as this, I could have answered for my courage: but now, to be sure, there is nothing to alarm one."

She looked round the room. The window curtains seemed in motion. It could be nothing but the violence of the wind penetrating through the divisions of the shutters; and she stepped boldly forward, carelessly humming a tune, to assure herself of its being so, peeped courageously behind each curtain, saw nothing on either low window seat to scare her, and on placing a hand against the shutter, felt the strongest conviction of the wind's force. A glance at the old chest, as she turned away from this examination, was not without its use; she scorned the causeless fears of an idle fancy, and began with a most happy indifference to prepare herself for bed. "She should take her time; she should not hurry herself; she did not care if she were the last person up in the house. But she would not make up her fire; that would seem cowardly, as if she wished for the protection of light after she were in bed." The fire therefore died away, and Catherine, having spent the best part of an hour in her arrangements, was beginning to think of stepping into bed, when, on giving a parting glance round the room, she was struck by the appearance of a high, old-fashioned black cabinet, which, though in a situation conspicuous enough, had never caught her notice before. Henry's words, his description of the ebony cabinet which was to escape her observation at first, immediately rushed across her; and though there could be nothing really in it, there was something whimsical, it was certainly a very remarkable coincidence! She took her candle and looked closely at the cabinet. It was not absolutely ebony and gold; but it was japan, black and yellow japan of the handsomest kind; and as she held her candle, the yellow had very much the effect of gold. The key was in the door, and she had a strange fancy to look into it; not, however, with the smallest expectation of finding anything, but it was so very odd, after what Henry had said. In short, she could not sleep till she had examined it. So, placing the candle with great caution on a chair, she seized the key with a very tremulous hand and tried to turn it; but it resisted her utmost strength. Alarmed, but not discouraged, she tried it another way; a bolt flew, and she believed herself successful; but how strangely mysterious! The door was still immovable. She paused a moment in breathless wonder. The wind roared down the chimney, the rain beat in torrents against the windows, and everything seemed to speak the awfulness of her situation. To retire to bed, however, unsatisfied on such a point, would be vain, since sleep must be impossible with the consciousness of a cabinet so mysteriously closed in her immediate vicinity. Again, therefore, she applied herself to the key, and after moving it in every possible way for some instants with the determined celerity of hope's last effort, the door suddenly yielded to her hand: her heart leaped with exultation at such a victory, and having thrown open each folding door, the second being secured only by bolts of less wonderful construction than the lock, though in that her eye could not discern anything unusual, a double range of small drawers appeared in view, with some larger drawers above and below them; and in the centre, a small door, closed also with a lock and key, secured in all probability a cavity of importance.

Catherine's heart beat quick, but her courage did not fail her. With a cheek flushed by hope, and an eye straining with curiosity, her fingers grasped the handle of a drawer and drew it forth. It was entirely empty. With less alarm and greater eagerness she seized a second, a third, a fourth; each was equally empty. Not one was left unsearched, and in not one was anything found. Well read in the art of concealing a treasure, the possibility of false linings to the drawers did not escape her, and she felt round each with anxious acuteness in vain. The place in the middle alone remained now unexplored; and though she had "never from the first had the smallest idea of finding anything in any part of the cabinet, and was not in the least disappointed at her ill success thus far, it would be foolish not to examine it thoroughly while she was about it." It was some time however before she could unfasten the door, the same difficulty occurring in the management of this inner lock as of the outer; but at length it did open; and not vain, as hitherto, was her search; her quick eyes directly fell on a roll of paper pushed back into the further part of the cavity, apparently for concealment, and her feelings at that moment were indescribable. Her heart fluttered, her knees trembled, and her cheeks grew pale. She seized, with an unsteady hand, the precious manuscript, for half a glance sufficed to ascertain written characters; and while she acknowledged with awful sensations this striking exemplification of what Henry had foretold, resolved instantly to peruse every line before she attempted to rest.

The dimness of the light her candle emitted made her turn to it with alarm; but there was no danger of its sudden extinction; it had yet some hours to burn; and that she might not have any greater difficulty in distinguishing the writing than what its ancient date might occasion, she hastily snuffed it. Alas! It was snuffed and extinguished in one. A lamp could not have expired with more awful effect. Catherine, for a few moments, was motionless with horror. It was done completely; not a remnant of light in the wick could give hope to the rekindling breath. Darkness impenetrable and immovable filled the room. A violent gust of wind, rising with sudden fury, added fresh horror to the moment. Catherine trembled from head to foot. In the pause which succeeded, a sound like receding footsteps and the closing of a distant door struck on her affrighted ear. Human nature could support no more. A cold sweat stood on her forehead, the manuscript fell from her hand, and groping her way to the bed, she jumped hastily in, and sought some suspension of agony by creeping far underneath the clothes. To close her eyes in sleep that night, she felt must be entirely out of the question. With a curiosity so justly awakened, and feelings in every way so agitated, repose must be absolutely impossible. The storm too abroad so dreadful! She had not been used to feel alarm from wind, but now every blast seemed fraught with awful intelligence. The manuscript so wonderfully found, so wonderfully accomplishing the morning's prediction, how was it to be accounted for? What could it contain? To whom could it relate? By what means could it have been so long concealed? And how singularly strange that it should fall to her lot to discover it! Till she had made herself mistress of its contents, however, she could have neither repose nor comfort; and with the sun's first rays she was determined to peruse it. But many were the tedious hours which must yet intervene. She shuddered, tossed about in her bed, and envied every quiet sleeper. The storm still raged, and various were the noises, more terrific even than the wind, which struck at intervals on her startled ear. The very curtains of her bed seemed at one moment in motion, and at another the lock of her door was agitated, as if by the attempt of somebody to enter. Hollow murmurs seemed to creep along the gallery, and more than once her blood was chilled by the sound of distant moans. Hour after hour passed away, and the wearied Catherine had heard three proclaimed by all the clocks in the house before the tempest subsided or she unknowingly fell fast asleep.

CHAPTER
Thirty-Seven

IT MIGHT BE SURMISED from the previous account that only Catherine felt all the distress brought about by the storm, with its reverberations against her window, while the rest of the household fell into an easy sleep. This would be a falsehood, as she was kept company in her wakefulness by the rest of the Tilneys, albeit each in their separate quarters, and left to their particular affairs. None sought her out, and she was never the wiser to their dispositions in relation to the violent climate, but this single point kept them all unified in their solitude.

Eleanor was unable to sleep because of the fury of the rain. This was not a new occurrence, as she had been a victim of such events since her youth. Rainstorms terrified her, always had. Even in her youth, that nervousness could not be lessened by her mother's comfort. This reaction was hardly out of the ordinary; a child's mind could be a sea of imagined terrible figures that moved about in the night, unspoken things hiding inside the closet and under the bed, fairy worlds that might exist alongside ours, and fantastic creatures who called the distant woods their home, venturing out only when they could move about unseen. For such an imagination, the brilliant flashes of lightning and intense thunder rumblings became an extension of those ideas. Demons of all sorts might travel on the winds of the storm, delivered to that very window of a child huddled in under the covers of their bed. Fear acted as a constant bedmate for the unnerved boy or girl during these times.

So it was with Eleanor, and it would be easy to dispel such a reaction in her youth as that of the normal childish mind, but her feelings were due to other experiences related indirectly to the nighttime rains. If asked, she would be unable to explain the specifics, so intangible were her feelings, as were her memories of those times, but she could tell you how, upon more than one occasion, she thought she heard additional noises within the storm. What it might be, she could also offer no explanation, but it had reminded her of the sounds of frogs, as if a multitude of the creatures formed an orchestra, and it was this cacophony that would underlie the pounding of the rain. On one occasion, she was able to muster up the courage to rise from her bed and look out the window, but all she could see was the torrential rain, with the background lit only in brief flashes from the lightning, and even that revealed nothing.

If she were to mention the sounds to those around her who might have heard the same from their rooms, the notion was quickly scoffed at; neither father, brother, servants nor attendants claimed to have heard anything, so surely it must have been purely her imagination. Even her mother, always so comforting, paused but a moment before reassuring her that there was nothing out there. Eleanor grew into adulthood, having remembered all this, and even with the knowledge that the rain was just that, nothing more, there was still something that kept her from resting easily, till the skies calmed down and the rain ceased to fall.

Her brother, Henry, told her there was nothing to the storm. In his heart, he believed this, and had endured many a rainy night in his room as his window rattled from its wrath, sleeping comfortably in ignorance of the sound. He gave it little mind, secure in the rationale of weather conditions and their function. For him, it was an event as natural as the growth of the grass, the movement of the ocean, or the change in days from overcast to a bright blue sky. Even so—and he would never admit it, even to himself—a torrential storm could still cause an unexplainable shiver to rise upon his spine.

On this particular night, Eleanor was wide awake, hoping against hope for a calm to the weather so that she might sleep. In his room, Henry was likewise alert, reclined in his chair with a book in hand, and positioned near a candle so as not to strain his eyes. It was a fascinating volume, one that he had been working on, and was eager to finish. Why he had not given up to sleep was nothing more than an active mind, so he chose to read until a time that he would grow tired. Then he would retire.

He also considered their guest with the hope that she was comfortable in her room. More than anything, he realized that it was her presence, more than anything, that kept him awake. Despite the distractions, be it the storm with its torrential rains and loud claps of thunder, or the book he tried to focus on, in the end, Catherine dominated his thoughts.

Sleep proved to be an elusive element for these three, all with their reasons for not succumbing to the realm of dreams. The common element that they all shared was that of discomfort against the night. As much as they wished, sleep would not come, and no degree of effort to bring it on was of any use.

This was not the case with General Tilney, who likewise remained awake and quite comfortable in his private library, deep in thought as he hovered over an oversized book, with a goblet of wine at his side along with the associated half-filled bottle. He enjoyed the night. For him, this was a private time, when he could be attentive to his concerns without any worries about being disturbed. He treated this room as a sanctuary, strictly barred from everyone else, secure that if his time spent here fell to distraction, it was his fault alone, as the blame could not be set on any visitor.

Even the rage of the weather outside served no cause of unease. On the contrary, he found the intensity of the rain to be an aid to his focus, the steady patter against the panes of the small window serving as a comfort. The room was well-lit by numerous candles, giving him ample light to indulge in his interests. Here, he paused, extended his arms to stretch his muscles, and gave up an inadvertent yawn. No, he was not tired yet, but soon, and then he would retire for the night.

There was another flash outside, lightning crossing the sky, then gone as quickly as it had appeared. Seconds later, its brother sound rumbled. The general looked up and considered the burst of light, just as another flash erupted. Such power, he thought, such unequaled power of the elements. Only if man had the ability to harness for his desires all that beyond his understanding.

CHAPTER

Thirty-Eight

THE HOUSEMAID'S FOLDING back her window-shutters at eight o'clock the next day was the sound which first roused Catherine; and she opened her eyes, wondering that they could ever have been closed, on objects of cheerfulness; her fire was already burning, and a bright morning had succeeded the tempest of the night. Instantaneously, with the consciousness of existence, returned her recollection of the manuscript; and springing from the bed in the very moment of the maid's going away, she eagerly collected every scattered sheet which had burst from the roll on its falling to the ground, and flew back to enjoy the luxury of their perusal on her pillow. She now plainly saw that she must not expect a manuscript of equal length with the generality of what she had shuddered over in books, for the roll, seeming to consist entirely of small disjointed sheets, was altogether but of trifling size, and much less than she had supposed it to be at first.

Her greedy eye glanced rapidly over a page. She started at its import. Could it be possible, or did not her senses play her false? An inventory of linen, in coarse and modern characters, seemed all that was before her! If the evidence of sight might be trusted, she held a washing-bill in her hand. She seized another sheet, and saw the same articles with little variation; a third, a fourth, and a fifth presented nothing new. Shirts, stockings, cravats, and waistcoats faced her in each. Two others, penned by the same hand, marked an expenditure scarcely more interesting, in letters, hair-powder, shoe-string, and breeches-ball. And the larger sheet, which had enclosed the rest, seemed by its first cramp line, "To poultice chestnut mare"—a farrier's bill! Such was the collection of papers (left perhaps, as she could then suppose, by the negligence of a servant in the place whence she had taken them) which had filled her with expectation and alarm, and robbed her of half her night's rest! She felt humbled to the dust. Could not the adventure of the chest have taught her wisdom? A corner of it, catching her eye as she lay, seemed to rise up in judgment against her. Nothing could now be clearer than the absurdity of her recent fancies. To suppose that a manuscript of many generations back could have remained undiscovered in a room such as that, so modern, so habitable!—Or that she should be the first to possess the skill of unlocking a cabinet, the key of which was open to all!

How could she have so imposed on herself? Heaven forbid that Henry Tilney should ever know her folly! And it was in a great measure his own doing, for had not the cabinet appeared so exactly to agree with his description of her adventures, she should never have felt the smallest curiosity about it. This was the only comfort that occurred. Impatient to get rid of those hateful evidences of her folly, those detestable papers then scattered over the bed, she rose directly, and folding them up as nearly as possible in the same shape as before, returned them to the same spot within the cabinet, with a very hearty wish that no untoward accident might ever bring them forward again, to disgrace her even with herself.

Why the locks should have been so difficult to open, however, was still something remarkable, for she could now manage them with perfect ease. In this there was surely something mysterious, and she indulged in the flattering suggestion for half a minute, till the possibility of the door's having been at first unlocked, and of being herself its fastener, darted into her head, and cost her another blush.

She got away as soon as she could from a room in which her conduct produced such unpleasant reflections, and found her way with all speed to the breakfast-parlour, as it had been pointed out to her by Miss Tilney the evening before. Henry was alone in it; and his immediate hope of her having been undisturbed by the tempest, with an arch reference to the character of the building they inhabited, was rather distressing. For the world would she not have her weakness suspected, and yet, unequal to an absolute falsehood, was constrained to acknowledge that the wind had kept her awake a little. "But we have a charming morning after it," she added, desiring to get rid of the subject; "and storms and sleeplessness are nothing when they are over. What beautiful hyacinths! I have just learnt to love a hyacinth."

"And how might you learn? By accident or argument?"

"Your sister taught me; I cannot tell how. Mrs. Allen used to take pains, year after year, to make me like them; but I never could, till I saw them the other day in Milsom Street; I am naturally indifferent about flowers."

"But now you love a hyacinth. So much the better. You have gained a new source of enjoyment, and it is well to have as many holds upon happiness as possible. Besides, a taste for flowers is always desirable in your sex, as a means of getting you out of doors, and tempting you to more frequent exercise than you would otherwise take. And though the love of a hyacinth may be rather domestic, who can tell, the sentiment once raised, but you may in time come to love a rose?"

"But I do not want any such pursuit to get me out of doors. The pleasure of walking and breathing fresh air is enough for me, and in fine weather I am out more than half my time. Mamma says I am never within."

"All the better for you. My father—" he began, and at this, his voice took on a less lighthearted tone, "as no doubt you will find, has his affection for a garden, although I think it more to do with a sense of order and status. His are very clean, and everything is in their place. Roses stand at attention. Perennials are in their quartered division. Shrubs and climbers all know their position. Even the lowly weeds know where to stand."

"It is good to enjoy a garden."

"The garden is one of his particular likes, which are as pronounced as his dislikes. He is particularly keen on history, as you might imagine, and has often dragged the family off to particular sites of some obscure significance: The flattened hill of Uley Bury, the burrow in Notgrove, battle sites in Tewkesbury and Stow on the Wold. More than once, we have ended up at Belas Knap—it looks much like an overgrown mound of earth with some ancient stones—but for him, it is a place of particular interest. This is one of the things he seems to share with my brother, this fascination with the old. Even I, with my interest in portraiture, have yet to find the beauty in the place. It still looks like a mound of dirt."

"Perhaps the weeds that grow there are to his favor?"

Henry laughed at her jest, and she, realizing that she had inadvertently found humour at another's expense, particularly one who had been so kind to her, attempted to find some words of apology. He found her response even more amusing, but gently reassured her that no offence was taken.

"At any rate, however, I am pleased that you have learnt to love a hyacinth. The mere habit of learning to love is the thing; and a teachableness of disposition in a young lady is a great blessing. Has my sister a pleasant mode of instruction?"

Catherine was saved the embarrassment of attempting an answer by the entrance of the general, whose smiling compliments announced a happy state of mind, but whose gentle hint of sympathetic early rising did not advance her composure. He was again most complimentary to her attire, paying special attention to the pattern and weave of the fabric, and clearly demonstrating an appreciation and understanding of well-made clothing.

The elegance of the breakfast set forced itself on Catherine's notice when they were seated at table; and, lucidly, it had been the general's choice. He was enchanted by her approbation of his taste, confessed it to be neat and simple, thought it right to encourage the manufacture of his country; and for his part, to his uncritical palate, the tea was as well flavoured from the clay of Staffordshire, as from that of Dresden or Save. But this was quite an old set, purchased two years ago. The manufacture was much improved since that time; he had seen some beautiful specimens when last in town, and had he not been perfectly without vanity of that kind, might have been tempted to order a new set. He trusted, however, that an opportunity might ere long occur of selecting one—though not for himself. Catherine was probably the only one of the party who did not understand him.

Shortly after breakfast Henry left them for Woodston, where business required and would keep him two or three days. They all attended in the hall to see him mount his horse, and immediately on re-entering the breakfast-room, Catherine walked to a window in the hope of catching another glimpse of his figure. "This is a somewhat heavy call upon your brother's fortitude," observed the general to Eleanor. "Woodston will make but a sombre appearance today."

"Is it a pretty place?" asked Catherine.

"What say you, Eleanor? Speak your opinion, for ladies can best tell the taste of ladies in regard to places as well as men. I think it would be acknowledged by the most impartial eye to have many recommendations. The house stands among fine meadows facing the south-east, with an excellent kitchen-garden in the same aspect; the walls surrounding which I built and stocked myself about ten years ago, for the benefit of my son. It is a family living, Miss Morland; and the property in the place being chiefly my own, you may believe I take care that it shall not be a bad one. Did Henry's income depend solely on this living, he would not be ill-provided for. Perhaps it may seem odd, that with only two younger children, I should think any profession necessary for him; and certainly there are moments when we could all wish him disengaged from every tie of business. But though I may not exactly make converts of you young ladies, I am sure your father, Miss Morland, would agree with me in thinking it expedient to give every young man some employment. The money is nothing, it is not an object, but employment is the thing. Even Frederick, my eldest son, you see, who will perhaps inherit as considerable a landed property as any private man in the county, has his profession."

The imposing effect of this last argument was equal to his wishes. The silence of the lady proved it to be unanswerable.

Something had been said the evening before of her being shown over the house, and he now offered himself as her conductor; and though Catherine had hoped to explore it accompanied only by his daughter, it was a proposal of too much happiness in itself, under any circumstances, not to be gladly accepted; for she had been already eighteen hours in the abbey, and had seen only a few of its rooms. The netting-box, just leisurely drawn forth, was closed with joyful haste, and she was ready to attend him in a moment. "And when they had gone over the house, he promised himself moreover the pleasure of accompanying her into the shrubberies and garden." She curtsied her acquiescence. "But perhaps it might be more agreeable to her to make those her first object. The weather was at present favourable, and at this time of year the uncertainty was very great of its continuing so. Which would she prefer? He was equally at her service. Which did his daughter think would most accord with her fair friend's wishes? But he thought he could discern. Yes, he certainly read in Miss Morland's eyes a judicious desire of making use of the present smiling weather. But when did she judge amiss? The abbey would be always safe and dry. He yielded implicitly, and would fetch his hat and attend them in a moment. He left the room, and Catherine, with a disappointed, anxious face, began to speak of her unwillingness that he should be taking them out of doors against his own inclination, under a mistaken idea of pleasing her; but she was stopped by Miss Tilney's saying, with a little confusion, "I believe it will be wisest to take the morning while it is so fine; and do not be uneasy on my father's account; he always walks out at this time of day."

Catherine did not exactly know how this was to be understood. Why was Miss Tilney embarrassed? Could there be any unwillingness on the general's side to show her over the abbey? The proposal was his own. And was not it odd that he should always take his walk so early? Neither her father nor Mr. Allen did so. It was certainly very provoking. She was all impatience to see the house, and had scarcely any curiosity about the grounds. If Henry had been with them indeed! But now she should not know what was picturesque when she saw it. Such were her thoughts, but she kept them to herself, and put on her bonnet in patient discontent.

She was struck, however, beyond her expectation, by the grandeur of the abbey, as she saw it for the first time from the lawn. The whole building enclosed a large court; and two sides of the quadrangle, rich in Gothic ornaments, stood forward for admiration. The remainder was shut off by knolls of old trees, or luxuriant plantations, and the steep woody hills rising behind, to give it shelter, were beautiful even in the leafless month of March. Catherine had seen nothing to compare with it; and her feelings of delight were so strong, that without waiting for any better authority, she boldly burst forth in wonder and praise. The general listened with assenting gratitude; and it seemed as if his own estimation of Northanger had waited unfixed till that hour.

The kitchen-garden was to be next admired, and he led the way to it across a small portion of the park.

The number of acres contained in this garden was such as Catherine could not listen to without dismay, being more than double the extent of all Mr. Allen's, as well her father's, including church-yard and orchard. The walls seemed countless in number, endless in length; a village of hot-houses seemed to arise among them, and a whole parish to be at work within the enclosure. The general was flattered by her looks of surprise, which told him almost as plainly, as he soon forced her to tell him in words, that she had never seen any gardens at all equal to them before; and he then modestly owned that, "without any ambition of that sort himself—without any solicitude about it—he did believe them to be unrivalled in the kingdom. If he had a hobby-horse, it was that. He loved a garden. Though careless enough in most matters of eating, he loved good fruit—or if he did not, his friends and children did. There were great vexations, however, attending such a garden as his. The utmost care could not always secure the most valuable fruits. The pinery had yielded only one hundred in the last year. Mr. Allen, he supposed, must feel these inconveniences as well as himself."

"No, not at all. Mr. Allen did not care about the garden, and never went into it."

With a triumphant smile of self-satisfaction, the general wished he could do the same, for he never entered his, without being vexed in some way or other, by its falling short of his plan.

"How were Mr. Allen's succession-houses worked?" describing the nature of his own as they entered them.

"Mr. Allen had only one small hot-house, which Mrs. Allen had the use of for her plants in winter, and there was a fire in it now and then."

"He is a happy man!" said the general, with a look of very happy contempt.

Having taken her into every division, and led her under every wall, till she was heartily weary of seeing and wondering, he suffered the girls at last to seize the advantage of an outer door, and then expressing his wish to examine the effect of some recent alterations about the tea-house, proposed it as no unpleasant extension of their walk, if Miss Morland were not tired. "But where are you going, Eleanor? Why do you choose that cold, damp path to it? Miss Morland will get wet. Our best way is across the park."

"This is so favourite a walk of mine," said Miss Tilney, "that I always think it the best and nearest way. But perhaps it may be damp."

It was a narrow winding path through a thick grove of old Scotch firs; and Catherine, struck by its gloomy aspect, and eager to enter it, could not, even by the general's disapprobation, be kept from stepping forward. He perceived her inclination, and having again urged the plea of health in vain, was too polite to make further opposition. He excused himself, however, from attending them: "The rays of the sun were not too cheerful for him, and he would meet them by another course." He turned away; and Catherine was shocked to find how much her spirits were relieved by the separation. The shock, however, being less real than the relief, offered it no injury; and she began to talk with easy gaiety of the delightful melancholy which such a grove inspired.

"I am particularly fond of this spot," said her companion, with a sigh. "It was my mother's favourite walk."

Catherine had never heard Mrs. Tilney mentioned in the family before, and the interest excited by this tender remembrance showed itself directly in her altered countenance, and in the attentive pause with which she waited for something more.

"I used to walk here so often with her!" added Eleanor; "though I never loved it then, as I have loved it since. At that time indeed I used to wonder at her choice. But her memory endears it now."

"And ought it not," reflected Catherine, "to endear it to her husband? Yet the general would not enter it." Miss Tilney continuing silent, she ventured to say, "Her death must have been a great affliction!"

"A great and increasing one," replied the other, in a low voice. "I was only thirteen when it happened; and though I felt my loss perhaps as strongly as one so young could feel it, I did not, I could not, then know what a loss it was." She stopped for a moment, and then added, with great firmness, "I have no sister, you know—and though Henry—though my brothers are very affectionate, and Henry is a great deal here, which I am most thankful for, it is impossible for me not to be often solitary."

"To be sure you must miss him very much."

"A mother would have been always present. A mother would have been a constant friend; her influence would have been beyond all other."

"Was she a very charming woman? Was she handsome? Was there any picture of her in the abbey? And why had she been so partial to that grove? Was it from dejection of spirits?"—were questions now eagerly poured forth; the first three received a ready affirmative, the two others were passed by; and Catherine's interest in the deceased Mrs. Tilney augmented with every question, whether answered or not. Of her unhappiness in marriage, she felt persuaded. The general certainly had been an unkind husband. He did not love her walk: could he therefore have loved her? And besides, handsome as he was, there was a something in the turn of his features which spoke his not having behaved well to her.

"Her picture, I suppose," blushing at the consummate art of her own question, "hangs in your father's room?"

"No; it was intended for the drawing-room; but my father was dissatisfied with the painting, and for some time it had no place. Soon after her death I obtained it for my own, and hung it in my bed-chamber—where I shall be happy to show it you; it is very like." Here was another proof. A portrait—very like—of a departed wife, not valued by the husband! He must have been dreadfully cruel to her!

Catherine attempted no longer to hide from herself the nature of the feelings which, in spite of all his attentions, he had previously excited; and what had been terror and dislike before, was now absolute aversion. Yes, aversion! His cruelty to such a charming woman made him odious to her. She had often read of such characters, characters which Mr. Allen had been used to call unnatural and overdrawn; but here was proof positive of the contrary.

She had just settled this point when the end of the path brought them directly upon the general; and in spite of all her virtuous indignation, she found herself again obliged to walk with him, listen to him, and even to smile when he smiled. Being no longer able, however, to receive pleasure from the surrounding objects, she soon began to walk with lassitude; the general perceived it, and with a concern for her health, which seemed to reproach her for her opinion of him, was most urgent for returning with his daughter to the house. He would follow them in a quarter of an hour. Again they parted—but Eleanor was called back in half a minute to receive a strict charge against taking her friend round the abbey till his return. This second instance of his anxiety to delay what she so much wished for struck Catherine as very remarkable.

CHAPTER
Thirty-Nine

AN HOUR PASSED AWAY before the general came in, spent, on the part of his young guest, in no very favourable consideration of his character. "This lengthened absence, these solitary rambles, did not speak a mind at ease, or a conscience void of reproach." At length he appeared; and, whatever might have been the gloom of his meditations, he could still smile with them. Miss Tilney, understanding in part her friend's curiosity to see the house, soon revived the subject; and her father being, contrary to Catherine's expectations, unprovided with any pretence for further delay, beyond that of stopping five minutes to order refreshments to be in the room by their return, was at last ready to escort them.

They set forward; and, with a grandeur of air, a dignified step, which caught the eye, but could not shake the doubts of the well-read Catherine, he led the way across the hall, through the common drawing-room and one useless antechamber, into a room magnificent both in size and furniture—the real drawing-room, used only with company of consequence. It was very noble—very grand—very charming!—was all that Catherine had to say, for her indiscriminating eye scarcely discerned the colour of the satin; and all minuteness of praise, all praise that had much meaning, was supplied by the general: the costliness or elegance of any room's fitting-up could be nothing to her; she cared for no furniture of a more modern date than the fifteenth century. When the general had satisfied his own curiosity, in a close examination of every well-known ornament, they proceeded into the library, an apartment, in its way, of equal magnificence, exhibiting a collection of books, on which an humble man might have looked with pride. Catherine heard, admired, and wondered with more genuine feeling than before—gathered all that she could from this storehouse of knowledge, by running over the titles of half a shelf, and was ready to proceed. But suites of apartments did not spring up with her wishes. Large as was the building, she had already visited the greatest part; though, on being told that, with the addition of the kitchen, the six or seven rooms she had now seen surrounded three sides of the court, she could scarcely believe it, or overcome the suspicion of there being many chambers secreted. It was some relief, however, that they were to return to the rooms in common use, by passing through a few of less importance, looking into the court, which, with occasional passages, not wholly unintricate, connected the different sides; and she was further soothed in her progress by being told that she was treading what had once been a cloister, having traces of cells pointed out, and observing several doors that were neither opened nor explained to her, excepting one.

"There," whispered Eleanor, while gesturing to a larger of the doors. "That is my father's private study."

"And is it a nice study?" asked Catherine, in an equally quiet voice.

"I would not know—as it is private—and he has never allowed us in."

"Not once? Even when you were young?"

"Never. He has always been particular to his confidential affairs."

At length, she found herself successively in a billiard-room, and in the general's private apartment, without comprehending their connection, or being able to turn aright when she left them; and lastly, by passing through a dark little room, owning Henry's authority, and strewed with his litter of books, guns, and greatcoats.

From the dining-room, of which, though already seen, and always to be seen at five o'clock, the general could not forgo the pleasure of pacing out the length, for the more certain information of Miss Morland, as to what she neither doubted nor cared for, they proceeded by quick communication to the kitchen— the ancient kitchen of the convent, rich in the massy walls and smoke of former days, and in the stoves and hot closets of the present. The general's improving hand had not loitered here: every modern invention to facilitate the labour of the cooks had been adopted within this, their spacious theatre; and, when the genius of others had failed, his own had often produced the perfection wanted. His endowments of this spot alone might at any time have placed him high among the benefactors of the convent.

With the walls of the kitchen ended all the antiquity of the abbey; the fourth side of the quadrangle having, on account of its decaying state, been removed by the general's father, and the present erected in its place. All that was venerable ceased here. The new building was not only new, but declared itself to be so; intended only for offices, and enclosed behind by stable-yards, no uniformity of architecture had been thought necessary. Catherine could have raved at the hand which had swept away what must have been beyond the value of all the rest, for the purposes of mere domestic economy; and would willingly have been spared the mortification of a walk through scenes so fallen, had the general allowed it; but if he had a vanity, it was in the arrangement of his offices; and as he was convinced that, to a mind like Miss Morland's, a view of the accommodations and comforts, by which the labours of her inferiors were softened, must always be gratifying, he should make no apology for leading her on. They took a slight survey of all; and Catherine was impressed, beyond her expectation, by their multiplicity and their convenience. The purposes for which a few shapeless pantries and a comfortless scullery were deemed sufficient at Fullerton, were here carried on in appropriate divisions, commodious and roomy. The number of servants continually appearing did not strike her less than the number of their offices. Wherever they went, some pattened girl stopped to curtsy, or some footman in dishabille sneaked off. Yet this was an abbey! How inexpressibly different in these domestic arrangements from such as she had read about—from abbeys and castles, in which, though certainly larger than Northanger, all the dirty work of the house was to be done by two pair of female hands at the utmost. How they could get through it all had often amazed Mrs. Allen; and, when Catherine saw what was necessary here, she began to be amazed herself.

They returned to the hall, that the chief staircase might be ascended, and the beauty of its wood, and ornaments of rich carving might be pointed out: having gained the top, they turned in an opposite direction from the gallery in which her room lay, and shortly entered one on the same plan, but superior in length and breadth. She was here shown successively into three large bed-chambers, with their dressing-rooms, most completely and handsomely fitted up; everything that money and taste could do, to give comfort and elegance to apartments, had been bestowed on these; and, being furnished within the last five years, they were perfect in all that would be generally pleasing, and wanting in all that could give pleasure to Catherine. As they were surveying the last, the general, after slightly naming a few of the distinguished characters by whom they had at times been honoured, turned with a smiling countenance to Catherine, and ventured to hope that henceforward some of their earliest tenants might be "our friends from Fullerton." She felt the unexpected compliment, and deeply regretted the impossibility of thinking well of a man so kindly disposed towards herself, and so full of civility to all her family.

The gallery was terminated by folding doors, which Miss Tilney, advancing, had thrown open, and passed through, and seemed on the point of doing the same by the first door to the left, in another long reach of gallery, when the general, coming forwards, called her hastily, and, as Catherine thought, rather angrily back, demanding whether she were going?—And what was there more to be seen?—Had not Miss Morland already seen all that could be worth her notice?—And did she not suppose her friend might be glad of some refreshment after so much exercise? Miss Tilney drew back directly, and the heavy doors were closed upon the mortified Catherine, who, having seen, in a momentary glance beyond them, a narrower passage, more numerous openings, and symptoms of a winding staircase, believed herself at last within the reach of something worth her notice; and felt, as she unwillingly paced back the gallery, that she would rather be allowed to examine that end of the house than see all the finery of all the rest. The general's evident desire of preventing such an examination was an additional stimulant. Something was certainly to be concealed; her fancy, though it had trespassed lately once or twice, could not mislead her here; and what that something was, a short sentence of Miss Tilney's, as they followed the general at some distance downstairs, seemed to point out: "I was going to take you into what was my mother's room—the room in which she died—" were all her words; but few as they were, they conveyed pages of intelligence to Catherine. It was no wonder that the general should shrink from the sight of such objects as that room must contain; a room in all probability never entered by him since the dreadful scene had passed, which released his suffering wife, and left him to the stings of conscience.

She ventured, when next alone with Eleanor, to express her wish of being permitted to see it, as well as all the rest of that side of the house; and Eleanor promised to attend her there, whenever they should have a convenient hour. Catherine understood her: the general must be watched from home, before that room could be entered. "It remains as it was, I suppose?" said she, in a tone of feeling.

"Yes, entirely."

"And how long ago may it be that your mother died?"

"She has been dead these nine years." And nine years, Catherine knew, was a trifle of time, compared with what generally elapsed after the death of an injured wife, before her room was put to rights.

"You were with her, I suppose, to the last?"

"No," said Miss Tilney, sighing; "I was unfortunately from home. Her illness was sudden and short; and, before I arrived it was all over."

Catherine's blood ran cold with the horrid suggestions which naturally sprang from these words. Could it be possible? Could Henry's father—? And yet how many were the examples to justify even the blackest suspicions! And, when she saw him in the evening, while she worked with her friend, slowly pacing the drawing-room for an hour together in silent thoughtfulness, with downcast eyes and contracted brow, she felt secure from all possibility of wronging him. It was the air and attitude of a Montoni! What could more plainly speak the gloomy workings of a mind not wholly dead to every sense of humanity, in its fearful review of past scenes of guilt? Unhappy man! And the anxiousness of her spirits directed her eyes towards his figure so repeatedly, as to catch Miss Tilney's notice. "My father," she whispered, "often walks about the room in this way; it is nothing unusual."

"So much the worse!" thought Catherine; such ill-timed exercise was of a piece with the strange unseasonableness of his morning walks, and boded nothing good.

After an evening, the little variety and seeming length of which made her peculiarly sensible of Henry's importance among them, she was heartily glad to be dismissed; though it was a look from the general not designed for her observation which sent his daughter to the bell. When the butler would have lit his master's candle, however, he was forbidden. The latter was not going to retire. "I have many pamphlets to finish," said he to Catherine, "before I can close my eyes, and perhaps may be poring over the affairs of the nation for hours after you are asleep. Can either of us be more meetly employed? My eyes will be blinding for the good of others, and yours preparing by rest for future mischief."

But neither the business alleged, nor the magnificent compliment, could win Catherine from thinking that some very different object must occasion so serious a delay of proper repose. To be kept up for hours, after the family were in bed, by stupid pamphlets was not very likely. There must be some deeper cause: something was to be done which could be done only while the household slept; and the probability that Mrs. Tilney yet lived, shut up for causes unknown, and receiving from the pitiless hands of her husband a nightly supply of coarse food, was the conclusion which necessarily followed. Shocking as was the idea, it was at least better than a death unfairly hastened, as, in the natural course of things, she must ere long be released. The suddenness of her reputed illness, the absence of her daughter, and probably of her other children, at the time—all favoured the supposition of her imprisonment. Its origin—jealousy perhaps, or wanton cruelty—was yet to be unravelled.

In revolving these matters, while she undressed, it suddenly struck her as not unlikely that she might that morning have passed near the very spot of this unfortunate woman's confinement—might have been within a few paces of the cell in which she languished out her days; for what part of the abbey could be more fitted for the purpose than that which yet bore the traces of monastic division? In the high-arched passage, paved with stone, which already she had trodden with peculiar awe, she well remembered the doors of which the general had given no account. To what might not those doors lead? In support of the plausibility of this conjecture, it further occurred to her that the forbidden gallery, in which lay the apartments of the unfortunate Mrs. Tilney, must be, as certainly as her memory could guide her, exactly over this suspected range of cells, and the staircase by the side of those apartments of which she had caught a transient glimpse, communicating by some secret means with those cells, might well have favoured the barbarous proceedings of her husband. Down that staircase she had perhaps been conveyed in a state of well-prepared insensibility!

Catherine sometimes started at the boldness of her own surmises, and sometimes hoped or feared that she had gone too far; but they were supported by such appearances as made their dismissal impossible.

The side of the quadrangle, in which she supposed the guilty scene to be acting, being, according to her belief, just opposite her own, it struck her that, if judiciously watched, some rays of light from the general's lamp might glimmer through the lower windows, as he passed to the prison of his wife; and, twice before she stepped into bed, she stole gently from her room to the corresponding window in the gallery, to see if it appeared; but all abroad was dark, and it must yet be too early. The various ascending noises convinced her that the servants must still be up. Till midnight, she supposed it would be in vain to watch; but then, when the clock had struck twelve, and all was quiet, she would, if not quite appalled by darkness, steal out and look once more. The clock struck twelve—and Catherine had been half an hour asleep.

CHAPTER

Forty

THE NEXT DAY afforded no opportunity for the proposed examination of the mysterious apartments. It was Sunday, and the whole time between morning and afternoon service was required by the general in exercise abroad or eating cold meat at home; and great as was Catherine's curiosity, her courage was not equal to a wish of exploring them after dinner, either by the fading light of the sky between six and seven o'clock, or by the yet more partial though stronger illumination of a treacherous lamp. The day was unmarked therefore by anything to interest her imagination beyond the sight of a very elegant monument to the memory of Mrs. Tilney, which immediately fronted the family pew. By that her eye was instantly caught and long retained; and the perusal of the highly strained epitaph, in which every virtue was ascribed to her by the inconsolable husband, who must have been in some way or other her destroyer, affected her even to tears.

That the general, having erected such a monument, should be able to face it, was not perhaps very strange, and yet that he could sit so boldly collected within its view, maintain so elevated an air, look so fearlessly around, nay, that he should even enter the church, seemed wonderful to Catherine. Not, however, that many instances of beings equally hardened in guilt might not be produced. She could remember dozens who had persevered in every possible vice, going on from crime to crime, murdering whomsoever abhey chose, without any feeling of humanity or remorse; till a violent death or a religious retirement closed their black career. The erection of the monument itself could not in the smallest degree affect her doubts of Mrs. Tilney's actual decease. Were she even to descend into the family vault where her ashes were supposed to slumber, were she to behold the coffin in which they were said to be enclosed—what could it avail in such a case? Catherine had read too much not to be perfectly aware of the ease with which a waxen figure might be introduced, and a supposititious funeral carried on.

The succeeding morning promised something better. The general's early walk, ill-timed as it was in every other view, was favourable here; and when she knew him to be out of the house, she directly proposed to Miss Tilney the accomplishment of her promise. Eleanor was ready to oblige her; and Catherine reminding her as they went of another promise, their first visit in consequence was to the portrait in her bed-chamber. It represented a very lovely woman, with a mild and pensive countenance, justifying, so far, the expectations of its new observer; but they were not in every respect answered, for Catherine had depended upon meeting with features, hair, complexion, that should be the very counterpart, the very image, if not of Henry's, of Eleanor's—the only portraits of which she had been in the habit of thinking, bearing always an equal resemblance of mother and child. A face once taken was taken for generations. But here she was obliged to look and consider and study for a likeness. She contemplated it, however, in spite of this drawback, with much emotion, and, but for a yet stronger interest, would have left it unwillingly.

Her agitation as they entered the great gallery was too much for any endeavour at discourse; she could only look at her companion. Eleanor's countenance was dejected, yet sedate; and its composure spoke her inured to all the gloomy objects to which they were advancing. Again she passed through the folding doors, again her hand was upon the important lock, and Catherine, hardly able to breathe, was turning to close the former with fearful caution, when the figure, the dreaded figure of the general himself at the further end of the gallery, stood before her! The name of "Eleanor" at the same moment, in his loudest tone, resounded through the building, giving to his daughter the first intimation of his presence, and to Catherine terror upon terror. An attempt at concealment had been her first instinctive movement on perceiving him, yet she could scarcely hope to have escaped his eye; and when her friend, who with an apologizing look darted hastily by her, had joined and disappeared with him, she ran for safety to her own room, and, locking herself in, believed that she should never have courage to go down again. She remained there at least an hour, in the greatest agitation, deeply commiserating the state of her poor friend, and expecting a summons herself from the angry general to attend him in his own apartment. No summons, however, arrived; and at last, on seeing a carriage drive up to the abbey, she was emboldened to descend and meet him under the protection of visitors. The breakfast-room was gay with company; and she was named to them by the general as the friend of his daughter, in a complimentary style, which so well concealed his resentful ire, as to make her feel secure at least of life for the present. And Eleanor, with a command of countenance which did honour to her concern for his character, taking an early occasion of saying to her, "My father only wanted me to answer a note," she began to hope that she had either been unseen by the general, or that from some consideration of policy she should be allowed to suppose herself so. Upon this trust she dared still to remain in his presence, after the company left them, and nothing occurred to disturb it.

In the course of this morning's reflections, she came to a resolution of making her next attempt on the forbidden door alone. It would be much better in every respect that Eleanor should know nothing of the matter. To involve her in the danger of a second detection, to court her into an apartment which must wring her heart, could not be the office of a friend. The general's utmost anger could not be to herself what it might be to a daughter; and, besides, she thought the examination itself would be more satisfactory if made without any companion. It would be impossible to explain to Eleanor the suspicions, from which the other had, in all likelihood, been hitherto happily exempt; nor could she therefore, in her presence, search for those proofs of the general's cruelty, which however they might yet have escaped discovery, she felt confident of somewhere drawing forth, in the shape of some fragmented journal, continued to the last gasp. Of the way to the apartment she was now perfectly mistress; and as she wished to get it over before Henry's return, who was expected on the morrow, there was no time to be lost. The day was bright, her courage high; at four o'clock, the sun was now two hours above the horizon, and it would be only her retiring to dress half an hour earlier than usual.

It was done; and Catherine found herself alone in the gallery before the clocks had ceased to strike. It was no time for thought; she hurried on, slipped with the least possible noise through the folding doors, and without stopping to look or breathe, rushed forward to the one in question. The lock yielded to her hand, and, luckily, with no sullen sound that could alarm a human being. On tiptoe she entered; the room was before her; but it was some minutes before she could advance another step. She beheld what fixed her to the spot and agitated every feature. She saw a large, well-proportioned apartment, an handsome dimity bed, arranged as unoccupied with an housemaid's care, a bright Bath stove, mahogany wardrobes, a writing desk, and neatly painted chairs, on which the warm beams of a western sun gaily poured through two sash windows! Catherine had expected to have her feelings worked, and worked they were. Astonishment and doubt first seized them; and a shortly succeeding ray of common sense added some bitter emotions of shame. She could not be mistaken as to the room; but how grossly mistaken in everything else!—in Miss Tilney's meaning, in her own calculation! This apartment, to which she had given a date so ancient, a position so awful, proved to be one end of what the general's father had built. There were two other doors in the chamber, leading probably into dressing-closets; but she had no inclination to open either. Would the veil in which Mrs. Tilney had last walked, or the volume in which she had last read, remain to tell what nothing else was allowed to whisper? No: whatever might have been the general's crimes, he had certainly too much wit to let them sue for detection. She was sick of exploring, and desired but to be safe in her own room, with her own heart only privy to its folly; but here she was, and decided to walk throughout the room, if nothing else than to acknowledge respect to the lady who had once lived in there.

This was, she accepted, a lovely room, and decorated in a simple but exquisite taste. She let her hands pass across the cotton fabric of the bed, feeling its smooth texture, and she wondered how the room might have given some sanctuary or pleasure to its occupant. Then to the neighbouring wardrobe, made of fine inlaid wood and left only as decoration to the room; she casually opened it, looking inside and through the empty drawers. By moments, a sense of peace came across her, so that if the room was of any reflection of Mrs. Tilney, then she must have been as great a comfort as indicated by her daughter.

Catherine approached the writing desk, the top bare of any correspondence materials, and pulled open the single drawer, which proved likewise to be empty, but in doing so, there was a soft noise from within, causing the drawer to extend further to one side. She pushed it back, only to find that the drawer was now blocked in some fashion and would recede only halfway. A cold panic swept over her, as her presence might be detected if the desk was not returned to its original condition, and so with a sense of urgency, she jiggled the drawer from side to side to get it back into place. Her efforts were to no avail; something had obstructed the drawer from the rear and would not give way. In desperation, she pulled the drawer forth, nearly dislodging it from its runners, and then pushed it back with more force. This time, the obstruction was cleared, falling to the floor as the drawer slid neatly into place. Catherine looked below and found the source of the problem: a small book bound in fabric, with delicate straps to both covers that might be tied together. After examining the exterior she leafed through the pages, finding it to contain not printed words, but handwriting, which filled a good two-thirds of the book, and it became clear to her what she held. This was a private journal, most likely that of the late Mrs. Tilney.

Acting upon suspicion, she reopened the drawer and ran her hand along the inside, feeling the upper contours of the wood. Sure enough, she discovered within the recesses, a pocket large enough to hold such an item, but hidden away from the casual observer. To retrieve the book, a person must reach into the back and pull the object from its hidden shelf. For some unexplained reason, it must have slid forward when she opened the desk, thereby falling and blocking the drawer from closing, and was freed only when she pulled it further back.

A dilemma confronted Catherine at this point; that being the insurmountable curiosity over such a journal, with the secrets that it might hold, and the proper respect that should in all accounts be given to an individual's privacy. If she were to follow the guidance of her conscience, she should replace the book in its original resting spot, but alas, she had read too many novels not to be enthralled by the possibility of its contents. In addition, she knew that she had already spent far too much time in the room and should make her way back—indeed she was on the point of retreating as softly as she had entered, when the sound of footsteps, she could hardly tell where, made her pause and tremble. To be found there, even by a servant, would be unpleasant; but by the general (and he seemed always at hand when least wanted), much worse! She listened—the sound had ceased; and resolving not to lose a moment, she hid the journal within the folds of her dress, then she passed through and closed the door. At that instant a door underneath was hastily opened; someone seemed with swift steps to ascend the stairs, by the head of which she had yet to pass before she could gain the gallery. She had no power to move. With a feeling of terror not very definable, she fixed her eyes on the staircase, and in a few moments it gave Henry to her view. "Mr. Tilney!" she exclaimed in a voice of more than common astonishment. He looked astonished too. "Good God!" she continued, not attending to his address. "How came you here? How came you up that staircase?"

"How came I up that staircase!" he replied, greatly surprised. "Because it is my nearest way from the stable-yard to my own chamber; and why should I not come up it?"

Catherine recollected herself, blushed deeply, and could say no more. As if by its own mind, her hand slid over the folds covering the book, keeping it safe and secret. He seemed to be looking in her countenance for that explanation which her lips did not afford. She moved on towards the gallery. "And may I not, in my turn," said he, as he pushed back the folding doors, "ask how you came here? This passage is at least as extraordinary a road from the breakfast-parlour to your apartment, as that staircase can be from the stables to mine."

"I have been," said Catherine, looking down, "to see your mother's room."

"My mother's room! Is there anything extraordinary to be seen there?"

"No, nothing at all. I thought you did not mean to come back till tomorrow."

"I did not expect to be able to return sooner, when I went away; but three hours ago I had the pleasure of finding nothing to detain me. You look pale. I am afraid I alarmed you by running so fast up those stairs. Perhaps you did not know—you were not aware of their leading from the offices in common use?"

"No, I was not. You have had a very fine day for your ride."

"Very; and does Eleanor leave you to find your way into all the rooms in the house by yourself?"

"Oh! No; she showed me over the greatest part on Saturday—and we were coming here to these rooms—but only"—dropping her voice—"your father was with us."

"And that prevented you," said Henry, earnestly regarding her. "Have you looked into all the rooms in that passage?"

"No, I only wanted to see—Is not it very late? I must go and dress."

"It is only a quarter past four" showing his watch—"and you are not now in Bath. No theatre, no rooms to prepare for. Half an hour at Northanger must be enough."

She could not contradict it, and therefore suffered herself to be detained, though her dread of further questions made her, for the first time in their acquaintance, wish to leave him. They walked slowly up the gallery. "Have you had any letter from Bath since I saw you?"

"No, and I am very much surprised. Isabella promised so faithfully to write directly."

"Promised so faithfully! A faithful promise! That puzzles me. I have heard of a faithful performance. But a faithful promise—the fidelity of promising! It is a power little worth knowing, however, since it can deceive and pain you. My mother's room is very commodious, is it not? Large and cheerful-looking, and the dressing-closets so well disposed! It always strikes me as the most comfortable apartment in the house, and I rather wonder that Eleanor should not take it for her own. She sent you to look at it, I suppose?"

"No."

"It has been your own doing entirely?" Catherine said nothing. After a short silence, during which he had closely observed her, he added, "As there is nothing in the room in itself to raise curiosity, this must have proceeded from a sentiment of respect for my mother's character, as described by Eleanor, which does honour to her memory. The world, I believe, never saw a better woman. But it is not often that virtue can boast an interest such as this. The domestic, unpretending merits of a person never known do not often create that kind of fervent, venerating tenderness which would prompt a visit like yours. Eleanor, I suppose, has talked of her a great deal?"

"Yes, a great deal. That is—no, not much, but what she did say was very interesting. Her dying so suddenly" (slowly, and with hesitation it was spoken), "and you—none of you being at home—and your father, I thought—perhaps had not been very fond of her."

"And from these circumstances," he replied (his quick eye fixed on hers), "you infer perhaps the probability of some negligence—some"—(involuntarily she shook her head)—"or it may be—of something still less pardonable." She raised her eyes towards him more fully than she had ever done before. "My mother's illness," he continued, "the seizure which ended in her death, was sudden. The malady itself, one from which she had often suffered, a bilious fever—its cause therefore constitutional. On the third day, in short, as soon as she could be prevailed on, a physician attended her, a very respectable man, and one in whom she had always placed great confidence. Upon his opinion of her danger, two others were called in the next day, and remained in almost constant attendance for four and twenty hours. On the fifth day she died. During the progress of her disorder, Frederick and I (we were both at home) saw her repeatedly; and from our own observation can bear witness to her having received every possible attention which could spring from the affection of those about her, or which her situation in life could command. Poor Eleanor was absent, and at such a distance as to return only to see her mother in her coffin."

"But your father," said Catherine, "was he afflicted?"

"For a time, greatly so. You have erred in supposing him not attached to her. He loved her, I am persuaded, as well as it was possible for him to—we have not all, you know, the same tenderness of disposition—and I will not pretend to say that while she lived, she might not often have had much to bear, but though his temper injured her, his judgment never did. His value of her was sincere; and, if not permanently, he was truly afflicted by her death."

"I am very glad of it," said Catherine; "it would have been very shocking!"

"If I understand you rightly, you had formed a surmise of such horror as I have hardly words to—Dear Miss Morland, consider the dreadful nature of the suspicions you have entertained. What have you been judging from? Remember the country and the age in which we live. Remember that we are English, that we are Christians. Consult your own understanding, your own sense of the probable, your own observation of what is passing around you. Does our education prepare us for such atrocities? Do our laws connive at them? Could they be perpetrated without being known, in a country like this, where social and literary intercourse is on such a footing, where every man is surrounded by a neighbourhood of voluntary spies, and where roads and newspapers lay everything open? Dearest Miss Morland, what ideas have you been admitting?"

They had reached the end of the gallery, and with tears of deepest shame she ran off to her own room, closing the door behind her, and tossing the secreted journal onto the bed. There she fell beside it, allowing tears to come as they would, and knowing that she had done a great wrong to Mr. Tilney and his family. At length, she composed herself and gave fresh consideration to the book beside her. In her heart, she knew that she should have left it where it belonged, and would now have to make another journey to the same room, to return it to its proper place. For the moment, the book would remain with her, so she slid it under her pillow, where it would be safe until she saw it home.

CHAPTER

Forty-One

THE VISIONS OF ROMANCE were over. Catherine was completely awakened. Henry's address, short as it had been, had more thoroughly opened her eyes to the extravagance of her late fancies than all their several disappointments had done. Most grievously was she humbled. Most bitterly did she cry. It was not only with herself that she was sunk—but with Henry. Her folly, which now seemed even criminal, was all exposed to him, and he must despise her forever. The liberty which her imagination had dared to take with the character of his father— could he ever forgive it? The absurdity of her curiosity and her fears—could they ever be forgotten? She hated herself more than she could express. He had—she thought he had, once or twice before this fatal morning, shown something like affection for her. But now—in short, she made herself as miserable as possible for about half an hour, went down when the clock struck five, with a broken heart, and could scarcely give an intelligible answer to Eleanor's inquiry if she was well. The formidable Henry soon followed her into the room, and the only difference in his behaviour to her was that he paid her rather more attention than usual. Catherine had never wanted comfort more, and he looked as if he was aware of it.

The evening wore away with no abatement of this soothing politeness; and her spirits were gradually raised to a modest tranquillity. She did not learn either to forget or defend the past; but she learned to hope that it would never transpire farther, and that it might not cost her Henry's entire regard. Her thoughts being still chiefly fixed on what she had with such causeless terror felt and done, nothing could shortly be clearer than that it had been all a voluntary, self-created delusion, each trifling circumstance receiving importance from an imagination resolved on alarm, and everything forced to bend to one purpose by a mind which, before she entered the abbey, had been craving to be frightened. She remembered with what feelings she had prepared for a knowledge of Northanger. She saw that the infatuation had been created, the mischief settled, long before her quitting Bath, and it seemed as if the whole might be traced to the influence of that sort of reading which she had there indulged.

Charming as were all Mrs. Radcliffe's works, and charming even as were the works of all her imitators, it was not in them perhaps that human nature, at least in the Midland counties of England, was to be looked for. Of the Alps and Pyrenees, with their pine forests and their vices, they might give a faithful delineation; and Italy, Switzerland, and the south of France might be as fruitful in horrors as they were there represented. Catherine dared not doubt beyond her own country, and even of that, if hard pressed, would have yielded the northern and western extremities. But in the central part of England there was surely some security for the existence even of a wife not beloved, in the laws of the land, and the manners of the age. Murder was not tolerated, servants were not slaves, and neither poison nor sleeping potions to be procured, like rhubarb, from every druggist. Among the Alps and Pyrenees, perhaps, there were no mixed characters. There, such as were not as spotless as an angel might have the dispositions of a fiend. But in England it was not so; among the English, she believed, in their hearts and habits, there was a general though unequal mixture of good and bad. Upon this conviction, she would not be surprised if even in Henry and Eleanor Tilney, some slight imperfection might hereafter appear; and upon this conviction she need not fear to acknowledge some actual specks in the character of their father, who, though cleared from the grossly injurious suspicions which she must ever blush to have entertained, she did believe, upon serious consideration, to be not perfectly amiable.

Her mind made up on these several points, and her resolution formed, of always judging and acting in future with the greatest good sense, she had nothing to do but to forgive herself and be happier than ever; and the lenient hand of time did much for her by insensible gradations in the course of another day. Henry's astonishing generosity and nobleness of conduct, in never alluding in the slightest way to what had passed, was of the greatest assistance to her; and sooner than she could have supposed it possible in the beginning of her distress, her spirits became absolutely comfortable, and capable, as heretofore, of continual improvement by anything he said. There were still some subjects, indeed, under which she believed they must always tremble—the mention of a chest or a cabinet, for instance—and she did not love the sight of japan in any shape: but even she could allow that an occasional memento of past folly, however painful, might not be without use.

Of the journal, she knew that a trip back to Mrs. Tilney's room was inevitable to replace the book in its secreted location as it was meant to be. On more than one occasion, she considered telling Henry about the find, or even more, Eleanor, who would surely be most grateful to know of such an artifact associated with her mother; but, no, it would then mean a confession as to why she had taken to exploring the room. She could not expose herself to such an embarrassment, even to one as kind as Eleanor. Instead, she kept the book hidden, having moved it from under her pillow to a safer place, inside the black cabinet, beside the laundry list she had been so taken by on her first night at the abbey.

The anxieties of common life began soon to succeed to the alarms of romance. Her desire of hearing from Isabella grew every day greater. She was quite impatient to know how the Bath world went on, and how the rooms were attended; and especially was she anxious to be assured of Isabella's having matched some fine netting-cotton, on which she had left her intent; and of her continuing on the best terms with James. Her only dependence for information of any kind was on Isabella. James had protested against writing to her till his return to Oxford; and Mrs. Allen had given her no hopes of a letter till she had got back to Fullerton. But Isabella had promised and promised again; and when she promised a thing, she was so scrupulous in performing it! This made it so particularly strange!

For nine successive mornings, Catherine wondered over the repetition of a disappointment, which each morning became more severe: but, on the tenth, when she entered the breakfast-room, her first object was a letter, held out by Henry's willing hand. She thanked him as heartily as if he had written it himself. "'Tis only from James, however," as she looked at the direction. She opened it; it was from Oxford; and to this purpose:

Dear Catherine,

Though, God knows, with little inclination for writing, I think it my duty to tell you that everything is at an end between Miss Thorpe and me. I left her and Bath yesterday, never to see either again. I shall not enter into particulars—they would only pain you more. You will soon hear enough from another quarter to know where lies the blame; and I hope will acquit your brother of everything but *the folly of too easily thinking his affection returned. Thank God! I am undeceived in time! But it is a heavy blow! After my father's consent had been so kindly given—but no more of this. She has made me miserable forever! Let me soon hear from you, dear Catherine; you are my only friend; your love I do build upon. I wish your visit at Northanger may be over before Captain Tilney makes his engagement known, or you will be uncomfortably circumstanced. Poor Thorpe is in town: I dread the sight of him; his honest heart would feel so much. I have written to him and my father. Her duplicity hurts me more than all; till the very last, if I reasoned with her, she declared herself as much attached to me as ever, and laughed at my fears. I am ashamed to think how long I bore with it; but if ever man had reason to believe himself loved, I was that man. I cannot understand even now what she would be at, for there could be no need of my being played off to make her secure of Tilney. We parted at last by mutual consent—happy for me had we never met! I can never expect to know such another woman! Dearest Catherine, beware how you give your heart.*

Believe me, &c.

Catherine had not read three lines before her sudden change of countenance, and short exclamations of sorrowing wonder, declared her to be receiving unpleasant news; and Henry, earnestly watching her through the whole letter, saw plainly that it ended no better than it began. He was prevented, however, from even looking his surprise by his father's entrance. They went to breakfast directly; but Catherine could hardly eat anything. Tears filled her eyes, and even ran down her cheeks as she sat. The letter was one moment in her hand, then in her lap, and then in her pocket; and she looked as if she knew not what she did. The general, between his cocoa and his newspaper, had luckily no leisure for noticing her; but to the other two her distress was equally visible. As soon as she dared leave the table she hurried away to her own room; but the housemaids were busy in it, and she was obliged to come down again. She turned into the drawing-room for privacy, but Henry and Eleanor had likewise retreated thither, and were at that moment deep in consultation about her. She drew back, trying to beg their pardon, but was, with gentle violence, forced to return; and the others withdrew, after Eleanor had affectionately expressed a wish of being of use or comfort to her.

After half an hour's free indulgence of grief and reflection, Catherine felt equal to encountering her friends; but whether she should make her distress known to them was another consideration. Perhaps, if particularly questioned, she might just give an idea—just distantly hint at it—but not more. To expose a friend, such a friend as Isabella had been to her—and then their own brother so closely concerned in it! She believed she must waive the subject altogether. Henry and Eleanor were by themselves in the breakfast-room; and each, as she entered it, looked at her anxiously. Catherine took her place at the table, and, after a short silence, Eleanor said, "No bad news from Fullerton, I hope? Mr. and Mrs. Morland—your brothers and sisters—I hope they are none of them ill?"

"No, I thank you" (sighing as she spoke); "they are all very well. My letter was from my brother at Oxford."

Nothing further was said for a few minutes; and then speaking through her tears, she added, "I do not think I shall ever wish for a letter again!"

"I am sorry," said Henry, closing the book he had just opened; "if I had suspected the letter of containing anything unwelcome, I should have given it with very different feelings."

"It contained something worse than anybody could suppose! Poor James is so unhappy! You will soon know why."

"To have so kind-hearted, so affectionate a sister," replied Henry warmly, "must be a comfort to him under any distress."

"I have one favour to beg," said Catherine, shortly afterwards, in an agitated manner, "that, if your brother should be coming here, you will give me notice of it, that I may go away."

"Our brother! Frederick!"

"Yes; I am sure I should be very sorry to leave you so soon, but something has happened that would make it very dreadful for me to be in the same house with Captain Tilney."

Eleanor's work was suspended while she gazed with increasing astonishment; but Henry began to suspect the truth, and something, in which Miss Thorpe's name was included, passed his lips.

"How quick you are!" cried Catherine: "you have guessed it, I declare! And yet, when we talked about it in Bath, you little thought of its ending so. Isabella—no wonder now I have not heard from her—Isabella has deserted my brother, and is to marry yours! Could you have believed there had been such inconstancy and fickleness, and everything that is bad in the world?"

"I hope, so far as concerns my brother, you are misinformed. I hope he has not had any material share in bringing on Mr. Morland's disappointment. His marrying Miss Thorpe is not probable. I think you must be deceived so far. I am very sorry for Mr. Morland—sorry that anyone you love should be unhappy; but my surprise would be greater at Frederick's marrying her than at any other part of the story."

"It is very true, however; you shall read James's letter yourself. Stay—There is one part—" recollecting with a blush the last line.

"Will you take the trouble of reading to us the passages which concern my brother?"

"No, read it yourself," cried Catherine, whose second thoughts were clearer. "I do not know what I was thinking of" (blushing again that she had blushed before); "James only means to give me good advice."

He gladly received the letter, and, having read it through, with close attention, returned it saying, "Well, if it is to be so, I can only say that I am sorry for it. Frederick will not be the first man who has chosen a wife with less sense than his family expected. I do not envy his situation, either as a lover or a son."

Miss Tilney, at Catherine's invitation, now read the letter likewise, and, having expressed also her concern and surprise, began to inquire into Miss Thorpe's connections and fortune.

"Her mother is a very good sort of woman," was Catherine's answer.

"What was her father?"

"A lawyer, I believe. They live at Putney."

"Are they a wealthy family?"

"No, not very. I do not believe Isabella has any fortune at all: but that will not signify in your family. Your father is so very liberal! He told me the other day that he only valued money as it allowed him to promote the happiness of his children." The brother and sister looked at each other. "But," said Eleanor, after a short pause, "would it be to promote his happiness, to enable him to marry such a girl? She must be an unprincipled one, or she could not have used your brother so. And how strange an infatuation on Frederick's side! A girl who, before his eyes, is violating an engagement voluntarily entered into with another man! Is not it inconceivable, Henry? Frederick too, who always wore his heart so proudly! Who found no woman good enough to be loved!"

"That is the most unpromising circumstance, the strongest presumption against him. When I think of his past declarations, I give him up. Moreover, I have too good an opinion of Miss Thorpe's prudence to suppose that she would part with one gentleman before the other was secured. It is all over with Frederick indeed! He is a deceased man—defunct in understanding. Prepare for your sister-in-law, Eleanor, and such a sister-in-law as you must delight in! Open, candid, artless, guileless, with affections strong but simple, forming no pretensions, and knowing no disguise."

"Such a sister-in-law, Henry, I should delight in," said Eleanor with a smile.

"But perhaps," observed Catherine, "though she has behaved so ill by our family, she may behave better by yours. Now she has really got the man she likes, she may be constant."

"Indeed I am afraid she will," replied Henry; "I am afraid she will be very constant, unless a baronet should come in her way; that is Frederick's only chance. I will get the Bath paper, and look over the arrivals."

"You think it is all for ambition, then? And, upon my word, there are some things that seem very like it. I cannot forget that, when she first knew what my father would do for them, she seemed quite disappointed that it was not more. I never was so deceived in anyone's character in my life before."

"Among all the great variety that you have known and studied."

"My own disappointment and loss in her is very great; but, as for poor James, I suppose he will hardly ever recover it."

"Your brother is certainly very much to be pitied at present; but we must not, in our concern for his sufferings, undervalue yours. You feel, I suppose, that in losing Isabella, you lose half yourself: you feel a void in your heart which nothing else can occupy. Society is becoming irksome; and as for the amusements in which you were wont to share at Bath, the very idea of them without her is abhorrent. You would not, for instance, now go to a ball for the world. You feel that you have no longer any friend to whom you can speak with unreserve, on whose regard you can place dependence, or whose counsel, in any difficulty, you could rely on. You feel all this?"

"No," said Catherine, after a few moments' reflection, "I do not—ought I? To say the truth, though I am hurt and grieved, that I cannot still love her, that I am never to hear from her, perhaps never to see her again, I do not feel so very, very much afflicted as one would have thought."

"You feel, as you always do, what is most to the credit of human nature. Such feelings ought to be investigated, that they may know themselves."

Catherine, by some chance or other, found her spirits so very much relieved by this conversation that she could not regret her being led on, though so unaccountably, to mention the circumstance which had produced it.

From this time, the subject was frequently canvassed by the three young people; and Catherine found, with some surprise, that her two young friends were perfectly agreed in considering Isabella's want of consequence and fortune as likely to throw great difficulties in the way of her marrying their brother. Their persuasion that the general would, upon this ground alone, independent of the objection that might be raised against her character, oppose the connection, turned her feelings moreover with some alarm towards herself. She was as insignificant, and perhaps as portionless, as Isabella; and if the heir of the Tilney property had not grandeur and wealth enough in himself, at what point of interest were the demands of his younger brother to rest? The very painful reflections to which this thought led could only be dispersed by a dependence on the effect of that particular partiality, which, as she was given to understand by his words as well as his actions, she had from the first been so fortunate as to excite in the general; and by a recollection of some most generous and disinterested sentiments on the subject of money, which she had more than once heard him utter, and which tempted her to think his disposition in such matters misunderstood by his children.

They were so fully convinced, however, that their brother would not have the courage to apply in person for his father's consent, and so repeatedly assured her that he had never in his life been less likely to come to Northanger than at the present time, that she suffered her mind to be at ease as to the necessity of any sudden removal of her own. But as it was not to be supposed that Captain Tilney, whenever he made his application, would give his father any just idea of Isabella's conduct, it occurred to her as highly expedient that Henry should lay the whole business before him as it really was, enabling the general by that means to form a cool and impartial opinion, and prepare his objections on a fairer ground than inequality of situations. She proposed it to him accordingly; but he did not catch at the measure so eagerly as she had expected. "No," said he, "my father's hands need not be strengthened, and Frederick's confession of folly need not be forestalled. He must tell his own story."

"But he will tell only half of it."

"A quarter would be enough."

CHAPTER
Forty-Two

CURIOSITY made her actions inevitable. How could it have been otherwise?

For many days, the journal had been left sequestered in the cabinet of such mystery, there in the company of the rolled manuscript and its details of stockings, waistcoats, and the like. While Catherine knew that she would at some point be required to return the book to its rightful place, she kept putting off the inevitable, partially out of shame of her behavior. There was also the fear of being caught in the act, just as she was in her first excursion, but with a greater possibility that the party finding her could be far less gracious in their understanding.

Beneath these valid points resided an underlying reason; one that she was less accepting to admit, even to herself, it being her desire to know the book's contents firsthand. She had come to terms with the folly of her earlier thoughts, and having pardoned the general of the very deeds that her imagination had created, there was no longer a need to search its writings as a source of his guilt. If any one person was guilty of misdeeds, it was she in her suspicions and actions. Instead, there was something there that had enveloped her upon entering Mrs. Tilney's room, it being a need to know the former lady of the house better. Thus far, she had only the description offered by Eleanor, memories related secondhand, a portrait, and a church memorial. These added up to an enigma for Catherine, and having never known the matriarch, the journal offered a means to make her acquaintance, if not in body, then in words and thoughts.

Simultaneously, she knew that she was in the wrong. These were introspections never meant to be shared with another, and if she were to open the journal, she would be invading the privacy of the very person she had come to admire.

If anyone were to be the proper steward of those observations, it should be her daughter—and this brought Catherine back to that dilemma of being unable to disclose this to Eleanor, due to the nature of its discovery.

So the book remained where it was, while often on Catherine's mind. In more than one instance, she removed the journal from the drawer and held it in her hands. Her fingers trailed across the texture of the fabric as if to detect some small measure of its secrets. Then, with a sigh, she would replace it and close the cabinet door.

Her resolve could only withstand so much; at last, she gave in, reminding herself that she would only look at a page, or possibly two. Surely no harm could come from that? From there came another page, and then another, and all of her best intentions gave way to insight.

From the initial pages, it was clear that few surprises might be found, as all were accounts of the most ordinary sort. On the first was simply a date, written in large numerals in the center of the page. This was followed on the next, as was throughout the succession of pages, with daily accounts written in the most delicate and elegant of penmanship.

Before the end of the first page, and for reasons completely unexplainable based on the generality of the writing, Catherine Morland had fallen under an enchantment, in wanting to know all she might about Eleanor's mother, and in doing so, felt drawn equally close to the daughter, as one sister to another.

At the same time, so unremarkable was the prose that it appeared that the authoress lived an existence of mundane plainness, unshackled by any form of excitement or sandal. Only in the details did the colour of her life emerge, showing clearly a woman capable of great amounts of emotion, and a passion confined by situation. So read the first entry:

Northanger, 3 June
Today was as fine a day as I could hope for. A simple breakfast of toast and juice, followed by a brief walk out of doors. Edward is still away, as he has been for the last month. The afternoon was spent in the company of Mrs. Malleson for cards and pleasantries. Her company is always a delight. There looked to be rain in the afternoon but it never came.

This was followed by another entry of equal inconsequential occurrences, suggesting that her life at the abbey was one of placid sameness.

> *Northanger, 5 June*
> *The rain that threatened to come for the last two days has arrived, so there was no morning walk. No company due to weather. My needle-point is nearly complete and will make a lovely gift for Mrs. Ripper. No word when Edward will return, such is the way of the military.*

From her usage, it was clear that the Edward in question was that of the general, and Catherine considered how the name sat upon his shoulders. Until now, she had not thought of him other than General Tilney, or as the father to her friends, but of course, he would have a Christian name, even if she had not thought of him with such an identity. In retrospect, it suited him well, and certainly more than a Billy or Johnny.

It was in a later entry that a reference was made to the daughter, bringing Catherine's attention to each word.

> *The hours pass far easier when Eleanor is nearby, even though her preference is to run and play rather than offer conversation. I do not mind this, as I was just like her at that age, and would not change her, or in any way diminish her spirit. In this home dominated by the other sex, she is my dearest companion, and no number of acquaintances, the Rippers or Mallesons, Fishers or Bakers could take her place.*

There it was, a sentiment as clearly spoken by the mother as later observed in the daughter, and a loneliness not consolable by the males of the house. Henry had alluded to Eleanor's need for companionship, of which he, with all his affection for her, was of inadequate support. So it was with Mrs. Tilney as well.

The substance of the writing changed in tone at the end of the month, and Catherine could only surmise its cause was from the individual noted as absent in the previous entries.

> *Edward is home. He returned at dusk two days ago, and as is his nature, set the house to a select structure. I am well used to it, knowing that it is from his background that he runs his life. He likes his*

precise schedule, and I cannot fault him for it, as he is a good man, despite his tendencies, and I care for him all the same. Yet how he scolds the servants makes me uneasy, and I wonder at their capacity of endurance as not to quit their employment.

The change in the children is all the more noticeable; they are quiet and obedient to a fault ¬—at least the younger two. Frederick is as impulsive as ever, and even his father's rule does not always cause him to conform. Yet it is this very thing that I believe Edward appreciates in his son, so alike are they. Henry is far more respectful, and dear Eleanor only shrinks into her shell when he is near, so alarmed she is of coming under his scrutiny. If only she could see him as I do. Under that stern exterior, there is a kinder man, even if it is not always apparent.

If a deeper understanding of General Tilney's nature was key to her tenderness, it was nevertheless not weakened in resolve when called upon, as indicated in his authoritarian rule of the house. A later entry made special note of this and was as indicative of his nature as hers.

Sometimes I feel so much for the children, especially Eleanor. Unfortunate girl, she arrived late to dinner today. Edward was so angry and took her to task on the account, that she cried throughout the rest of the meal, and afterward ran straight up to her room. I spoke in her defense but he would have no part of it. Later he said his actions may have been overly dictatorial, but I feel he said it more for my sake than hers. I know what she feels, as I have been a victim of his temper as well. As harsh as his tongue may be, he has never raised a hand.

The following entry from the next day was short.

I found flowers in a vase in my room, picked from the garden outside. I know it was his doing. He also left a single flower for Eleanor in her room. It was his way to make amends. If only he was always so considerate.

There followed a succession of pages with little to note, Mrs. Tilney recording the basics of the day, the menu for breakfast and dinner, acquaintances that might have visited, or more times, did not, and the time spent with Henry and Eleanor. Then in the second week of July, this observation:

It seems at times that I see my husband as little now as when he was away. He attends the meals, but he has been spending so much time closeted away in his private library, of which no one is ever allowed in. He has always been a secretive man, but he seems more distant than ever. How I yearn for the early days of courtship when he paid as much attention to me as I to him. I am duly aware that he is a man of business but must it come at such an expense?

Her journaling through the following week recorded more of the same behavior, with her husband there in body, but never in attendance emotionally, and mostly cloistered away in his private sanctuary. The time spent with family was kept to his standards of rigidity, and on more than one occasion, had cause to reprimand one of the children in the harshest terms. Never did he use the same tactics with his wife, but through her writings, it appeared that she received the blunter end of his behavior, through his indifference and cold responsiveness. If it was love that nurtured her, there was little to be found to sustain her from the general.

Through these accounts, Catherine gleaned a greater understanding of the family to which she had been invited, while there remained a great deal unspoken. For all this, she found the general's behavior towards her always congenial and respectful, and so unlike the individual personified in the writings. To what end was this consideration based, she wondered, as she surely merited no better position than that of his own family? Was his personality that divided? As kind as he had been on her behalf, she had also seen his shortened temper with his children, and could only imagine what would erupt if he were truly enraged.

As detailed in the next entry, his departure the following week was just as abrupt as his arrival, with the servants undoubtedly breathing a collective sigh of relief.

Edward left yesterday on business and will not be back for a fortnight. Already, the household has lapsed back into such comfort and pleasantries as I wish were a constant at all times. The children are more jovial and talkative. Eleanor laughs constantly, reminding me of how much I miss that joyful exuberance. As always, I am saddened to see Edward go, to which I am then inclined to give close analysis, for as my husband and the father of my children, he is as part of me as the air that I breathe. If only he might relearn some gentler graces which he had demonstrated so early on in our relations. I cannot help but wonder what has become of that man who I fell so earnestly in love with those years ago, for surely he is still there somewhere.

Until he does find his gentle mercies, perhaps it is best that he occupies himself in his library, in whatever he does there to pass the hours, and to which remains a great mystery.

The lateness of the hour brought a reluctant Catherine to pull the ribbon marker across the page and close the journal, having become as enraptured with its contents as she had with the individuals on which it was based. It was placed back in the cabinet, the drawer closed, and the doors shut. With a mind still reeling from all that she had read, she took to bed and waited for a sleep that came only after multiple attempts to still the mind from its adventures, of sons and daughters, a mother now departed, and an enigma of a father who gave of himself not in tenderness, but in too much structure.

CHAPTER

Forty-Three

A DAY OR TWO PASSED away and brought no tidings of Captain Tilney. His brother and sister knew not what to think. Sometimes it appeared to them as if his silence would be the natural result of the suspected engagement, and at others that it was wholly incompatible with it. The general, meanwhile, though offended every morning by Frederick's remissness in writing, was free from any real anxiety about him, and therefore was unchanged in attitude when a letter from the son did arrive. He took no effort to excuse himself to read the delivery but opened it there in the parlour where they had gathered. Henry, Eleanor, and Catherine all watched him as he read the communique, looking for some small indication from his manners as to its contents, however he offered no expression of satisfaction or displeasure, on the whole suggesting that the matter of Isabella Thorpe was either mentioned in such vague terms as to elicit no reaction, or was left out altogether. With stone-faced indifference, he folded the letter and slipped it into his pocket.

"And how is our brother faring?" asked Henry.

With a response targeted to everyone present and to no one in particular, he answered simply, "Satisfactory," and it became clear that he would give no further details to the contents. Without pause, he took paper in hand at the writing desk and penned a letter, so brief as it must have been only a sentence, two at the most.

"You will, of course, send Frederick all our love and affection," commented Henry in humour, knowing of the disdain the brother had for overt endearments. The general neither smiled nor replied, but finished the letter, and after folding it, handed it over to his footman, and from there set in the entry hall, as was any correspondence either received or outgoing, where it would be sent later on in the morning.

The matter at hand concluded, the general resumed his consistent solicitude of making Miss Morland's time at Northanger pass pleasantly. He often expressed his uneasiness on this head, feared the sameness of every day's society and employments would disgust her with the place, wished the Lady Frasers had been in the country, talked every now and then of having a large party to dinner, and once or twice began even to calculate the number of young dancing people in the neighbourhood. But then it was such a dead time of year, no wild-fowl, no game, and the Lady Frasers were not in the country. And it all ended, at last, in his telling Henry one morning that when he next went to Woodston, they would take him by surprise there some day or other, and eat their mutton with him. Henry was greatly honoured and very happy, and Catherine was quite delighted with the scheme. "And when do you think, sir, I may look forward to this pleasure? I must be at Woodston on Monday to attend the parish meeting, and shall probably be obliged to stay two or three days."

"Well, well, we will take our chance some one of those days. There is no need to fix. You are not to put yourself at all out of your way. Whatever you may happen to have in the house will be enough. I think I can answer for the young ladies making allowance for a bachelor's table. Let me see; Monday will be a busy day with you, we will not come on Monday; and Tuesday will be a busy one with me. I expect my surveyor from Brockham with his report in the morning; and afterwards I cannot in decency fail attending the club. I really could not face my acquaintance if I stayed away now; for, as I am known to be in the country, it would be taken exceedingly amiss; and it is a rule with me, Miss Morland, never to give offence to any of my neighbours, if a small sacrifice of time and attention can prevent it. They are a set of very worthy men. They have half a buck from Northanger twice a year; and I dine with them whenever I can. Tuesday, therefore, we may say is out of the question. But on Wednesday, I think, Henry, you may expect us; and we shall be with you early, that we may have time to look about us. Two hours and three quarters will carry us to Woodston, I suppose; we shall be in the carriage by ten; so, about a quarter before one on Wednesday, you may look for us."

A ball itself could not have been more welcome to Catherine than this little excursion, so strong was her desire to be acquainted with Woodston; and her heart was still bounding with joy when Henry, about an hour afterwards, came booted and greatcoated into the room where she and Eleanor were sitting, and said, "I am come, young ladies, in a very moralizing strain, to observe that our pleasures in this world are always to be paid for, and that we often purchase them at a great disadvantage, giving ready-monied actual happiness for a draft on the future, that may not be honoured. Witness myself, at this present hour. Because I am to hope for the satisfaction of seeing you at Woodston on Wednesday, which bad weather, or twenty other causes, may prevent, I must go away directly, two days before I intended it."

"Go away!" said Catherine, with a very long face. "And why?"

"Why! How can you ask the question? Because no time is to be lost in frightening my old housekeeper out of her wits, because I must go and prepare a dinner for you, to be sure."

"Oh! Not seriously!"

"Aye, and sadly too—for I had much rather stay."

"But how can you think of such a thing, after what the general said? When he so particularly desired you not to give yourself any trouble, because anything would do."

Henry only smiled. "I am sure it is quite unnecessary upon your sister's account and mine. You must know it to be so; and the general made such a point of your providing nothing extraordinary: besides, if he had not said half so much as he did, he has always such an excellent dinner at home, that sitting down to a middling one for one day could not signify."

"I wish I could reason like you, for his sake and my own. Good-bye. As tomorrow is Sunday, Eleanor, I shall not return."

He went; and, it being at any time a much simpler operation to Catherine to doubt her own judgment than Henry's, she was very soon obliged to give him credit for being right, however disagreeable to her his going. But the inexplicability of the general's conduct dwelt much on her thoughts. That he was very particular in his eating, she had, by her own unassisted observation, already discovered; but why he should say one thing so positively, and mean another all the while, was most unaccountable! How were people, at that rate, to be understood? Who but Henry could have been aware of what his father was at?

From Saturday to Wednesday, however, they were now to be without Henry. This was the sad finale of every reflection: Captain Tilney's letter had arrived but had apparently said little, giving way to the possibility of another letter of full disclosure, and would certainly come in his absence; and Wednesday she was very sure would be wet. The past, present, and future were all equally in gloom. Her brother so unhappy, and her loss in Isabella so great; and Eleanor's spirits always affected by Henry's absence! What was there to interest or amuse her? She was tired of the woods and the shrubberies—always so smooth and so dry; and the abbey in itself was no more to her now than any other house. The painful remembrance of the folly it had helped to nourish and perfect was the only emotion which could spring from a consideration of the building. What a revolution in her ideas! She saw clearly now, set straight through Mr. Tilney's reprimand, as well as the insights gained from his mother's pen. For all his faults, she could now accept the general as an individual of limited patience and rigid mind, but not without a level of generosity. This was but one aspect of the change in her interests; She, who had so longed to be in an abbey! Now, there was nothing so charming to her imagination as the unpretending comfort of a well-connected parsonage, something like Fullerton, but better: Fullerton had its faults, but Woodston probably had none. If Wednesday should ever come!

It did come, and exactly when it might be reasonably looked for. It came—it was fine—and Catherine trod on air. By ten o'clock, the chaise and four conveyed the two from the abbey, and upon departure, Catherine felt a relief come over her, leaving her novel-induced fantasies, her subsequent embarrassment, and the journal behind. Of the book, she had progressed only a few pages deeper from her initial read, and those had offered nothing more than daily accounts of little import. After an agreeable drive of almost twenty miles, they entered Woodston, a large and populous village, in a situation not unpleasant. Catherine was ashamed to say how pretty she thought it, as the general seemed to think an apology necessary for the flatness of the country, and the size of the village; but in her heart she preferred it to any place she had ever been at, and looked with great admiration at every neat house above the rank of a cottage, and at all the little chandler's shops which they passed. At the further end of the village, and tolerably disengaged from the rest of it, stood the parsonage, a new-built substantial stone house, with its semicircular sweep and green gates; and, as they drove up to the door, Henry, with the friends of his solitude, a large Newfoundland puppy and two or three terriers, was ready to receive and make much of them.

Catherine's mind was too full, as she entered the house, for her either to observe or to say a great deal; and, till called on by the general for her opinion of it, she had very little idea of the room in which she was sitting. Upon looking round it then, she perceived in a moment that it was the most comfortable room in the world; but she was too guarded to say so, and the coldness of her praise disappointed him.

"We are not calling it a good house," said he. "We are not comparing it with Fullerton and Northanger—we are considering it as a mere parsonage, small and confined, we allow, but decent, perhaps, and habitable; and altogether not inferior to the generality; or, in other words, I believe there are few country parsonages in England half so good. It may admit of improvement, however. Far be it from me to say otherwise; and anything in reason—a bow thrown out, perhaps—though, between ourselves, if there is one thing more than another my aversion, it is a patched-on bow."

Catherine did not hear enough of this speech to understand or be pained by it; and other subjects being studiously brought forward and supported by Henry, at the same time that a tray full of refreshments was introduced by his servant, the general was shortly restored to his complacency, and Catherine to all her usual ease of spirits.

The room in question was of a commodious, well-proportioned size, and handsomely fitted up as a dining-parlour; and on their quitting it to walk round the grounds, she was shown, first into a smaller apartment, belonging peculiarly to the master of the house, and made unusually tidy on the occasion; and afterwards into what was to be the drawing-room, with the appearance of which, though unfurnished, Catherine was delighted enough even to satisfy the general. It was a prettily shaped room, the windows reaching to the ground, and the view from them pleasant, though only over green meadows; and she expressed her admiration at the moment with all the honest simplicity with which she felt it. "Oh! Why do not you fit up this room, Mr. Tilney? What a pity not to have it fitted up! It is the prettiest room I ever saw; it is the prettiest room in the world!"

"I trust," said the general, with a most satisfied smile, "that it will very speedily be furnished: it waits only for a lady's taste!"

"Well, if it was my house, I should never sit anywhere else. Oh! What a sweet little cottage there is among the trees—apple trees, too! It is the prettiest cottage!"

"You like it—you approve it as an object—it is enough. Henry, remember that Robinson is spoken to about it. The cottage remains."

Such a compliment recalled all Catherine's consciousness, and silenced her directly; and, though pointedly applied to by the general for her choice of the prevailing colour of the paper and hangings, nothing like an opinion on the subject could be drawn from her. The influence of fresh objects and fresh air, however, was of great use in dissipating these embarrassing associations; and, having reached the ornamental part of the premises, consisting of a walk round two sides of a meadow, on which Henry's genius had begun to act about half a year ago, she was sufficiently recovered to think it prettier than any pleasure-ground she had ever been in before, though there was not a shrub in it higher than the green bench in the corner.

A saunter into other meadows, and through part of the village, with a visit to the stables to examine some improvements, and a charming game of play with a litter of puppies just able to roll about, brought them to four o'clock, when Catherine scarcely thought it could be three. At four they were to dine, and at six to set off on their return. Never had any day passed so quickly!

She could not but observe that the abundance of the dinner did not seem to create the smallest astonishment in the general; nay, that he was even looking at the side-table for cold meat which was not there. His son and daughter's observations were of a different kind. They had seldom seen him eat so heartily at any table but his own, and never before known him so little disconcerted by the melted butter's being oiled.

At six o'clock, the general having taken his coffee, the carriage again received them; and so gratifying had been the tenor of his conduct throughout the whole visit, so well assured was her mind on the subject of his expectations, that, could she have felt equally confident of the wishes of his son, Catherine would have quitted Woodston with little anxiety as to the How or the When she might return to it.

CHAPTER

Forty-Four

UPON HER RETURN from Woodston, and just prior to her retiring, Catherine found the time to retrieve the journal once more from its drawer and continue from where she had left off.

Northanger, 11 August

I dreamt of an idyllic existence, where the children are always happy and respectful, the man acts as a provider during the day but is a loving father and husband in the remaining hours, in all a setting that is condition-free of concern, and the affection of one is felt by all. I dream of warmth of the heart, compassion, and understanding. Most of all, I dream of companionship. Would that this were the reality, and in considering this, I put forth the question—am I asking that much?

At times, Edward can be extremely hard to bear. At others, he can be a ghost of his former self, with nary a word spoken. His time spent with family is in expectation of all things set his way, or he goes from silent to stern rebuke at the offender. This was not the man that I pledged my faith to all those years ago, but it is the man I still care for.

I have often wondered how Edward spends his hours here, as he mostly keeps to himself, sequestered in the private library below. I have seen the door, but to that extent, its contents remain a mystery. It would not bother me terribly, as men need their domains to rule, if he were to give some time to conversation. I miss his insights and wisdom, and yes, even the humour of his that has been vacant for far longer than I dare to consider.

And so I dream. And hope. And pray.

Northanger, 10 August

I lost all composure yesterday. Fortunately, the children were not around to see it. I pleaded my case to Edward, that I needed him as much in confidence as in presence, but he was giving little in return of either. He was resolute that nothing had changed in his care for me, but he had pressing affairs that could not be altered and required his time. He is wrong. He has changed.

Northanger, 11 August

I have come to a decision, one that has been on my mind for a great length of time, more than bears recounting. I must consider the fact that the esteem I hold for my husband is no longer reciprocated in kind, or if so, has transformed into a thing I cannot fathom. We share the same house, but not his contemplations, and only a minimum of time or conversation. I feel my heart breaking at this, but if I am no longer allowed to his private thoughts as I once was, then I shall at least have a better understanding of the nature of my rival. I cannot say whether exploring his library will give me any satisfaction, but it is a thing I feel compelled to take on. Is this a betrayal of his trust? Yes; and this is why I have put it off for so long, however, I feel that he has lost my trust by shutting me out—not from his private room but the chamber of his heart.

13 August

My first opportunity to gain entry to his library today was unsuccessful as it was locked. I should have expected as much. There may be a solution, but it cannot be accomplished before he returns. I will try again soon.

23 August

At last, another opportunity, as he has left for the city. I established where he kept the key—I only had to do some careful questioning of the house servants. Today, then.

24 August

I hardly know how to begin this entry, except to say that for all time that I thought I knew my husband, I was terribly mistaken. I have been to the library, the one he has kept under lock and key from all observers, and can now say that I understand why it was barred from view, even if not to explain the whys of its contents. The cell was set up like any library, as to be expected, and at first, I noticed nothing out of the ordinary. Only when I began a closer examination of the books and artifacts therein did I grow cold in horror. It is a room of dark material, such as I never knew existed, even though I do not comprehend its meaning. Many of the books are very old, and in foreign languages that I cannot discern, but of the ones that I could read over, and the diagrams and sketches, I know that it has something to do with black magic so vile that it is an offence to all things of a Christian mind. Alongside this were maps of both local and worldly views, marked with lines and writings, and a journal that must have been his, but which I could not bring myself to inspect. What was most disturbing, to which I cannot get out of my mind, was a bas relief on the shelf of some horrid creature, neither man nor animal, but something else, surrounded by human figures in either a state of group agony or ecstasy.

I cannot begin to understand why my husband would be involved with such a thing. I can only state that I cannot remain in this house as long as those obscenities remain, and though it means admitting my invasion to his domain, I must plead my case to rid this house of them forever. It can be no other way.

29 August
Edward returned yesterday, and while I was not able to speak immediately, but wait another day, I found the time and courage to face him tonight. It is the hardest thing I have ever done, knowing he would be angry beyond measure at my actions, apparent betrayal, and subsequent demand. I told him all, followed by my request for his library to be cleared of its contents.

To my surprise, after his initial shock, he was not consumed by rage but kept calm. He spoke softly, with the tone of affection I have not heard in so long, and even what I believe must have been the beginnings of tears. He apologized for causing me such distress, but the work was part of a larger scheme that even now he could not divulge its true meaning, only to say that it had to do with his work. As such, I must not speak of it to a soul. He would, in turn, remove the whole from the abbey, if not immediately, then as soon as possible, and would be done with the whole affair soon enough. He held me in his arms, for which it has been so long since his last embrace, and I spoke my love for him, and he told me to rest easy, that he would take care of everything.

Have I found my dear Edward once more? More importantly, has he found his way back to me?

Catherine pulled the ribbon across the page and closed the book. For all that she might have thought of the general, never would she have considered something as this, even if he had come to his senses through Mrs. Tilney's intervention. The account had left her uneasy in the knowledge that even the children may not be aware of—or should know—as it would surely colour their opinion of their father. An understanding was dawning on Catherine of the responsibility of reading another's thoughts, becoming privy to their secrets, and all it might mean. Filled with such a mixture of feelings as this, she was forced to put the journal away.

She could read no further tonight.

CHAPTER
Forty-Five

THE NEXT MORNING BROUGHT the following very unexpected letter from Isabella:

Bath, April

My dearest Catherine, I received your two kind letters with the greatest delight, and have a thousand apologies to make for not answering them sooner. I really am quite ashamed of my idleness; but in this horrid place one can find time for nothing. I have had my pen in my hand to begin a letter to you almost every day since you left Bath, but have always been prevented by some silly trifler or other. Pray write to me soon, and direct to my own home. Thank God, we leave this vile place tomorrow. Since you went away, I have had no pleasure in it—the dust is beyond anything; and everybody one cares for is gone. I believe if I could see you I should not mind the rest, for you are dearer to me than anybody can conceive. I am quite uneasy about your dear brother, not having heard from him since he went to Oxford; and am fearful of some misunderstanding. Your kind offices will set all right: he is the only man I ever did or could love, and I trust you will convince him of it. The spring fashions are partly down; and the hats the most frightful you can imagine. I hope you spend your time pleasantly, but am afraid you never think of me. I will not say all that I could of the family you are with, because I would not be ungenerous, or set you against those you esteem; but it is very difficult to know whom to trust, and young men never know their minds two days together. I rejoice to say that the young man whom, of all others, I particularly abhor, has temporarily left Bath. You will know, from this description, I must mean Captain Tilney, who, as you may remember, was amazingly disposed to follow and tease me, before you went away. Afterwards he got worse, and became quite my shadow. Many girls might have been taken in, for never were such attentions; but I knew the fickle sex too well. He went away to his regiment two days ago, and I trust I shall never be plagued with him again, although he boasted to return before my departure. He is the greatest coxcomb I ever saw, and amazingly disagreeable. The last two days he was always by the side of Charlotte Davis: I pitied his taste, but took no notice of him. The last time we met was in Bath Street, and I turned directly into a shop that he might not speak to me; I would not even look at him. He went into the pump-room afterwards; but I would not have followed him for all the world. Such a contrast between him and your brother! Pray send me some news of the latter—I am quite unhappy about him; he seemed so uncomfortable when he went away, with a cold, or something that affected his spirits. I would write to him myself, but have mislaid his direction; and, as I hinted above, am afraid he took something in my conduct amiss. Pray explain everything to his satisfaction; or, if he still harbours any doubt, a line from himself to me, or a call at Putney when next in town, might set all to rights. I have not been to the rooms this age, nor to the play, except going in last night with the Hodges, for a frolic, at half price: they teased me into it; and I was determined they should not say I shut myself up because Tilney was gone. We happened to sit by the Mitchells, and they pretended to be quite surprised to see me out. I knew their spite: at one time they could not be civil to me, but now they are all friendship; but I am not such a fool as to be *taken in by them. You know I have a pretty good spirit of my own. Anne Mitchell had tried to put on a turban like mine, as I wore it the week before at the concert, but made wretched work of it—it happened to become my odd face, I believe, at least Tilney told me so at the time, and said every eye was upon me; but he is the last man whose word I would take. I wear nothing but purple now: I know I look hideous in it, but no matter—it is your dear brother's favourite colour. Lose no time, my dearest, sweetest Catherine, in writing to him and to me, Who ever am, etc.*

Such a strain of shallow artifice could not impose even upon Catherine. Its inconsistencies, contradictions, and falsehood struck her from the very first. She was ashamed of Isabella, and ashamed of having ever loved her. Her professions of attachment were now as disgusting as her excuses were empty, and her demands impudent. "Write to James on her behalf! No, James should never hear Isabella's name mentioned by her again."

On Henry's arrival from Woodston, she made known to him and Eleanor their brother's safety, congratulating them with sincerity on it, and reading aloud the most material passages of her letter with strong indignation. When she had finished it—"So much for Isabella," she cried, "and for all our intimacy! She must think me an idiot, or she could not have written so; but perhaps this has served to make her character better known to me than mine is to her. I see what she has been about. She is a vain coquette, and her tricks have not answered. I do not believe she had ever any regard either for James or for me, and I wish I had never known her."

"It will soon be as if you never had," said Henry.

"There is but one thing that I cannot understand. I see that she has had designs on Captain Tilney, which have not succeeded; but I do not understand what Captain Tilney has been about all this time. Why should he pay her such attentions as to make her quarrel with my brother, and then fly off himself?"

"I have very little to say for Frederick's motives, such as I believe them to have been. He has his vanities as well as Miss Thorpe, and the chief difference is, that, having a stronger head, they have not yet injured himself. If the effect of his behaviour does not justify him with you, we had better not seek after the cause."

"Then you do not suppose he ever really cared about her?"

"I am persuaded that he never did."

"And only made believe to do so for mischief's sake?"

Henry bowed his assent.

"Well, then, I must say that I do not like him at all. Though it has turned out so well for us, I do not like him at all. As it happens, there is no great harm done, because I do not think Isabella has any heart to lose. But, suppose he had made her very much in love with him?"

"But we must first suppose Isabella to have had a heart to lose—consequently to have been a very different creature; and, in that case, she would have met with very different treatment."

"It is very right that you should stand by your brother."

"And if you would stand by yours, you would not be much distressed by the disappointment of Miss Thorpe. But your mind is warped by an innate principle of general integrity, and therefore not accessible to the cool reasonings of family partiality, or a desire of revenge."

Catherine was complimented out of further bitterness. Frederick could not be unpardonably guilty, while Henry made himself so agreeable. She resolved on not answering Isabella's letter, and tried to think no more of it.

CHAPTER
Forty-Six

ALL OF CATHERINE'S OPINIONS regarding Isabella were further challenged the following day with a second letter from the same, forcing her to weigh the fact from falsehood, and decide once again on the value of such a friendship.

Bath, April

Dear Catherine,

    I beg your patience again as I feel I must set myself straight with you, as honestly as I can. Please tear up my letter from yesterday; I said a great many things that were not from the heart and should not have been set to paper—except the plea for James, that much was truthful.

    I have committed some terrible wrongs to those around me, to you, and especially to your brother, and I now think I may be in a position beyond which I can safely remove myself. So I write once more for your help, your advice, and most importantly, your forgiveness. I cannot excuse my past actions. They are mine to own, but I quickly lost sight of having something far dearer than I realized at the time. Only after destroying any chance of that happiness did I realize what I had done.

At the same time, I aligned myself with someone who has proved to be far more harmful than I ever imagined. I cannot explain myself better without a full incrimination of my actions which I am too ashamed to admit, even to myself, so please allow me to not dwell there. Let me state in short that he has shown himself to be persuasive and heartless, selfish for his ends—and while I cannot give any solid evidence of this, I feel that he is capable of doing terrible wrongs. Because of this, I hope to leave Bath and never be found by him again.

As for James, I have never regretted anything more in my life. Let him know this, from one who is now the most sorrowful creature upon the earth.

You may think this letter to be written by someone else, as its tone and frankness are so unlike me. I am used to hiding behind my words without showing any of what is underneath. Now, for once, I must speak true, and I pray that you recognize it as honest.

I am sad and frightened. I have consorted with the worst kind of person—you know of whom I speak—and even now, I can feel some vague threat. I am done with him, but I am afraid that he is not done with me. Dearest Catherine, as absurd as it sounds, I fear for my life and I know not what to do.

If you could find it in your heart to forgive a foolish girl who has not thought as clearly as she aught, please write back. Write me soon.

With all my heart,
Isabella

Catherine knew not what to make of the letter, so unlike anything before said by Isabella, either on paper or in direct conversation. She had already come to terms with the lengthy series of falsehoods presented by her former friend, accepted it for what it was, and therefore aligned herself rightfully with her brother. The shallowness of the previous letter was so pronounced, that she had dismissed the whole as complete artifice. So what was she to make of this?

She considered taking in either of the Tilneys as counsel but quickly discounted it as a possibility. Isabella's letter accused their brother of such behaviour that it would surely be held in offence, as to influence their opinion to an even greater degree. She could not bring herself to insult them in that way. Miss Thorpe's words were meant for Catherine alone, and despite all her uncertainties about its validity, she felt she must honour at least that privacy. As to its true meaning, that was a matter she would have to consider without outside help.

What captured her attention most was its sense of urgency, as if Isabella's life depended on it; and what about the final line? If she was in genuine trouble, surely there were others closer to her who might offer whatever aid she needed, her brother and mother among them. The more she contemplated its meaning, the more she weighed in on its honesty.

Isabella had demonstrated an inability to truthfulness; her previous letter was as clear validation as any. Could she accept the latest as anything else than more of the same? Despite the change in tone, it might be another set of falsehoods, spoken from another approach.

Still injured from how her brother had been treated, and the lies previously told to her, Catherine reluctantly concluded that the letter was no different in content from the last. How could she honestly think otherwise? With a heavy heart—or was it guilt?—she put the letter away and again resolved to do nothing.

CHAPTER
Forty-Seven

SOON AFTER THIS, the general found himself obliged to go to London for a week; and he left Northanger earnestly regretting that any necessity should rob him even for an hour of Miss Morland's company, and anxiously recommending the study of her comfort and amusement to his children as their chief object in his absence. His departure gave Catherine the first experimental conviction that a loss may be sometimes a gain. The happiness with which their time now passed, every employment voluntary, every laugh indulged, every meal a scene of ease and good humour, walking where they liked and when they liked, their hours, pleasures, and fatigues at their own command, made her thoroughly sensible of the restraint which the general's presence had imposed, and most thankfully feel their present release from it. Such ease and such delights made her love the place and the people more and more every day; and had it not been for a dread of its soon becoming expedient to leave the one, and an apprehension of not being equally beloved by the other, she would at each moment of each day have been perfectly happy; but she was now in the fourth week of her visit; before the general came home, the fourth week would be turned, and perhaps it might seem an intrusion if she stayed much longer. This was a painful consideration whenever it occurred; and eager to get rid of such a weight on her mind, she very soon resolved to speak to Eleanor about it at once, propose going away, and be guided in her conduct by the manner in which her proposal might be taken.

Aware that if she gave herself much time, she might feel it difficult to bring forward so unpleasant a subject, she took the first opportunity of being suddenly alone with Eleanor, and of Eleanor's being in the middle of a speech about something very different, to start forth her obligation of going away very soon. Eleanor looked and declared herself much concerned. She had "hoped for the pleasure of her company for a much longer time—had been misled (perhaps by her wishes) to suppose that a much longer visit had been promised—and could not but think that if Mr. and Mrs. Morland were aware of the pleasure it was to her to have her there, they would be too generous to hasten her return." Catherine explained: "Oh! As to that, Papa and Mamma were in no hurry at all. As long as she was happy, they would always be satisfied."

"Then why, might she ask, in such a hurry herself to leave them?"

"Oh! Because she had been there so long."

"Nay, if you can use such a word, I can urge you no farther. If you think it long—"

"Oh! No, I do not indeed. For my own pleasure, I could stay with you as long again." And it was directly settled that, till she had, her leaving them was not even to be thought of. In having this cause of uneasiness so pleasantly removed, the force of the other was likewise weakened. The kindness, the earnestness of Eleanor's manner in pressing her to stay, and Henry's gratified look on being told that her stay was determined, were such sweet proofs of her importance with them, as left her only just so much solicitude as the human mind can never do comfortably without. She did—almost always—believe that Henry loved her, and quite always that his father and sister loved and even wished her to belong to them; and believing so far, her doubts and anxieties were merely sportive irritations.

No further pages had been turned in Mrs. Tilney's journal, in part due to the unsettling contents that had been revealed when Catherine had last taken the book in hand. What the mother had discovered in the library had been vaguely described, but her subsequent reactions were enough to convince Catherine of its unwholesome nature. Even after reading those pages, she had dwelt on its particulars, and knowing that the general had agreed to relent on the dark materials gave her only marginal reassurance. She now found it difficult to be in his presence without all this fresh knowledge ever on her mind, even though the events took place a good many years in the past. True, she had always felt a trifle uncomfortable in his presence, either due to his overwhelming attention to her comfort, or his otherwise stern demeanor. This only intensified her trepidations. On their last dinner, the night before his departure, she felt especially nervous at his continued doting and attention to her fashion, while feeling ashamed that she should react in such a way to the individual who had shown nothing but the greatest favoritism to her. It was in bad form to hold any such grievance, even though she nevertheless looked forward to his absence and the exclusivity it would give to Henry and Eleanor.

As that evening drew to a close, she withdrew the journal once more from its drawer and continued to read.

Northanger, 3 September

I have not been feeling myself for the last day, a level of nausea making it difficult to rise to my normal spirits. I hope that it passes quickly. Mine has never been the sturdiest of constitutions, with a stomach more delicate than most. I missed my walk today, but as the weather was not cooperative, it was of little consequence.

4 September

I confess to feeling worse today, possibly a fever. Edward has been most kind, looking after me, wiping my head with a damp cloth when needed, and serving me a medicinal tea that will help to calm the stomach. He stayed at my side so that we were able to talk. It has been an eternity since he has given me his time to such a degree and is proof that the man that I married is still there within.

5 September

I should be feeling better, but instead, I have grown worse. Nothing will stay down and the fever has continued. Mr. Munro, our physician to whom I have placed all my trust in the past, has been called upon for me. I have had digestive ailments before, but there is something about this that is different. There is nothing I have been able to do to lessen the symptoms. Edward continues to look after me and bring me my food. He has been so kind.

6 September

I can barely write from weakness. Mr. Munro visited earlier. I think he has called for other opinions. Edward has insisted I continue the medicinal teas, but it tastes horrible. My insides feel raw. For the first time, I have thought of death. I am terrified, not for myself but for the children.

7 September
I have had the most horrible thoughts. Surely it is a delusion. Could the teas be making me feel worse—and if that is the case—I shudder at the implications. Please, do not let it be so.

8 Sept
Edward, why have you done this?

There were no further entries in the journal. Catherine closed the book, and a coldness swept over her as the full ramification of the words took hold, and its suggestion of actions far more foul than she, with an imagination ripe from wildly spun novels, could have conjured. She flipped through the remaining pages once more, in hopes of a further account she might have missed, but there were none—only blank sheets.

Edward, why have you done this?

It was more than a question; it was an accusation, a condemnation. With her last entry, Mrs. Tilney had spoken aloud a revelation as much as a question from beyond the grave, condensed to the single word, "Why?" Catherine could only pretend to identify with what she must have felt, knowing that the man that she had promised her love to, had spent a life with, and from whom she had borne children, might have wronged her in such a fashion. Surely, she must have meant something else, and it was Catherine's interpretation of the words that suggested the betrayal. She went back through the book, rereading the pages carefully, noting every word, every nuance, in hopes that she had been incorrect in its meaning, but in the end, she was unable to conclude any different outcome.

Mrs. Tilney died shortly after the last entry, of complications from bilious fever, a diagnosis concluded by the physicians, and held as accurate by the children. Her previous history of symptoms was confirmed by her earlier comments, but to offer such suspicions with her last words suggested only two alternatives: she was delusional from the fever, and the accusations were nothing more than a paranoia not based on reality—or it was the truth.

If the latter was accurate, what would have been the reason for such an action? Catherine realized that she knew very little about the family, its background, and all the minuscule particulars that made up their lives. All she had to go on was what she had been told by Henry and Eleanor, the physical surroundings of which she had spent the last weeks, and the daily accounts from the journal, the combination of which still gave a scattered tapestry of their existence. From all she could determine, the general could be cold and indifferent, but clearly, there was far more to him than was visible on the surface, evident from his wife's memoirs.

Just as possible was his honest intent to nurse her back to health by means of the teas and medicinals he must have believed would resuscitate her, and later still, the physicians when his remedies failed to take hold. Henry had made clear that his father was overwhelmed by the loss of his wife, surely clear evidence of his innocence.

But still—what if he had become false in his affections, or perhaps those feelings had turned to another woman? Might all the feelings of passion and endearment have transformed into boredom, even hatred? How was one to truly know the heart of another? The one event of any consequence that stood out was the mother's excursion to General Tilney's private library, and her subsequent confrontation afterward. Based on her account, there had been no anger on his side, and if anything, a gentler reaction than was his normal disposition. He had agreed to set things right for her. Were the contents of the library of such importance, and of such a secretive nature, that it could require the permanent silencing of his wife? The idea was beyond any normal level of comprehension, and yet—

Edward, why have you done this?

Catherine found herself shivering uncontrollably, and unable to calm herself directly, she set the journal on the bed and began to pace her room, taking in deep breaths to soothe the nerves. At once, she felt the imposing claustrophobic quality of the abbey, the very thing that she had initially envisioned prior to her arrival, with its dark secrets, hidden chambers, and even a skeleton hidden behind the veil. At that time, the idea was intoxicating, and she could hardly wait to uncover every secret. With her arrival and subsequent time spent there, it ceased to be anything more than an overly large dwelling, and her concocted mysteries were dispersed to a mundane reality. Now, she had come full circle, without any advance warning, and the possibility of dark intrigue weighed in upon her to a degree that she could hardly bear. As her body continued in its involuntary shudders, she wished to be back in Bath, or even Fullerton, anywhere but this.

Her first thought was to reveal all to Henry—he would surely know what actions to take—but just as quickly realized that this was impossible. Already he had admonished her for such thoughts, thus sending her running to her room in tears. How could she explain the finding of the diary, and in a blatant act of propriety, keeping it in her room to read at her leisure? If ever she were to lose all respect in his eyes, then that would surely accomplish the fall from grace. Even to explain the compartment of the writing desk from which the book was hidden would have been an embarrassment. No, she would have to remain silent.

Just as improper would have been to take Eleanor in as counsel as she possessed a far weaker stamina for unsettling news. She was still in mourning for her mother, even after all the passed time, under the belief that the death was of a natural, although tragic, illness. Revealing that her mother had died under such a reprehensible cause was far too great a cruelty to bestow upon her.

A further puzzle remained, this being how the journal might have survived all these years without detection, just as how it might have been secreted after the final entry. Surely Mrs. Tilney had grown so ill as to make its return unbearably difficult. It was apparent from the poor penmanship in the latter writings that her strength was failing. It must have taken a great degree of will to write her last thoughts and put it back in its place of safety, where it remained for these many years—and its authoress, being the only person to know of the compartment, took that secret to her grave.

All this and more settled upon Catherine with a stifling finality, and she suddenly understood in full what care a person should take in wanting a thing too much, because it was entirely possible to get it, regardless of their actual desire.

When the morning dawned, she felt no better, as the night had been long and troubling, making a decent rest all but impossible. She joined Henry and Eleanor in the breakfast-parlour and initially found herself reticent to conversation, but was soon drawn out by his agreeable manner to the degree that she was able to respond in kind. Even with the weight of the journal's disclosures upon her mind, she found it possible to set the thoughts aside for the moment, as much for her own need of comfort as the simple truth—what had taken place was many years behind her, and her dwelling on it at present, would change nothing.

The morning passed, with ever-present thoughts of Mrs. Tilney. Time and again, she reconsidered speaking to Henry, but he was never far away from his sister, making such a conversation impossible; nor was it prudent, as it would only incriminate her, she kept reminding herself. What good would it do?

In all this, a germ of an idea developed, at first being a passing thought, but it soon took a stronger hold, centering on General Tilney's private study and what part it had played in earlier events. Were the contents of that room and its unwelcome discovery the keys to the mother's ill health and eventual death? Furthermore, what exactly was it that she had come across that could have brought about such an ending? When confronted, the general agreed to clear the study of the offending contents, and if he were true to his word, the removal would have taken place. With his wife's passing so soon afterward, particularly if he had played some part in the outcome, there was the notable possibility of the study being left intact, for whatever value it held of more importance over the life of his wife. If this was true, and his study retained its contents at that time, what then was it to be at the present? Clearly, it was still used in its private capacity by the general, as Eleanor had noted during their tour of the abbey, but was still kept as secret as it had been when Mrs. Tilney was alive.

What was beyond the door? The question vexed Catherine increasingly as the day progressed, thus bringing the inevitable conclusion; that the answer might be found by venturing forth to the very place that fools would fear to tread, and repeating that act that cost the lady of the abbey so dear. By degrees, she began to map out a plan for the following day, a limitation being her securing an hour away from Eleanor, surely more than enough time to commit the deed and return undiscovered. What she might do with the discovery was another matter to which she had no immediate answer; in fact, she preferred to give it as little thought as possible. The window of opportunity was specific to the afternoon, due to the brother's own travels.

Henry was not able to obey his father's injunction of remaining wholly at Northanger in attendance on the ladies, during his absence in London, the engagements of his curate at Woodston obliging him to leave them on Saturday for a couple of nights. His loss was not now what it had been while the general was at home.

So it was that on the following day, Henry reluctantly took his leave and the girls spent a pleasant morning together, even with Catherine appearing to be distracted on more than one occasion. By pure fortuitous chance, the afternoon arrived, and Eleanor, feeling less than favourable to the day, excused herself by stating her need for rest, and unknowingly allowing her friend the opportunity to set her plan into motion.

CHAPTER
Forty-Eight

BY ALL RIGHTS, Catherine should have been more nervous. What she prepared to do was foolhardy, inconsiderate, reckless, deceitful—even dangerous. Not for the first time in her life had she plunged into an action best described as witless, and indeed, her present intention was imbecilic in the extreme; however, she was determined to see it through. Instead of nervousness, she felt a combination of excitement mixed with caution to her excursion through the abbey. The two people she would have least wanted to confront—Henry and the general—were both away, and with Eleanor retired to her room, there were only the various housekeepers and servants to avoid. If she were careful, she might navigate the trip undetected. It occurred to her that even though she had sworn off all her novel scenarios from entering real life, this had all the symptoms of such a plot. To counter this were the words Henry had spoken, played over in her mind: "Miss Morland, what ideas have you been admitting?"

By retracing her steps from the earlier tour of the abbey, passing by the kitchen with all its modern improvements, the dining-room and billiard-room, and only getting turned around on one occasion, she was soon able to find what once was the monastery's cloister, there with the bare markings on the floor to the individual cells. How they had been removed and what they might have contained at one time were additional mysteries not to be entertained at present, although they might have given way to some fanciful speculation. What was foremost on her mind were the set of doors nearby, and the largest one that Miss Tilney had pointed out as they passed by. Soon enough, she found herself standing opposite the set, having reached her destination without encountering a single servant.

Now facing the door, an unease overtook her; up to now, she had done nothing untoward, but merely exploring the confines of the abbey. Going any further marked a point of invasion, to which she could, if caught, offer no reasonable explanation. At present, she could simply turn and walk away, with no one the wiser to her intentions. Even with these thoughts, she knew there would be no retreat—after all, she had come this far, hadn't she?

She tried the door handle. Of course, it was locked; she expected as much, but there were advantages to reading so many novels, with their wide and varied storylines, mysterious castles, hidden chambers, and dark secrets. Getting through locked doors had been a common occurrence in these tales, as were methodologies for getting through. She had come prepared with several hairpins, and with little effort was able to release the old mechanism, even a bit surprised that the technique detailed in her reading was accurate. With a final look to both sides, making sure that no one was nearby, she opened the heavy door just enough to slide in.

The first thing she noticed was the illumination, unique to the closeted nature of the room; its source was a single-paned window, as well as a set of architectural improvements certainly contrived by the general to allow additional light in. Her concern of needing a candle for her investigation proved to be invalid. As to the room itself, the whole was of moderate size, no bigger than she might have expected, but more cluttered than any other in the estate. To one side were shelves of books and artifacts, alongside tables piled with manuscripts and loose pages. In the center, a table and chair were set, with a large volume left open, aside sheets of paper and a well-used writing set. On the whole, it looked like any other library, excepting the older age of the books and the general disorder of the room, the latter suggesting the importance of study over organization. She found it a curious fact, as the general seemed to be so fastidious and orderly in every other aspect of his life.

With all the objects that filled the room, it was peculiar that she noted a minor detail, that being the ceiling, its stone as old as the surrounding walls, but far darker in the center. Upon closer examination, it appeared to be charred, as if a great fire had been set, with soot caked across the surface. The discolouring appeared to be quite old, causing Catherine to wonder what the room might have been used for at that time.

She worked her way across the study, examining the tables and shelves, noting their contents but not recognizing anything in particular. The volumes appeared to be in any number of languages—Latin, German, Arabic, as well as

English, but even those in her native tongue were in names incomprehensible to her. Thus must be the interests and mentality of a general, with no books to read for casual pleasure, but business, academia, and more than likely, warfare. The one constant was in their advanced age, some looking to be hundreds of years old, if not more. She pulled a book from the shelf at random, and after a cursory glance at its weathered cover, opened it. The smell of antiquity washed over her, and in gingerly leafing through the pages, she could feel the brittle texture of each sheet. As to its contents, being in some unknown language, she could only take it at face value, acknowledge its age and possible rarity, and then replace it on the shelf.

On a nearby table was a set of maps of various ages, indicating different regions, the topmost being of a section of Gloucestershire, with handwritten lines and notes all directed to the area near Winchcombe labeled as Belas Knap. Next to this was an illustration of a landscape, likewise labeled as the same. The name struck her as familiar, and she remembered Henry telling her of his father's fascination for the locale. What his preoccupation was with the spot was unclear, even with the notations before her, but the general must be well informed on the geographical formations of many sites, this stemming from his occupation.

Her attention returned to the shelves, and the occasional sculpture, bas relief, and objects d'art set at intervals between the books, examining one after another. As a whole, they were of the most peculiar subjects, many representing strange creatures that were neither man nor wholly beast, but some sort of mixture of the two. These she took to be representations derived from some sort of ancient mythology, although it did not strike her as distinctly Roman, the lore to which she was most familiar. One in particular looked distinctly aquatic, but with the lines depicting tentacle-like formations, she discounted it as being Poseidon. More possible was its similarity to one of his minions, with a head resembling an octopus, but with the crouching body more akin to an animal, sharpened claws on the front and hind feet, and long, narrow wings on its back. The statue, from head to base, measured some seven to eight inches in height. To the other side of the shelf was a closeted set of vials, each bearing different liquids and herbs. Hanging from a brass nail inset to an upper shelf was a gold chain bearing a pendant comprised of a trio of geometric shapes, a triangle containing a circle, and divided vertically by a single line.

On the whole, she could not see the reason for the private study being off limits to all but the general, its contents being far too obscure to lure any other family member, and only by degrees did she begin to register an uncomfortable chill unrelated to the temperature of the room. The books and their subjects were of no recognizable theme, but she nevertheless felt a growing disgust for the library, and even the book titles that could be read— Ars Magna et Ultima, De Vermis Mysteriis, Cryptomenysis Patefacta, Saducismus Triumphatus, and Cthäat Aquadingen—suggested things of an unpleasant nature, but with specifics she could not begin to describe.

Only then did she bring herself to the central table, there bearing the largest volume, with other parchments and books alongside, and sheets of notes, perhaps set by the general's hand. Like other volumes in the study, this was one of the ages, bound in dark leather, evidently penned by hand, and judging from the contents, it being some form of Latin. She shifted it over to view the cover, the surface void of text, and then to the front page in search of a title. This she found, reading only the first two syllables, Necron—, before it ran into a succession of others, and leaving her unable to pronounce the whole as a single entity. What she did recognize—not from any great knowledge of Latin, but from the novel by Ludwig Flammenberg so well loved by Isabella, and its title, Necromancer of the Black Forest—was its reference pertaining to the dead.

The book was set back in its place to peruse its pages, but neither its text nor arcane symbology offered any better understanding, except that its subject was wholly vile. She looked at the neighbouring parchments, finding further illustrations of the beings depicted in sculpture on the shelf, and here did the real horror settle under her skin. Before her eyes were drawings of creatures alongside humans, all depicted in acts and rituals too obscene to recount, and in offence to all that was holy. Beside this was an open book filled with notes, the handwriting that of the general's judging from the nearby pen and ink.

She began to read and was filled with a terror as she had never before felt, not fully comprehending the words before her, but seeing a dark design through the various books, drawings, and artifacts within the chamber. This was no benign mythology of ancient lore; she had been educated enough on the deities of Rome and Greece, and to a small extent Norse and Egypt, to detect the differences. The entities depicted on the pages before her were of something else entirely, wholly alien and repugnant to the senses. That the library had been dedicated to its study made the subject all the more tangible, leading her to question why the general held this fixation.

In a burst of clarity, Catherine Morland grasped the truth about Mrs. Tilney's obscure accounts and subsequent death. Indeed, she had come down to this library, found her way in, and made the same discovery. Her reaction would have been not unlike what Catherine now felt, but with the additional fact of the materials residing in her estate. She had confronted her husband and demanded its removal. She died shortly thereafter, to a cause now evident, for whatever the true meaning of this material was, the general surely meant to keep it secret.

To what degree was his arcane knowledge of importance? If the mere awareness of it by any other could be considered a risk, then the general had been faced with a problem of the worst kind. Many a wife had been held in confidence of her husband's private activities throughout history, either in the nature of politics or social fare. Were the contents of these ancient texts beyond that to which a life companion might be entrusted? If so, then the obvious alternative meant obtaining the silence of his wife at all costs.

Catherine thought back to Mrs. Tilney's journal, and those final entries, noting the herbal teas and her weakened constitution. She posed the question in her last words: *Edward, why have you done this?*

Catherine could bear no more, knowing that she had to get out of the chamber immediately, and in fear for her safety. She was now in possession of the same knowledge that had brought about the mother's premature death, and if the general were to find out—

The thought was far too horrible to contemplate. She quickly turned to exit the room, and in her haste, caught the fabric of her dress on the corner of the table, ripping a section in the process. She tugged at the material, tearing it from the table and leaving a noticeable hole in the weave. Wasting no time, she fled the study, closing it shut, and quickly made her way back to her chamber, there to compose herself to this new unwanted knowledge.

In her haste, she did not attempt to relock the study door as she left.

CHAPTER
Forty-Nine

THE ACQUISITION OF KNOWLEDGE can be either a blessing or a curse, depending on the variables of the individual and their surroundings, as well as the information itself. Many will spend a lifetime in pursuit of knowledge, while others accept it only as it comes to them. Either way, it also comes with a price, that being the responsibility of its bearer.

The great weight of this now bore down on Catherine Morland, who for the first time in her life, felt wholly alone, without a person to turn to for assistance. Behind the closed door of her chamber, she curled herself up upon her bed, rocking back and forth, tormented over the newfound knowledge she had foolishly pursued, and not knowing what to do with it. She had allowed her curiosity to lead her on without any consideration of the consequences, and having discovered the truth, realized the peril it now placed upon her own life.

Time and again, she thought of revealing all to Henry, who would surely know what to do. Just as quickly, the idea was discarded for all the same reasons as not telling him of the journal earlier. After all, this was not some stranger of whom they might speak, but his father, with incriminations regarding the death of his mother, no less. How could she, who had been so reprimanded by him earlier, confess that she did not heed his good words, but meddled in their private affairs to prove the father's guilt? This was no way to repay all the kindness shown to her. How could she do such a thing to the man she had come to regard in feelings that were becoming more confusing by the day in terms of her affection? His reaction to any disparaging words would surely be more than she could bear.

Nor could she confess to Eleanor, who would be likewise horrified at the account, and just as easily see Catherine poorly for her investigations. Unlike Henry, she would not have the resolve to deal with the information, other than to turn to Henry, this being the same as telling him directly. In addition, such a revelation would only put the sister in possible jeopardy as well.

There were no others at the abbey to disclose the information to, as all the servants reported directly to the general, and she knew not who to trust beyond the brother and sister.

Might she get word out to some authority, so that it might be dealt with in an official capacity? Aside from the difficulty in doing so, there would then be the matter of supplying the proof, and assuming that it was taken as accurate, it would not take long for Henry to find out how it came to be. Surely, he would be even more affronted for not being taken in confidence. As to the general, such a strategy would lead to him knowing of her discovery and subsequent invasion of his private study.

The more she thought of it, her options dwindled. There were her parents, to whom she could write and explain, but already she knew their answer. If she were to be believed at all, they would tell her to leave at once—after she was to offer the most cordial words of thanks for the hospitality—and come home directly. While this might be the safest, it left a stone unturned, that being Henry and Eleanor. As long as they were uninformed of the affair, they were surely safe. However, if either were to find out in their own time, without any advance warning, they could be in danger. This avenue of thought led back to telling Henry directly, which in turn led back to all the arguments for not telling him. With this, the never-ending conundrum continued.

With all her heart, she regretted having taken the journal, and in those days prior, having the colour of mind to suspect such acts in the first place, which led her to seek out Mrs. Tilney's room; the journey to the private chamber; even the act of befriending the Henry and Eleanor, for all the love she had for them both. What had it gained her?

The other, more obvious solution was to simply keep quiet, reveal nothing, and pretend that all was as it should be. Mrs. Tilney had died of natural causes. The general was a loving husband who cared for his wife above all else and had no secrets to hide. The general would never, under any circumstances, willfully do harm to her—would he?

If she were to keep her silence, but was nevertheless found out by the general, what then? Having not told a soul, if she were eliminated as the mother was, the unpardonable would be even greater than before, without anyone else the wiser. In her heart, she knew that atonement for such deeds would be found, if not on Earth, then when he met his end—even so, she had to tell someone, or at the very least let them know that not all was right at the abbey.

After all the considerations of those she knew, and those she did not know, and finding no clear answer, she turned to the one she could always count on to listen, just as she would always listen and give comfort in return, in all their years of living together. Dearest Sarah might not be able to offer any advice, but she was the best shoulder to lean on in this time of need, and she needed desperately to unload the burden. She sat at the writing desk, looking for long moments at the blank page before her, pen in one hand, while letting her free hand trail over the decorative inkwell, and then to the nearby letter opener, fingers guided across its long, slender surface, the elegant curves of the embellishments in the handle, and down the edge of the blade to the sharpened end tip. At last, finding a commitment to the opening words, and after wiping tears from her eyes, she dipped the pen in ink and began.

Dear, sweet Sarah,

I write to you from Northanger Abbey, the residence of the Tilneys, of which I disclosed details in my last letter. My stay has been, for the most part, pleasant, due to the endearments of Henry Tilney and his sister Eleanor. Their father, General Tilney, is now away on business.

This letter is short due to necessity, but I must disclose some information that has left me so unnerved as to have trouble in even the act of writing. It concerns the death of the mother, who departed the family some years back. I have reason to believe that it may not have been of normal causes as was diagnosed by the physicians of the time, but by the guiding hand of her husband. Having pursued this idea for solid proof, I have found my way into the general's private study, and found in its contents, things that are most foul. I am terribly frightened as this may be why the mother died so suddenly. While I know that I should tell Henry of this in full, I cannot bring myself to do so—most ashamed would I be to fall under his gaze again. I know I have done wrong, but it is a minor offence to my suspicions of what else has been done in this house.

I know you cannot advise properly, and it may not be safe to do so—but I felt that you should know. Please keep this to yourself and tell none.

With all my love forever and always.
Cathy

Catherine sealed the letter, and ran it downstairs to the entry hall, leaving it on the table with the other outgoing letters to be sent the following day. With a final glance at the letter, for whatever good it would do, she went back upstairs and prepared herself to rejoin Eleanor, in pretended spirits as gay as if she had not a care in the world.

It was the second mistake she made in as many hours and one that would cost her dearly.

CHAPTER

Fifty

THE GENERAL RACED through the night, ever closer to home, and not soon enough. If his anger might drive the horses any faster, he would have already arrived hours earlier. There were dire corrections to be made there, and he would not waste a minute.

He had been misled, and in the worst way, fully by fault of John Thorpe. All his designs had been based on Thorpe's good word, given of Miss Morland, and of her family's fine standing and economic status. This misdirection would have continued if not for an encounter of pure chance and unexpected outcome. The trip to London had been a most productive one, the general meeting with several associates to address key issues of business, and taking in some recreation of the feminine kind while he was there. Most important was the procuring of a package from a local book dealer with whom he had a long outstanding arrangement. Their exchange conducted, he had exited the shop with the parcel in hand when, in an encounter of astronomically long odds for a city of its size, he nearly bumped into Mr. Thorpe as he passed. They quickly exchanged pleasantries before the general made a casual reference to Miss. Morland.

At this, young Thorpe's countenance changed to one of abject distain hastened to contradict all that he had said before to the advantage of the Morlands— confessed himself to have been totally mistaken in his opinion of their circumstances and character, misled by the rhodomontade of his friend to believe his father a man of substance and credit, whereas the transactions of the two or three last weeks proved him to be neither; for after coming eagerly forward on the first overture of a marriage between the families, with the most liberal proposals, he had, on being brought to the point by the shrewdness of the relator, been constrained to acknowledge himself incapable of giving the young people even a decent support. They were, in fact, a necessitous family; numerous, too, almost beyond example; by no means respected in their own neighbourhood, as he had lately had particular opportunities of discovering; aiming at a style of life which their fortune could not warrant; seeking to better themselves by wealthy connections; a forward, bragging, scheming race.

The terrified general pronounced the name of Allen with an inquiring look; and here too Thorpe had learnt his error. The Allens, he believed, had lived near them too long, and he knew the young man on whom the Fullerton estate must devolve. The general needed no more. Enraged with almost everybody in the world but himself, he set out the next day for the abbey.

By the time he had reached his estate, a plan had been formed fully in his mind, that being the immediate ejection of Miss Morland from their home. She would be given time to collect herself, and then be removed by carriage on the following morning, and taken back to where she properly belonged. That would be the end of her dealings with them, and he with her.

He arrived at Northanger an hour before midnight, and hastened inside, ready to set his orders into motion. This would come second, only after he put his bound package into the safety of his study. Upon entering the grand hall, he gave brief attention to the mail on the table, inspecting the several letters that had arrived for him, and noting the outgoing letter, it being by Miss Morland's hand. Seeing her letter only intensified his resolve, and he made his way down to his private library.

Here, then, was the first indication that something was wrong as he arrived at the door, only to find it unlocked. He considered this, and the possibility that he might have absentmindedly forgotten to lock the door after his last visit—but no, he had never left the room before without securing the door. While possible, it was hardly probable.

Tilney entered the study, taking in the whole for anything that might be amiss; upon first glance, the room appeared to be in order. Only after a closer examination did he find smaller indications of change, papers set differently than he last had them, as well as the book on the center table, set to a different page from where he last had been reading.

Clearly, someone had been in this room, even finding a way to unlock the door to gain access. With an eye keen from his years of study and observation, he examined the library in full, searching for any further indication of disturbance.

At the same time, his anger grew, building up from the level already established when he had arrived. He had nearly finished his sweep through the library when he detected one small thing he had initially missed. On the metal corner of the table hung a small scrap of fabric, evidently caught and torn from a larger piece. He removed the cloth and held it up to the light, examining it in detail, he having a keen eye for fabric.

In a revelation so strong, he nearly buckled to the floor; he knew who had been there, recognizing the fabric from the very garment she had worn before. The very person he wanted to be rid of so venomously had found her way into his private chambers, surely discovering the secrets he guarded so closely. In an instant, all the plans he had set for her expulsion from their home were scattered, he knowing that she could not be allowed to reveal her discovery to another.

The general began to pace the study, considering the possible options in dealing with the meddlesome girl, and soon approached the shelf set with vials and bottles. He removed one, holding it up for consideration, and becoming more somber with it in hand. He could do as he did before, with this very vial, using just a few drops each day to render his problem solved—but even as he considered the option, he knew it could not be. Having done it once robbed him of whom he had loved most, a loss he still regretted, even while knowing he had no other choice. This was not a path he could follow again.

Only then did another plan form, one better suited to the time at hand, and fitting to the dark work he had been laboring over for so long. The minor details quickly followed, this being the nature of a general used to such strategies, and in short order, he reformed the actions to be taken. He set the vial back on the shelf for some future use.

General Tilney exited his private study, locking it securely behind him, before returning to the main hall. Once there, he retrieved the letter that Catherine Morland had written, addressed to her sister in Fullerton. Without hesitation, he opened the letter and read its contents.

With that, he knew in full of her guilt, and assumed the harshest resolve to set his plan—and her fate— into motion. He ripped the letter in two and placed it in his pocket. Then taking pen and paper in hand, he wrote out a detailed directive, sealed it, addressed the letter, and called for a servant, with directions for it to be delivered immediately, regardless of the hour. As the servant left the room, he heard footsteps behind him, that being his daughter who had come to find out who had arrived.

CHAPTER
Fifty-One

CATHERINE SHOULDERED THE WEIGHT of the general's true nature as capably as an heroine might but with much distress. By the time she rejoined Eleanor earlier that afternoon, she had composed herself to the best of her abilities and was able to find comfort in the sister's companionship. Henry's absence was also a source of melancholy for the pair; it lessened their gaiety, but did not ruin their comfort; and the two girls agreeing in occupation, and improving in intimacy, found themselves so well sufficient for the time to themselves, that it was eleven o'clock, rather a late hour at the abbey, before they quitted the supper-room on the day after Henry's departure. They had just reached the head of the stairs when it seemed, as far as the thickness of the walls would allow them to judge, that a carriage was driving up to the door, and the next moment confirmed the idea by the loud noise of the house-bell. After the first perturbation of surprise had passed away, in a "Good heaven! What can be the matter?" it was quickly decided by Eleanor to be her eldest brother, whose arrival was often as sudden, if not quite so unseasonable, and accordingly she would go downstairs in due course to welcome him.

Catherine walked on to her chamber, making up her mind as well as she could, to a further acquaintance with Captain Tilney, and comforting herself under the unpleasant impression his conduct had given her, and the persuasion of his being by far too fine a gentleman to approve of her, that at least they should not meet under such circumstances as would make their meeting materially painful. She trusted he would never speak of Miss Thorpe; and indeed, as he must by this time be ashamed of the part he had acted, there could be no danger of it; and as long as all mention of Bath scenes were avoided, she thought she could behave to him very civilly. In light of Isabella's last letter, and her intimations of the Captain's darker qualities, she could not be certain of either the truth of the author or the nature of the subject. Either way, she preferred to keep her distance as much as respectfully possible. In such considerations time passed away, and it was certainly in his favour that Eleanor should be so glad to see him, and have so much to say, for half an hour was almost gone since his arrival, and Eleanor did not come up.

At that moment Catherine thought she heard her step in the gallery, and listened for its continuance; but all was silent. Scarcely, however, had she convicted her fancy of error, when the noise of something moving close to her door made her start; it seemed as if someone was touching the very doorway—and in another moment a slight motion of the lock proved that some hand must be on it. She trembled a little at the idea of anyone's approaching so cautiously; but resolving not to be again overcome by trivial appearances of alarm, or misled by a raised imagination, she stepped quietly forward, and opened the door. Eleanor, and only Eleanor, stood there. Catherine's spirits, however, were tranquillized but for an instant, for Eleanor's cheeks were pale, and her manner greatly agitated. Though evidently intending to come in, it seemed an effort to enter the room, and a still greater to speak when there. Catherine, supposing some uneasiness on Captain Tilney's account, could only express her concern by silent attention, obliged her to be seated, rubbed her temples with lavender-water, and hung over her with affectionate solicitude. "My dear Catherine, you must not—you must not indeed—" were Eleanor's first connected words. "I am quite well. This kindness distracts me—I cannot bear it—I come to you on such an errand!"

"Errand! To me!"

"How shall I tell you! Oh! How shall I tell you!"

A new idea now darted into Catherine's mind, and turning as pale as her friend, she exclaimed, "'Tis a messenger from Woodston!"

"You are mistaken, indeed," returned Eleanor, looking at her most compassionately; "it is no one from Woodston. It is my father himself." Her voice faltered, and her eyes were turned to the ground as she mentioned his name. His unlooked-for return was enough in itself to make Catherine's heart sink, and for a few moments she hardly supposed there were anything worse to be told. She said nothing; and Eleanor, endeavouring to collect herself and speak with firmness, but with eyes still cast down, soon went on. "You are too good, I am sure, to think the worse of me for the part I am obliged to perform. I am indeed a most unwilling messenger. After what has so lately passed, so lately been settled between us—how joyfully, how thankfully on my side!—as to your continuing here as I hoped for many, many weeks longer, how can I tell you that your kindness is not to be accepted—and that the happiness your company has hitherto given us is to be repaid by—But I must not trust myself with words. My dear Catherine, we are to part. My father has recollected an engagement that takes our whole family away on Monday. We are going to Lord Longtown's, near Hereford, for a fortnight. Explanation and apology are equally impossible. I cannot attempt either."

"My dear Eleanor," cried Catherine, suppressing her feelings as well as she could, "do not be so distressed. A second engagement must give way to a first. I am very, very sorry we are to part—so soon, and so suddenly too; but I am not offended, indeed I am not. I can finish my visit here, you know, at any time; or I hope you will come to me. Can you, when you return from this lord's, come to Fullerton?"

"It will not be in my power, Catherine."

"Come when you can, then."

Eleanor made no answer; and Catherine's thoughts recurring to something more directly interesting, she added, thinking aloud, "Monday—so soon as Monday; and you all go. Well, I am certain of—I shall be able to take leave, however. I need not go till just before you do, you know. Do not be distressed, Eleanor, I can go on Monday very well. My father and mother's having no notice of it is of very little consequence. The general will send a servant with me, I dare say, half the way—and then I shall soon be at Salisbury, and then I am only nine miles from home."

"Ah, Catherine! Were it settled so, it would be somewhat less intolerable, though in such common attentions you would have received but half what you ought. But—how can I tell you?—tomorrow morning is fixed for your leaving us, and not even the hour is left to your choice; the very carriage is ordered, and will be here at seven o'clock, and no servant will be offered you."

Catherine sat down, breathless and speechless. "I could hardly believe my senses, when I heard it; and no displeasure, no resentment that you can feel at this moment, however justly great, can be more than I myself—but I must not talk of what I felt. Oh! That I could suggest anything in extenuation! Good God! What will your father and mother say! After courting you from the protection of real friends to this—almost double distance from your home, to have you driven out of the house, without the considerations even of decent civility! Dear, dear

Catherine, in being the bearer of such a message, I seem guilty myself of all its insult; yet, I trust you will acquit me, for you must have been long enough in this house to see that I am but a nominal mistress of it, that my real power is nothing."

"Have I offended the general?" said Catherine in a faltering voice, knowing that she had—in her heart, in her mind, and certainly in action. How might he have figured it out so quickly, having just arrived back from London?

"Alas! For my feelings as a daughter, all that I know, all that I answer for, is that you can have given him no just cause of offence. He certainly is greatly, very greatly discomposed; I have seldom seen him more so. His temper is not happy, and something has now occurred to ruffle it in an uncommon degree; some disappointment, some vexation, which just at this moment seems important, but which I can hardly suppose you to have any concern in, for how is it possible?"

It was with pain that Catherine could speak at all; and it was only for Eleanor's sake that she attempted it. "I am sure," said she, "I am very sorry if I have offended him. It was the last thing I would willingly have done. But do not be unhappy, Eleanor. An engagement, you know, must be kept. I am only sorry it was not recollected sooner, that I might have written home. But it is of very little consequence."

"I hope, I earnestly hope, that to your real safety it will be of none; but to everything else it is of the greatest consequence: to comfort, appearance, propriety, to your family, to the world. Were your friends, the Allens, still in Bath, you might go to them with comparative ease; a few hours would take you there; but a journey of seventy miles, to be taken post by you, at your age, alone, unattended!"

"Oh, the journey is nothing. Do not think about that. And if we are to part, a few hours sooner or later, you know, makes no difference. I can be ready by seven. Let me be called in time." Eleanor saw that she wished to be alone; and believing it better for each that they should avoid any further conversation, now left her with, "I shall see you in the morning."

Catherine's swelling heart needed relief. In Eleanor's presence friendship and pride had equally restrained her tears, but no sooner was she gone than they burst forth in torrents. Turned from the house, and in such a way! Could it truly be that the general discovered her suspicions, and therefore wanted to rid himself of her presence? It seemed the most likely answer for a dismissal so abrupt. How he might have found her out was a complete mystery, as he had only been home a short while. Of course, it was equally possible that Eleanor spoke the truth: that an urgent trip to Lord Longtown's required her immediate departure, but even so, to be sent away in such a manner went beyond any proper behavior—without any reason that could justify, any apology that could atone for the abruptness, the rudeness, nay, the insolence of it. Henry at a distance—not able even to bid him farewell. Every hope, every expectation from him suspended, at least, and who could say how long? Who could say when they might meet again? And all this by such a man as General Tilney, so polite, so well bred, and heretofore so particularly fond of her! It was as incomprehensible as it was mortifying and grievous. From what it could arise, and where it would end, were considerations of equal perplexity and alarm. The manner in which it was done so grossly uncivil, hurrying her away without any reference to her own convenience, or allowing her even the appearance of choice as to the time or mode of her travelling; of two days, the earliest fixed on, and of that almost the earliest hour, as if resolved to have her gone before he was stirring in the morning, that he might not be obliged even to see her. What could all this mean but an intentional affront? By some means or other she must have had the misfortune to offend him. Eleanor had wished to spare her from so painful a notion, but Catherine could not believe it possible that any injury or any misfortune could provoke such ill will against a person not connected, or, at least, not supposed to be connected with it.

Heavily passed the night. Sleep, or repose that deserved the name of sleep, was out of the question. That room, in which her disturbed imagination had tormented her on her first arrival, was again the scene of agitated spirits and unquiet slumbers. Yet how different now the source of her inquietude from what it had been then—how mournfully superior in reality and substance! Her anxiety had foundation in fact, her fears in probability; and with a mind so occupied in the contemplation of actual and natural evil, the solitude of her situation, the darkness of her chamber, the antiquity of the building, were felt and considered without the smallest emotion; and though the wind was high, and often produced strange and sudden noises throughout the house, she heard it all as she lay awake, hour after hour, without curiosity or terror.

There was also the matter of Mrs. Tilney's journal and the secrets it had revealed. Only yesterday, a time that seemed so long ago, she had been torn over confessing to either Henry or Eleanor and had decided against it. Now with her premature departure only hours away, she reconsidered her actions. Henry, at the very least, should know in full what she had uncovered; if not, his mother's death might forever be one never justified to its true nature.

With a hand unsteady from nerves and lack of sleep, she wrote out a letter to Henry, knowing that it might be her last opportunity to speak to him in any manner, the thought of which made her all the worse in despair.

Henry,

I will have left by the time you read this, to which I am saddened so greatly, for the hospitality that you and your sister have shown me. Your father has sent me home with no advance notice. Otherwise, I would have wanted to state my farewells to you in person. I must be honest with you in certain details I have uncovered, and you may deal with them as you see fit. Attached to this letter is a journal. It is your mother's. I discovered it in a hidden compartment of the desk in her room. To my great shame, I did not follow your advice from that day, but read the journal, and was made aware of the details of her death that even you may not know. I also made the same discoveries as she, visited the same study she described, and have been likewise unnerved by its contents. I cannot explain more, asking only that you read it. Then you may understand, and I hope, think somewhat kindly of me. For my part, I think all the world of you and your dear sister. I pray that you both take care and be safe.

Catherine

Nothing more could she add, although there was so much she wanted to express, her hopes and regrets of her time there at the abbey, as well as her deepest fears. If only he were here before her, she might be able to let loose her reservations and speak her heart. Then, with the floodgates released, words came, enough to fill volumes. With only the paper before her and little time left, she could only leave him with a few sentences to set things right. Both the letter and book were wrapped in one of her scarves and set aside. She would hand it to Eleanor for delivery to her brother before she left. For now, she must pack for the long trip home.

Soon after six Eleanor entered her room, eager to show attention or give assistance where it was possible; but very little remained to be done. Catherine had not loitered; she was almost dressed, and her packing almost finished. The possibility of some conciliatory message from the general occurred to her as his daughter appeared. What so natural, as that anger should pass away and repentance succeed it? And she only wanted to know how far, after what had passed, an apology might properly be received by her. But the knowledge would have been useless here; it was not called for; neither clemency nor dignity was put to the trial—Eleanor brought no message. Very little passed between them on meeting; each found her greatest safety in silence, and few and trivial were the sentences exchanged while they remained upstairs, Catherine in busy agitation completing her dress, and Eleanor with more goodwill than experience intent upon filling the trunk. When everything was done they left the room, Catherine lingering only half a minute behind her friend to throw a parting glance on every well-known, cherished object, and went down to the breakfast-parlour, where breakfast was prepared. She tried to eat, as well to save herself from the pain of being urged as to make her friend comfortable; but she had no appetite, and could not swallow many mouthfuls. The contrast between this and her last breakfast in that room gave her fresh misery, and strengthened her distaste for everything before her. It was not four and twenty hours ago since they had met there to the same repast, but in circumstances how different! With what cheerful ease, what happy, though false, security, had she then looked around her, enjoying everything present, and fearing little in future, beyond Henry's going to Woodston! Happy, happy breakfast! For Henry had been there; Henry had sat by her and helped her. These reflections were long indulged undisturbed by any address from her companion, who sat as deep in thought as herself; and the appearance of the carriage was the first thing to startle and recall them to the present moment. Catherine's colour rose at the sight of it; and the indignity with which she was treated, striking at that instant on her mind with peculiar force, made her for a short time sensible only of resentment. Eleanor seemed now impelled into resolution and speech.

"You must write to me, Catherine," she cried; "you must let me hear from you as soon as possible. Till I know you to be safe at home, I shall not have an hour's comfort. For one letter, at all risks, all hazards, I must entreat. Let me have the satisfaction of knowing that you are safe at Fullerton, and have found your family well, and then, till I can ask for your correspondence as I ought to do, I will not expect more. Direct to me at Lord Longtown's, and, I must ask it, under cover to Alice."

"No, Eleanor, if you are not allowed to receive a letter from me, I am sure I had better not write. There can be no doubt of my getting home safe."

Eleanor only replied, "I cannot wonder at your feelings. I will not importune you. I will trust to your own kindness of heart when I am at a distance from you." But this, with the look of sorrow accompanying it, was enough to melt Catherine's pride in a moment, and she instantly said, "Oh, Eleanor, I will write to you indeed. But there is something of such importance I must ask of you, a favor that I hope is not too great."

Catherine pulled forth the scarf bearing the journal and letter, placing it in Eleanor's hands. "Please see to it that your brother is given this and that he reads it in full. It is for his eyes only, so please forgive my not explaining it further. Will you do this for me?" To this, the sister agreed without hesitation.

There was yet another point which Miss Tilney was anxious to settle, though somewhat embarrassed in speaking of. It had occurred to her that after so long an absence from home, Catherine might not be provided with money enough for the expenses of her journey, and, upon suggesting it to her with most affectionate offers of accommodation, it proved to be exactly the case. Catherine had never thought on the subject till that moment, but, upon examining her purse, was convinced that but for this kindness of her friend, she might have been turned from the house without even the means of getting home; and the distress in which she must have been thereby involved filling the minds of both, scarcely another word was said by either during the time of their remaining together.

Short, however, was that time. The carriage was soon announced to be ready; and Catherine, instantly rising, a long and affectionate embrace supplied the place of language in bidding each other adieu; and, as they entered the hall, unable to leave the house without some mention of one whose name had been previously mentioned only in reference to being given the scarf and its contents, she paused a moment, and with quivering lips just made it intelligible that she left "her kind remembrance for her absent friend." But with this approach to his name ended all possibility of restraining her feelings; and, hiding her face as well as she could with her handkerchief, she darted across the hall, jumped into the chaise, and in a moment was driven from the door.

CHAPTER
Fifty-Two

CATHERINE WAS TOO WRETCHED to be fearful. The journey in itself had no terrors for her; and she began it without either dreading its length or feeling its solitariness. Leaning back in one corner of the carriage, in a violent burst of tears, she was conveyed some miles beyond the walls of the abbey before she raised her head; and the highest point of ground within the park was almost closed from her view before she was capable of turning her eyes towards it. Unfortunately, the road she now travelled was the same which only ten days ago she had so happily passed along in going to and from Woodston; and, for fourteen miles, every bitter feeling was rendered more severe by the review of objects on which she had first looked under impressions so different. Every mile, as it brought her nearer Woodston, added to her sufferings, and when within the distance of five, she passed the turning which led to it, and thought of Henry, so near, yet so unconscious, her grief and agitation were excessive.

The day which she had spent at that place had been one of the happiest of her life. It was there, it was on that day, that the general had made use of such expressions with regard to Henry and herself, had so spoken and so looked as to give her the most positive conviction of his actually wishing their marriage. Yes, only ten days ago had he elated her by his pointed regard—had he even confused her by his too significant reference! And now—what had she done, or what had she omitted to do, to merit such a change? Ah, but such a question; she might guess at the answer, if not how it had been made known to him.

There was only one offence against him of which she could accuse herself. Certainly, its beginnings had been such that it was scarcely possible to reach his knowledge. Henry and her own heart only were privy to the shocking suspicions which she had so wildly entertained; and equally safe did she believe her secret with each. Designedly, at least, Henry could not have betrayed her. If, indeed, by any strange mischance his father should have gained intelligence of what she had dared to think and look for, of her fancies and injurious examinations, she could not wonder at any degree of his indignation. If aware of her having viewed him as a murderer, she could not wonder at his even turning her from his house. But a justification so full of torture to herself, she trusted, would not be in his power. Then, again, if Mrs. Tilney's words were indeed true, and she had been silenced to keep his secrets safe, what else might he be capable of? The expulsion of a house guest in this manner might not be any more extraordinary than his other actions.

Anxious as were all her conjectures on this point, it was not, however, the one on which she dwelt most. There was a thought yet nearer, a more prevailing, more impetuous concern. How Henry would think, and feel, and look, when he returned on the morrow to Northanger and heard of her being gone, was a question of force and interest to rise over every other, to be never ceasing, alternately irritating and soothing; it sometimes suggested the dread of his calm acquiescence, and at others was answered by the sweetest confidence in his regret and resentment. To the general, of course, he would not dare to speak; but to Eleanor—what might he not say to Eleanor about her?

Then there was the journal, a final good-bye in the form of her scarf along with the unsettling contents in his mother's own words. Once read its entirety, what would he think? What would he do?

In this unceasing recurrence of doubts and inquiries, on any one article of which her mind was incapable of more than momentary repose, the hours passed away, and her journey advanced much faster than she looked for. The pressing anxieties of thought, which prevented her from noticing anything before her, when once beyond the neighbourhood of Woodston, saved her at the same time from watching her progress. Salisbury she had known to be her point on leaving Northanger; but after the first stage she had been indebted to the post-masters for the names of the places which were then to conduct her to it; so great had been her ignorance of her route. She met with nothing, however, to distress or frighten her. Her youth, civil manners, and liberal pay procured her all the attention that a traveler like herself could require; and stopping only to attend to the horses, she journeyed on.

Though no object on the road could engage a moment's attention, she found no stage of it tedious. From this, she was preserved too by another cause, by feeling no eagerness for her journey's conclusion; for to return in such a manner to Fullerton was almost to destroy the pleasure of a meeting with those she loved best, even after an absence such as hers—an eleven weeks' absence. What had she to say that would not humble herself and pain her family, that would not increase her own grief by the confession of it, extend a useless resentment, and perhaps involve the innocent with the guilty in undistinguishing ill will? She could never do justice to Henry and Eleanor's merit; she felt it too strongly for expression; and should a dislike be taken against them, should they be thought of unfavourably, on their father's account, it would cut her to the heart.

Her contemplations were abruptly interrupted by a sound from outside the carriage, the increase in volume soon apparent in another set of hooves against the ground, along with an exchange of voices, the whole completely unintelligible from inside. This continued for a good minute, eventually prompting her to find the source of the commotion. She looked out one side and saw nothing, and was moving to the opposite side as the carriage slowed, there seeing a figure on horseback alongside, shouting commands at their driver. Her view was brief, as the rider brought the horse up front, but he had appeared to be in disguise, a hat covering much of his head, and a cloth wrapped over the lower part of his face.

In an instant, the multitude of fictional brigands she had read of came to the fore in her mind, the difference being that this was real, and happening before her eyes. Likewise, there existed none of the excitement she had felt in her novels; instead, a cold fear ran up the back of her spine, all the more intensified as a single shot rang out. Her carriage came to a stop, followed by silence, excepting the occasional noise made by the horses.

Had all this taken place several months earlier, prior to Bath and her stay at the abbey, before her discovery of the journal and eventual expulsion by the general, she might have reacted with the youthful thrill of a new adventure, waiting to see what might happen next. The Catherine Morland returning to Fullerton was not the same as the one who had left, and the series of experiences she had endured had brought about a more mature perception of that around her. In recent days, she had contemplated a fuller scope of behaviors of which the human mind is capable, and in doing so, began to comprehend the ramifications of a single act, for good or ill. She dwelt upon life and death, and the delicate thread that bound them together—as well as what might exist on either side of that filament. In short, she had discovered her mortality.

As the seconds stretched themselves to an indefinable length, she withdrew to the furthest corner of the carriage, unsure of what had just happened, nor wanting to know. If anything, she wished more than ever to be somewhere else and escape the silence—a desire made all the more emphatic when a single arm fell into view from one of the windows, that belonging to the coachman. From the lack of movement, she knew him to now be dead. A fresh wave of horror took hold as she saw the hand covered in blood, a few drops of which dripped down from the fingers.

There came a scream, which must have been her own, and at that moment, the door to the carriage was yanked open, she coming face to face with the figure she had just seen on horseback. There was little to the intruder not covered, only his dark eyes and part of his cheeks. With a motion so fast she had no time to react, he grabbed her arm and pulled her forth, bringing her within a mere inches of his face. Only then did she recover her ability to fight, in a futile struggle against his brute strength. In desperation, she clawed at his face, leaving a set of three red lines across his cheek.

"Damn you, girl," he growled, yanking her forth out from the carriage. As he did so, he held his other hand aloft, clutching a white handkerchief, and mashed it over her nose and mouth. She smelt a strong aroma of chemicals before becoming light of head, the dizziness intensifying within seconds. The last thing she remembered seeing was the trickle of red oozing from one of the deep scratches she had left upon his face.

CHAPTER
Fifty-Three

ONLY A FEW HOURS after Catherine's departure from Northanger did Henry return, far sooner than originally planned, but hastened by his desire to spend as much time as possible while she was there as a guest. After finding her gone, Eleanor related to him in short order the events leading up to Miss Morland's departure. Henry was, in turn, astonished, saddened, and ultimately furious at the actions of the general, leading to a direct and antagonistic confrontation between father and son. Henry's indignation on hearing how Catherine had been treated, on comprehending his father's views, and being ordered to acquiesce in them, had been open and bold. The general, accustomed on every ordinary occasion to give the law in his family, prepared for no reluctance but of feeling, no opposing desire that should dare to clothe itself in words, could ill brook the opposition of his son, steady as the sanction of reason and the dictate of conscience could make it. But, in such a cause, his anger, though it must shock, could not intimidate Henry, who was sustained in his purpose by a conviction of its justice. He felt himself bound as much in honour as in affection to Miss Morland, and believing that heart to be his own which he had been directed to gain, no unworthy retraction of a tacit consent, no reversing decree of unjustifiable anger, could shake his fidelity, or influence the resolutions it prompted.

The encounter took place outside the front entry as the general was having his carriage readied, he just having set several travelling bags along with two wrapped packages inside when approached by the son. The general had planned to be away for the greater part of the day, expecting to return and then depart once more for Herefordshire for the arranged visit with Lord Longtown. With

Henry's early arrival, plans were altered only that he too would travel with them, a plan unacceptable in light of Miss Morland's expulsion. Henry steadily refused to accompany his father into Herefordshire, an engagement formed almost at the moment to promote the dismissal of Catherine, and as steadily declared his intention of offering her his hand. The general was furious in his anger, and they parted in dreadful disagreement. Only then, after the departure of General Tilney, did the brother and sister talk in full, culminating in the delivery of the journal and letter into his hands, still wrapped in Catherine's scarf.

His father's behavior baffled Henry, knowing well how rough his demeanor might be when upset, but not a side he had displayed in its entirety to Catherine. If anything, he had gone out of his way to show her every kindness, leading both son and daughter to conclude his intentions to be favourable to the extreme. His actions in sending her off were so counter the former made no sense, and Eleanor soon left her brother to look over the contents of the scarf in private, neither being any closer to understanding what had occurred.

Any confusion soon took on a new light, as he read first the letter, and then in an alarmed state, the day-by-day memoirs of his mother, spoken as clearly as if she were there by his side, and with hand upon hand, recounted her final days. Henry did not rush through, but took his time, absorbing every word, as everything he believed crumbled; the details of her passing, the diagnosis given by the physicians, and above all, an aspect of the father that, although distant in many ways, now was an individual that he knew not at all. By the time he reached the last entry, he realized that a whole portion of his life had been a lie, perpetuated by his father.

For long minutes afterward, he sat with the volume in hand, trying to form some understanding of the two disparate events, the one that took place years earlier, and that of Catherine's departure, as there was surely a connection between the two. What was evident to him was that to fully comprehend the chain of events, he would need to see for himself the study that first his mother, and then Catherine, had visited.

Locked doors to the abbey were not an obstacle to him as he had managed in his youth to secure entrance to every other room in the abbey, save that one, and only due to the fear of his father's wrath, should he be found out. With parental discovery not an issue now, he wasted no time in scouring the elder Tilney's room, soon finding the key hidden in the back of a dresser. Soon after, he gained access to the study held private by his father since childhood. Having always been studious and alert, he was able to deduct that the man he had called father was dealing in matters so unwholesome and vile that it was no wonder that he had kept it hidden from view, not that resolved him in any manner. The books, letters, manuscripts, and artifacts all dealt with all things unholy. There was also no wonder that his mother had asked for its removal, but even with the materials before him, he still found it incomprehensible that a man would take such actions to keep the matter secret from all other eyes.

The outcome, as indicated by his mother's own words, was clear. She was dead. Likewise, Catherine had been sent away, and if this was due to her finding out about these dark artifacts, and then being caught in that knowledge, then might it be that her own life might be in jeopardy?

The final piece, the one that tipped the scales while causing Henry's blood to run cold, was spread out on the table, a simple map, marked with inscriptions and lines, forming a pattern around a location he had known from visits since childhood. Suspicions grew outward, based on the events before him, and in an agitation of mind that would take more solitary hours to compose, he began to fear for the well-being of another, of whom could be in the greatest of danger.

CHAPTER
Fifty-Four

HOW LONG CATHERINE had been unconscious was uncertain; she recalled no dreams, just a lingering blackness, and even when it lifted, her thoughts oozed to a slow and groggy pace. Only by degrees did she pull herself to full consciousness, and then to realize the change in her circumstances.

The first thing she sensed was the prickling of grass against her back, cool and slightly damp, the ends tickling against the skin. It was this that brought her to full awareness, realizing that there was no barrier of fabric between grass and flesh. She tried to shift her weight and found herself unable to do so, both arms and legs secured in some manner as to keep her from moving.

She gazed at the sky above her, bright with stars and the moon at its fullest, giving ample illumination to the surroundings, which were likewise augmented by several torches set in positions around her. The lanterns offered sufficient light to observe how she had been restrained: both wrists were bound with ropes that stretched approximately one foot in length and tied to wooden stakes, these secured to the ground. Both arms were outstretched, as were her legs, pulled far apart and bound in a similar manner. Only then did the truth about her condition strike her, feeling the grass underneath, the rope pulling hard on her extremities, and the breeze cold against her skin.

All of her clothes had been removed. Whoever had kidnapped her had committed the unpardonable act of stripping her of every article of clothing she had worn, and had tied her to the ground in a position so vulnerable and so immodest as to leave nothing to the imagination. She raised her head to better view her condition, and to her shock, found that her body was not entirely bare; it had been covered with a series of symbols and patterns, painted upon her skin by some unseen hand with a pigment of a dark brown colour. She had seen the writings before but it took a minute for the recollections to become clear. Memories struck her of Bath and the dead woman who had been pulled from the river, whose body had the same markings.

Catherine let out a gasp, followed by another as she found herself unable to breathe properly, each successive intake of air ending abruptly. She closed her eyes, hoping to calm herself, before opening them again, taking in her surroundings. Before her stood an enormous mound, part of a vast field, and the hill inset with a stone entrance to the front, apparently some sort of ancient landmark from a bygone time that seemed somehow familiar. Then it came to her; what she saw around her closely resembled the landscape rendering that she had viewed in the general's study. To one side were several piles of clothing, one of which she recognized as her own. As to the other?

A soft whimpering nearby of a feminine nature drew her attention. By degrees, she looked to her right to see another figure, also naked and tied down in a position much like her own, apparently awake and sobbing. Due to the illumination, she could not make out the details, but even at the distance, she recognized the profile and texture of the hair as Isabella Thorpe.

In a voice just loud enough to carry, but still a whisper, Catherine tried calling to the other but received no reply, not even an acknowledgment of being heard. Isabella continued to cry softly to herself.

"Don't you go worrying about her, girl," came a voice from beyond her range of vision, the figure soon appearing before her, and one she knew. Captain Frederick Tilney knelt before her, looking up and down the length of her body, adding, "You are a pretty little thing. More's the pity." As he drew closer, she could see his face clearly, and the cruelty behind his eyes that Isabella recently came to know firsthand. More notable was a set of three long scratches across his face, still red in the torchlight.

"Indeed, I do not appreciate the little love marks you bestowed upon me earlier," he said, noticing her line of sight and touching the deep cuts left by her fingernails. "But by the time our evening is over, you will have something more to show, mark my words."

"Why?" she managed to whisper.

"Because it was ordained—and you know more than is prudent for one as sweet as yourself. It will all be set and complete soon enough." With that, he ran his index finger slowly from her chin down the length of her body to her legs.

Catherine responded out of impulse, an action well beyond her normal behavior. She had never been one to display a confrontational quality, neither strong of will nor dominant in personality. In any lesser situation, she would have gone silent, pleaded, begged, cried, or given some other passive response. However, for whatever reason, and in an act wholly spontaneous, she reacted contrary to her usually passive nature.

She raised her head toward Tilney and spat, hitting the intended target directly across his face, the second such offence she had left there. His response was swift, slapping her hard across the cheek, and leaving a sharp sting on one side.

"Enough!" shouted another voice from behind, and even without a visual, she knew the sound, the intonation, from a thousand words spoken previously. It was that of General Tilney. "Leave her be. We have business to attend to, and as we now have a pair instead of one, the outcome should be most auspicious."

The general came into her range of sight, dressed in robes of darkest black, and holding a large book, the same that had rested open in his study. He looked at her with something she could not quite discern—sadness, pity, regret. "I am most sorry Miss Morland that it has come to this. I had such different plans initially for you, but apparently, you were not who I thought you were." He paused, thinking of these words, before adding, "No, you were someone quite different." At this, his face hardened, and with a glance to his son, moved to a spot between the two girls, stating simply, "Let us begin."

Again, Catherine called out to Isabella; this time, the call was received and the erstwhile companion turned her head, their eyes meeting for the first since Pulteney-Street, a stretch of seconds that seemed an eternity. The Isabella that confronted her now was one so different in nature than the girl of the past. Gone was the lighthearted confidence the young Thorpe once possessed, instead replaced with a cold fear that shone forth across her face, and causing her whole body to tremble. She mouthed words, barely audible, but recognizable nevertheless. "Please. Help me."

Catherine could offer no reply of assurance, no promise of comfort outside of being there as an unwilling ally beside her, so she only nodded. Their feelings were the same, two hearts beating as one.

The general pulled from the folds of his robes a ceremonial dagger, made of some silver alloy that gleamed in the light, holding it aloft before him, and chanting a few indistinguishable phrases below his breath. The sight of the blade, and the possible use it might have, caused Catherine to tense, her hands clenched.

That she and Isabella had been tied down, the book of such abominations before her, and the man now reciting some ritualistic words with a knife in hand, all formed the obvious in her mind. This was all part of some sacrificial rite, with her and Isabella evidently bound as victims, the end of which was clear from the knife held for them both to see. Her foreboding became all the more clear as the younger Tilney took a spot directly in front of them and set down a small sculpture, the same octopus-like figure that she had seen on the study shelf.

General Tilney began to mark off a shape around them, walking off the parameters to three points and stopping at each, drawing sigils in the air with the athame, and finally returning to the center before them. He then pointed the tip of the blade at Catherine, again reciting words while drawing invisible symbols in the air above her, and then bringing the tip down to her stomach. She felt the cold point of the blade as it touched the skin below her naval, and she clenched her teeth, unable to breathe as it rested there for some moments. From there, he might only give it a quick thrust for the blade to bury itself in her abdomen. She began to pray while waiting for him to complete the deed—but the athame was then pulled back and the whole procedure repeated over Isabella, who gasped as the metal descended to touch her bare flesh.

Taking a step back, he raised his arms, and proclaimed, as if addressing the landscape surrounding him, "The Old Ones were, the Old Ones are, the Old Ones shall always be."

With a final glance at the two women before him, he turned his back on them, now facing the mound of earth, and opened the book. The words then spoken were not of any tongue Catherine had ever heard, but something far more primal, a guttural series of utterances that formed an unknown language.

"Ph'nglui mglw'nafh Cthulhu R'lyeh wgah'nagl fhtagn."

His recitations continued, but with no further recognizable words, and being partially drowned out by Isabella's incessant sobbing, Catherine looked to all sides for any means of breaking herself loose. Nothing lay nearby, excepting the occasional twig, and an abundance of grass. Further off, she thought she saw something reflecting through the leaves of an outgrowth of greenery, like a small set of eyes, soon finding them to be that of a small rabbit, staring back at her. She found a ludicrous quality to this, causing her to laugh—of all things, laugh—and in desperation, how she might plead to the little bunny for help, possibly to nibble through the ropes or run to fetch help. After some moments, the creature wandered off past the remains of some stone fence, leaving her to her fate.

The stream of utterances from the general paused as he gestured with his left hand, drawing sigils in the air. His actions were that of solemn reverence but of a sort that Catherine had never witnessed in any church, and it reeked of all things foul in the sight of Almighty God. Once completed, he returned his gaze to the book before him, examining its contents before starting anew with a fresh set of incantations.

Tears welled up in her eyes, her nose getting equally congested, as she knew the finality of her situation. There was nothing she could do but wait for whatever conclusion they had devised, and hoped it would be swift. She closed her eyes in an unsuccessful attempt to quell the tears that continued to flow, making her vision of the scene around her a blur. Then, as another sound began to form, she realized that the wetness of her eyes had not fully caused the haze. Something had formed around the base of the mound, extending up and outward in both directions, a misty substance that diffused the overall appearance. As the haze grew in density, there came an accompanying sound, something akin to a low rumble, but distorted, almost wet. To this, the general's recitations became more pronounced and louder to the activity around him.

The ground began to shift. Catherine felt it against her bare back, a bucking of rock against rock, adding this noise to the rest, just as the mound began to split open. Whole sections of earth fell away as other sections of stone shot forth, like a small, controlled earthquake, isolated to the terrain in front of her, and as the opening grew wider, something else began to form from the vortex.

Equal in substance to the mist, it assumed a more pronounced shape, solidifying in distinct highlights and shadows. Just as she might find a figure disguised in an ordinary cloud overhead, she observed a figure before her, a shape forming a torso, arms to either side, and the head above that continued to undulate in form. As the face coalesced into a series of lengthy feelers stemming from its lower half, a cold panic ran throughout her body, recognizing the thing for what it must have been—the same as the sculpture now positioned only a short distance in front of her. As above, so below.

The entity took on substance, not a solid mass, but gelatinous and semi-transparent, even as another set of shapes rose from the crater. These were of the same wet material, all writhing independently of one another, and clearly recognizable as some sort of long tentacles.

At once, Catherine found her voice and screamed.

The general continued in his monotone long chant, encouraging the shape that formed before them to continue in growth and solidity. It was then that

Catherine noticed that one set of limbs had stretched forth, making its way slowly along the ground, directly toward Isabella. She noticed it as well, having raised her head, looking at it in abject terror, and unable to do anything but watch and mouth a word over and over again.

"No. No. No."

The distance quickly closed, and the first tentacle fell upon her arm, moving over the surface as if exploring. Soon came another, this falling across her waist, and probing in a similar manner. If Isabella had wanted to scream in terror, the ability must have frozen deep within her. A third appendage slid up from the ground, wrapping and unwrapping itself around Isabella's leg, causing her to cry, her voice now freed. It caressed her leg, as a hand might stroke a pet, but with it came a thick sound, and looking at it closer, Catherine saw that the tentacles were covered with small suckers along the underside and at the tip, each resembling a sort of deformed mouth that opened and closed with an obscene sound. The limb worked its way up Isabella's leg, passing the knee. As Catherine turned her head from the horror, Isabella screamed, a long, drawn-out cry of pain, disbelief, and invasion. All too soon, the cry dwindled into a gurgle deep within her throat, and finally to a series of low whimpers.

The inhuman entity before them continued to shift in solidity and mass, just as the sounds around them shifted in intensity. To the writhing appendages from the chasm, there appeared other entities, smaller and independent from the rest, and with nondescript shapes, blending into the shadows as if not wholly there. Catherine kept looking to one side, unable to look back at the one who had been her dear friend and confidant in Bath, and only the sound near her feet brought her vision back to that in front of her. Another tentacle, just like the one that savaged Isabella, rose before her, only a foot distant, hovering as if examining her in full—then apparently satisfied, the appendage lowered itself down and forward, the sickeningly wet lips of the suckers making contact with the bare skin of her ankle.

Now it was Catherine's time to scream, louder and more vehemently than she ever had before, as if her life depended on it.

Three things took place at almost the same time, each relating to the other. There erupted another shout, this being a different voice, followed by the sound of someone running. A figure came into view, throwing himself at the general, the two of them falling to the ground. Above them, the gelatinous creature rose in height, as if standing erect to view all before its rule, and the shapes that might have been its wings began to spread outward. As small as they were in the sculpture, here they appeared to grow in size as they extended to the left and right, and in doing so, became the one part of the shape to take on full opacity, blocking out everything in its periphery. The mass of tentacles, all at once, began to react in an erratic manner, moving about in a frenzy, and even the one on her leg had ceased its upward motion.

To this, another figure raced into view, that being Frederick Tilney, rushing to the couple now wrestling upon the ground. He pulled the attacker off of the general, and as he rose, Catherine was able to see who the newcomer was.

Henry.

The two brothers faced off, even as the general retrieved the fallen book, flipping madly through the pages in order to continue with his incantation. Behind them, multiple tentacles flopped around in mad disarray. The one on Catherine's leg had resumed its slow progression.

"Let them go," Henry demanded, causing the older brother only to laugh and shake his head.

"Go home, baby brother. Leave men's work to those who have the will."

There had always been a disconnect between the two brothers, so unlike in so many ways, but there remained the ties of blood. Now, none of that mattered; the years growing up together, the occasions of rare comradery, or the bonds set from parentage were all immaterial. Henry faced a person who was as much a stranger as his father. In a peculiar yet horrifying way, it made sense to find them both here with a common intention.

"You were right. You are just like our father."

Frederick sneered while pulling out his revolver from his cloak. "You have no idea."

Henry stepped back, aware that he was defenseless against the weapon. His brother aimed the weapon and pulled the trigger. At that precise moment, one of the tentacles wrapped itself around Frederick's leg and pulled, causing the shot to pass mere inches from Henry's head. It rose, dragging him into the air, where he attempted to free himself of its grip. In a motion so quick as to blur, it retreated into the chasm, pulling Frederick down with it as he struggled against its slimy hold. There was a final scream from beyond the rocks, and then nothing.

The Elder Tilney had found his place in the volume and returned to his chanting, his voice drowned out by Catherine's screams for help as the pulsating mouths of the appendage worked their way along her leg, now reaching her knee. Henry launched himself at his father once more, this time taking hold of the book with both hands. The general, having had a lifetime of training and experience in various forms of combat, defended himself accordingly, striking back with blows meant to take Henry down. One such offence left the son momentarily dazed, but not to the point of releasing his grip.

Instead, he threw his weight forward again, taking them both to the ground, the book momentarily forgotten beside them. The general responded with a blow to the throat, before climbing on top of him, now in a position to finish the duel. Pulling the athame from his belt, he pointed it downward, positioned directly over Henry's chest—hesitating as he looked directly at his son, and something flashed across his face, an expression suggesting the myriad of thoughts underneath.

For one even as trained as the general, it is one thing to eliminate an enemy in the heat of war, but by far another to completely do away with that innate humanity that separates man from beast, especially when confronted by those tied by blood. Henry saw this as well.

Henry then noticed the familiar necklace that hung from his father's neck, the locket with Mrs. Tilney's image inside.

"Is this it?" he sputtered. "Are you to kill off your entire family?"

General Tilney looked up in the direction of the crevice, to the spot where his eldest and favourite son had been dragged away, and a hard resolve now took him, raising the athame high so that it might better do its work.

"I've lost that already," he replied through gritted teeth. "My legacy lies below."

A pair of tentacles now fell across them, one wrapping around the elder Tilney's left hand and dragging him backward, and the other narrowly snaring Henry's leg. As if aware of the book as a protective talisman, the general reached for it with his free hand, pulling it just beyond his son's reach. Possession lasted but a moment. The thing squeezed the general tight, and at once, his fingers slipped from the book, leaving it behind as another tentacle rose and took hold of his other arm. The two tentacles now began to pull in opposite directions as they retreated to the chasm, stretching General Tilney taut between them—and just as he disappeared from view, there came a loud snapping noise, that of a body being ripped in two.

As Henry rose, he heard another scream and looked back at Catherine, her eyes wide in terror as the thing slid up to the top of her leg. Without thinking of the consequences, he seized the book and hurled it the remaining distance into the chasm where it merged with the semi-transparent substance of the monstrosity ascending from the depths. In what appeared to be a direct reaction to its contact, the whole area took on a fiery glow while causing the shape to lose its solidity. The ancient book erupted into what might be best described as flames, but of an opaque blackness that no fire might possess.

Henry saw none of this; instead, his attention returned fully to Catherine and the unspeakable monstrosity sliding across her body. He retrieved the fallen athame, the same that had been pointed at his own heart only a minute before, and threw himself at the writhing limb, driving the sharpened blade deep into its foul skin. He pulled the knife out, before plunging it again into the flesh in an attempt to cut through the thing while causing it to writhe in apparent pain. The mouth-like suckers along the length of the tentacle now opened and closed spasmodically, making wet sucking noises as they convulsed.

A sound erupted overhead, indescribable in tone but if ever the creature towering over them was to scream out, it would make this ungodly noise. Just as the being lost its shape, so did the mass of tentacles, now dissolving into a sort of sticky putrescence, including the nearly severed one that Henry had attacked. The shape faded as the vortex folded in on itself, leaving behind only a liquid residue of all that it once was, with a stench equally foul.

Henry knelt beside Catherine who, while partially covered with a sticky mucous substance, and in a state of shock, appeared unharmed; and taking her head in his arms, asked if she was hurt in any way. "No," she answered in a whisper, "I-am-all right." The last word choked in the back of her throat as her body shuddered once more. He locked his eyes on hers, and in doing so, was confirmed of his feelings and his worst fears, that she might have been lost to him forever; and she, being an heroine in the truest sense of the word, in turn had her own feelings of safety and adoration reinforced, for being rescued by her hero.

Only after some moments lost in each other's gaze did he remember the inappropriateness of his embrace and her current state of vulnerability, although they might have been well past such concerns of discretion, having just dealt with abominations far beyond any proper moral code. Thus, he placed a single kiss on her forehead, before retrieving the garments piled nearby. He severed the cords that bound her arms and legs, and allowed her the opportunity to make herself presentable, all the while averting his eyes to that which he wanted more than anything to idolize.

As Catherine dressed, he gave her all the privacy required, turning his immediate attention to her friend and fellow ritual victim. The gathering of clothes belonging to Isabella Thorpe lay a few yards distant on the ground and four stakes marked the spot where she had been restrained, the cords now loose—but of the unfortunate young woman, there was no trace.

He spent the following minutes searching for young Thorpe, at length reluctantly abandoning hope. He collected the various items strewn across the field, the ritual knife, statue, and leather carrying bags, all to be taken back to Northanger. He would decide what to do with them later.

Nearby stood a carriage, most likely used to transport the two ladies, and the absence of a coachman suggested that either the father or son had taken the reins.

As to the general and Frederick, both had been dragged into the abyss, and Henry had neither the will nor the bravery to approach its edge for examination. For now, the most important thing was to get Catherine back to the safety of the abbey, where he and Eleanor might see to her care and right the wrongs done to her.

With her now dressed and upon her feet, although unsteady and requiring his aid to walk, Henry guided her back to the carriage while speaking soft words of comfort. Once she had been situated inside, and after gathering the few items and placing them in the front—for it would be a wholly uncaring thing to set them next to her inside the carriage—he climbed up and took the reins in hand. They departed Belas Knap, for the security and unyielding affection offered by Northanger Abbey and its remaining occupants.

CHAPTER

Fifty-Five

AMONG THE TRUTHS universally acknowledged is that between brother and sister, a secret is never long kept before it is discovered by the other. Having been born from the same source, and in spending so many years in each other's company, even the slightest nuance is recognized, every fallacy flagged, and hidden agendas uncovered.

For the two younger Tilneys, whose affection for one another had grown with their years, it was all the harder for any wool to be pulled over the relation's eyes.

Henry had fully intended to shield Eleanor from much of the details leading up to and including Catherine's abduction, knowing that it would be impossible to tell but a little without telling all. Such accounts would assuredly be a strain on his sister with her acute sensitivity, especially regarding the well-being of others. Even on the journey back from Belas Knap, he weighed hard on how to explain Catherine's return, especially considering her current state. Upon arriving at Northanger, he could only tell her that Catherine was in need of care and comfort, both of which Eleanor could exceed at supplying. Further explanations must wait until later.

Catherine was in no state to either elaborate on any details, or resolve the sister's questions, she being too distraught over the evening's events, and was therefore given every accommodation, made as comfortable as possible, a glass of wine to settle her nerves, the time to cleanse herself of the putrid residue that clung to her skin, followed with a change of clothes before finally being set to bed.

Above all, rest was what she needed the most—as if she could sleep peaceably in the near future.

Only after she was secure in her chamber were the siblings able to talk at length, and all Henry's resolutions to hold details back were scattered to the winds, under his sister's precise questions. He began with the journal, handing it to her, and allowing her the time to read it to the end, as he waited nearby, catching her occasional looks at him in disbelief. It was best this way; if she were to know the truth, it should begin with the words from her mother whom she had missed so terribly.

All too soon, she closed the book, sitting in silence for some time, coming to terms with the many beliefs she held that were false. Once she had prepared herself, he began his account, showing her Catherine's letter to him, and then detailing his discoveries and theories, culminating in his race to Belas Knap and its grim events. He deliberately omitted many of the harsh details, as well as the particulars found in their father's study, but even with these exclusions, and as a master artisan might, he painted a detailed and nuanced picture for the sister. Hardest for her to accept was that her father, whom she had long accepted to be harsh, even brutal at times, could be capable of such heinous acts; that their brother had taken the same pursuits made the matter all the worse.

"Why is it," she asked, "that as shocked as I am at these events, in my heart, I cannot be wholly surprised? Was his blackness that evident?"

"Only by a counterbalance in goodness in the observer; because you feel so deeply, might the shadows be felt rather than be seen? It is a question to be considered."

"You compliment me unnecessarily."

"Do I? Then I will endeavour to speak of you in the opposite."

"Please do not jest. These matters are not light, and I have difficulty comprehending what it means."

"Then please accept my apology. I will speak as direct as possible, for I cannot have you any more distressed than I—and please believe that I am equal to the pain that you feel."

She smiled at his understanding, and knew him to be true, as he always had been. He was correct; there would be a great many questions to consider in the days to come, and possibly some answers might follow. For now, both knew that their chief concern should be their guest, who had been invited originally under false pretenses beyond their control, and then dismissed with the worst of intentions. Together, it was their responsibility to regain the faith that had been assuredly lost.

Soon thereafter, Eleanor checked on Catherine, finding her in a deep but fitful sleep, apparently restless in her dreams, and remaining in one position for only a few minutes before shifting into another. With rest offering the best restorative, they hoped that she might be in a better condition in the morning, so brother and sister talked for another hour before retiring, each knowing that their ability to sleep would be likewise strained.

Their hopes were dashed the following morning when Catherine appeared in the breakfast-parlour, looking far frailer than she had on the previous evening, her complexion pale and lips dry, and in spirits equal to her appearance. She took her breakfast only a little, showing a lack of appetite, and despite the attention shown by both brother and sister, she responded with pleasant but minimal answers. Only when she rose did her condition exhibit its greater hold, as her legs gave way and she collapsed beside the table.

It was soon apparent that she had been taken ill, most likely from her prolonged exposure to the elements the night before, exaggerated by the emotional strain from the same evening's horrors, the result causing a lethargy of body as well as mind. She was seen back to her chamber, Eleanor taking charge of her comforts while Henry called for the apothecary. In this, she was seen to, prescriptions given, all in order to quicken her healing.

With the evening, it was clear that her condition had worsened, with a fever taking hold, and causing much distress to the Tilneys as a delirium settled in, they having done as much as they might to nurse her condition. The night passed slowly, the second night offering relatively little rest for either host or guest and with Catherine checked upon every hour. Hopes were again defeated as the fever continued to fall, only to rise again, with chills and shivering suggesting the symptoms of the ague, and Catherine now having difficulty in keeping any food down.

Eleanor had taken to spending her time at her side, being able to do little more than watch her condition and keep her forehead cool with a damp cloth. Another visit by the apothecary, and another diagnosis, suggested that time would be the best healer, along with the treatments he recommended. As little as Eleanor might do, Henry fared less, and was left to pace the halls in worry, and as the day progressed, decided to send word to the family in Fullerton on the morrow if her condition had not improved.

Catherine's delirium reached its zenith that evening, as she began to cry and plead for help. Only when Henry listened closely to her ramblings did he realize that she was re-experiencing the nightmarish events at Belas Knap, and no amount of persuasion on their part could dislodge the hallucinations. Henry felt lost, having saved her once from the terrors in the tangible world, but found himself helpless at a second attempt. He left her in Eleanor's care, exiting the room on the verge of tears.

As if to match the storm taking place within the abbey, the weather outside countered with a fury of its own, bringing torrential rains against the walls, and emphasizing the pounding with thunder and flashes of lightning. The intensity of the storm had not been matched since the first night of Catherine's stay at Northanger, she then being unable to sleep due to the fierce rainfall and the mystery of her new surroundings. By comparison, she barely stirred, and her fever a match to the severity of the pounding rain and succession of loud cracks and rumbles.

By the strangest of coincidences, the climax and resolution of the weather fell parallel to the dissipation of the fever, each drawing down in an almost symbiotic manner, so that by the dawn, a calm had settled upon both. While this marked the turning point in her recovery, the rigors of the previous days had left her in a weakened state so acute, that it would be another day before she could rise on her own. The happy Tilneys saw to her recovering strength, and taking of solid foods, so that the day passed into night without any relapse or further cause for alarm—and for the first night since her expulsion by the general, all three slept soundly.

CHAPTER
Fifty-Six

CATHERINE WAS THE FIRST to wake the following morning at the break of dawn, with the initial fleeting rays of light streaming in through the window. Her initial thoughts, though exceedingly slowed from her illness, were of appreciation: of feeling better and in the comfort of a soft bed, of the care given her during her convalescence, and of being alive. Her slumber initially roused by a sound nearby, she turned her head to find the chair by her bed occupied. In the dimness of the light, she first believed it to be Eleanor, or possibly one of the housemaids, but in hearing the familiar voice, recognized it to be neither.

"So you are awake at last," said Isabella, in a hushed tone, in keeping with the hour. "I have been ever so worried."

Seeing her friend brought about some disbelief, even to wonder if she still might be caught in some residue fantasy left over from a fevered mind. It was unclear how many days had passed since she first became ill, or what had taken place in the interim. While she recalled being looked after by both Tilneys and some unnamed servants, this was the first she had seen of Miss Thorpe, who might have likewise been there for days.

Yet how could this be? After all, she had witnessed the unspeakable take place involving her friend—or thought she had, the events now being equally in question, and its aftermath a blur in her mind. Might it all have been some dream or other delusion of thought? Regardless, Isabella sat before her, as clear and real and solid as possible.

"How did you come to be here?" she asked.

Isabella smiled. "Nothing could keep me from you, not for the world. We are as sisters, you and I."

There was no easy reply for this, as Catherine was still perplexed at how Miss Thorpe's appearance, and the casual air she gave in her answer, one that was so typical of her nature. Unable to form a better response, and in being not quite herself, she offered the most basic of answers. "Yes." To this, she added that which was foremost on her mind. "But I thought you had been—" The words trailed off, as she was too unnerved to complete either the sentence or the thought.

"You dear creature, I am quite fine, as you can see. It is your well-being that is of concern, for you surely have been unwell—I can see how it has left you weak, even though your colour has returned. But enough of this. I have a thousand things to tell you, and am sure you have as much to tell me in return."

"Indeed, yes, but, please, I must know directly; tell me the truth of what happened when we last saw one another. Were you not there beside me? Did you experience the same awful things that I saw? Or was this some wild imagination so real that I cannot know the difference? I must hear you speak the words for my sanity."

"Please, let us not speak of such things for the moment," replied Isabella with a shake of her head. "You are here, as am I. Is that not enough?"

"Perhaps. I only want to understand. It was all so dreadful, and to see you in such a state, especially after receiving your letters, so different from one another, I could scarcely know what to believe. You had expressed a concern for your safety, and with such words against Captain Tilney. I could never have thought such a thing had I not seen him in so terrible a fashion for myself."

At his mention, Isabella lowered her head and responded after some moments in a quieter voice. "Yes, Frederick Tilney could be a great many things, not all of them immediately apparent on the surface. For all his charm, he could be equally cruel and selfish. I could not know that at first, but by the time I wrote to you, he had shown me his true face. By then, I was lost."

"You hurt James terribly." Catherine was surprised that she spoke so directly, as she would normally avoid any form of direct criticism, but the words spilled out as easily as they might pass across her mind. In response, Isabella nodded in shameful agreement, clearly aware of how she had destroyed her chances as well as his.

"I know, and I must live with that upon my heart forever. I was—persuaded in ways that I am not proud of."

"Is he how you came to be there beside me that night? Was it Captain Tilney's doing?"

"Dear, sweet Catherine, there are things far beyond what I could hope to fathom, and of which had been mercifully ignorant of before. Frederick Tilney was a man of great passion—the path he followed was but one of them. You see, he comprehended who he was with great clarity—and knew me as well, even more so than I knew myself. How could I have perceived his motivations until then?"

There was something in her voice that had changed, a subtlety in tone that suggested an affinity for the very thing she spoke against. It may have been how freely she used the captain's name without a trace of scorn. Could it be that after all that had occurred, she still felt something for the man? Surely, that was not possible.

"What are you saying, for it sounds as if you still find him as likable?"

"I—understand him. That is neither like nor dislike."

"But how could you? I, for one, hate him, as well as his father."

"More is the pity, then, for your lack of understanding."

Catherine was more astonished at this remark than anything else. Isabella's words, her attitude, were so far different from the girl befriended in Bath, but there she sat with the same expectations of companionship as ever before.

"Dear creature, let us not fault any differences. We know each other too well for that. Please, let us talk about ourselves." With that, she placed her hand upon Catherine's in a gesture of love and affection.

The moment of contact sent a chill across Catherine's arm, as the hand was clammy, cooler to the touch than it should have been, even to the point of dampness. Her reaction was involuntary, a short gasp in surprise as she tensed her fingers. Isabella laid her other hand on the first, with a caress meant to offer reassurance, but causing the opposite effect. Indeed, her hands were quite cool. Could it be that Isabella had come down with the same contagion that Catherine had managed to heal herself from?

"Isabella, your hand is cold. Are you sure you are well?"

Isabella smiled, and replied in the affirmative, noting that she had never felt better. But there was something in how she spoke that rang as untrue, as revealing as the lowered temperature of her touch. She ran her fingers along the length of Catherine's arm, thus causing the skin to rise in goose bumps from the chill. It was then that Catherine noticed the wetness glistening upon Isabella's arm, as some sort of translucent liquid oozed out from under her sleeve, and trailed slowly downward. A feeling of revulsion suddenly overtook Catherine, who pulled her hand back and edged slowly to the opposite side of the bed.

Isabella gave no reaction to this but stared back, and only when Catherine managed to climb from the bed on unsteady legs did she rise as well. The days of constant fever and little food had left Catherine in a weakened state, making it all the harder to keep her balance; still, she managed to step backward to the far wall near the window, only to have Isabella move around the bed to face her directly.

With her erect body fully in view, it was all the more apparent that something was terribly wrong with Isabella, even with her declarations to the contrary. Her slim figure, which had always been so elegantly shaped, now appeared to have lost some of its natural form and had instead taken on an unusual curvature without following the conventional lines of the body. With each step, the bulges seemed to move as if on their own, and Catherine considered that she might have something concealed under her dress. As she moved more into the streaming light from the window, there became visible the splotches of moisture that discoloured her dress. More distressing was the fluid so apparent on her arm had also formed around her legs and feet, as she left a moist trail behind her with each step.

The full measure of fear gripped Catherine as the bottom of Isabella's dress began to move, outward at first, and then up as if being lifted, even though her hands were nowhere near, instead raised forward as if beckoning for an embrace; then the tip of what resided underneath came into view, prodding and moving the fabric out of the way, and the wet mouths that lined the appendage began to expand and contract, all the while making a disgusting sound.

"Dearest Catherine," she said in a mockery of a bedroom voice. "Sweet sister. You know there is nothing I would not do for those who I love. Do you not feel the same?"

Catherine felt the unyielding surface of the wall behind her, with no place to turn, and could only watch as Isabella Thorpe stepped ever closer, arms outstretched, and the writhing obscenity moving out from her dress into clear view.

"Hold me, dearest," she cooed while closing the final yards and taking Catherine into her arms. A scream formed somewhere in Catherine's throat, but was unable to find its way out, just as she felt the tentacle rise upward against her back, and slowly wrap around her waist, pulling her forward. She could feel the sticky mucus from its moist skin, even through the fabric.

Simultaneously, another appendage appeared, snaking around her with its dampness soaking through her clothing. Then the scream that had been pent up was blocked as Isabella sealed their mouths together in a kiss, forcing herself deeply, and leaving a foul taste that was bitter and thick, salty like that of seawater.

Her passions enflamed, Isabella pulled her friend tight. Catherine felt the tentacles slide across her body, seeking spots for exploration, and filling her with revulsion, mixed with dark pleasure, an ecstatic delight that frightened her more than anything else. She found herself unable to move her arms; they hung limply to her side, even as she wanted to push herself away, and yet she didn't. Sensing this, Isabella opened her mouth wider, sharing and releasing the floodgates to the ocean, and drawing the other into the surging waves of her infectious desire. Catherine felt her strength of will fade, and while still overwhelmed with repugnance, found herself equal to the desire—and wanting even more.

Isabella moved her head to the side, whispering in her ear, "Dear Catherine, let me love you," while running her tongue along the lobe. She then began to pull Catherine's garments up with her hands, even as the mouthed tentacles moved their way across her shivering body, offering kisses of seduction.

Their eyes met, Catherine's wide with fear, and something more, something primal while Isabella's eyes were cool, wet, and of a desire that would only be quenched through the other's fluids. She smiled and whispered, "Be mine, sweet sister"—

Then she screamed.

A loud guttural cry issued from Isabella Thorpe, one mixed with blood and water, surprise and anguish, and death. The twin tentacles that had been probing Catherine's body now shot forth in a frenzy of convulsions, even as she stumbled back and fell to the floor, revealing the silver letter opener that had been plunged into her back—and above her, Eleanor Tilney, her hand still raised from delivering the blow. The Thorpe-thing writhed on the floor for another minute, blood seeping out from the wound and from her mouth, and gelatinous fluids oozing from the mouth-like openings of the tentacles. With a final jerk, her body tensed then went still.

Catherine's legs, barely able to sustain her weight against the assault, now gave way, and she slid to the floor, looking at the horror before her that had once been her friend; and then, finally, up to the one who had saved her, just as the brother had a few days before.

For no reason she could explain, a thought occurred to her, that being the comment once made by John Thorpe during their carriage ride in Bath, of the nightjars that call out for an individual's soul when death comes to call. In this early dawn, she heard not a sound outside, no birds, and she could only think this explainable as the soul that Isabella had possessed was lost days ago, and the creature before her had none to give.

She raised her hand, as much for aid in getting to her feet as in need of comfort. Eleanor responded, showing as much compassion and affection at this moment as she had demonstrated in bravery beyond her nature only minutes before.

"I never did find her very agreeable," said Eleanor.

CHAPTER

Fifty-Seven

THERE IS NOTHING more conducive to the bonding of individuals than a communal experience, the results of which can bring to each member the respect, endearment, and affection of the others, and as a result, form family ties out of its separate strands. The most meaningful of these, from engagements of a single afternoon to those extended over weeks, even months, may produce lasting relationships in many varied forms.

For the trio at Northanger Abbey, the circumstances of the last six days had forged bonds in a manner more extreme than might ever be normally considered, the events including murder, attempted murder, rape, abduction, seduction, revelations of falsehoods and deceits, abject cruelty, and a host of unmentionable activities beyond the pale of civilized society. To state that each of the three, in their way, had come from the experienced unaltered would be the slightest of descriptions; their individual epiphanies ran far, far deeper.

For Eleanor, the entire framework of her family had been uprooted, along with her preconceived beliefs about her mother, father, and brother. Through the experience, she found within an inner strength that she never knew she might possess. Despite all her losses, she gained a sister as dear as if the ties of blood had bound them since birth. For Henry, also dealing with newfound revelations of his own family, he recognized the feelings that had been forming since his first encounter with Miss Morland in Bath, and her response when asked of her visitations to the upper rooms, concert, and theater; as such, he was assured of the full measure of his devotion therein. As his sister had gained another from the extremes of care, he affirmed his obsession out of passion as well as love.

The collected change in Catherine, greater than either brother or sister, could be found in every singular trait she already possessed; the naivety of youth was chiseled into caution and doubt, and never would she be as trusting ever again, being misled by both Thorpes, as well as the general. Like Eleanor, she also found that inner resolve that she might tap into when required. In the weeks beginning in Bath, and culminating with Isabella's return to the abbey, she had grown far older than the time allotted, shedding many of the qualities of her youth, while taking on a maturity of personality and intellect.

In short, she had advanced from a girl to a woman with all the varied nuances and contradictions to be expected in the sex. For all her development, the gain most pronounced was in the affection for the two Tilneys, the likewise bonds of sisterhood with Eleanor, and the feelings of far more depth and complexity for Henry, along with the dearest hope that those emotions might be reciprocated in kind.

The Tilneys had been concerned that the reappearance of Miss Thorpe and its horrific aftermath might have brought about a relapse in Catherine's condition, so soon after her fever and related symptoms had abated. This was not the case, with Catherine making a quick recovery in body, although her mental state was far more shaken. Indeed, the ordeal had given her to occasional tremors, as unwanted memories would surface without warning. Henry had felt that it was best to leave explanations to a minimum, at least for the time being until she was better equipped to deal with the details, if ever that time came, and Eleanor agreed.

Therefore, as Catherine asked for them on one specific or other particular to the event at Belas Knap, or all that led up to those moments, she was given only generalities, much to her ire. Instead, she was asked to be patient until the brother gleaned a greater understanding. This was, in fact, true, as in being thrust into the dynamics of his father's hidden life, Henry now had as much to decipher to his satisfaction.

What was also clear was that Catherine's time at Northanger Abbey was nearing an end, at least for the present. With Isabella's appearance at the house, and in gaining access within the walls without anyone's knowledge until it was nearly too late, it was evident that the estate was not as secure as might have been otherwise thought. Henry's chief concern was in Catherine's safety, and if he was unable to offer sanctuary within the walls of the abbey, then he would need to guide her to safe haven elsewhere. The most logical alternate was back in the familiar surroundings of Fullerton. In deciding this, and wanting her away as soon as possible in case of any other breach, the siblings agreed that in one or two days, she would depart, showing enough recovered health to sustain the journey.

The plan was presented to Catherine who, while disappointed at leaving those to whom she held most dear, understood their motivations, and thereby reluctantly agreed. Her somber attitude brightened when presented with the additional option, that being that Eleanor might accompany her for the journey, to stay afterward at Fullerton for an unspecified time, if this was agreeable to Catherine as well as her parents. The possibility was more than Catherine could hope for and she eagerly accepted the companionship, expressing that there would be little worry of Eleanor not being welcomed at Fullerton.

The day passed, and then another as plans were set in full, bags packed, and final arrangements were made for the journey, with the two girls set to leave on the morrow. It was at this time that a messenger from Prestbury arrived with a communication for Henry. The remains of two bodies had been found in the area of Belas Knap, and it was thought, by nature of evidence found in the vicinity, that there might be a connection of relation. He was thereby asked if he might make the journey and offer assistance. This came as no surprise; Henry had previously assumed that if there were any remains to be found, it would be a matter of time before the discovery was made. Had it not been for Catherine's subsequent illness, he might have already returned to the site, if nothing else, than to confirm that which had taken place that night. Now that a letter of notification had arrived, he felt duty-bound to oblige and confirm what he already knew. The communication was acknowledged, and he made his preparations to depart.

The direct consequence was a delay in the return to Fullerton, as Eleanor was now obliged to remain, in preparation for the possible funerals of either father, brother, or both. In active defiance, Catherine now refused to leave without the sister, instead headset on staying to offer whatever support and solace she might. She would not back down despite their appeals for her safety, and she, knowing them perhaps too well for her ends, was secure that they would relent in her favor. With instructions to the house staff to be on watch for anything out of the ordinary, and determined to return as quickly as possible, Henry set off for Prestbury.

The distance was covered by morning's end, with Henry arriving in Prestbury to weather most favourable, a distinction that he noted to counter the village's reputation, with its numerous folk stories of being haunted. Most every town could boast of at least one ghostly yarn, usually being wild fabrications based on lesser-known historical events, but Prestbury seemed to have more than its fair share: a spectral abbot that wandered the burial grounds of the Prior of Lanthanum; more than one female apparition, one being a young girl playing a spinnet; a spectral shepherd and his herd usually seen in Swindon Lane; a ghostly horseman that rode Shaw Green Lane, and another at the Burgage, this being a messenger that, in heading for Edward IV's camp, had been intercepted, tortured, and executed by Parliamentary troops.

Some visitors in the area around Cleeve Corner had claimed that they had experienced the feeling of being choked; reportedly, a woman was once strangled in her bed in that area. In all, the town's ghastly reputation, however fictitious, was more than the sum of its parts. This offered no comfort to Henry as he arrived, already knowing what he might find, and seeing it somehow fitting to the surroundings.

Tilney met up with two men, Collinson and Shelley by name, who had sent the communication. He was informed that the discovery was made not by them, but by a resident nearby Belas Knap, who had heard some disturbance in that direction a few nights earlier but made no immediate attempt to investigate. When he did at last venture onto the grounds, he found the mound in a state of upheaval, from what cause was uncertain, and upon looking down into the crevice, found two bodies. Due to the severe nature of the injuries done, it was impossible to make any identification directly, and only from some personal belongings found on the bodies were they able to relate one to the name of Tilney. This evidence, with additional investigation and some guesswork, led them to send the letter, upon the chance of a relationship between the two.

Henry was escorted to a building where the bodies were kept so that he might confirm their identity, while forewarned of the gruesome nature of the remains. Even at this, their warnings were understated, and Henry was hard-pressed to keep from fleeing the room upon the viewing. He found it hard to accept that the carcasses before him were those of his brother and father, but even in their mutilated states, he knew it to be them. Of particular note, the locket, which the general had worn around his neck was missing, apparently pulled from the necklace during the scuffle.

Arrangements were made for the bodies to be sent home, where he would make the proper arrangements, and he further put forth that he would attempt to return at a later time, then to see the site for himself, and asked if they might be of assistance to him at that time. To this, they agreed, and he soon began his return trip to Northanger, reaching the abbey well before nightfall.

With the deaths confirmed of both General Tilney and his son, under circumstances never fully explained publicly, the plans for Fullerton were set back indefinitely, and due to Catherine's obstinance at remaining, Henry accepted her extension with both extremes of emotion; a grave concern for her well-being while remaining under their care, and the constant pleasure of her presence; and this all under the shroud of the funerals and aftermath, with appropriate black attire, ringing of bells, letters of condolence, and the expectations of their mourning.

The general had been held in high esteem in various circles, due to his military associations, thus attracting wider attention, and was even more apparent at the funeral, to the extent that any possibility of it being a traditional gathering comprised only of closest friends and family fell asunder. Some for whom the general had either served for or with were present, including General Courteney, a very good and old friend, and even the Marquis of Longtown, for whom his hastily planned visit had been staged. For the closer relations that attended, there were also the larger numbers, largely uninvited but who were present, nevertheless, and who were unknown to either Henry or Isabella.

For the Tilney children and Catherine, it was a pretense bordering on charade; only they knew the manner of the deaths, and the dark arts that both had been practicing, to such a degree that every word spoken at the service, and all wishes of condolence rang counter to the truth. Those who spoke highly of the general, his upstanding qualities and his care for his fellow man, obviously had no clue about his other characteristics. Likewise, similar sentiments for Frederick Tilney fell counter to his genuine nature, although it was equally possible that some knew exactly what kind of men the two were, but were too polite to comment, given the circumstances.

It was noticed that there was a young woman, exceedingly attractive in appearance, who had arrived alone and spoke to no one but gave all the mannerisms of genuine sorrow in favor of the son. After a period, she wiped her eyes, rose, and left without a word, causing Eleanor to wonder who she was, and how she had come to know her brother. What was clear was that she held high affection and great loss for the brother, and as women have a way of knowing things, especially in the affairs of other women, Eleanor was sure that this was a lover of Frederick's. Whether he had reciprocated with more than his body was another matter.

Most troubling was the internment. Father was laid to rest next to Mother, and the son nearby. That he would be given his final resting place next to the woman he had murdered was reprehensible in every way possible, causing Henry to barely restrain himself in disgust. She deserved far better than that. There was little to be done to counter the arrangement as it had been planned far in advance, probably before the general even entertained the idea of her death. Any alteration would have inevitably led to revealing their disfavor for their father or some of the details that might bring undue damage to the family name, and as both children had come to understand, what good would it do in the larger scheme of things? They knew the truth, and that was enough.

Catherine served as a calming presence to them both, and when the degrees of Henry's agitation had grown intolerable, her hand upon his arm helped to soothe the injustice. Since her abduction and rescue, the three had come to depend equally on the affections and better natures of each other, in order to make sense of the madness around them. It was hoped that a normality might again come into their lives, sooner rather than later.

Henry realized the uncertainty of that hope as he paid attention to the strangers at the service, some of whom had such distinct features that it marked them as exceedingly unusual, and whose presence seemed equally out of place. Even with a few inquiries made, he discovered practically nothing about the individuals—but their presence made him all the more uncomfortable, comprehending that the father's interests undoubtedly led to forming associations with others of dubious character. He found their presence invasive but had no due reason to have them put out.

This general feeling of unease grew as he was approached by not one but three at separate times after the service, they offering their condolences before asking a line of questions fully inappropriate to the time, and largely centered on the father's activities. One, who had introduced himself as Mr. Carreras, specifically asked what was to become of his private collections, and if there was to be any dispersion of them outside of the family. If such a liquidation were to take place, he would be most keen on setting arrangements, and even confident to offer a good price that would make the transaction worthwhile. His intensity as he spoke, visually exaggerated by his large eyes and thin lips, caused Henry to sense a quality of desperation, even malevolence, under the man's proper decorum, and wondered to what lengths he might endeavor to meet his desires.

A card was exchanged, and Henry slipped it into his coat pocket, even while restraining the urge to toss it aside as quickly as possible. With this and other similar thoughts present, and equally unsure if any others had been involved in the events at Belas Knap, he once more became concerned about the security of the abbey and its grounds, should someone want to gain access without invitation.

Having considered the possibilities, and still thinking in the best interests of the ladies, he concluded that the plans for Fullerton should be resumed in as short a time as possible. Their safety would be better ensured away from the abbey until such a time that he could address the matter of his father's dark interests, and be certain that the former monastery might be as much of a sanctuary as it once was. When informed of these considerations, Eleanor agreed and was sure of Catherine's equality to the idea. As to the timing, Henry was defiant to the decorum of extended mourning, confident that they were better served in a safe haven without the black, than following the custom inside the abbey walls. Again, plans were set and bags repacked for the journey.

For his part, Henry was most depressed, not wanting to see Catherine depart, and his sister as well, so he set his plans to pay a visit to Fullerton as soon as possible. Their final night at the abbey was as pleasant as could be hoped for, so they remained awake well past a normal hour if only to extend the enjoyment of their company for a final time. Amid their objections to quitting the evening too early, then came the inevitable, when one, then another, followed by the last, all went to their respective chambers to sleep off the remaining hours.

The morning came far too soon for the three, with the girls now readied and bags set in the carriage. Good-byes were said, and for both Catherine and Henry, even more was felt, but not expressed in words, each still cautious of the other's feelings, but hoping for so much in return.

"I hope to visit as soon as I might," he said, brightening Catherine's countenance considerably, the result of which was even more resolve to make it so, and in as little lapse of time as possible. Final words were spoken. Hands were clasped in farewell. Embraces were exchanged between brother and sister. With that, Eleanor and Catherine stepped into the carriage and were away.

Neither Catherine nor Eleanor asked him what became of young Isabella's body. Had they, Henry likely would not have divulged the details, only that she had been honored with a proper burial in sight of the Almighty. Beyond this fact, Isabella's disappearance from the world remained a mystery. He took matters into hand, even with the knowledge that her parents would forevermore anguish over what became of their daughter, and his guilt over her final repose would last a lifetime. In this deed, he demonstrated himself to be as much of a man of action as his father but differed with sanctified intent. Deep within a secretive wooded plot near the abbey, Henry prayed over the grave for her eternal salvation while mourning what might have been under different circumstances a beloved addition to the Morland family.

CHAPTER
Fifty-Eight

THE RETURN TO BELAS KNAP followed soon after. Regardless of any apprehension of the journey, Henry felt steadfast in putting the particulars related to his father's alignments to rest, thereby burying the affair—the difference being his intention to leave behind no marker in memoriam.

He arrived in Prestbury, and after meeting up with Mr. Collinson and Mr. Shelley, they soon set off for Belas Knap, with Shelley taking some minutes to pack what he considered to be necessary provisions into a set of bags on his horse. This was undoubtedly due to some description given by the local who had originally discovered the bodies. During the interim, and in conversation with Collinson, Henry found the gentleman to be involved in the livestock trade, having a keen sense of business to make the profession suitable as well as profitable. Mr. Shelley was the proprietor of a small shop, carrying the goods and wares that the residents found necessary. The shop also served as a meeting spot for other business, as well as idle gossip, and was thus the logical place to first hear of the nearby disturbance.

The three men made their way to the ancient mound, travelling past the Humblebee Woods to the site, edged to one side by the forest, and on all sides by the remnants of a stone wall, now reduced to a scattered line of rock. In the broad daylight, it was much as Henry remembered from past visits with his father, the central structure of the mound rising some thirteen feet, and stretched horizontally for approximately seventy-five yards from north to south. But now the rise in the earth had undergone a radical change. The once-smooth hill of grass was broken asunder as if a great earthquake had fractured the ground apart across the center of the mound while causing great sections of rock to cut through the surface. Even upon their approach, it was clear that some tremendous force had caused this destruction. Henry recalled the chaos from his last time there, at that time giving more attention to father, brother, and Catherine than the lay of the land; the terrible apparitions and the creatures that had emerged from the mound were indelible images that even at present were hard to dispel, with the terrain now still, the sun shining brightly, and no indication of the monstrosities that had been there before.

Without a word, he dismounted his horse and closed in on the ancient formation, even with those recent memories fresh on his mind. In front were the two sets of posts with severed lengths of rope still attached to each. Shelley and Collinson both eyed the stakes, and from their expressions, clearly had some idea of what its purpose had been, but said nothing, excepting wary glances to each other. Henry knelt at one set, examining the grass, covered in sections with some partially dried residue that, when rubbing his fingers across it, came up tacky, and pungent in aroma. This angle offered visibility to the cracked doorway of the mound, but it was in the area above that he knew he must go. At the same time, he searched for any sign of his father's missing locket.

The two men from Prestbury were more reticent but followed behind as he made his way up the slope of the mound, soon finding himself at its edge, looking down into the abyss formed by the cracked earth. The drop was hardly an extreme distance, only as much as he had climbed, but straight down to an unearthed area. Based on the structure itself and the scattering of bones, both animal and human, the space had at one time been part of a Neolithic burial chamber. At the ledge, only a few yards away, the earth was slathered with a dark brown colour, this being where he last saw his father, and his stomach turned, as he knew the source of the discolouring.

At the bottom of the chambered burrow, a jagged crack in the earth ran the full distance of the interior, just wide enough to discern the shift in rock from one side to the other, while at the far end, it disappeared into the blackness of another fissure near the side wall. From the positioning of the earth around the opening, it appeared to have been cracked apart in the same manner as above, more than likely occurring when the tremors opened up the outer shell of the mound. The opening was of perhaps seven feet in length, and half that in width, but with a depth uncertain. The last detail, possibly the most unnerving of all, were the markings that stretched along the burrow floor from the hole, indicating that something had been dragged out from the chasm, or back in.

After examining the ledge for usable footholds, he climbed downward into the burrow for a better look at the opening, and once at the bottom, he looked up at his companions, who were likewise above looking down at him. In unison, they shook their heads, clearly indicating their reluctance to join him; their position at the top was close enough for their comfort. Henry responded with a half-hearted smile and a nod of understanding. This was not their business to resolve as they were only observers. Still, he was satisfied to have them there, even at this distance. He would have been more unnerved if he had made this trip alone.

Now at the edge of the inner crater, he could see the details that were not visible from above, most notable being a series of horizontal stone slabs, set at intervals inside the periphery, and looking much like roughly carved steps, these leading downward into the darkness below. Henry moved from one side to the other and then to his knees, hoping to gain a clearer view of those depths, but after only a few yards, it was a solid inky black. He remained in a crouching position for some minutes, considering the options, but equally aware of the one possible choice if he was to find out what was inside; and at last resolved, he turned back to the men, explaining what he intended to do.

"Are you sure you'd be wanting to do that, sir?" asked Collinson, clearly uncomfortable at the thought of someone descending into the crack in the earth.

"I see no other option," Henry replied. "Not if I want to find out what happened here." There was more to his statement than expressed. His father's final words had not left him.

My legacy lies below.

If he was to know what his father intended, he would have to travel downward. In addition, he hoped to find the locket with his mother's portrait. Having not found it above, it must have been torn off below.

"I should not be long, but you may remain where you are."

Collinson took this with great relief while Shelley, giving the whole an estimation, nodded and stated, "Then I will be having something you will likely need. Wait but a minute." He stepped from Henry's line of sight and was absent for some minutes while Henry continued to examine the interior of the mound, noting its series of chambers, and another splattering of brown liquid upon the earth, most likely the spot where Frederick met his end.

"Oy!" came a voice from overhead. Shelley had returned, now holding a lantern aloft. Clearly, he had been thinking ahead to what might be needed and had packed it before their trip. In his other hand, he held a coiled length of rope. A clever man, he.

While not thrilled to be doing so, he made his way down to the bottom of the burrow, accessories in hand, and in reaching the floor, held them out to Henry. "Now don't be expecting me to follow you any further. I don't care to know what's down there, if you catch my meaning." Henry understood precisely, knowing that even in this enlightened age, superstitions ran deep, and after having seen the things he had experienced, perhaps that was a prudent way of thinking. There was some truth to Hamlet's words to Horacio, with the many things found in both Heaven and Hell—and he doubted that Shakespeare had seen even half the things he had.

Henry accepted the gifts with appreciation and thanks while reassuring the merchant that his presence would not be required a foot lower than where they already stood. The lantern was lit, rope wrapped over his shoulder, and after a few steps inside the opening, he began his descent. The stone steps were clearly of some ancient age, roughly carved from stone and set at angles not entirely even. The walls themselves were nothing more than bare rock cut out from the earth by some distant hand, but at about eight feet in depth, there came a change, this not being visible from the surface.

The walls became even in texture, much like large slabs that had been set into place, and after another few more feet were the first of the carvings set into the walls. These were diagrams and symbols, the meanings of which were unknown to Henry, but were obviously of some relevance at the time they were etched into the rock. He held the lantern close for examination while wishing that he had also brought about something to make notes, as he would never remember the specifics after his return to the surface—momentarily, he considered going back, and looked above him at the bright light that was now partially visible due to an outcropping of rock that put him in the shadows. No, he would proceed, and try to remember as best as he could.

The steps continued in their haphazard downward direction, and with each step, he could feel the air growing cooler, but seeing no end in sight, the steps faded into the darkness, while the light above became dimmer, as the passage moved downward at crooked angles. These visuals being considerably disconcerting, a level of claustrophobia crept over him, from the narrowness of the wall on all sides and the lack of light except for his lantern. There came a point where he considered a retreat, but with a deep breath and fresh resolve, he continued forth.

At some level, which he surmised to be about fifty to seventy feet down, the steps came to an end, reaching a flat expanse, and Henry found himself in a level tunnel, much wider than what he had descended from, it progressing a short distance then opening into an even wider area of perhaps ten to fifteen feet in each direction. The chamber was barren of content, except an ornate far wall with a single door on the opposite side, and smaller openings, about two feet square, set at intervals at the base of the floor on the left and right side, to which no amount of light could reveal what lay beyond. In the center of the room stood a rectangular slab raised a good three feet in height. Like the previous walls, the room and the slab were covered with intricate designs and symbology, and in holding the lantern closer, he could see that the topmost surface of the slab was stained in a dark colour, collected also in the deep lines of the carvings. It took no imagination to understand what disturbing purpose the platform had been used for. Whether it was this realization or the distance from the surface, he now realized how cold it had gotten, having not dressed for such cooler climates. He spent a few more minutes examining the room, along with the ceiling, with its own set of diagrams that he soon recognized as some set of map of the constellations, but not resembling any that he had before seen.

On the far end on either side of the door was a set of massive statues that extended the full height of the room, all lined in a row and inset to the wall. There was a striking familiarity to the figures, and as Henry drew closer, he recognized their similarity to the same bust that had been found above following Catherine's rescue. The shapes were distinctly animal-like in nature, crouched into a sitting position, with small wings that extended down each side, and front claws that held to the base of the wall. Of the head, it was as much octopus as land animal, with long tentacles that extended from the lower part of the face.

Henry exited the room through the opposing doorway, finding yet another set of steps, these being less crude than the previous, and beginning with this descent, the whole about him changed. Immediately noticeable, in addition to the cold, was a musky dampness, along with a putrid smell that made the ever-present claustrophobia even more acute. After a few steps, the surrounding walls changed in texture, the roughened rock giving way to something much smoother. In rubbing his fingers across the surface, which was slightly damp from the moisture in the air, it hardly felt like rock, but a material as sleek as glass, but wholly without colour, an opaque black that seemed to suck up any light shone against it. Like above, there were etchings, but these appeared somehow different in what way, he could not define.

After another dozen steps, the downward tunnel began to take on particular angles quite unlike the previous, set to some unusual precision. Again, the steps came to an end, also opening into a wider area, and in this, Henry realized that he was now inside something completely alien to anything he had ever before encountered. For that matter, it was unlike anything that a normal person might consider to be rational.

The whole seemed to defy normal architectural possibilities, non-Euclidean, with walls set at bizarre angles that were neither convex nor concave. There was a disorienting quality to it that threw off his equilibrium, as what should have been horizontal ceased to be level. Inset at intervals were strange bas-reliefs and etchings of unknown origin or meaning. In addition to this was the unique texture of the flooring, walls, and ceiling, all made from the same material, the light seemed to create strange patterns against the surface, offering no reflection to the illumination, but with light refracted from the water dripping out of certain areas in the construct.

Only now did Henry become aware of the other that had been absent throughout his descent. Until now, the only sound had been his alone, feet connecting against stone as he progressed. Within this chamber, there came to his ears another set of sounds. A liquid, either water or a similar wet substance, could be heard in the constant drips, and further away, some flowing, as if from a distant underground channel. The sounds echoed from the smooth surface of the walls, somehow amplifying the whole. To this was another, far more disturbing sound–that of a distant padding, like feet moving across puddles of water collected on the floor, but without the solidity of a normal foot, much more akin to a flopping sound. Henry envisioned the slapping of fish against a damp surface as the best visual to the noise, as faint as it was, but seeming to grow in intensity.

More than anything else—the darkness, the narrow chamber, the isolation, or complete strangeness to the surface—it was this sound that caused Henry to encounter an intense level of fear that could be felt throughout his body and brought forth a cold sweat. It all seemed too much, and the dense smell became even more noxious to the point of choking. For long minutes, he remained perfectly still, listening to the sound that seemed to come from no specific direction, but from all around and growing louder by the minute. Then for whatever reason he could not define, he continued onward, to find the source of the noise that simultaneously filled him with dread.

Angles of floor, wall, and ceiling bent in upon themselves, creating an abstract dynamic as the chamber narrowed and angled downward. He found himself walking up steps that took him downward, in complete defiance of normal logic, thereby leading out to a multiple set of pathways, the largest of these also angled up in a downward direction. From here, the sound seemed the loudest, along with something comparable to croaking, like the sound of a thousand frogs merged into one distinct noise.

And there, deep in the shadows, he witnessed something moving.

Henry raised his lantern aloft, directing the beam into the blackness to reveal the thing—or multiple things, as it was hard to discern the shape in full. To call it anything but an abomination would be inaccurate, the manifestation being similar to a toad or fish, or something in-between, but mutated to the degree that defied description. With the light, it recoiled slightly, letting out a scream, resembling a guttural croak that droned on well after it had closed its misshapen mouth. How it detected the light was uncertain, as it bore no apparent eyes, only a massive blank surface covered with a slimy wetness, but was some sort of head. As it moved, other shapes shifted about it, suggesting either more than one such creature or smaller appendages of the same. On the whole, this was the stuff of nightmares unlike anything Henry might have envisioned.

To the monstrosity's call, there were other replies from chambers far and wide, each echoing through the walls, and he realized that this was not a singular entity, but part of a breed of subterranean creatures. With a coolness of mind that surprised him, he cautiously retracted the light, moving backward to a safe distance, and in preparation to make as quick a retreat as possible. He had seen enough for a lifetime.

He made a sharp turn, causing the lantern to flicker, and brought about a horrible mental picture of the light going out, leaving him in complete darkness, and to the mercy of these vile things. The thought caused him to take more care with the lantern, all the while retracing his steps through the distorted angles of the chamber, and nearly getting lost from disorientation caused by their illusion. At length he found the steps leading upward, even as the croaking surrounded him, the sound growing louder, and he knew that the amphibious monstrosities were closing in, arriving from unseen tunnels. He reached the stone chamber, there with the central slab before him, and again he had the insight to what might have taken place there. This brought about a fresh sense of revulsion, at the horror that those unfortunate enough to have been laid there must have endured.

As he entered the chamber, pain shot through his back as his shoulder was jerked backward, nearly causing him to stumble. At first thinking it was from one of the subterranean creatures, he shot a glance behind him and saw that the rope he had coiled around his shoulder had snagged against an outcropping of rock. He quickly fumbled with the rope, dropping it from his arm, having no need of it. Ahead was the opening and the stairs leading upward, so he quickly made his way forward.

Shadows shifted outward at the walls, and he saw that the diminutive openings that lined the base on both sides of the walls were no longer vacant; shapes slithered out from them, similar in appearance to the thing he had seen previously, each causing wet slapping sounds against the floor as their bodies fell against the surface while emitting low croaking noises. Henry experienced a moment of sheer panic as his body froze, unable to move in horror at the sight before him. Only when one of the creatures brushed his leg with its paw did he find the will to act, rushing forth to escape the room. With only a foot away from the exit, he felt something wet and clammy wrap itself around his leg, and in looking down, saw it restrained by one of the things. Several attempts were made to shake his leg loose, but the thing only tightened its grip, so he swung the lantern around within inches of its head, and either its brightness or its heat caused the beast to emit a loud cry and let loose its grip, allowing him to pull away. In that brief moment, Henry was given a glimpse of the thing at a range of only a few feet. In that moment he knew the sight would haunt him for the rest of his days.

The monstrosity measured roughly the size of a large dog, but wider and squat, looking much in body like an enormous frog, and with longer arms that ended in talon-like fingers. The whole of the body was rough, similar to an amphibian, including a series of raised indentions that followed the line of the spine on the back. Perched on top was the head, an enormous misshapen mass of damp flesh void of eyes, and a wide toothless mouth that extended, revealing strings of mucus extending from upper to lower lip. The thing produced a stench of decay, as noticeable as the slimy coating of the body, and the residue it left in its wake. All this was visible in the short seconds before Henry pulled his leg away and turned, running as best as possible in the dim space of the chamber for the exit, and knowing that many other such creatures were behind him. To all this was a scream that might chill the blood, and only after did he realize that it had been his own.

The roughened steps were taken two at a time. He slammed against one side of the cramped space, then the other, ever upward as the sounds of multiple croakings echoed against the walls behind him. For the time it took for him to ascend, reaching the point where the stone inscriptions first began, it seemed to be an eternity; at any moment, he expected to feel the damp claws pulling him back, and the ensuing terror urged him all the more to climb as fast as possible.

Then came the first rays of light from above. He progressed ever upward until, at about ten feet below the ground, he found himself fully in some visible ray of sunlight, and at this point, he found he could run no more. He fell back against the steps, sitting there and listening for the horrible sounds, which had now faded into nothingness. Some minutes passed, in which he embraced some level of composure, feeling secure that the creatures below would not venture to this height where they would be exposed to the illumination of the day. Only then did he see a reflection of something metallic wedged into a crevice in the rock. Recognizing the object, he claimed the now-scuffed locket, examining it before putting it in his pocket. At last, he found the strength to rise to his feet and take the final steps up to the surface.

As he stepped out from the fissure, he found the two men sitting at the top of the mound looking down, Collinson rather pale and nervous while Shelley appeared all the more composed, sitting calmly and smoking his pipe. They eyed him closely as he climbed out, before asking him what he found below.

Henry considered the best way to answer, then replied in a calm voice, "Nothing. It is an ancient burial site—but there are rats down there. It should be sealed immediately due to disease, as they surely carry the plague."

The thought of such a possibility was enough to incite an immediate reaction from both men, they instinctively took several steps back from the ledge. Henry managed to restrain a grim smile, knowing that his variation of the facts would serve its purpose. At the top of the mound, he returned the lantern, along with fervent thanks for its usage, and apologies for having lost the rope along the way. In way of replacement and for services rendered, he offered compensation for which Mr. Shelley, being a good businessman, accepted without pause, and caused Mr. Collinson to regret not thinking of bringing such provisions himself.

Not to leave things unequal, Henry presented Collinson with more than adequate recompense for his own time. In short order, the two men left for the village, richer in pocket, and already set with the intention of sealing the opening. Henry estimated that such a closure would take place soon thereafter as word spread of even the remote possibility of an outbreak.

There was nothing else to be done. Henry Tilney departed Belas Knap for the last time, with fervent hopes that it would likewise never fill his thoughts again.

CHAPTER

Fifty-Nine

AN HEROINE RETURNING, at the close of her career, to her native village, in all the triumph of recovered reputation, and all the dignity of a countess, with a long train of noble relations in their several phaetons, and three waiting-maids in a travelling chaise and four, behind her, is an event on which the pen of the contriver may well delight to dwell; it gives credit to every conclusion, and the author must share in the glory she so liberally bestows. But my affair is different in certain respects; had she not uncovered anything formidable at Northanger Abbey, and had the general not altered his initial plan after his revelations from Mr. Thorpe, then my heroine would have returned home in solitude and disgrace; and no sweet elation of spirits could lead me into minuteness. An heroine in a hack post-chaise would be such a blow upon sentiment, as no attempt at grandeur or pathos can withstand. Swiftly therefore should her post-boy drive through the village, amid the gaze of Sunday groups, and speedy should be her descent from it. She would have prepared no enjoyment of no everyday nature for those to whom she went; first, in the appearance of her carriage—and secondly, in herself. That, however, is another ending, belonging to the fabric of another very different narrative.

In this story, I bring back my heroine safely to her home after experiencing the most horrifying and perilous of adventures, and in the company of a dearest friend. Their trip from the abbey had been a delight, due to the pleasure of the other's company, and without accident or alarm, thereby between six and seven o'clock in the evening found themselves entering Fullerton.

The chaise of a traveler being a rare sight in Fullerton, the whole family was immediately at the window; and to have it stop at the sweep-gate was a pleasure to brighten every eye and occupy every fancy—a pleasure quite unlooked for by all but the two youngest children, a boy and girl of six and four years, who expected a brother or sister in every carriage. Happy the glance that first distinguished Catherine! Happy the voice that proclaimed the discovery! But whether such happiness was the lawful property of George or Harriet could never be exactly understood.

Her father, mother, Sarah, George, and Harriet, all assembled at the door to welcome her with affectionate eagerness, was a sight to awaken the best feelings of Catherine's heart; and in the embrace of each, as she stepped from the carriage, she found herself soothed beyond anything that she had believed possible. So surrounded, so caressed, she was happy beyond measure! Brief introductions were made for Eleanor, who was likewise greeted with smiles and embraces. In the joyfulness of family love everything for a short time was subdued, and the pleasure of seeing her, leaving them at first little leisure for calm curiosity, they were all seated round the tea-table, which Mrs. Morland had hurried for the comfort of the two travelers.

Excitedly, and with numerous pauses for questions or additional comments from Eleanor, did she then begin what might perhaps, at the end of half an hour, be termed, by the courtesy of her hearers, an account of her stay, both at Bath with the Allens, and then at Northanger; but scarcely, within that time, could they at all collect the particulars. For all the telling of stories, there were just as many avoided, mainly dealing with the general and his darker interests, as well as the death of his wife. Naturally, they said nothing of the strange business at Belas Knap. Sarah pressed her sister for details of the abbey and its many hidden chambers: indeed she indulged in the sweets of incomprehensibility.

"I am most happy for the two of you," said Mrs. Morland; "You must have had a memorable time of it, and now Catherine is back at home, and Eleanor is most welcome. It is always good for young people to have their adventures; and you know, my dear Catherine, you always were a sad little scatter-brained creature; but I hope you must have been forced to have your wits about you, with so much excitement."

To this last comment, her mother could have no idea of either the excitement Catherine had endured or the extent to which her wits played a part. On both accounts, such ignorance served her mother the best.

This first evening back in Fullerton was spent in lively conversation, both sides telling what the other had missed, even though the scales tipped far to Catherine, as there was very little to be addressed as newsworthy from her home. Eleanor was given every courtesy, and true to Mrs. Morland's words, was most welcome as an addition to the family. This hospitality helped lighten any nervousness or insecurity on Eleanor's part, being given such generosity and affection for one whose acquaintance spanned only a few hours. Even with the best spirits exhibited, the day's journey had left both girls exhausted, and readily agreed to her mother's next counsel of going early to bed.

Sleep came fast and deep, of the most rejuvenating kind for both Catherine and Eleanor, so that when they all met the next morning well after the sun had risen, there remained no trace of fatigue or lowered spirits. Following breakfast, they walked outside for a time, and by being back home with such companionship as was present, Catherine was confirmed in her strength of feelings, in valuing Eleanor's merits and kindness, and knowing that she could never enough commiserate her for the care and affection given during those last days at the abbey, it all deserving the thousand good wishes of a most affectionate heart.

During lunch, conversation had come to the Allens and the acquaintances made at Bath. "This has been a most fortunate acquaintance, the two of you," observed Mrs. Morland, causing Catherine to think of the other person she would have liked to have made the journey. As if picking up on these thoughts, she added in reference to Eleanor, "Mrs. Allen thought highly of both you and your brother; but you were sadly out of luck too in your Isabella. Ah! Poor James! Well, we must live and learn; and the next new friends you make I hope will be better worth keeping."

Catherine coloured as she warmly answered, "No friend can be better worth keeping than the present company." This remark brought about an equal flush to Eleanor's cheeks.

The thoughts of Henry persisted, with hopes of meeting again quite soon, and with equal unsubstantiated fears that had no rationale might he forget her, and in that case, no longer be interested in resuming their familiarity. Her eyes unexpectedly filled with tears as she pictured her acquaintance so renewed; and her mother, incorrectly perceiving her emotions due to her return to Fullerton, proposed, as another expedient for restoring her spirits, that they should call on Mrs. Allen.

The two houses were only a quarter of a mile apart; and, as they walked, Mrs. Morland quickly dispatched all that she felt on the score of James's disappointment.

"We are sorry for him," said she; "but otherwise there is no harm done in the match going off; for it could not be a desirable thing to have him engaged to a girl whom we had not the smallest acquaintance with, and who was so entirely without fortune; and now, after such behaviour, we cannot think at all well of her. Just at present it comes hard to poor James; but that will not last forever; and I dare say he will be a discreeter man all his life, for the foolishness of his first choice."

At this, Catherine fell silent, feeling all the worse for what befell poor Isabella, who could never have deserved so inhumane a fate. Despite her inconsistencies of preference, and in thinking of her interests too much, she was far from a person with no redeeming qualities. Catherine had wondered if her friend had openly invited the horrors of her own free will, or was lured in as a victim; but she could no longer hate her former friend for the wrongs done to James. Poor, unfortunate James. He would never know what had become of the enticing young woman who had stolen his heart, only to have it dashed afterward. The same applied to the remaining Thorpes—Isabella's brother, sisters, and mother— to never know the full account of her premature demise. Already, her mother had contacted the authorities regarding her daughter's mysterious disappearance. For their part, Catherine, Eleanor, and James were understood not to speak a further word of it. How could they without appearing to be not of a right mind?

Mrs. Morland said no more on the subject, as was for the best. This was just such a summary view of the affair as Catherine could listen to; another sentence might have endangered her complaisance, and made her reply less rational; for soon were all her thinking powers swallowed up in the reflection of her own change of feelings and spirits since last she had trodden that well-known road. It was not three months ago since, wild with joyful expectation, she had there run backwards and forwards some ten times a day, with an heart light, gay, and independent; looking forward to pleasures untasted and unalloyed, and free from the apprehension of evil as from the knowledge of it. Three months ago had seen her all this; and now, how altered a being did she return!

Both Catherine and Eleanor were received by the Allens with all the kindness which their unlooked-for appearance, acting on a steady affection, would naturally call forth; and warm was their pleasure, on hearing of her stay at the abbey—though its representation bypassed the same details that had been eliminated in the earlier recollections with the Morlands. At some point, the conversation shifted to the time spent in Bath, and Mrs. Allen expressed herself to all the particulars of the city. "Only think, my dear, of my having got that frightful great rent in my best Mechlin so charmingly mended, before I left Bath, that one can hardly see where it was. I must show it you some day or other. Bath is a nice place, Catherine, after all. I assure you I did not above half like coming away. Mrs. Thorpe's being there was such a comfort to us, was not it? You know, you and I were quite forlorn at first."

"Yes, but that did not last long," said Catherine, her eyes brightening at the recollection of what had first given spirit to her existence there.

"Very true: we soon met with Mrs. Thorpe, and then we wanted for nothing. My dear, do not you think these silk gloves wear very well? I put them on new the first time of our going to the Lower Rooms, you know, and I have worn them a great deal since. Do you remember that evening?"

"Do I! Oh! Perfectly."

"It was very agreeable, was not it? Mr. Tilney drank tea with us, and I always thought him a great addition, he is so very agreeable. I have a notion you danced with him, but am not quite sure. I remember I had my favourite gown on."

Catherine could not answer; and, after a short trial of other subjects, Mrs. Allen again added—"And such friends you have made, with Miss Tilney now here with us, and her brother—what an upstanding man he is—and their father. Such an agreeable, worthy man as he seems! I do not suppose, Mrs. Morland, you ever saw a better-bred man in your life. His lodgings were taken the very day after he left them, Catherine. But no wonder; Milsom Street, you know."

As they walked home again, Mrs. Morland endeavoured to impress on her daughter's mind the happiness of having such steady well-wishers as Mr. and Mrs. Allen, and the kindness of the Tilneys, while she could preserve the good opinion and affection of her earliest friends. It is the best intentions of those closest that can make the difference. There was a great deal of good sense in all this, and Catherine's feelings were aligned with almost every position her mother advanced, knowing that it was also the ill-begotten deeds of others can cast it all asunder. It was upon the behaviour of the closest of these very acquaintances that all her present happiness, and all her unspoken yearnings had sprung; and while Mrs. Morland was successfully confirming her own, Catherine was silently reflecting what Henry might be doing at that minute, and knowing only that he was not there with her.

CHAPTER

Sixty

THERE IS A TIME FOR EVERYTHING—a time for balls and plays, and a time for work. This was a sentiment often expressed by Mrs. Morland, and repeated once again after Catherine had made one too many references to her stay in Bath. "My dear Catherine," she said, no longer able to refrain from the gentle reproof, "I am afraid you are growing quite a fine lady. I do not know when poor Richard's cravats would be done, if he had no friend but you. Your head runs too much upon Bath; but there is a time for everything—a time for balls and plays, and a time for work. You have had a long run of amusement, and now you must try to be useful." Apparently, even the accompaniment of a friend could no longer detain her from the normal chores she had been expected to carry out.

Catherine took up her work directly, saying in some defiance that "her head did not run upon Bath—much." This, of course, was simply not true. She knew it. Her mother knew it as well and had used the excuse to get some housework in order. Eleanor volunteered to help as well, but the offer was declined, as she was a guest and it was not proper for her to assist. She smiled, accepted the dismissal, and then proceeded to help anyway.

As an afterthought when Eleanor was out of earshot in another room, Mrs. Morland added, "I hope, my Catherine, you are not getting out of humour with home because it is not so grand as Northanger. That would be turning your visit into an evil indeed. Wherever you are, you should always be contented, but especially at home, because there you must spend the most of your time. I did not quite like, at breakfast, to hear you talk so much about the French bread at Northanger."

"I am sure I do not care about the bread. It is all the same to me what I eat, however, I did feel it a kindness and compliment to Eleanor and her family to say so."

"There is a very clever essay in one of the books upstairs upon much such a subject, about young girls that have been spoilt for home by great acquaintance—The Mirror, I think. I will look it out for you some day or other, because I am sure it will do you good."

Catherine said no more, and, with an endeavour to do right, applied to her work. It may have been that Mrs. Morland was prompted to make the comments, feeling that her own home was being held up for comparison, however, any such possibilities were held solely in her mind; never had such an idea occurred to Catherine, who did love the French bread at Northanger, but no more and no less than the bread at Fullerton, both being equally delicious for their distinct qualities.

Mrs. Morland left the room to fetch the book in question, anxious to lose no time in attacking so dreadful a malady as a spoilt child. It was some time before she could find what she looked for; and other family matters occurring to detain her, a quarter of an hour had elapsed ere she returned downstairs with the volume from which so much was hoped. Her avocations above having shut out all noise but what she created herself, she knew not that a visitor had arrived until a loud outpouring of cries became so great as to shake the house to its foundation, and on entering the room, the first object she beheld was a young man whom she had never seen before. With a look of much respect, he immediately rose, and being introduced to her by her conscious daughter as "Mr. Henry Tilney," with the embarrassment of real sensibility began to apologize for his unannounced appearance there, and stating his impatience to be assured of Miss Morland and his sister having reached the home in safety as the cause of his intrusion. He did not address himself to an uncandid judge.

Mrs. Morland had been always kindly disposed towards both brother and sister—the latter from her appearance there, and the former from the high praise offered by both girls—and instantly, pleased by his appearance, received him with the simple professions of unaffected benevolence; thanking him for such an attention to her daughter, assuring him that the friends of her children were always welcome there.

His heart was greatly relieved by such warmness, and in returning in silence to his seat, therefore, he remained for some minutes most civilly answering all Mrs. Morland's common remarks about the weather and roads. Eleanor was quite pleased to see her brother, as to be expected from their bonds as siblings, as well as intimate friends of extended absence. Catherine meanwhile—the anxious, agitated, happy, feverish Catherine—said not a word; but her glowing cheek and brightened eye made her mother trust that this good-natured visit would at least set her heart at ease for quite a time, and gladly therefore did she lay aside the first volume of "The Mirror" for a future hour.

Desirous of Mr. Morland's assistance, as well in giving encouragement, as in finding conversation for her guest, Mrs. Morland had very early dispatched one of the children to summon him; but Mr. Morland was from home—and being thus without any support, at the end of a quarter of an hour she had nothing to say. After a couple of minutes' unbroken silence, Henry, turning to Catherine for the first time since her mother's entrance, asked her, with sudden alacrity, if Mr. and Mrs. Allen were now at Fullerton? And on developing, from amidst all her perplexity of words in reply, the meaning, which one short syllable would have given, immediately expressed his intention of paying his respects to them, and, with a rising colour, asked her if she would have the goodness to show him the way.

"You may see the house from this window, sir," was information on Sarah's side, which produced only a bow of acknowledgment from the gentleman, a knowing smile from Eleanor, and a silencing nod from her mother; for Mrs. Morland, thinking it probable, as a secondary consideration in his wish of waiting on their worthy neighbours, that he might have further interest in her daughter than only her safe arrival, would not on any account prevent her accompanying him. They began their walk, and Mrs. Morland was not entirely mistaken in his object in wishing it. Some explanation on his father's account he had to give; but his first purpose was to explain himself, and before they reached Mr. Allen's grounds he had done it so well that Catherine did not think it could ever be repeated too often. She was assured of his affection; and that heart in return was solicited, which, perhaps, they pretty equally knew was already entirely his own; for, though Henry was now sincerely attached to her, though he felt and delighted in all the excellencies of her character and truly loved her society, I must confess that his affection originated in nothing better than gratitude, or, in other words, that a persuasion of her partiality for him had been the only cause of giving her a serious thought. It is a new circumstance in romance, I acknowledge, and dreadfully derogatory of an heroine's dignity; but if it be as new in common life, the credit of a wild imagination will at least be all my own.

A very short visit to Mrs. Allen, in which Henry talked at random, without sense or connection, and Catherine, rapt in the contemplation of her own unutterable happiness, scarcely opened her lips, dismissed them to the ecstasies of another tete-a-tete; and before it was suffered to close, she had already thought through all he had told her and all she had experienced during the last week at Northanger Abbey.

Henry had never disclosed in full the details leading up to her abduction, which she had not already uncovered, in part due to his unwillingness to expose her to any more distress than she had already experienced; this was especially true during her severe illness following the events at Belas Knap. In addition, there were great parts to the mystery that he still attempted to understand, and would not fully comprehend until well after her return to Fullerton. The walk to the Allens, therefore, in a pace taken like that of a tortoise, offered the opportunity to give up the remaining details previously held from her, along with that he had so hoped to express.

On his return from Woodston, he had been met outside the abbey by his impatient father, hastily informed in angry terms of Miss Morland's departure, and ordered to think of her no more. After a heated argument, they went their separate ways in defiance of the other. Only afterward was he able to piece together the threads that led to his father's outrage, including the one that at first had nothing to do with the secrets hidden away in his study.

Its beginnings fell into place in Bath, with John Thorpe being the originator of the misconception. The general, perceiving his son one night at the theatre to be paying considerable attention to Miss Morland, had accidentally inquired of Thorpe if he knew more of her than her name, and was thereby given the false bill of goods, suggesting in grand terms Catherine's family to be far more than they were, along with the ties to the Allens. Upon such intelligence the general had proceeded; for never had it occurred to him to doubt its authority. Thorpe's interest in the family, by his sister's approaching connection with one of its members, and his own views on another (circumstances of which he boasted with almost equal openness), seemed sufficient vouchers for his truth; and to these were added the absolute facts of the Allens being wealthy and childless, of Miss Morland's being under their care, and—as soon as his acquaintance allowed him to judge—of their treating her with parental kindness.

Catherine herself could not be more ignorant at the time of all this, than his own children. Henry and Eleanor, perceiving nothing in her situation likely to engage their father's particular respect, had seen with astonishment the suddenness, continuance, and extent of his attention; and though latterly, from some hints which had accompanied an almost positive command to his son of doing everything in his power to attach her, Henry was convinced of his father's believing it to be an advantageous connection, it was not till the late explanation at Northanger that they had the smallest idea of the false calculations which had hurried him on. That they were false, the general had learnt from the very person who had suggested them, from Thorpe himself, whom he had chanced to meet again in town, and who, then spun a completely different story. With this new account, the general rushed home to cast Catherine out in as short a period as possible.

The affrighted Catherine, amidst all the terrors of expectation, as she listened to this account, could not but rejoice in the kind caution with which Henry had saved her from the necessity of a conscientious rejection, by engaging her faith before he mentioned the subject; and as he proceeded to give the particulars, and explain the motives of his father's conduct, her feelings soon hardened into even a triumphant delight. The general had had nothing to accuse her of, nothing to lay to her charge, but her being the involuntary, unconscious object of a deception which his pride could not pardon, and which a better pride would have been ashamed to own. She was guilty only of being less rich than he had supposed her to be. Under a mistaken persuasion of her possessions and claims, he had courted her acquaintance in Bath, solicited her company at Northanger, and designed her for his daughter-in-law. On discovering his error, to turn her from the house seemed the best, though to his feelings an inadequate proof of his resentment towards herself, and his contempt of her family.

It was upon the general's return that his plans again changed, no doubt from the discovery of his private study being entered, and the possibility of his being found out. Henry was not sure of how the discovery was made, but the evidence detailed in Catherine's letter to her sister, found in the general's coat pocket, suggested that the father had seen the letter on the hall table, and for whatever reason he might have had, suspected her to the extent of opening the letter for himself. He then altered his strategy for Miss Morland's safe return home.

For every man, there is a mixture of dark and light, saint and sinner. With the general, an aspect of his character had long been fascinated with the occult sciences, leading him into dark alleyways beyond the pale of accepted beliefs. It had become an obsession with him, in particular, the cults dealing with certain secret texts and ancient beings purported to have held dominion over the Earth well before the dawn of man. The material contained within his library was obscene in every way, and it was clear why he would have kept his interests secret except for those in his inner circle.

That his wife found out, forced him to do what he felt he must, and bringing about her death was the cause of his deep regret ever after. His agony was clear from his preservation of her room intact while unable to bear even the thought of her. Even the memorial placed at the church was a constant reminder of what he did, not by choice but by his misguided necessity. It was no wonder that when he found Catherine out, she would not have been given any better treatment.

It was also of no surprise that Frederick would have been drawn into the same unholy alliance and was therefore enlisted to kidnap Catherine from the carriage, for the vile ritual they had already planned out with another victim—Isabella Thorpe, who had been unfortunate enough to have fallen for Captain Tilney's deceitful charms. The plan enacted, both girls found themselves held captive at Belas Knap. Had it not been for Henry's deduction, first from the letter and journal given to him by Eleanor, and then by examining the contents of the study, and in particular, the map, Catherine would not be present at the moment.

I leave it to my reader's sagacity to determine how much of all this it was possible for Henry to communicate at this time to Catherine, how much of it he could have learnt from his father, in what points his own conjectures might assist him, and what portion must yet remain to be told in a letter from James. I have united for their case what they must divide for mine. Catherine, at any rate, heard enough to feel that in suspecting General Tilney of either murdering or shutting up his wife, and finding out that he was capable of far worse, she had scarcely sinned against his character, or magnified his cruelty.

Henry, in having such things to relate of his father, was almost as pitiable as in their first avowal to himself. He blushed for the wicked counsel which he was obliged to expose. The conversation between them at Northanger had been of the most unfriendly kind. Henry's indignation on hearing how Catherine had been treated, on comprehending his father's views, and being ordered to acquiesce in them, had been open and bold. The general, accustomed on every ordinary occasion to give the law in his family, prepared for no reluctance but of feeling, no opposing desire that should dare to clothe itself in words, could ill brook the opposition of his son, steady as the sanction of reason and the dictate of conscience could make it. But, in such a cause, his anger, though it must shock, could not intimidate Henry, who was sustained in his purpose by a conviction of its justice. He felt himself bound as much in honour as in affection to Miss Morland,

and believing that heart to be his own which he had been directed to gain, no unworthy retraction of a tacit consent, no reversing decree of unjustifiable anger, could shake his fidelity, or influence the resolutions it prompted. That is how they parted at Northanger, only to confront each other one last time, even as the demons from some unspeakable hell hovered over them, and ultimately took the general for their own.

As to the private study, Henry returned after the funeral and subsequent visit into the subterranean chambers of Belas Knap to examine the contents in detail. What he found only confirmed what he already knew with every fibre of his being; that the materials therein were of a content of such unspeakable horror that it should be eradicated from the Earth. By his hand, and without help from the servants, he took the entire contents of the library to the lawn outside the abbey, there to be set on fire and destroyed. As the flames consumed that which the general held so dear—the books and manuscripts, the charts and drawings, statues and obscure artifacts, jewelry, baubles, and ritual objects, he thought he might have heard something upon the wind, like a high-pitched wail, or the call a nightjar might make in the early hours, just as the sun was set to claim another day.

CHAPTER
Sixty-One

MR. AND MRS. MORLAND'S surprise on being applied to by Mr. Tilney for their consent to his marrying their daughter was, for a few minutes, considerable, it having never entered their heads to suspect an attachment on either side; but as nothing, after all, could be more natural than Catherine's being beloved, they soon learnt to consider it with only the happy agitation of gratified pride, and, as far as they alone were concerned, had not a single objection to start. His pleasing manners and good sense were self-evident recommendations; and having never heard evil of him, it was not their way to suppose any evil could be told. Goodwill supplying the place of experience, his character needed no attestation. "Catherine would make a sad, heedless young housekeeper to be sure," was her mother's foreboding remark; but quick was the consolation of there being nothing like practice.

There was no obstacle on Henry's side. Any opposition died with the general, who had, until his final return to Northanger, given every impression of desiring Catherine Morland as an addition to the family. His death, along with that of their brother, Frederick, left Henry to answer to none but himself, or at least until he took Catherine for his own, and would then be required to answer to her. Such is the proper resolution for any storybook, be it novel or otherwise.

He could not help but appreciate the irony of his father's actions, once he was informed of Mr. Morland's true circumstances, and understood how the general had been scarcely more misled by Thorpe's first boast of the family wealth than by his subsequent malicious overthrow of it; that in no sense of the word were they necessitous or poor, and that Catherine would have three thousand pounds.

Indeed, Henry was a practical man, and understood the importance of such things, but essential to him was the care and affection of Catherine, certainly worth more than could be calculated in coinage, as well as the high esteem of her mother and father. As only he and Eleanor remained of the family line, the Morlands were the closest he now had to family.

It might be considered, if this was a different story, with no trace of occultism or dark forces about, and the general being simply misguided, what could have been the eventual outcome. Had Catherine's expulsion from the abbey been based on family station, it would surmise that, until such a time that his father softened his heart, it must be impossible for them to sanction the engagement. Their tempers were mild, but their principles were steady, and while his parent so expressly forbade the connection, they could not allow themselves to encourage it. That the general should come forward to solicit the alliance, or that he should even very heartily approve it, they were not refined enough to make any parading stipulation; but the decent appearance of consent must be yielded, and that once obtained—and their own hearts made them trust that it could not be very long denied—their willing approbation was instantly to follow. His consent was all that they wished for. They were no more inclined than entitled to demand his money. Of a very considerable fortune, his son was, by marriage settlements, eventually secure; his present income was an income of independence and comfort, and under every pecuniary view, it was a match beyond the claims of their daughter. The young people could not be surprised at a decision like this. They felt and they deplored—but they could not resent it; and they parted, endeavouring to hope that such a change in the general, as each believed almost impossible, might speedily take place, to unite them again in the fullness of privileged affection. Henry returned to what was now his only home, to watch over his young plantations, and extend his improvements for her sake, to whose share in them he looked anxiously forward; and Catherine remained at Fullerton to cry. Whether the torments of absence were softened by a clandestine correspondence, let us not inquire. Mr. and Mrs. Morland never did—they had been too kind to exact any promise; and whenever Catherine received a letter, as, at that time, happened pretty often, they always looked another way.

The end of such a story would follow an expected change in the father's disposition, by one literary device or another, thereby bringing together the two in affection and matrimony, thus resolving any final disputes, and allowing the reader to close the book in satisfaction of a pleasant ending. That particular finale is reserved for another book that, although independent, would share certain similarities of resolution.

It should also be noted that any anxiety—be it any other hindrance to a blessed union must be the portion of Henry and Catherine, and of all who loved either; as to its final event, can hardly extend, I fear, to the bosom of my readers, who will see in the tell-tale compression of the pages before them, that we are all hastening together to perfect felicity.

The means by which their early marriage was affected bears the least notation, as since there were no further obstacles, it was arranged, conducted, and executed with the sameness as most any other; save that for the two principals, it was an event to be forever cherished. Henry and Catherine were married, the bells rang, and everybody smiled; and, as this took place within a twelvemonth from the first day of their meeting, it will not appear, after all the dreadful events occasioned by the general's cruelty, that they were essentially hurt by it. To begin perfect happiness at the respective ages of twenty-six and eighteen is to do pretty well; and professing myself moreover convinced that the general's monstrous conduct, so far from being really injurious to their felicity, was perhaps rather conducive to it, by improving their knowledge of each other, and adding strength to their attachment, I leave it to be settled, by whomsoever it may concern, whether the tendency of this work be altogether to recommend such occult activities, murder, and human sacrifice, or reward filial disobedience.

Theirs was not the only marriage of which to end this story, the other being Eleanor with a man of fortune and consequence, which took place in the course of the summer—a union that, had the general been alive to see it, would have likely thrown him into a fit of good humour, from which he might have been truly pleasant to be in the company of.

The marriage of Eleanor Tilney, her removal from all the tragic memories of such a home as Northanger, to the home of her choice and the man of her choice, is an event that I expect to give general satisfaction among all her acquaintance. My own joy on the occasion is very sincere. I know no one more entitled, by unpretending merit, or better prepared by habitual suffering, to receive and enjoy felicity. Her partiality for this gentleman was not of recent origin; and he had been long withheld only by inferiority of situation from addressing her. His unexpected accession to title and fortune had removed all his difficulties. Her husband was deserving of her; independent of his peerage, his wealth, and his attachment, being to a precision the most charming young man in the world. Any further definition of his merits must be unnecessary; the most charming young man in the world is instantly before the imagination of us all. Concerning the one in question, therefore, I have only to add—aware that the rules of composition forbid the introduction of a character not connected with my fable—that this was the very gentleman whose negligent servant left behind him that collection of washing-bills, resulting from a long visit at Northanger, by which my heroine was involved in one of her most alarming adventures.

How Eleanor met up once more with Michael —for this is the same man for whom she had been so favourable to these many years, and had kept a discreet correspondence with—was a contrivance of pure coincidence, he being in Fullerton on some business, and in a chance meeting with Henry, inquired to the health of the family, and in particular, the sister. Without giving the particulars, he was told of the unfortunate passing of both father and older brother, of which he offered his sincere condolences. His demeanor changed significantly upon hearing that Eleanor was staying with friends nearby; and after asking if she might be receptive to him paying a visit, and being answered in the affirmative, there was little to keep him away.

The intervening years since his visit to Northanger had strengthened his already handsome appearance, causing his bright blue eyes to be larger, his jaw more square, and mouth wider, however, any change in his appearance, either beneficial or to his detriment, made no difference to Eleanor, who was as hopelessly in love with him, as she always had been. His visit was an unexpected pleasure, and the first of many, culminating in a proposal, as there were no longer any barriers in the way to their attachments. She accepted before he could finish asking.

The wedding took place in Norwich in Norfolk, just west of his home in Adaraborne, with Henry and the entire Morland family making the trip for the event, so bonded had Eleanor become to their family. The ceremony was intimate, with those in attendance mainly being from the groom's side, due to the proximity to his home, and was, as all such events should be, a joyous affair. Most of the attendees were of either direct or distant relations, he being tied to the Everett line, as well as the Waites, a few of whom had only recently returned from Innsmouth in America.

Even with the uplifting nature of the events, Henry found himself, at times perplexed by the mixture of guests in attendance, noting the similarity in appearance as rather peculiar, with a commonality of features. Many of them seemed to have overly large eyes that seldom seemed to blink, and skin pulled taut, causing the lips to appear thin and elongated. It was a similarity of feature he had noticed in some of the attendees at his own father's service. As unusual as they seemed in appearance, he assumed it to be a regional distinction.

The one other event of note during the celebration was a gift, given from one of the American Waites, it being an elegant tiara of unusual shape. At first glance, it appeared to be solid gold, but with a subtle luster suggesting another alloy in combination. The craftsmanship was exquisite in every detail and of a design not immediately recognizable to any specific period or style. Its shape, somewhat high in front and of an irregular periphery, suggested it as an antique heirloom, but for a head far more elliptical than Eleanor's, as was evident when she tried it on. "I should not worry," said the American Waite, "in time, your head may grow into it."

Eleanor accepted the gift graciously, and exchanged smiles with her Michael, finding it so easy to get lost in the sea of his eyes; so captivating that she could spend an eternity looking into them, and drown in the ocean therein.

So concludes the adventures of our heroine, with an imagination equal to that which could be found in reality, and who sought out far more than she expected to find. No one would have supposed her to be born an heroine, nor would she have seen herself as one, except as a fantasy from one of her novels. However, heroines are just as much made as born, and as one settles back into a life of uneventful domesticity, another may rise to the challenge, and usually without any expectations from the ordinary, thrust into the unexpected by the most ordinary of things, be it a hidden journal, the memory of a long-dead mother, a hidden chamber—or even a diadem of exquisite craftsmanship, but with its unique dark mysteries.

ABOUT THE AUTHORS

Jane Austen (1775–1817) was an English novelist known primarily for her six novels along with other shorter and unfinished works. Those completed novels are *Sense and Sensibility, Pride and Prejudice, Mansfield Park, Emma, Northanger Abbey* (posthumous), and *Persuasion* (posthumous). While her writing went largely unrecognized during her lifetime, her use of social commentary, wit, and realism earned her worldwide acclaim in the two centuries since her death. Austen's works have been adapted and reinterpreted countless times into other mediums including stage, radio, television, and film.

David Welling is a writer, artist, and graphic designer. His first book, *Cinema Houston*, was published in 2007 by the University of Texas Press. The non-fiction book chronicles the history of movie theatres in Texas' largest city. It is the recipient of the 2008 Julia Ideson Award and the Society of Architectural Historians' 2009 Antoinette Forrester Downing Award. He has since shifted to fiction. David is the author of *Midwinter Tales*, a collection of seasonal short stories, and is developing a series of novels centered on fictional auteur film director F.O. Steiner. He lives in Houston along with his wife, furry pooch, and kitties.